Silver Hammer, Golden Cross
Book Six of
The Circle of Ceridwen Saga

Also by Octavia Randolph

The Circle of Ceridwen

Ceridwen of Kilton

The Claiming

The Hall of Tyr

Tindr

Light, Descending

The Tale of Melkorka: A Novella

Ride: A Novella

Silver Hammer, Golden Cross

Octavia Randolph

Silver Hammer, Golden Cross is the Sixth Book in The Circle of Ceridwen Saga by Octavia Randolph

ISBN 978-1-942044-07-9

Bookcover design: DesignForBooks.com

Textures, graphics, photo manipulation, hammer and cross illustrations, and maps by Michael Rohani.

Photo credits: Left gold chain: Fotolia @ Valerii Zan, right gold chain: Fotolia @ Gitanna; clouds and earth, DesignForBooks.com.

Pyewacket Press

The Circle of Ceridwen Saga employs British spellings, alternate spellings, archaic words, and oftentimes unusual verb to subject placement. This is intentional. A Glossary of Terms will be found at the end of the novel.

He suffers that much less, who knows a number of songs. –
The Exeter Book

List of Characters

Ceric, son of Ceridwen and Gyric, grandson of Godwulf of Kilton

Worr, the horse-thegn of Kilton

Raedwulf, bailiff of Defenas

Modwynn, Lady of Kilton, widow of Godwulf

Hrald, son of Ælfwyn and Sidroc, heir of the Danish keep of Four Stones in Lindisse

Ashild, daughter of Ælfwyn and Yrling, Hrald's older half-sister

Ælfwyn, mother to Ashild and Hrald, widowed of Yrling; marriage dissolved with Sidroc

Asberg, brother-in-law to Ælfwyn

Jari, a warrior of Four Stones, body-guard to Hrald

Gunnulf, Jari's younger brother

Sigewif, Abbess of Oundle, sister to slain King Edmund of Anglia

Sparrow, known now as Bova, a novitiate of Oundle

Wilgot, the priest of Four Stones

Ceridwen, Mistress of the hall Tyrsborg on Baltic island of Gotland

Sidroc, her husband, formerly Jarl of South Lindisse

Rannveig, a brewster on Gotland

Tindr, her hunter son, and Šeará, his Sámi wife

Ælfred, King of Wessex

Eadward, Prince of Wessex, son of Ælfred

Begu, a village woman of Kilton

Edwin, Ceric's younger brother, heir to Kilton

Edgyth, Lady of Kilton, mother by adoption to Edwin, widow of Godwin

Cadmar, a warrior-monk

Thorfast, nephew to Danish King Guthrum

Haesten, a Danish war-chief

Silver Hammer, Golden Cross Map Year 890

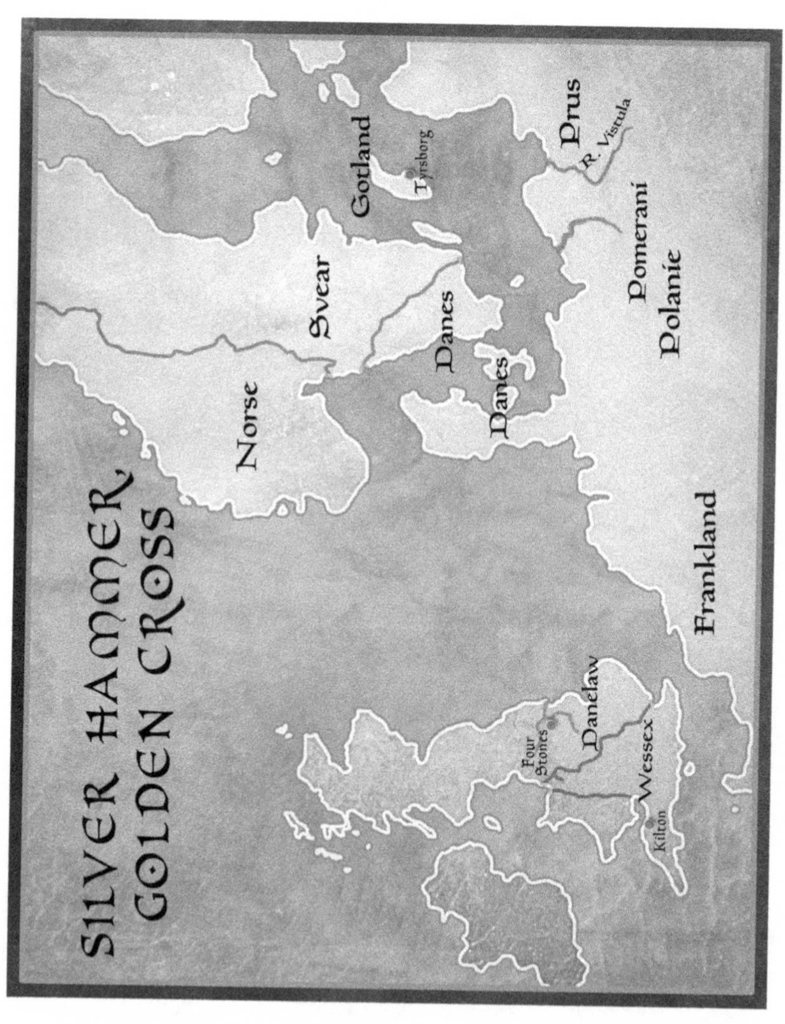
SILVER HAMMER,
GOLDEN CROSS
Norse
Svear
Gotland
Tyrsborg
Prus
R. Vistula
Pomerani
Polanie
Danes
Danes
Danes
Frankland
Danelaw
Four Stones
Wessex
Kilton

Contents

Silver Hammer, Golden Cross

Preface

Peace is wrought in the words of men, strong links to bind two folk together. War is wrought in the deeds of men, sundering with blood what words had forged in ink.

After long and bloody war, a Peace had been made by Ælfred, King of Wessex, and the Dane Guthrum. This Peace cleaved the country in two, and left Guthrum King of East Anglia. For over ten years it held.

One signer of that Peace was Sidroc the Dane, one of Guthrum's war-chiefs. Sidroc had won much treasure in his warring against the Angles and Saxons, and ruled over the keep of Four Stones. But for most of the years of that Peace Sidroc was hundreds of leagues East, on the Baltic island of Gotland. Four Stones fell to his second child, Hrald, whose older sister Ashild could not inherit. As a maid with a brother she was destined to wed a powerful lord, either Saxon or Danish, to join two houses and increase the riches of both.

Away in Wessex was another great keep, that of Kilton. The older son of that hall, now of eighteen years, rode to Four Stones to see his best friend…

Part One: Peace

Chapter the First: The Sword of Godwulf

Angle-land

The Year 890

CERIC OF KILTON leant forward over his saddle pommel. He had just tested the tie-lines on the saddle bags of the pack horse he led; all was secure. He turned his head and grinned at Worr, the horse-thegn of Kilton, who rode on his right, then shot a quick look and a nod to the bailiff of Defenas on his left. The four thegns they rode with touched their heels to their mounts in response. They were off.

The troop was now only a two days' ride from Four Stones. Ceric and the six who accompanied him had been on the road for ten days, and his goal was near. They were seven men and five pack horses, a considerable train, for they carried not only provision for themselves but a number of gifts for the family of Four Stones. A long ride in Wessex would not have occasioned the carrying of so many staples for their provisioning, as in Ælfred's realm they would be welcome anywhere; one look at the embroidered golden dragon on the pennon affixed to one of the thegn's saddles would have made them so. But they were riding across Kingdoms, and had been for several days in that ruled by the Danish King of Anglia, Guthrum. The Peace forged between Ælfred and the Danish invaders more than ten years ago had remained largely unbroken, but the Lady of Kilton, Modwynn, Ceric's grandmother, had insisted Ceric take no fewer than five thegns with him. That Worr would ride with him was assumed from the start. Worr was Ceric's pledged man, and had once been the pledged man of Gyric, Ceric's father, and then that of

Ceric's uncle, Godwin, the Lord of Kilton. Godwin had been felled in single combat by a Dane four years ago, on an island far to the East, two seas away. Both Ceric and Worr had witnessed the killing. It was one of many ties that bound them.

The dragon pennon proclaimed the party to be men of Wessex. The safe-conduct in Ceric's saddle bag was signed by none less than his godfather, King Ælfred himself. No man had challenged their crossing, and he had had no need to draw it from its hardened leathern tube. Before they had crossed the border from Wessex to Anglia they had taken care to fully restock their provender so that they might keep their need to buy along the road to a minimum. They wanted as few as possible to mark their progress. It was a welcome surprise that when they did meet folk along the road in the Danish Kingdom they had been cordially greeted. Passing a small farm not far from the border into Anglia a woman had lifted her head from her wash tub and watched them progress down the dusty trail just outside the stone-walled border of her vegetable plot. She turned and called out to someone unseen, her alarm clear in her voice. Then her eyes fixed on the pennon jutting upright on its short staff from the cantle of the thegn's saddle. The flag barely moved in the slight breeze, but shifted enough for her to see it as the standard of Ælfred. By the time her husband emerged from the barn her fear was abating. The three men who led the troop of warriors had done nothing more than lift their hands to her in greeting as they moved along. It was her husband, who stood blinking in the strong light, who called out to them, and Worr reined to a halt.

The man was a Dane, his wife of Angle-land. He was one of many former warriors who had helped secure the border, claimed land and a woman, and stayed on; the boy and two girls who emerged from around the back of their small wooden house told that their union was as old as Guthrum's conquest of Anglia.

Their farm was remote and nearly a day's walk to the nearest village. Both man and wife were glad to see some of whom they could ask news. The woman led them to the little crock of ale keeping cool in a spring-house, bidding them bring their own wooden cups, as she had not enough serving ware of her own to dip in to slake the thirst of so many. The Dane hauled water for their horses from his well, eyeing the thirsty beasts and the weapons the thegns bore with that adept worth-judging that Danes always seemed to practice.

Worr did the talking, telling the questioning Dane they were headed for Guthrum at the fortress at Headleage, with a message from Ælfred. Ceric knew to keep quiet, noting that the turning point for Headleage was half a day's ride ahead, and even if the man and his now-scattered brethren thought to plot any mischief against those seemingly headed for their own king, they would not find them on that road.

Ceric was the youngest by a decade of any of the men he rode with, and so plainly dressed that none would know that five of the six served as his bodyguard. If his garb drew any interest at all, it was the distinction of its extreme soberness. His wool leggings and leathern leg wrappings were a blue so dark to show almost black, and his tunic was also of the same dusky hue. Ceric's copper-gold hair was a shock above it, his green eyes almost startling. When his shoulders were not covered by his mantle, a flash of the golden chain he wore about his neck might be seen, but he kept the golden cross it bore against his skin, well-hidden. Except for feast days this was the way Ceric had dressed since becoming a man, in the dark hues that recalled his dead uncle. One of the pack horses carried Ceric's ring-tunic, which he had blackened, just as Godwin had blackened his.

After they had regained their road Ceric spoke.

"I would we were going to Guthrum; I would like to look upon him."

Worr smiled over his horse's mane. Worr had thick brown hair, the colour of a wet river stone, and he pushed one side of it back over his ear.

"You already have, when the Peace was signed and Ælfred and he came to Kilton."

Ceric had been so little then he could have no hope of any recollection. He only nodded in chagrin, having called to mind his youth in this way.

"He does not impress," Worr went on, reading Ceric's briefly furrowed brow. "Short, old and grey; that is my memory of him."

Ceric watched his friend's face as it bobbed with the steady walk of his mount. "Also a great warrior," Worr finished.

Worr's eyes had lifted, as if taking in all about them. This is what Guthrum's prowess had won, this immense kingdom, the greater part of the huge island riven down the centre and divided up, Danes and their winnings on one side, Ælfred and his defenders on the other.

They met with others who welcomed them in Anglia. On the banks of a lively stream they found a hamlet of cottars, crofts tidy, cattle and sheep thriving. Ten years ago Danes had swept through, carrying all the livestock away with them, and leaving a few resistant cottars dead in their wake. But that had been all. No Danes settled there, either then or after, and after a hungry year the folk gradually replenished what had been lost. They had rebuilt the stone preaching cross the Danes had thrown down, and a priest came every month just past the waxing of the Moon to help them pray at it. The folk knew

Guthrum, the war lord of the Danes, was now their King. It meant little to them; they had never seen the King of their own people, and as long as they were left in peace they cared not which man was called such.

It was a vast and largely empty land the men of Kilton crossed. Ceric's goal was across the Trent, in the South of Lindisse. The first time he had travelled to Four Stones he had been a boy of nine years, going by sea from Swanawic in the South all around the coast of Wessex, and parts of the coast of Mercia and Anglia too. Three years later he had ridden much this same route with Worr and Godwin, Lord of Kilton. The three had travelled hard and fast, his uncle simmering with a rancour that would erupt and seal his Fate when they found Ceric's mother.

Another had witnessed the killing of the Lord of Kilton that day, the son of his killer: Hrald, Ceric's best friend. Worr had started his return journey for Angle-land two days later, but Hrald and he had sojourned on with his mother, Ceridwen, and Hrald's father, Sidroc. They had nearly ten months together on the green island of Gotland, living at the hall Tyrsborg set above the eastern shore of the Baltic. Then they too must return, Ceric to Kilton, and Hrald to his mother and sisters at Four Stones. More than four years had passed since their parting. In two more days Ceric would see Hrald again.

A long ride invites the unspooling of thoughts. Ceric rocked steadily in his saddle, recalling that time at Tyrsborg. The shock of his uncle's death had receded, day by day over the first few weeks on Gotland, soothed by the routines of the small hall and the freedoms he and Hrald had known there. There was a clarity about their smallest actions, even now. He was returned to his mother, and Hrald to his father, the blood-ties reaffirmed. With his uncle dead, and the great distance between Angle-land and Gotland, he was somehow less the nephew of the Lord of Kilton, and more his mother's son. The simplicity and directness of his life with her, and with Hrald, had changed him. He had need to care for his own horse, to help Tindr with the wood-store, and with Hrald and his mother's small offspring, pull weeds from the bean patch and to gather up hens' eggs. He had liked these things, more than he had imagined. At night at Tyrsborg all sat together at one table, even the serving woman and the cook. When he returned to Kilton he found himself stopping to help a serving man who seemed over-ladened with the bundle of kindling strapped to his back, or pausing to help a woman pull the heavy draw-bucket over the lip of the stone-rimmed well. He did this unthinking, seeing it as the right and reasonable thing to do. But after a time the serving folk themselves deterred him, stammering their thanks red-facedly, then waving him away. Perhaps it was unseemly for them to accept the aid of one of the sons of Kilton; and, worse, proof they were not up to the tasks set for them. As the weeks passed he returned to his expected role, one of great privilege, but ringed with limitations. He felt the same must be true for his friend.

A special gift for Hrald burdened one of the pack horses: a ring-tunic. Ceric had thought long and hard about a worthy gift for his friend. He knew the treasure room at Four Stones housed a whole chest of fine swords; he and Hrald had opened it several times after the Lady Ælfwyn had unlocked it for them. They had drawn out weapon after weapon, swaddled in sheep fleece and still bright due to the oily wool-wax therein. They had lifted and tested each grip, exclaiming over the rippled dance of pattern-welded steel in the edged blade as they turned the swords in the shaft of white light piercing the room from high in the wall. They had run their fingers over pommels and grips embellished with beaten silver and even gold wire, making a sinuous dance of form under their hands' grip. Sidroc, the Jarl of South Lindisse, Lord of Four Stones, had kept none but the best weapons of the Saxons and the Danes for himself and his son, and Hrald would have the pick of them.

No, he would not bring a sword, nor any blade, and it was not just the surplus of weaponry his friend possessed that stopped him. And Hrald would have almost sixteen years now; a sword already at his side when warranted. But a well-wrought ring-tunic – something made anew, and just for Hrald, one of length enough to suit his friend's height and long arms – this was a worthy gift. He had had the weapon-smith of Kilton fashion one, choosing a thegn both tall and lean to be measured for it, for if Hrald had been taller than Ceric then, at two years his junior, he was sure to approach his Danish father in height as he grew.

"My friend is thin," Ceric advised the armourer as he watched the man stretch the measuring thong across the thegn's back and note the tick marks.

"Aye," the man assured him with a grin. "But he will mend of that with the years, fill out, grow into the shoulders as he grows in years. Let me make it for the man he will be, not the lad he is."

Ceric bobbed his head with his own grin, yes, of course.

The gift tunic now lay shining, rolled in a fleece-lined pouch of tooled leather. Its heft was such he took care to place it high across his pack-horse's shoulders to better bear the weight.

Other gifts lay in special pouches, all things he had chosen himself. One in particular he had asked his aunt, Edgyth, to sew a wrapping for, and she, with her gentle smile, had readily complied. Inside the linen bag lay a gown of silk, destined for Hrald's elder sister, Ashild.

After his mother had vanished while departing Four Stones to return to Kilton, all her treasures were carefully kept, taken by Ceric's grandmother Modwynn to her own bower house in hope of her return. When Ceridwen's letter arrived, carried by Worr, telling all at Kilton that Ceric would stay the year on Gotland with her, it also asked Modwynn to distribute her 5,000 coins of silver between her two sons. Two thirds were to be given to Ceric, and one third to the younger Edwin, made Godwin and Edgyth's child through adoption.

Ceridwen's other belongings she bade Modwynn dispose of as she felt just. Ceridwen had been her beloved second son Gyric's wife, and the reason he had survived to return, maimed as he was, to Kilton; and Modwynn had loved Ceridwen for her own sake, seeing in her spirit and courage the makings of a woman well-formed to one day be Lady of Kilton. That Fate had led, even driven her from this path had not caused Modwynn's hand to waver above the store of treasure Ceridwen left behind. She placed all aside for Ceric, gemstones and ornaments of silver and of gold, and two gowns of heavy shimmering silk. They were of green and of yellow, the match in beauty of the two of red and blue which Ceridwen had presented to Modwynn on the day she first arrived at Kilton so many years past.

It was the yellow Ceric chose to take to Ashild. When they had first met as toddling babes Ashild's hair had been the flaxen shade of Lady Ælfwyn's hair, her mother. When Ceric saw Ashild again, they both had nine Summers, and he saw it had darkened to a honey hue. The last time he had seen her, on his and Hrald's return from Gotland, it was the colour of old oak, a rich light brown enlivened with ashy strands where the Sun had left its mark. It suited her eyes, which were of a dark blue-grey, eyes which Ceric had seen storm often enough in their childish games together. The gown of yellow silk was that shade of a hen's yolk, a strong and vibrant gold. He pictured her darker hair coming down from underneath her linen head-wrap and falling upon the sleeves.

"This is a gown fit for a Queen," Modwynn had told him, as she lifted it from a chest and handed it to him. His request to carry it with him to Four Stones had taken her quietly aback, yet it was her grandson's to give. She watched him shake the dazzling thing out in front of them.

"Or a bride," she added.

His cheek coloured then, and his eyelashes dropped over his green eyes.

"Lucky the maid who will wear it," she went on, her thoughts running ahead. She had known all about the costly ring-shirt Ceric was having made for his friend Hrald, who would soon rule Four Stones. But of Ashild Modwynn knew little. This gift was telling her much.

As an alliance it could hardly be bettered; she saw that at once. Ceric's abiding friendship with Hrald had been valuable enough to have made Ælfred give his eager assent to Ceric making the journey. The Peace forged between the King of the Saxons and that of the Danes was fraying, and word was that Guthrum was ailing. The Danish war chief had been canny enough to unite a myriad of war-bands into an army so formidable that the division of Kingdoms, and the paying of much tribute, was the only road to the cessation of hostilities. In return Guthrum and his chief men had taken baptism, become Christian, at least in name, and had permitted the return and even flourishing of priests, nuns, and monks in the lands they now controlled. If Guthrum should die soon, all of East Anglia could disintegrate into vying war-chiefs, eager to be called King, or content to resume raiding.

The daughter of Four Stones coming as bride to Ceric of Kilton would serve as a powerful bond between Saxons and Danes. The distance between Kilton and Four Stones was great enough that such travelling as Ceric was about to commence could not be undertaken lightly, perhaps not again for years. And Danes would also vie for the hand of such a maid; Modwynn knew this well. Yet Ceric had only eighteen years.

Such an age was fine for a bride, but too young to make a settled and responsible husband.

The Lady of Kilton stood looking at her grandson. He had seen bloody violence and travelled, at his young age, far further than any but the most wandering of Holy Men – or Danish raider. Yet he was untested. His own father had died when he was but a small child, and his uncle when he was twelve. She and Godwin's widow Edgyth had done what they could in raising him. Cadmar, an old retainer of her father's turned monk, had guided and trained the boy, as had the trusted Worr. And she fully knew the awkwardness of Ceric's position. Four years older than his younger brother Edwin, he was but second in line at Kilton; if Edwin lived to manhood he would almost assuredly be named ealdorman of the great burh, not Ceric. A match between Edwin and Ashild of Four Stones would be one she or any other counsellor of Edwin's would not only consider, but welcome.

Modwynn saw in her grandson's gift the import of his feelings towards the maid. In surrendering their newborn son to Godwin, her son and daughter-in-law had surrendered too their elder son's claim as heir. She would not let Ceric lose the woman he wanted to Edwin as well.

Ceric still held the golden gown in his hands, though he had dropped his arms. She moved to him, picked up the skirts of it now resting on the wooden planks of her bower house floor, made to fold it up again.

"And so you have decided on her?" she asked Ceric, her tone matter-of-fact, her eyes lowered upon the shimmer of silk as she turned it in her hands.

The slightest intake of air from her grandson made her lift her eyes back to his face.

"I like her – well," he said at last.

Modwynn had memory of the yellow curls of the toddling Ashild, and also of the two babes tussling together in the herb beds, of them sleeping nestled next to each other in the broad ox-drawn waggon the Lady Ælfwyn had arrived at Kilton in.

For a moment she thought of he who was that lady's husband then. She had with her own hands filled the cup of that scarred Dane who would years later cut down her eldest. She checked herself an instant later; she had known when she first saw Ashild that her real father was dead, slain by Godwin himself. If it had been otherwise, if Ceric sought to wed the natural daughter of the man who had killed his uncle – yes, such marriages were made, but she found it hard to countenance her welcoming of such a bride. Yet here was Ceric, perhaps already decided upon her, a maid left fatherless through Godwin's act of revenge.

Modwynn was not one to run from conclusions she had drawn. She finished folding the gown and laid it aside on the white wool coverlet of her bed.

"Ceric," she cautioned. "I would not have you wed at so young an age. If Ashild of Four Stones is to be your wife, if you are to seek her hand, far better it be in three years, or at least two. There is much to consider, treasure to be exchanged, her bride price to be set, argued over, and accepted. And would Guthrum – if he still lives then – look kindly on such a match?"

She paused a moment, watching his face change as he listened to her words, then went on. "These are only a few of the questions to be resolved." The furrows in her brow had deepened, recounting all this.

Of a sudden Ceric felt trapped, as if a door he had not known he had stepped through had slammed shut behind him.

His eyes swept over the bundle of silk on his grandmother's bed. "I bring a gown to her, that is all..." he said in excuse, his words trailing off in the stillness her conditions had created.

Her answer was calm, but the firmness in her voice forced his eyes back to her. He took in her face, one lined with years but not without the comeliness Ceric had been taught to see in his elders. In form she was still straight and tall, her hands strong and expressive. He had never known her as less than a commanding figure of a woman.

"You take a gift of a silken gown to her, a gift not only of great richness, but of intimate nature," she corrected.

He saw that now; bringing a maid a piece of silk from which she would cut and sew her own gown was somehow less personal than the gift of one made up, a gown which he had grasped in his hands, imagined her in, even held to his chest.

He lowered his eyes again. Women were always surprising him, but none surprised him more than his grandmother, who he thought he knew best.

"Will...will she find offence in this?" he managed to ask.

She studied his cheek, still rounded, the faint freckles dotting his nose, the tumble of beautiful reddish curls that fell from his brow.

"She will find delight in it," she said at last, and let herself smile.

She did not add that the gift would return a portion of the treasure Ælfwyn had forced upon Ceridwen. Ceric was not thinking of that, and there was at this moment no reason for him to. He saw only his own desire to give the richest gift he could to a girl he pursued.

It was early Summer, the roads dry, and rivers easy to ford. The troop from Kilton had made good time and would arrive next day. They had stopped a shepherd driving his flock across the road, and once the man had got over his fright he could tell them Four Stones was near. They made camp early that day, gauging they would reach Four Stones at midday. As they rode on in the morning they would meet a ward-corn or watch-man of some kind, and perhaps in this way those at Four Stones would have some little warning of their arrival, if a man of the place was sent ahead to tell them. When Worr and Ceric had ridden this way with Godwin that was what had happened, and they had not only a wary escort through the countryside and to the palisade walls, but another man who had found horse and ridden fast ahead of them.

They struck their final camp and made ready, brushing down their horses well, wiping the dust from their saddles and packs, and for Ceric, dressing in a fresh linen tunic and leggings. They slung their shields upon their backs, swung into their saddles, and began.

Now that he was so close, Ceric found it hard to think of his goal, growing ever nearer. He had spent part of everyday thinking on Hrald, imagining his grin, watching his face when he opened the heavy pouch that held the ring-tunic. He knew Hrald would be tall, but he had grown in height himself, and hoped the gap between them was not laughable.

He had found it harder to think of Ashild, to imagine her now, and almost impossible to think of what he would say when he gave her his gift. He could picture doing so alone with her, but not in front of all, which he knew he must do; they would not be left alone and together now they were older. He was aware he was almost holding his breath, and was seeing nothing of the ripening field of rye before him.

He brushed this from his mind, steadied himself. He shifted the reins. His right hand rose to his sword hilt, and he let his fingers curl around it.

The metal they closed around was gold. The sword he bore was the golden-hilted one of Godwulf, his dead grandsire, the great ealdorman of Kilton. That few inches of bright metal, as bright as Ceric's hair, stood out against his dark clothing. The blade of the sword was buried in a new scabbard, one dark and almost plain, the leather embossed with subtle whorls of spirals, with only a narrow bar of gold at its mouth, and gold again as a chape at its tip. But the sword itself was old.

Godwulf had been laid out with this sword on his chest when he died, that and all his war-kit surrounding him, and his thegns had circled the oak table which bore their lord's body and mourned aloud his passing from this Earth. But as a good Christian the revered warrior had been lowered into the ground beneath the stone floor of the little chapel with nothing more than the linen binding sheet Modwynn had woven and embellished for the task. His seax, spear, and shield had been taken by his widow and packed away, as had the sword of wonder he had worn since a young man. It had been a gift from Ælfred's own father, Æthelwulf, when he was King of Wessex, and was old even then, it was said.

This sword of Ceric's grandsire had been placed into his hands three years ago, and by the ealdorman's widow, Modwynn. He had turned fifteen, and a man, and Modwynn held a true symbel for his sword-bearing ceremony. Cups were raised to the young man, oaths of fidelity sworn, and on his behalf Modwynn bestowed rich gifts to those men who now became Ceric's pledged own. These were the thegns of Kilton who pledged their warrior arms to defend and support him, in battle and in life. Twenty of the five-and-sixty thegns of Kilton had been asked by the young man to be his; Worr and Cadmar had helped him make up the roll. All had accepted.

There were two tall and heavy carved oak chairs on the stone dais in the hall of Kilton, ordered made by Godwulf when he took the young Modwynn to wife. His was massive, hers less so, and both were covered in cleverly-wrought chiseled designs of circling beasts and soaring birds with ensnaring tails. These were the chairs at which they sat at table, yes, but when Godwulf's was set alone upon the dais it became the gift-stool, that seat of power in which he gave out gifts of treasure to his men. It was from this chair Godwulf had presented his elder son Godwin with his weapons at his sword-bearing ceremony.

The night after the old lord's death Godwin had lowered himself into it for the first time, and he had done so with the respect worthy of so hallowed a seat. He sat there each night he was at Kilton. Then Godwin sailed to reclaim the lost Ceridwen, and never returned. The oak chair with its now-smooth arm rests stood empty these past four years. But for his symbel Modwynn had the chair brought forward, and there she herself took her place for the night.

Cadmar carried the sword to her before all, holding it aloft so that the shining blade caught and threw the flickering light from the flames in the fire-pit. All eyes were on it; it had been wrapped away in the treasure room for nearly the length of Ceric's entire life. Cadmar laid it down across the lap of the Lady of Kilton and stepped to one side. Ceric stood before her, and at his right stood Worr, and at his left his aunt, Edgyth, who had nurtured the boy with loving kindness; and standing before Edgyth, her hands upon his shoulders, was Ceric's younger brother Edwin, who had then eleven years.

Behind them stood all the thegns of Kilton, and all their wives, and all their children, arrayed each of them in the finest clothes they owned, and Ceric in a newly-made tunic of sky blue, woven and sewn by his aunt, with silver wire and coloured thread stitched into the neck opening and hem.

Modwynn looked into the eyes of Ceric, and then down at the gleaming blade spanning her lap. The long fingers of her slender hands rose, and she touched the sword, hilt and naked blade both, and then looked back at her oldest grandson. Her words rang out, filling the ears of the eager listeners ranged under Kilton's peaked roof.

"Ceric of Kilton," she called. "Here is the sword of Godwulf.

"On its hilt he passed me the golden ring I wear to this day as his wife. With it he fought and won battles that brought him fame, and with it in hand he answered the call of five Kings. I give it now, into your hands and into your trust. With it may you serve Christ, Ælfred, and Kilton."

With a nod she gestured him forward. The words she spoke as she passed the weapon to Ceric were for him alone.

"It has rested long enough, my boy," she told him, her voice a murmur. "May bearing it give you the long life granted to Godwulf."

Thus came the sword of Godwulf to Ceric. And this was how he thought of it: The sword of Godwulf. That it was now his was the act of God and the often unfathomable and twisting ways of Fate. The bond he felt with it was as intense as that which any young warrior ever formed with his life-taking and life-preserving weapon. That first night he had not been able to leave it hang upon the wall inside his alcove, and found himself unashamedly taking the sheathed blade into his bed.

He thought back on that day, riding now far from home with his hand closed around the hilt. He had no memory of his grandsire, but he knew – he had been told – that Godwulf delighted in his long-awaited grandson, had held him, dandled him, tested the babe's strong grip upon his knotty finger.

And the bond went back even further than that; his mother had told him what the old lord had said to her, when he learnt she was with child: 'From today I know my name will live, and not die with this aged flesh of mine.'

Godwulf said this thinking the boy to be born would be his heir. And so Ceric knew himself to be. He felt somehow anointed by Godwulf, as much as if the old lord had lived long enough to lay his gnarled hands upon Ceric's head and bless him as he knelt before him.

He would not be ealdorman of Kilton and its Lord; his younger brother Edwin had been picked out for that. But Ceric had this sword. Through it he felt himself to be his grandsire's true heir.

He had come to see that Godwulf, and his weapon, were of far greater importance than either his Uncle Godwin, or his father Gyric. Godwin had been a warrior of renown, then thrown his life away in single combat on a distant island. His father, Gyric – his sword was taken from him, lost somewhere in a Dane's treasure room. Godwulf, father of them both, was the greater warrior.

And this sword had never failed Godwulf. There was power in its history, he who wielded it, the warriors who rallied round it, the folk it was raised to defend, the foes who fell before it. Ceric felt this. Godwulf had used the hilt of this sword to wed Modwynn, a vow on his warrior's worth to her. Oaths had been sworn upon its blade of dancing rippled steel. If Godwulf had been the symbol of Kilton and its wealth and might and valour, then this sword was the symbol of that great man himself, celebrated and recalled in his cherished weapon.

Now it was in Ceric's possession. It was Fated to be his, laid by and saved for him by Modwynn, Lady of Kilton, destined to be hung upon his chest. Now it was Ceric's hand that closed about it, a hand he prayed would be worthy of the honour, and the task.

Chapter the Second: Two Women

Four Stones in Lindisse

RAEDWULF, the bailiff of Defenas, rode steadily by Ceric's left side. He was the oldest of any of the men there by a decade, and was in fact the father of Wilgyfu, who had almost four years ago wed Worr, the horse thegn of Kilton. His girl had left him then, gone north and to the sea to Kilton, a place which had suited her well, for she had already presented Worr with two healthy boys.

Raedwulf rarely saw his grandsons, and the thought that he had been so blessed took some getting used to. His own wife had died in childbed after their daughter's birth, and he had raised Wilgyfu with the help of his nearby married sister. He and his daughter had travelled up to Kilton often enough to be noticed by Worr, who even as a youth had become a vital part of the household. Worr's ability with horses had led him to be set in charge of all the herd kept by Godwin, and the beasts' training, breeding, and care placed largely in his hands. That Worr was a stalwart fighter and superior at tracking only enhanced his value. His long-time attachment to Godwin's younger brother Gyric marked him nearly as close as kin, and when Gyric had returned, blind and weakened, from the treachery he had suffered it was Worr who became his steadfast companion.

It had been Worr who Godwin had chosen to take with him on the trip that would seal his Fate, Worr and Ceric both, and the boy had been raised seeing almost as much of the former as the latter. At Ceric's sword-bearing the Lady

Modwynn had presented Worr with a parcel of fertile land to honour his oath to her grandson.

Raedwulf's love for his only child was such that he would have gone to almost any length to secure her happiness. Wilgyfu eased his path by confiding that the raw-boned but good-looking Worr had made it clear in a few words exchanged at feast times in the hall of Kilton that he would like leave to speak to her father.

For all this Raedwulf did not know his son-in-law well; it was only now after two weeks on the road with Worr that he could truly claim a knowledge of the man. What he had seen confirmed his view of the young man's worth, and that of his young daughter's judgement. The few times Wilgyfu and Worr had seen each other prior to their betrothal – and never, to his knowledge alone – could scarcely have been enough to instill the confidence they shared from the beginning that their match would be a good one. Yet so it had proved. He recalled the wintery day at Kilton Wilgyfu had come to him, the very morning of their setting off to return to Defenas, and surprised him with her declaration that she had met the man she would wed.

He was taken aback, not so much by her shining eyes, but by the determination in her low and quiet voice. He had needed a moment to gather himself. Love could strike like this; he had seen it once.

A wood-cock, flushed by their nearness to the road, took flight from the tall wild grasses they now passed, causing his horse to toss his head and snort. Raedwulf glanced over to Ceric at his right. The lad seemed lost in his own thoughts, and the hand closed around his sword hilt suggested they might be of unsettled nature. Raedwulf's role as bailiff of Defenas brought him at regular intervals to Kilton on the King's business. He had seen Ceric almost from birth, having made the journey to mourn that infant's grandsire, but only now could take the measure of the young man who represented half of the entire issue which remained of the great Godwulf.

The bailiff, concerned as he was with matters of justice and the law, was not alone in his concern for the future of so vital a stronghold, so vast a fortune, as Kilton. Only two males of Kilton remained, and one was still a boy. But consider Æthelwulf, Ælfred's own father: four sons to his name, yet the first three would die in rapid succession after bearing the crown of Wessex. It had been left to the youngest, once destined for the Church, to rally all the forces he could scrape and save the final Kingdom from falling to the Danes. It was not the number of heirs but their quality that mattered. Ælfred had proved that.

Of Edwin, Raedwulf had yet to form an opinion; he was but thirteen. Raedwulf had been present at the symbel at which Ceric had been given arms, including that famed sword which hung from the black baldric Ceric now wore. The bailiff remembered Edwin looking on with awe at his older brother, all that night through. When he returned to Kilton to join this party travelling to Lindisse he noted the younger's pride in, and admiration of, Ceric. Up to the age of ten Edwin had been much kept with women. The boy knew himself to be, like his brother, the child of the Lady Ceridwen, but had, as was just, always named Edgyth, Mother. Godwin's widow was learned, and had begun early to school him, as had the priest, in letters and sums, all things needful to a man who would someday rule. Even then his training-in-arms had started, though, first as an outgrowth of the blunted wooden sword and spear he was given as play-things as a child, and now under the tutelage of Worr and Cadmar. But when war came, as Raedwulf was certain it would, it would be his son-in-law's role to fight next to Ceric, not Edwin, and he felt the older boy favoured at least in this.

A horn sounded, almost as if they stood on the field of battle Raedwulf was thinking of. In the warm and still air it startled. So they had been spotted. All reined to a halt, awaiting the coming of he who had blown it. The open country they had just passed through now had a thicket of trees flanking the dusty road, a perfect place for a watch-man to wait.

The horn-blower showed himself, not entirely willingly, for he was alone, his pale ox horn now hanging from his neck, his spear in both hands. He stayed on the side, not stepping before the horses. He was an older, but wiry man, active-looking enough, and Raedwulf guessed he had dropped down from the tree he had settled himself in to confront them. Other than the spear he was unarmed, save for the knife at his side; but the long and double note he had blown would have been enough to alert the next man down the road. The man's eyes took them in at a glance, paused at the bright yellow of the pennon rising from the saddle of the horse at the rear, and returned, apparently counting, to the three who rode at the head.

Worr, having given the man time enough to assess them, now turned in his saddle and spoke. He was looking almost straight down the shaft of the spear pointed at him.

"We ride in peace to Four Stones. Ælfred, King of the Anglo-Saxons, sends greeting to the Lady Ælfwyn and her kin." He spoke slowly and clearly, and now made a slight gesture to Ceric to display the letter of safe-conduct.

As soon as Ceric reached for his near-side saddle bag the man jerked the spear towards him, thrusting it perilously close to his shoulder.

Worr returned his eyes to the watch-man. "Steady," Worr told him in a low tone, as if he were calming a horse.

Ceric's green eyes were round in his head, but after an initial pause he did not flinch. He pulled the lacing through the bag flap, and holding it open with one hand, slowly withdrew the leathern tube within.

He did not slide the parchment forth, only held its casing in his hand. The watch-man's eyes shifted to it.

"A letter from our King," Ceric said, with enough firmness so that the man nodded.

"You will wait," the watch-man said at last, enough for them to hear the lilting twang of the speech of the Danes in his answer.

Wait they did. It was not an easy task for any of the seven men to do so. Stopped as they were, reins slack, helmets in their saddle bags, weapons sheathed, mindful of their need for cool-headedness while a single Dane – an old one at that – pointed his spear in threat at the horse thegn of Kilton, riding as body-guard to Ceric of Kilton himself. Yet they had been trained to abide in such circumstances, much in the same way they had been trained to forfeit their lives in fighting to the death for their pledged lord.

They had been stopped in the shade of the trees; Raedwulf was grateful for that. Their horses swished their tails and shook their heads, wanting to crop the grasses just out of reach. They held them from doing so, just as Worr held the eyes of the watch-man. The man had shifted the point of his spear from Ceric back to Worr, and stood beneath him, feet braced. A spear held in offensive position for any length of time grows heavy, and the men could see this older Dane tire. Worr would have invited him to set the butt end of it down on the ground, but did not want to give offence by suggesting he had detected any weakness in he who held it.

At length they saw those who had been summoned. Four horsemen came riding at a canter towards them down the road, kicking up enough dust for twenty. They quickened the pace when they saw the number of men stopped on the road before them, then slackened when they saw they were held by a single spear-man.

Their horses were as good as he had remembered, Worr thought to himself. The four men upon those good mounts bore shields upon their backs and swords at their sides. They rode one-handed, a spear held upright in their right hands, ready at any time to level or launch them.

The Danes pulled up, faces searching the men stopped before them. One of them, with long yellow hair, squinted at the youth in the middle.

"Ceric," he called. He smiled through the grime on his face.

"Gunnulf," answered Ceric.

The watch-man let his spear butt hit the hard ground.

Ceric raised his hand in greeting to the mounted Dane. It was Jari's younger brother, only a year or two older than Ceric himself. Jari was Hrald's chief body-guard. Gunnulf was not as big as his older brother, but was just as well-knit, the legs that gripped his horse's barrel long and powerful.

"You are here at last," Gunnulf answered. His horse was wheeling beneath him, and he kept grinning as he turned. "Hrald will be glad. Follow me."

Ceric also recalled another young man, Onund, who rode just behind Gunnulf. Onund had dark brown hair over his shoulders, a broad face, and high colour in his cheeks. Ceric remembered a grappling match Onund had taunted Hrald to when they were boys; Hrald had handily pinned the chubby-faced boy to the ground. That face was more angular now, but the eyes which swept over Ceric did so appraisingly.

They left the watch-man to his trees and went on at a walk, Gunnulf and Onund falling in beside Ceric. Gunnulf had given Worr a nod; he recalled him as well, but had not seen the older man on Ceric's other side before.

Raedwulf was aware of the Dane Gunnulf prattling away at Ceric, and relieved at it; the tightness between his shoulder blades had relaxed, and the hand that had wished to touch his own sword hilt in reassurance did so. But his thoughts were turning to what lay ahead of him. They had gained the furthest reaches of the village fronting the fortress, and its palisade wall stood up at the end of the road. The bailiff had never ventured to Lindisse before, nor known the lands of the dead Merewala as anything more than an entry on a long list of Saxon, Mercian, or Anglian keeps which had been taken by the invaders. It had been so distant from his duties to the King as law-giver that it could be little else. It was only when Ælfred called him to Witanceaster that he learnt his mission here, what he would deliver. And to whom.

By the time Ceric rode through the open gates of the palisade, Gunnulf and the three riders with him had been joined by three more, picked up at another check-point just beyond the sheep folds of the village; all those guarding the approaches to Four Stones seemed ready to follow them in. His own party had dropped back a little, letting the men of his host surround him, as if to share some credit for bringing one long-looked for in. None had ridden ahead to give Hrald warning, and indeed any such would have been slight. But Gunnulf had told him Hrald was about Four Stones that day, and within a moment or two of entering the yard Ceric spotted his friend.

A horse had been tied outside the lead-roofed stable, and two men were bending over the upraised front hoof one of them held in his hand. The bigger of the two turned his head at the clatter of hooves behind him, then let fall the one he held. Hrald straightened up, and the stable man Mul beside him.

"Hrald," called Ceric. His face was wreathed in a smile, deepening as he watched Hrald's blue eyes open, and his own grin form. Ceric jumped from his horse and shrugged off his shield.

His friend strode closer.

"I should have stayed up there," Ceric told him, seeing how much taller Hrald had grown.

The long arms closed about him a moment, slapping his back, then Hrald stood back as Ceric took him in. His dark brown hair was now just long enough to be held in two plaits, one on either side of his face. His chin and cheeks displayed the beginnings of a dusky beard, one he had begun to shave every week. A few wisps of dark chest hair showed at the top of his split-neck collar. His green tunic and brown leggings were unadorned, but of cloth finely woven and carefully sewn; his leg wrappings tooled with spiraling designs stamped into their chestnut brown leather.

Hrald smiled now, his teeth white and strong.

"You are come," he said. His voice was quiet and Ceric could see a glistening in his eyes. "I had one letter from you, at Lady Day, three Summers ago. Did you ever receive mine?"

"Only one?" Ceric returned. "I gave two, one just after the first Hlafmasse to a priest coming to Oundle, then another last year before Yule, telling you I would try to come this Summer."

Hrald was shaking his head, in listening and also in wonder.

"I had no letter back from you," Ceric was saying now. The carrying of any such was fraught with uncertainty, even with the Peace holding as it had.

"Well, you are here now, that is all that matters," Hrald was saying.

He now saw Worr, who had dismounted, and went to him and gave him his arm in welcome. Ceric had gone on to greet Mul and a few others he remembered.

"Your Lady Mother?" Ceric now asked, tilting his head to the hall itself.

"I think she is within," Hrald guessed, "numbering cups and salvers or some such. We dent them so; there are always new ones she must order to be made."

They laughed together at this, for no reason than the other's nearness. They walked to the door, closed against the dust of the dry yard. All the men were off their horses now, and had formed up behind Ceric. The yard was busy with folk working, with many children too; and he nodded or called out to lads or maids he recalled who now were grown to young men and women.

Hrald pulled on the twisted iron bar of the door, and a shaft of light followed them in. At the far end of the hall, near the broad raven banner hanging on the wall, stood Hrald's mother and a few other women, looking down on an array of metal on a table. The side door was open, giving them light, and the women's faces turned and looked at those who approached. Ælfwyn's tallness and slenderness marked her at once, as did the bulky form of Burginde, who had served her since her birth. Hrald's aunt, Æthelthryth, was there, holding a ewer in her hands. Ceric's eye skipped from face to face of the women standing over the pile of metal on the table. Ashild was not amongst them.

Hrald's mother came around the end of the table she had been standing at.

"Is it – Ceric," she asked, and then answered herself with a laugh. She came at him, arms open, the fine linen of her head wrap trailing from her shoulders in her haste.

"My Lady Ælfwyn," Ceric was beginning, only to be smothered in her arms.

She kissed his brow, and both cheeks, all as he was trying to make his bow to her. She was laughing and crying both, and he of a sudden felt close to tears himself, thinking on his own mother.

Ælfwyn pulled back, sniffling, her smile broad in her thin face. She had his hands, warm and strong, in both of her own, and gave them a squeeze. She saw his mother in his green eyes.

He now found himself in the arms of Burginde, who hugged him with surprising strength.

"And quite a man you are," she appraised, with that deep and hearty laugh he remembered. She straightened her head-wrap, which had gone crooked as she pushed herself upon him. Her hair was wholly grey now beneath it, but her cheeks had almost the freshness of a maid's. She now had to look up at him, he had grown so.

Ælfwyn saw Worr, liked and remembered him well, and smiled on him as he came forward to her with his simple greeting.

The third man Ælfwyn did not know. She had never seen him before. He was her age, or above so; there were a few strands of grey in his brown hair, which fell tousled but evenly trimmed to the collar of his dark travelling tunic. The hair itself was striking, with enough wave in it to separate into individual locks; as a boy he must have been curly-headed. He was well but not richly dressed, with a sword and seax which she knew had been a royal gift, or the battle-gain taken from some war-chief of wealth; she had learnt to judge such things over the years. His mouth and chin were firm, so much so that they might run to grimness; his eyes a blue mild enough to belie that sternness. He stood erect, alert, his person the match of the younger men about him, a man of discipline, and action, still.

There was no arrogance in his bearing, and she had seen much of that in men of his estate, be they Saxon or Dane. There was rather the stance of one confident in the pursuit of his objective, but mindful of the needs of others. She wondered if he might attend upon the King.

The stranger stepped forward now, inclined his head to her.

"Ælfwyn of Cirenceaster," she heard him say.

His words stopped her where she stood, recalling her as they did to her girlhood self. She had not heard this name for over half a lifetime.

She felt her face change; she did not know how.

He then added, "Lady of Four Stones," placing her firmly in the present moment.

The slightest pause before he spoke again, the fine head inclined to her a second time.

"I am Raedwulf, bailiff of Defenas, in service to Ælfred, King of Wessex. I bring you his greeting, and also his gift."

He had it in his hands, carefully wrapped from dust and the jostle of the road, and had taken it from his saddle bag upon dismounting, so that the King's gift might be presented first.

His eyes dropped to what he held out to her, then lifted again to her face. He held them there long enough so that she herself must look away.

She let her eyes fix on the small package he held out.

"The King has my gratitude, as does Raedwulf of Defenas, for bearing his gift to me."

He took a step closer so she might take it, then stepped back. All, even Ceric and Worr who had seen what was within, watched closely as her white hand rose. Beneath the linen was a small box, one of hardened leather.

She almost dare not hope. She laid the linen on the table behind her, lifted the cover of the box, set it too down upon the dark surface of the scarred table. She gazed downward into what she held.

"A book." Her words came out gentle as a breath. "We have no books…"

"The Psalms, my lady. These were rendered from the Latin by Ælfred himself, then copied out and decorated by the monks of Athelney, at the King's command."

Her eyes sparkled as she lifted her gaze back to him. "How glad I am," she told Raedwulf. "How glad Wilgot will be. Our priest."

She had not yet taken the tiny volume out of the lower half of the box which protected it. Instead she pressed the whole to her bosom, against her heart.

Serving men and women were now come from a side passage, some carrying basins of water and towels, others tall bronze ewers and trays crowded with cups. One of the trays bore several cups of silver, and this was set down near to where Ælfwyn stood by the table.

They had come upon her without warning, and the bailiff of Defenas had presented himself and his rich gift so quickly, that only now could they pause and observe the ritual welcome she had held to for these many years, that which any hall in Wessex would provide. She took some little pride in this, her serving folk so well trained that they were at the ready with all which was needful. Even the riders of Four Stones who had served as escort knew what was expected of them, and took their turns rinsing their dusty hands when the basins were held before them; they had followed the Saxons in, and wanted to take part in the ale to follow.

She poured out ale into the silver cups first, then passed one to Ceric, then to Hrald, next to the bailiff, and to Worr. With a nod she told Æthelthryth and Burginde she would pour out as well into the bronze cups for the thegns of Kilton, and did so also for her own men. At this happy occasion all should have their drink poured by the Lady's own hand. When all held their cups she returned to the lone silver one on her tray, and filled it for herself.

"I welcome you, as Lady of Four Stones," she told her visitors, before her eyes fixed on Ceric where he stood next to Hrald. "And I bless your coming," she added, beaming at them both.

She looked now to her son, a look suggesting he must speak.

A little sound came from Hrald's throat, but he turned and faced his guests. Nearing sixteen years he was tall as the tallest man there. His face was as long and thin as the rest of him, his pointed chin still an echo of his mother's. His hair, dark as his father's, and bound in its two plaits, had not a trace of Sun in it. His eyes were a mid-blue, fringed with boyish dark lashes under surprisingly heavy dark eyebrows. Those eyebrows, in reflection of his thoughtfulness, now knitted themselves towards one another.

He looked at each man in turn, then at Ceric. "Well-come, friends, and well-met," was all he said, and all he need say.

They lifted the ale to their lips, and more than one tight throat was eased by the drinking of it.

Ceric gestured, and two of the thegns came forward. One of them held the gift for Hrald, the other the gifts for the rest of the family.

"Ashild…?" Ceric finally asked, looking at Hrald.

On the road one night when he had bedded down he had thought of the moment he would lift the welcome-cup to his mouth, and had pictured Ashild having poured it. Now he began to worry why he had not seen her. Hrald's letter to him had never arrived Kilton. Perhaps in it he told of Ashild's marriage…or…

But his friend shot a look at his mother.

Ælfwyn shook her head a moment, as if remembering. "The valley of horses – she is there; she went with Ealhswith to choose a horse for her."

Ealhswith was Ælfwyn's youngest girl; she would be, Ceric reckoned, of ten or so years now. That Ashild had taken it upon herself to select a suitable mount for her came as little surprise to him; she was always a good, even a venturesome rider.

Hrald turned to one of his men. "Go and fetch them," he said simply.

The man left and they turned to the gift-giving. Ælfwyn had set the book upon the table, replaced the hard cover to its box, and even draped the linen wrapping over it again, as if she would, alone and in private, have the delight of holding it in her hand, turning over the first leaf, studying the minute words and tiny pictures.

Ceric took the leathern pouch holding the ring-shirt from the thegn, its heaviness clear. He laid it next the box, and gestured his friend to it.

Hrald touched it, feeling its massed weight, and its mobility; it shifted slightly as he turned the pouch to open the flap. A sheepskin, fleece side out, had been sewn inside the heavy cow hide of the pouch. He saw the gleam of bright steel. He pulled the mass out, unrolled, and held it by the shoulders, the clinking of the links as it unfurled signaling to even those who could not see what it was.

Ceric and Hrald stood at the table, backs to the hall. Only Ælfwyn stood next them, watching as her son accepted his gift. The ring-tunic was still held up in Hrald's hands.

"To protect you," Ceric murmured.

Hrald's dark lashes had swept down over his eyes. He raised them a moment as he nodded to his friend. He had no words to answer with. It was there in his look.

He turned to those behind him, holding the heavy thing aloft. The men called out, Danes and Saxons both, the Danes in admiration of a rich gift, the Saxons in the pride of having given it. Onund had been standing in the front, arm draped over Gunnulf's shoulder, and now dropped his arm and took a step forward to better see the fine ring-shirt.

When the hall had quieted Ceric tilted his head close to Hrald's. "The other things…they are for your mother, and sisters," he told him.

Hrald nodded; it was time to dismiss the on-lookers. Their guests need be offered the chance to wash, and sleeping places found for them. And as there would be a feast tonight, he knew his mother would need to start giving orders for it. The ale went round a second time, and after this the group dispersed. The escort, satisfied at having taken part in the welcoming, took horse and rode back to their posts. Æthelthryth stayed with her sister, a smile of mild and sweet surprise still upon her lips. Burginde plopped down at a stool off to her mistress' left, but the other women vanished down the dim passageway to the kitchen yard. Mul was called in, and the thegns returned to the yard with him so that their weary horses might be unloaded and looked after. Ceric and Worr and the bailiff of Defenas stayed on, invited by the lady of the place to sit at the darkened oak table.

Raedwulf took note of what hung on the wall behind that table. It was a round warrior's shield, iron rimmed, the leathern face covering the wooden boards of it painted in a broad swirling design of red and black that issued from the pointed iron boss at the shield's heart. It was, he could see, a shield that had seen some action, battle-tested by the gashes on its face, and the fact that the rim had been patched.

Ceric saw it too, and knew it for what it was, the shield of Sidroc. He had clear memory of it laying on the table in front of the chair in which that jarl had once sat. Now Hrald went and sat there.

Ceric felt uncertain if he should give Hrald's mother her gift now, or wait until Ashild arrived. The second saddle bag holding the things meant for them sat lumpily before him. At that moment he wanted to be outside and alone with Hrald, walking, or maybe riding with him. They could go to the falcon house, or out to the valley of horses. This last thought brought Ashild back to mind. He gave his head a little shake, and was aware that the bailiff was studying him. He cleared his throat and pulled the bag closer.

"I have something for you, Lady," he told Ælfwyn. He pulled out a few small linen pouches, sewn into tiny drawstring bags. One was marked with the letter Ash, Æ, sewn into it, naming it as Ælfwyn's. He placed it in her hands.

She pulled on the ribband to release the puckered opening, and emptied the contents into her slender hand. It was a small circular pin of a coiled, long-limbed beast mouthing the tip of its own tail, beautifully wrought. It was also of gold.

Her mouth opened, but no sound came forth. Ceric saw her eyes fill, and knew there was no need to say the next.

"It was my mother's. I thought of anything I could bring, you would like something of hers best."

She had closed her fingers around it, and smiled at him. "I recall her wearing it at Kilton, when you and Ashild were but babes and I came to see her…"

Ceric was looking down now, gesturing to the other small pouches. "These are necklaces and bracelets the silver-worker at Kilton made up; please to give them to your sisters and to Ealhswith as you see fit."

His eyes went to the still full-looking saddle bag. "The big one – it is for Ashild," he managed.

Ælfwyn was thanking him for his generosity when the door at the far end of the hall was pulled open again. They all turned to it. There, outlined in the bright light of mid-day, stood a woman's form. She left the doorway, a child scampering at her side.

Ceric stood, aware of the heavy scraping of the double bench he had been seated on. He could scarcely make her out with the glare from the opened door surrounding her. Now that she was so close he felt something akin to dread. What if she had grown plain, or buck-toothed, or…He could not imagine that she was already wed or promised to some man; Hrald or his mother would have told him when he asked about her.

She hurried to where they sat, and came around the table to Ceric. She was slightly breathless, he could hear that, and he hoped she might fling herself into his arms in delighted surprise, allowing herself that liberty due to a childhood friend.

But no, she drew up short before him. He was taller than her, by more than a hand's width, and he was glad of it. She was smiling, almost grinning at him, and he saw she was neither plain nor had her teeth gone awry. He was surprised to see her dressed as a woman of the Danes: a sleeveless gown, with paired brooches of silver at the shoulder straps, over a long-sleeved linen shift. Her mother, and Burginde, still wore the long-sleeved gowns favoured by Saxon women. Other than the brooches she wore no jewels, save the small golden cross she had worn since a child.

"Ceric!" said Ashild, and then grasped him in the briefest of sisterly embraces. She smelt of horses and hay, and he saw the remains of a green and sappy leaf which had stuck to the hem of her head wrap. He could not see her hair, and thought for some fresh and terrible moment she had cut it off. But no, she tossed her head looking at her brother and mother, and he saw it was merely held in a plait trailing down her back. Ceric heard Burginde give a disapproving cluck from where she sat.

She was not alone in her assessment of the maid's entry.

"Ashild," the Lady of Four Stones said, and even given the smile on that lady's lips some little note of reproach found its way into her voice. She was standing herself now, looking apologetically at her guests. "Raedwulf of Defenas, this is my eldest, Ashild. And my youngest, Ealhswith," she added, as that child came to her mother's side.

"My ladies," answered Raedwulf, nodding at them both.

Ashild looked as if she might laugh, but did not. Ealhswith, suddenly shy, clung to her mother.

"Worr you will remember," Ælfwyn was going on to her eldest, who responded with a nod of her own.

"Ceric has brought us not only the happiness of his visit, but gifts from Kilton," she was telling Ashild. "A ring-shirt for Hrald. A golden pin which was his mother's, for me." Her voice had softened at this last. She looked to Ceric.

"Yes," he began, not knowing what more he would say; his brain had emptied. He reached for the saddle bag, and pulled out the bulk of what had filled it. The linen his aunt had used to sew the pouch was of pale yellow, and on it she had threaded a small line of embroidery in darker yellow.

"This…this is for you," he said, shoving it at Ashild.

She gave a little start, almost laughing, and he recalled the day he had thrown a toad at her. She had started like that then, and a moment later picked the ugly thing up and flung it right back at him. It had hit him in the face while he was laughing at her.

He hoped she would not shove it back, and she did not. Instead she took a moment gathering herself, looking down on it, and wiping her hands on her skirts. He saw its bulk surprised her, and that she had no idea what might be within.

She shook it out of the linen pouch and onto the surface of the table. It lay there, pooled like the yellow Sun, dazzling with its sheen even in the low light of the hall. She made a small sound, a gasp of wonder, he hoped. She took it in her hands, turned it, found the sleeves.

It was not only silk, she saw, but a made-up gown, and one of surpassing beauty.

She knew enough not to hold it up to herself; that would be unseemly in mixed company. But she must show it to the others, now she knew it for what it was, and she lifted it in her hands.

"A gown. Of silk."

This too Ælfwyn knew well, better even than the gold circle pin Ceridwen had worn. This yellow-gold gown of silk had been hers. She had worn it at Cirenceaster, as a maid Ashild's age.

Then it had been forfeit to the Dane she had been forced to wed, Yrling; bundled up with everything of worth her parents had ever given her, and much more too, and sent here to the then- ruined keep of Four Stones, which Yrling had conquered. Ashild's father.

The Lady of Four Stones felt almost faint, and sat down, gently, but without feeling her knees bend. For the second time since Ceric had arrived she was recalled to her girlhood home, first by the bailiff of Defenas calling her by her original name, and now by this gown, one of four given her by her parents so long ago.

Another at that table recalled that gown, but she was not looking at him.

Ashild held the gown in her hands. It was of such value that she did not know what to say. Her mother, always so good at prompting, had her own eyes cast down at the pitted face of the table, looking at what Ashild could not guess.

Ashild did not know the meaning of it. She knew a gift of this richness would be given only to a bride, as her bride-price; or by a very rich man to his new wife the first morning they awoke together, to thank her for the gift of her body. Or given, as her mother had once told her, by loving parents to their daughter. Here was her brother's friend – her friend – giving it. To her.

She was left alone. Ceric was staring at her, the smile on his lips wavering. Hrald was looking, blankly, she thought, from the pooled silk to her. The older man, the bailiff, was gazing away, off to one side. Only Worr looked normal, expectant, but not conveying any strain.

"I thank you, Ceric," she said at last. "It – it is wonderful."

"How strange that the bailiff should call you that," Æthelthryth said to her sister, when their guests had risen and they were alone a moment.

Ælfwyn simply nodded in assent. It had been one impress after another; Ceric's joyful coming, Raedwulf's salutation, seeing the silk gown once more.

Æthelthryth's face wore a smile, a wistful one, for their lost home. "But – it is your name," she answered herself.

Chapter the Third: Two Swords

THE feast that night would not be held for several hours. Before that time her guests must be accommodated. With quick decision Ælfwyn offered the weaving room up the side stairway to Raedwulf; she did not deem it fit that he should sleep in the hall with the men. Hrald himself slept there amongst them, as was right for an unmarried youth. But the bailiff would need a table, she thought, and had earned both comfort and privacy after the long ride from Wessex with the younger men.

She herself slept these days in her bower house, set at the end of her garden. Little Ealhswith and Burginde slept there too. Ashild and Ælfwyn's sister Eanflad slept in the house of Æthelthryth, wed to Asberg, the Dane who served well in keeping Four Stones for the day Hrald would command.

The treasure room was become just that, the stronghold in which the treasure was stored. When Hrald wed he would take his wife to it. Ælfwyn had left the wolf-skin spread upon the bed there; she had not slept under it since the day Ceridwen and Sidroc had been taken. It was the gift of her mother to her bridal night, packed in secret by her and Burginde amongst her barrels and chests of goods and only discovered on the day itself. It was meant to grace the bed of two. If her bed had been cold since, it was not due to the lack of its furred thickness.

She had taken Ælfred's gift to her bower house, and given herself a moment to admire it. She had slipped the linen pouch holding Ceridwen's gold pin within the case surrounding the book, and she took it out now and set it aside. She drew the book out. It was no longer than the length of her hand. The binding was of two thin wooden boards, covered over with sheets of silver, front and back. The spine was left open, the tough and thick red-dyed linen thread that laced the parchment quires together giving colour as they wound through the creamy folds so exposed. The silver-faced covers of the book had been impressed with wondrous skill. The front cover bore an image of God in Majesty, hands open and outstretched, his gown spilling over the cloud he stood on. There were rays of light, shown by lines issuing from behind Him. Surrounding Him were flying beings – angels, she thought; some carried swords, and all had feathered wings, like birds.

The back was simpler, yet somehow more mysterious. She looked down on a swirling mass of cloud forms, some large, some small, as if the skies had shifted and the God that had been so clear on the front of the Psalter had been obscured. The clouds now blocked the Sun, and Him. She thought on this. No, that was not a hopeful note on which to leave those who had added their own voice to the ancient King David's in praise. Perhaps it meant that all lay contained within, all the cosmos, everything.

She let herself sink down on her bed, considering this. She did not understand why Ælfred would send her this gift. She had known, even when she first arrived at Four Stones, that her father had ignored the call to arms of the then-king, Ælfred's brother. He did so to try and make a separate Peace with Yrling, and in doing so forfeited not only his daughter but later his own life. Her father could not be considered by Ælfred to have been a friend to his own family, or to greater Wessex. And all these long years later, she had been, of course, living under Danish law, and in a Danish Kingdom, nothing to do directly with the King of Wessex.

She had seen Ælfred several times, as a maid back at Cirenceaster. That was years ago…

She stopped herself in her thinking. Rich gifts were Ælfred's to give, and Ceric was his god-son. Right now she must go to the kitchen yard and see what could be done to make a fitting welcome feast.

She rose, took a small bronze key from the cluster at her waist, and carried the book in its box to the stout chest which held her remaining jewels. She set the gold pin in as well, vowing to wear it that night. As she was relocking the chest she heard a knock, and at almost the same time, Ashild call out, "Mother." The door opened and her daughter stood before her.

She had the yellow pouch in her hands. She left the door open behind her, and Ælfwyn could see by her face that Ashild was not thinking of that. She crossed behind her daughter and closed it.

"What does it mean?"

Ashild had many aspects to her temperament, but fretfulness was not one of them. Yet her worry sounded in her question to her mother.

She moved the pouch in her hand, lifting it slightly. "Ceric brings me this. And that man, the bailiff – he came all the way with Ceric, to bring you a book from Ælfred."

Her mother did not answer, but Ashild went on as if she did not expect her to.

"They are here for me," she proclaimed. "Here to bargain for me. To make of me a Peace-weaver."

The girl was always direct. This was so bald that Ælfwyn would have hazarded a short laugh, if her daughter's face had not betrayed fear.

Ælfwyn went to her, took the bundle and placed it on the small table there, and then pulled Ashild to her in a long and slow embrace. She felt her daughter's chest heave against her own, and tried to slow her breathing by the drawing of her own deep breaths. The girl smelt of the stable; that, and a whiff of the lavender flowers she liked to crush and rub through her hair.

"My dear girl," her mother whispered. Then she stepped back, her hands on her daughter's shoulders. She was still taller; Ashild would not reach her height, she thought. Nor would her daughter, at this moment, meet her eyes.

Ælfwyn let out another slow breath. "You have seventeen years. You are the daughter of Four Stones. Your brother will rule soon. Of course men seek your hand. This is not the first time one has shown his interest."

"So I am right," Ashild answered. "Ceric is here for me." She pulled away from her mother's hands, and looked around the room in such a way that Ælfwyn wondered if she thought Ceric was hiding in the alcove where at night Ealhswith slept, and listening to all.

Ælfwyn began to feel some concern now. "Does it displease you so much? You and Ceric are – friends. You and he – "

"Do not, please, tell me of how we slept together as babes in your waggon," she fired. "I have heard that tale enough."

"Your brother loves him," Ælfwyn tried. "And – he is Ceric of Kilton. The god-son of – "

"I know, the King of Wessex. I know all this."

The petulance in her tone made her mother swallow her own impatience. A gentle silence had generally been the best way to greet Ashild's anger. The girl was kind enough, and old enough, to come to her senses in a short while. If she did not always return, with lowered chin, to beg forgiveness, at least the storm would shortly blow over.

"Ashild, I think you read much into Ceric's gift. The ring-tunic he had made for Hrald was of great worth, and I think he wished to choose something equally so for his sister." Ælfwyn thought of the pin she had just locked away. "He brought me a gift of gold."

Ashild stood a moment longer, then nodded her head. Kilton, she thought; a Kingdom and a half away. And you would have me go there?

It was not something she could say; she did not wish to hear the answer.

She felt her mother's gaze upon her. She let her eyes drop to the table and what it held.

"The gown. I must wear it tonight?"

"You must wear it at some point in his visit. Not to do so would be to slight it." She considered the girl's reluctance. "If you do so tonight, at the welcome feast, it would not only be appropriate, but – it would be over with, and done."

Ashild took this in, and nodded. "Then I can lay it away."

"Yes. Then, if it does not please you, you could lay it away."

Ælfwyn would not point out that to do so to such a queenly gift would be a waste of its beauty and value; she did not herself think that way. Her surprise and disappointment was solely in the fact that the idea of Ceric being her suitor appeared distasteful to her daughter. They had been avid playmates as children; did not Ashild feel she knew Ceric, and well?

The girl was once more pulling the gown from its pouch. The silk, heavy as it was, was slippery, enough so that it fell with a soft and hissing crackle from the table where she had piled it. Ælfwyn bent to pick it up; her daughter was already unpinning her own gown so she could try the new one.

It was simply sewn, with long, narrow sleeves, a round neckline, and skirts that rustled with the expanse of fabric that had been lavished therein. It was not the yellow forced from the weld plant, but a far more vibrant and richer shade. No embroidery ornamented it; the vivid hue of the golden silk was enough. Such a gown demanded only the simplest but most striking of jewels. Ælfwyn thought of all those she had given to the abbess of Oundle. But Ashild was not one to layer on baubles.

"It is long; too long," her daughter decided, once she had dropped it over her head.

"Yes. I am taller than you. And it was once my gown," her mother told her.

Her daughter stopped in her fussing then.

"It was yours?"

"It was. One of four gowns, all of silk, my parents had given me when I turned sixteen. I gave all of them to Ceric's mother."

"So they have been at Kilton all this time?"

"Yes. When I visited her there, she told me she had given two of them to her mother-in-law, the Lady of Kilton, in thanks for the way she had received her as daughter. But two she kept."

"And Ceric has brought one of them to me."

Ashild sat down on the bed, her new yellow skirts billowing around her. Outside a bird called, and beyond that she could hear the fainter sounds of the bustle in the kitchen yard.

"I will wear it tonight," she told her mother, and rose to pull it off.

Hrald had taken Ceric down along the palisade to the trees in the hollow. The hall was noisy with serving folk setting up for the night, and Hrald had stopped just long enough to get his sword from the treasure room. Now they walked next the marshy wetland, trampling the grasses that rose tall along the path for want of use. They would meet no one here, and they could talk.

Ceric had been eyeing the sword Hrald had emerged from the treasure room wearing. Like all Danes, he wore it at his hip, just as Danes wore their knives hanging down from their weapon-belts.

"Which did you choose?" he asked his friend. He and Hrald had spent so much time with the trove of swords, he thought he would remember them all.

Hrald pulled it from its scabbard and handed it to Ceric. The hilt was fairly plain, two pieces of well-figured dark-veined horn held by silver rivets. The iron guard was broad and forward-curving. The crowning pommel was of iron, but well-shaped and smooth to the touch.

The blade itself was long, and the most impressive part of the whole, deeply etched in almost blue-grey rippling pattern-welding, every ripple signifying a different thin bar of steel the weapon-smith had hammered and twisted together to make the blade dance in the light.

Ceric turned it in his hand, admiring it.

"Good spring, too," Hrald told him. A moment passed as they both watched Ceric catch the Sun with it. "My father almost took it as his own. I remember him testing it, calling it a fine blade."

Ceric nodded, and passed it back.

"Yours," prompted Hrald. He had taken a moment to re-sheath the blade.

Ceric drew it forth from the simple black scabbard hanging high on his chest. Hrald had already seen the bright gold of the hilt, proclaiming it the weapon of a king or great war-lord.

"It is the sword of Godwulf," Ceric told him. "It was given him by King Æthelwulf."

Hrald let a low whistle escape his lips. With all the gold it was the costliest weapon he had ever seen, or could hope to see. It exceeded the seax Ceric wore across his belly, which he knew to have been that of Merewala, who had fallen defending Four Stones.

Hrald handed it back. He sized up his friend, dressed as he was in his dark clothing, as Ceric buried the blade in its near-plain scabbard.

"A lot of show," Hrald ribbed. "A scabbard to match would blind your enemy before you drew the blade."

The moment it was out of his mouth he regretted it. Ceric's father had been blinded by some Danes. It had happened years ago, but still –

"I...I did not mean that," he stammered. "Not like that."

Ceric had winced, but now shook his head. "Forget it. I understand."

Weapons sheathed, they resumed their walking.

"How was it given," Hrald asked.

"My grandmother Modwynn, the Lady of Kilton, held a symbel for my sword-bearing. She took Godwulf's gift-stool herself, and gave it me by her own hands. She was wed by it," he went on. "After Godwulf's death she took the sword and kept it by for me."

"For you?" Hrald repeated. "Of course," he answered himself a moment later. "You are eldest."

Hrald's thoughts ran on. "And Edwin, your brother?"

"Godwin's sword will be his. That and his seax."

It was only the open-handedness of Hrald's father that had made this possible, that the weapons of the Lord of Kilton could be carried back by Worr to be set aside for his heir. But Ceric could not quite say this. Hrald had witnessed it as well, and there was no need. Just as there was no need to mention who had killed Godwin.

"What else happened?" Hrald wanted to know.

"Men pledged to me," Ceric recounted. "I had asked twenty to do so, and they did."

"How...how do they do that?" Hrald asked.

"Cadmar – I have told you of him; he is a warrior, but a monk, too, and counsels my grandmother – Cadmar called out the names of the men. They came, one by one, and knelt before me. They offered me their hands – " here Ceric pressed his palms together, as if in prayer "– and swore, by their own lives, to defend mine. I placed my hands over theirs, to accept. Our priest Dunnere blessed each of them, and me, asking in Christ's name we be worthy of our vows."

They both thought on this, Ceric remembering, Hrald imagining. Many of the men would have been far older than Ceric, and to have seasoned warriors kneel before you and declare their arms to be yours must have struck him with awe.

"Worr was first," Ceric went on, "and will always be my chief man, serving as he has my father and uncle."

Hrald could look forward to no such swearing of fealty. His father's men had been bought with nothing more than treasure, and this he knew. It was not the only thing that bound them to him; he had heard his father refer to other Danes as his brothers often enough. And men like Asberg and Jari had been tied to his father through their actions on the field of battle, fighting shield-to-shield, providing cover, even saving each other's lives. But the bond was personal, unvoiced. And it did not extend to Hrald, or at least no further than Asberg's bond to him as uncle did. The men of Four Stones remained content after his father's disappearance because they had been treated fairly by him. They had settled, wed, and without grudging let Asberg and Jari continue to maintain what his father had won, just as his mother continued to run the hall.

There had been peace, as well. Asberg and Jari had been strong enough to keep internal dissent from growing, and had no need to marshal the men to fight a common enemy from without. Sidroc's shield upon the table reminded all of he who had been Jarl, and Hrald, sitting next to it, was his heir. But if there had been war when he was still a boy he did not know what would have happened.

"After they pledged to you?" Hrald asked now.

"Modwynn gave them all gifts of silver, or horses, to bind, and honour their pledges. To Worr she gave land. Then we drank – a lot." He was grinning now, and Hrald was grinning too, almost as if he had been there himself and had tasted the strong mead they must have been lifting.

"She gave me gifts too. A grant of land, her property at Sceaftesburh. It was my father's. And two new silver cups." He did not say that this last gift looked forward to his marriage, with one cup meant to be his, the second for his wife.

Ceric looked at the still-smiling Hrald.

"How was yours given?" Ceric asked him.

"Not – not a ceremony the way you had. My mother marked the month I was born. It was fifteen years past, last harvest-tide, near St Matthew's Day."

"Tell me of it," Ceric invited, just the same.

"Mother and Uncle Asberg came to me, and asked if I were ready to choose a sword from the treasure room. They both keep keys to the chest where the swords lay. Ashild was there too, but not teasing me, as she can do. Mother unlocked the chest. She said she would hold her key to it another three years, until I am eighteen."

Ceric nodded at this, but Hrald was looking straight ahead as they walked, recalling all this; and remembering who had not been there.

The person missing from the room was his father Sidroc. If his father had been there he would have chosen a sword for his son, marked out with his warrior's eye and experience the best weapon for Hrald. Hrald remembered sitting in the treasure room of Tyrsborg, off in Gotland, and his father speaking to him about this day, telling him he would have his pick.

The open chest held more than forty swords, lying in rows five deep, a sheep fleece between every layer. All Hrald could do was reach for the close second, the one his father would have worn if he had not selected that which he did. Because Hrald had often lifted it, it was in the first layer, on the top.

He picked up his story, moving his hand towards the sword at his side. "This one…was right there. I knew I wanted it.

"Asberg clapped me on the shoulder and praised my choice, told me it was one I would not outgrow however tall I got." The corners of his mouth turned up, remembering this. "And he promised me this new scabbard and belt, as his gift.

"Mother kissed me, a kiss of blessing."

He paused now, and felt Ceric was waiting to hear more. Compared to the symbel held for him his own sword-bearing seemed homely, and of no consequence. Yet something had happened, something more than choosing his sword. He decided to tell Ceric of it.

"Then Ashild made a gesture with her hand, that she wished to hold my sword herself.

"It surprised me. I waited long enough that she made a sound like a laugh.

'My touch will not blunt it, any more than my look, or mother's, would,' she said.

"She was almost taunting me. She knew I did not believe that old warning, that a woman could dull a man's weapon merely by looking on it, and so bring about his death. Why even mention it, I wondered.

"She reached her hand again, and I gave the sword over to her. Her right hand closed round the grip. She held it slightly down, then raised the blade up, straight to the roof between her and me.

"Then she spoke. 'This is the sword with which you will defend our home,' she said.

"She sounded almost – strange. My mother and uncle were watching her; their eyes were locked on her. I could not see her well; her face was split in two by the broad blade she held before it.

"She said something more. 'May you never fail it.'

"She lowered the blade then, so that it just touched my brow. I jerked back a little, even though she was going slowly. I remember how cold the steel felt on my brow-line. I saw her face now, her eyes staring at me. She looked a stranger.

"Then she pulled the sword back. She gave another short laugh, but one with some mirth in it."

He did not know what more he could say. That was all the ceremony he had, but somehow it had been Ashild who had made a rite of it. He had chosen the weapon, but then she made it also seem that it had somehow chosen him, as well.

Hrald knew women had power in their own way, and that they could use those powers to ruin a man; both the Saga-stories and those of the Holy Book were full of such tales. And he knew a maid had a power, just by her being still a maid. Ashild was a maid, so she had that power, and she was older than him, and she was clever and sharp-tongued, too. She saw things in her own way, and sometimes it was hard for Hrald to understand her.

That had been one such time, when she touched his sword's blade to his forehead. It was the duty of a man's sword not to fail him; if you felt your weapon had let you down, if you got hurt or your sword was not fast enough to protect one you tried to protect, then you killed your sword, took it to a Place of Offering and broke the blade, or bent it in two, rendering it useless forever as punishment. But when Ashild held the sword in her hand she changed that all round, and asked that he be worthy of the sword. It was almost a challenge, the way she said it, though she had kept her voice low.

He wondered what his friend thought about this. Ceric was walking on along at his side, listening, Hrald thought, with intent, but he had said nothing when he finished.

New words were rising in Hrald's throat, and now forming on his lips: Will you wed her, he meant to ask Ceric.

But Ceric was speaking again. Hrald was able to stop his question, making just a sound as they both spoke together. Hrald nodded, yielding to Ceric.

"The shield in the hall," Ceric noted, but said no more than this about it.

Then, "You sit in the high seat now," he guessed.

Hrald was looking down at the grass they trod. He was giving silent thanks to God that he had been stopped from asking such a question of Ceric, and just a few hours after his friend had arrived.

"Já. Yes," he answered, turning his thoughts. "That happened the year after you and I came back from Gotland."

Ceric thought back on what would occasion this; Hrald would have been only about Edwin's age then, thirteen years.

Hrald read his friend's face, and went on.

"It was the year that marked five since my father had vanished," he explained.

Ceric understood at least a part of it then. He knew that if any man or woman was gone for five years, the marriage they had entered into could be dissolved by law. Yet Hrald's mother had not taken another husband. Ceric counted to himself. She had been unto a widow for nine years now.

"I think…it was part of how mother, and my Uncle Asberg too, saw my…" Hrald paused so long, as if searching for the right words, that he had slowed. Ceric slowed too, at his side.

"My becoming one who could someday lead Four Stones," he finished.

Hrald's memory of that night was as clear as if it were last week. It had been St Mary's Day, that day nearing the end of Summer which nonetheless could be the hottest part of it. The day before St Mary's had been the day on which Hrald's father had ridden away as escort to Ceric's mother, and never returned. It was not a loss that, year-to-year, had been marked in any open way at the hall; yet he felt his mother was ever aware of it. That day had come round with the wheel of the year four more times without real mention. But this day she had spoken to him about it.

"Hrald," she called him as he came in through the side door from the stable yard. She was there just within, as if she had been waiting for him. He was a little late for the evening meal, the hall already crowded with men and women. He could smell the savour of browis with shredded pig-meat in it, and with it the warm scent of crusty loaves lately taken from their iron baking pans. The serving folk were massed in the passageway and at the end of the big table where he sat with his mother and uncle and the chief men of the place, Jari and the others.

"Walk with me to the table," his mother was telling him. "Your uncle awaits you. He will take your father's shield from the table, and give it you. You will hold it up a moment, then turn and hang it on the peg you will find on the wall behind you. Then turn to the hall – a moment will do. Take your seat." She paused just a moment in her instruction. "Your father's chair. You will sit there now."

He had no warning of this, but by the hushed seriousness of her tone knew he must do as he was bid. They stepped forward together over the floor of red and white stone, moving between trestle tables filled with those hungry for their supper. The sound of the hall was that of every night, voices raised in laughter or in calling out, riding above the rolling undercurrent of ringing cups and rattling salvers. From one of the benches his friend Gunnulf leant out to speak to him, asking a question about a colt they were training together, but Hrald knew to keep going.

Sure enough his uncle, Asberg, stood there at the centre-point of the big table, right at the spot at which he had five years earlier placed the shield of Sidroc, as reminder of that Jarl. It was odd seeing him there, standing and waiting; ordinarily he would be seated on Hrald's right side, the big chair his father had sat in empty between them. Now his uncle stood and watched him come, and Jari, seated where he ever sat, watched him too. Hrald became aware that those behind him must be seeing this, for the noise of the hall began to fall away somewhat.

When he and his mother reached the table, she went to stand behind the chair at which she sat. He moved closer to Asberg, who met his eyes. Then his uncle leant over the table and took up the red and black painted shield from its surface, handing it to Hrald so that he would take it by the rim edges and hold it, face first, before him.

It was awkward, but he did it. He held it aloft a moment, the bottom rim of it just clearing his eyes as they looked upon the folk of the hall of Four Stones. They were all looking back. Their noise had ebbed to a droning hum, a noise that thinned as he turned his back on them.

He lowered the shield, his arms near trembling, and saw the thick wooden peg that had been pounded in on the plank wall behind where he sat. He turned the shield, found the leathern shoulder strap, hooked it up and over the peg. The shield hit the wall as it settled, ringing out a dull and solid-sounding clang.

Then he turned back to the hall. Some of those he looked at cocked their heads in question, or glanced from him to Asberg or his mother, but none called out. A few nodded at him, and at what they had just seen. He looked at Asberg, at his mother. Their faces said he had done well. He began to move to the bench next his mother, checked himself, and stepped to the high backed-chair next to hers. It had already been pulled out enough for him to slip his slight frame in without making it scrape across the hard stones of the floor. He stood there a moment, until his mother began to sit. Then he lowered himself in his father's vacated chair.

"You have sat there for two years now," Ceric was summing.

Hrald nodded.

"Now you have your sword," Ceric went on. He thought on something he and the bailiff had spoken about, on the way here. "In three more years Guthrum is sure to name you Jarl."

Hrald again nodded. "So they say. There has been no trouble here amongst the men, thanks to Asberg and Jari. Guthrum has come a few times himself to see us."

"He must be well pleased, how you have held your lands and men," Ceric offered. "And the other things – your moving to the high seat at table, choosing your sword yourself – these were steps along the way to the day your King Guthrum names you true Jarl."

Hrald listened to his friend ticking off these benchmarks. Ceric looked and sounded like a man. Hrald had never felt the two years between them as sharply as he did at this moment. He felt himself a boy, with a boy's confusion.

I did not choose my sword myself, Hrald was saying silently. I chose that which my father had named a good one. I carried his shield to the wall and hung it there because my mother had told me to do so. I felt a traitor to him in moving it, but then he had betrayed me in not coming home –

He stopped himself, looked up. They had walked to the Place of Offering. The shallow pit which had once received the glitter of sacrificed weapons was clogged with drying grass. At the right end of it the wooden figure of Odin still stood. Dry-rot had cost him most of his face, and only a few spots on his tree-trunk body showed where the wood had been smoothed and once painted in bright pigments. Lichen grew over much of it. He had seen his father kill animals here, though he be Christian; Hrald had watched him in secret. He recalled the last time he had watched his father do so. He knew his father's act was wrong, but could neither try to stop him nor look away. He feared his father would burn in Hell for coming here, killing the piglet, and leaving it as Offering.

And he knew his father loved him, but that he was also somehow outside of his father's love, in this, and in other things.

Ceric was looking at the old beech tree at the other end. Its toothed and splaying leaves were at their fullest extent; it would be a few more weeks before they would begin to show any crinkle at their edges. Even so, he caught a dull glimmer of something hanging from one of the branches, dropping straight down in the greenish light. It was a silver necklace, left to the Old Gods. He knew that; he had seen it on past trips here with Hrald. The necklace was tarnished, but in the late afternoon Sun some brightness glittered from within its links. He wondered who had hung that necklace there, and why.

Chapter the Fourth: The Reflection in the Silver Disc

THE relief Ælfwyn felt at how well the feast was going was fully matched by the happiness she knew in having Ceric back again. She had only to look at Hrald to see his own joy in his friend's nearness. Her boy sat in the great carved chair, Ceric on the bench at his right hand, their heads often together as they talked and laughed together. Asberg and Æthelthryth were next along the benches, and then Jari, sitting with his wife Inga. On Ælfwyn's left sat the bailiff of Defenas, and then Worr. Wilgot the priest in his dark robes came next; he had sat at the high table since his arrival in the second year of her marriage to Hrald's father.

The table was filled out with those men who had always taken their places there, the most favoured of the warriors of Four Stones, who had helped win the place with Yrling, and then rode with Sidroc to its palisade walls to back him in his claim for it against his cousin Toki. Those who were wed sat with their wives at their sides. The four thegns from Kilton had been placed at the next table down, interspersed with some of the younger men of Four Stones; both Ælfwyn and Worr were keeping an eye on them, gauging their comfort, which seemed considerable, given the abundant food and drink.

For they were hungry. The seven who had ridden from Kilton had made camp anew each night, doing so without the benefit of a supply waggon and cook. They had carried salted and dried pig, and sacks of oats and barley. The small round loaves of bread and pots of soft cheese from Kilton's ovens and spring house were quickly consumed, giving way to the steady fare of grain browis boiled over a hastily laid camp-fire. Water from streams had been the drink of their horses, and theirs too, save for the time near the border they had been given ale.

Now they grasped deep cups in their fists. Ælfwyn had poured out for the high table, and Ashild, seated at the first woman's table, poured for the table which held the thegns and Four Stone's warriors of the second rank. Burginde also sat with Ashild, as did Ælfwyn's sister Eanflad, young Ealhswith, and a number of other unmarried women of the hall. Serving folk carried jugs amongst the rest of the trestles. Ælfwyn's guests at her own table all drank from the same stemmed goblets of silver they had taken their greeting-ale with. The thegns contented themselves with the large flared-wall cups of bronze she had been counting when they arrived.

She had not had time enough to do all she wished, but felt pride at what the kitchen yard had produced all the same. The leavened goodness of newly baked bread and the sweetness of butter would be what men on the road most craved, that and fresh meat. Two half-grown piglets had been basted in tangy verjuice dotted with crushed and resinous rosemary needles, then split and roasted until the skin was brown and crackling. Eggs were ever hard to come by on the road, and there were boiled hen's eggs, shelled and rolled in flaked salt and the tiny feathered leaves of green and pungent dill. A barley browis enlivened with fresh cress rounded out the meal, ladled steaming into deep pottery bowls.

Only one thing disturbed Ælfwyn's content, and that was the man seated at her left. Raedwulf of Defenas seemed distracted, almost ill at ease. He praised his hostess for her food and drink, but not in the smooth and practiced manner she might expect of a man of his rank and background. He did not attempt to impress her with tales of Ælfred's court, or display his familiarity with the leading families of Wessex by sharing seemingly private incidents for her amusement. Perhaps he did not feel his hunger with the acuteness of the younger men he had travelled with, for he ate and drank with notable restraint. She wondered if it were mere restlessness; he had delivered his King's gift to her, and perhaps was eager to be off. She did not yet know how long Ceric meant to remain with them, and could not in courtesy inquire how long the bailiff intended to stay; it could not be long, she assumed, a few days' rest for his horse and he would start back, with at least two of the thegns, she imagined.

"I must thank you again for bringing so precious a gift from Ælfred, King, to me," she said.

She had just offered the bailiff a small salver on which new apples, their juices sweetened by quick seething in butter, lay sliced. He reached for a crescent of fruit, then stopped himself with a jerk of his head.

"Forgive me. There is a second part to the King's gift to you, which lies still within my packs." He glanced up and across the crowded hall. The night was drawing to its close, and she must be as tired as he.

"It, like the book of Psalms, was created at the monastery Ælfred has founded at Athelney. It is the first such religious house to be created by the King; after so much destruction of our holy houses it gives him joy to have raised it up, and now to be able to commission gifts from it.

"If I may, I will present it on the morrow," he ended.

"Of course," she assented. "Although how the Psalter could be bettered, I cannot imagine."

Her smile was warm and sincere. It was for the book, he knew, but aimed at him. He saw how blue her eyes were, bright even by the glow of the tapers ranged about the table in front of them. Those blue eyes shifted to the left, as if she were thinking.

"Nor," she went on after a moment, "can I guess why the King so honours me with this gift, as grateful as I am to have it."

"Your benefactions to the foundation at Oundle are well-known to Ælfred," he answered. "Oundle alone has kept God's word alive in Lindisse these past many years, and you are largely responsible for this."

She demurred. "It is the work of Abbess Sigewif," she returned, lifting her hand slightly as if pushing away his praise. "If I have aided her with my treasure, I am grateful. But it is her work, her vision, that created and sustains Oundle."

"You undervalue your contribution. You must not do so, you who have done so much."

It was not just idle praise. There was some little strength in his words, and he ducked his chin as if he had heard the force in it, and would excuse himself.

"The bringing of the True Word to the heathen is a vital part of the Peace," he went on, in way of explanation. "King Æthelstan taking baptism, forsaking his idols, set a standard for his men, one which brings them closer to our own ways."

He spoke here of Guthrum, King of the Danes in Angle-land. As part of the Peace he had submitted to baptism, and been given the Christian name Æthelstan. The younger Ælfred had served as his god-father.

Ælfwyn had no ready answer for this. She had perhaps seen Guthrum more often than Raedwulf. And Sidroc, who had been there at Guthrum's side, had told her about it.

Guthrum was a shrewd and careful leader, well able to judge what would matter to his opponent in a peace treaty. Both sides must make concessions. The donning of a new linen tunic, presented as gift by his sponsor, Ælfred, and the sprinkling of water on Guthrum's head was important to the King of Wessex. Guthrum would agree to this, as would his chief men. He had tried in one final push to win all of Angle-land for himself, tried and failed. This young Ælfred had come from the marshes he had been driven into and somehow rallied men enough to beat his trained and hardened warriors.

It was the will of the Gods. Guthrum had made an earlier vow to Ælfred, made it with his own blood and the blood of his best men, on a great arm-ring of silver. Then he had broken that vow, felt forced to by the growing unease amongst those men of his who wanted more still. But he had angered the Gods, Odin and Tyr most deeply, in the oath-breaking. When the raven banner the Danes carried into the final battle fell, Guthrum knew his quest to rule all was over.

Keeping what he had already won became the goal. As part of the terms Ælfred asked that he accept a new God. As a demand it was slight enough, and besides Guthrum had his own curiosity about this God who had so aided his foe.

Ælfwyn did not think Guthrum's Christianity ran any deeper than this; like the white tunic he had been given on his baptismal day, he could take it off and put it on. And perhaps the bailiff of Defenas agreed with her. He had seen enough of the Danes, she was certain, to hold no illusions, though here with her now he must say the right and hopeful thing. At any rate, what was most important about the Danes accepting Christ was the new protection afforded nunneries and monasteries. These had been easy targets for the raiders, with their altars adorned as they were with silver and sometimes gold. Monks and priests had been slaughtered, and women consecrated as brides of Christ ravished, even carried off. With the taking of a new God the Danes understood His temples must not be desecrated, His holy men and women left in peace.

She had been attending to these thoughts, and glanced now at Raedwulf. His own eyes had travelled to the women's table, to rest on Ashild. The cressets lighting her table cast a flickering sheen on the deeper yellow of her gown. The bailiff seemed captivated by this play of light, and she spent a moment looking at him as he watched it. Then Ælfwyn saw Burginde looking fixedly back at him. She seemed to be studying the bailiff, and by her puckered lips Ælfwyn knew her brain was turning. An instant later Burginde's own gaze was broken by Ealhswith, pulling at the old nurse's sleeve, wanting her attention.

Ceric too was looking at the women's table, and also at Ashild. He had forgot that she would not be sitting there with them, but be away at her own table. Other than a nod and smile at him when she sat down, he had no contact with her.

She was wearing the golden gown he had brought her, and as she had entered the hall he had the pleasure of seeing her in it. She had combed out her hair so that it did indeed fall upon the shoulders of the gleaming fabric. The head-wrap she donned that night was as fine as the thin veils her mother favoured, and around Ashild's neck lay, as it ever did, the small cross of gold she had been given as a child. To this had been added a single round brooch, alight with the red of garnets, pinned near her neckline.

Ceric had taken ale twice at Four Stones, and not yet from Ashild's hand, as he had imagined on the road here. During the meal she had only risen once to pour out for the men at the second table; after this a serving woman had done so. But he had seen his thegns smile at her, seen that her sleeve of heavy silk had brushed the sleeve of one of them, and seen too the chaffing banter exchanged between her and the men of Four Stones she served. Gunnulf made her laugh with something he said about her gown; he could tell by the way she touched the neckline of it with her hand as she answered him. Of the men of the place he could do nothing, but he felt a thrill of envy towards his own pledged men, who held their cups before her as she dipped the bronze ewer their way. He tried to stifle this in his breast; he had never spoken of her to any of them, and they had no way of knowing that one day she would sit next him at the table upon the stone dais at Kilton.

"In the morning we will take falcons, and hunt," Hrald was telling him.

Some other young women had now come up to Ashild, come from the tables at which they sat with their own families, and he saw they were admiring her gown. Ceric turned his eyes and thoughts to Hrald.

"There are doves aplenty in the skies," Hrald went on, "and we will bring back enough to have a pie made with what they take."

A pie I would like to eat from a single salver, shared by Ashild, thought Ceric.

Four rode out with hawks upon their gloved left wrists in the morning: Hrald, Ceric, Worr, and Ashild. Raedwulf had been asked but had declined; he had spent enough time in the saddle, and bid the younger folk joy of their morning's sport.

The falcon house at Four Stones had three adult, trained birds in its mews, and they took all three with them, as well as a young female. Their path took them out along the palisade beyond the kitchen yard end of Four Stones, where the rivulet that ran at the tail of the yard passed under the wall and gradually flattened into a stream. Wild grasses grew plentifully there, though it was a short ride away; a horseman cannot comfortably ride one-handed, his other uplifted to hold a hunting bird, for long. They used no dogs, just flushed the doves by riding into the tall grasses in which the birds dipped and pecked at fallen seeds.

Before they set off Ceric and Worr acquainted themselves with the falcons by holding them and throwing out a lure tied to a leathern thong for them to pounce upon. When the bird returned to the wrist with it, they were given a morsel of fowl. In this way the birds learnt their voice and whistle. Ceric and Worr were given the most experienced birds, so that they might have the best hunting, but Hrald handed the young female to his sister.

"She is steadier with Ashild than with any one," he told his guests. The female, though young, was as large as the lone male they took with them. Her brown-feathered head swiveled over her folded wings, and her yellow eyes looked unblinkingly out at those looking back at her.

"We understand each other," Ashild said, checking the light tether at the falcon's feathered leg. "I have made what she wants, to be what I want. So we are both happy."

She was speaking to the others, but looking all the time at the young falcon on her wrist.

Yet the bird was flighty, and took to spreading her wings in protest if Ceric drew too near. He had a bird on his own wrist, and need attend to it.

At morning's end they had brought down six doves between them, and a wood-cock as well. The older birds would let their handlers take the downed prey from them, and were content to be allowed to rip into and devour what they wanted from the final birds they had snatched from the sky. But the female Ashild flew she allowed the entire wood-cock to. It was the only bird she had knocked out of the air, despite flying at two others.

"But she has taken the biggest prey of all," Ashild pointed out, as they watched the falcon rip the feathers from the wood-cock's plump body. "She will have her reward for setting her sights so high."

Each of the riders had a small woven basket of wicker-work at their saddle, and into it they dropped the gain from the morning's outing, Ashild's only remaining empty.

Riding back, Ceric moved his horse in alongside that of Ashild. Her falcon, having eaten, made no protest, though he could hear Ashild soothing it with her voice. Hrald and Worr were behind them. Ceric would at last have a moment to speak to her.

She looked over her bird at him. Her expression suggested she expected him to make some comment of the hunt just completed. When he did not speak, she smiled in a way that made him feel awkward, almost foolish. Her lips were pressed together, and curled to suggest she was holding back laughter.

She moved her gaze from his face to the walls ahead. He looked at the line of her face. Away from her, he had thought of her as being pretty. Now he saw she was not, or that it was the wrong word for her. Yet she was far from plain. There was something else she presented to the eye, at least to his.

Her face had not the narrowness of her mother's, nor Hrald's; her brow was broader, the chin not pointed, rather it was strong and round. Her nose was well-shaped, but neither very straight nor small, with the slightest of bumps up high at the bridge; nothing distinctive about it. The mouth too was mid-size, bowed as a woman's should be, but not, he knew, one to be overly remarked upon. The eyes of grey-blue were large enough, the lashes fringing them thick enough. Her eyebrows were a shade darker than her hair, which he still thought of as the colour of old oak, a warm light brown in which glints of pale gold shone. In form she was womanly, neither as tall nor as slight as her mother. He remembered as a boy thinking of her as sturdy, and she looked that, still.

Peering at her profile, he tried to guess of himself where his attraction lay. Her eyes, he thought; and yes, her lips. Those deep grey-blue eyes were active and searching, betraying the quickness of her brain. The expression of her mouth was ever-changing, and capable of conveying much without uttering a sound.

And although they looked nothing alike, parts of her reminded him of Hrald. Her thoughtfulness, for instance, though she could pierce that in an instant with a flare of temper, which Hrald never did. As a child, her demands to be included in their play amused and sometimes irked Ceric. As a maid there was much she was forbidden to do, but would do anyway, and most certainly if she saw Hrald and Ceric do so. She was older than Hrald, why had he freedoms she had not? She had been pulled away from their shared adventures many times the Summer he had spent here with them as a boy, pulled away by her mother or Burginde and punished. That the punishment was no greater than being forced to return to her spindle or yarn-winding made him brush it off. Such was woman's work, and she must learn it early, just as weapon-play with wooden swords and staffs had been his task, and that of Hrald, priming them for the day they took up true weapons.

She had still managed to become a good rider, and had as much ease about the falcon mews and in the field with the birds as her brother. For a moment he thought of his Aunt Edgyth, and the contrast between her quiet and learned self, and Ashild, riding next him, a falcon on her wrist. He hoped his uncle's widow would welcome her. Modwynn, he felt, would surely do so.

"Of what do you think?" she asked of a sudden.

The steady rhythm of their horses' pace, and his own thoughts, had lulled him. He saw she was watching him; the mouth he had been considering had curved into a slight smile.

He took an intake of breath. He could not tell her he had been judging her person, deciding her to be not pretty after all, and yet imagining the day he returned with her to his home and presented her to the ladies of Kilton.

"Of your gown," he lied, grasping at one of first things he had noted when he had seen her yesterday. "You dress as a woman of the Danes."

She was in fact again wearing the two-part dress of the Danish women of the place, with the same thick and round silver pins she wore yesterday holding her shoulder straps. That over-gown had been red; this one was blue, upon another long shift of white linen.

She gave the slightest of laughs, as if of surprise at his answer. "It is practical. If my over-gown soils, I can quickly change it for one clean."

He took this in with a nod.

"Last night," he said abruptly. "You looked – lovely."

It was her turn to take a breath. "I have not yet today thanked you for the splendid gown."

She paused, and Ceric thought she was about to say more about it, but did not.

"I must have surprised you," was what she did say.

He did not quite understand, and after a moment longer said so. "Surprised me?"

She had turned her lower lip in, and her white upper teeth now chewed it. "I do not know. Yes, I do. To those who know my mother, I am a surprise. Or worse."

"How so?"

"She is lovely. I am – not lovely. Despite what you said."

Ceric had done no courting, but knew enough that maids did not reject a given compliment. To attempt to refute her words, when he had had the same thought himself, was a disservice to them both. He told the truth.

"You are better than lovely. You are Ashild."

But he had missed his mark.

"Pretty words," she returned. "But at Kilton you must excel at them."

He was taken aback. What did she wish to hear; he could neither praise her nor share with her his thoughts about her attractions. And it was rude.

"Do I deserve that? Does Kilton?"

She pondered a moment.

"Kilton I do not know," she conceded.

"But me you do," he prodded.

She smiled now, and nodded her head, her tone much the milder. "Yes. Since we were babes together, as mother and Burginde keep reminding me."

She took a breath, began anew.

"Thank you for the gown, Ceric. It is wonderful, as I said when you gave it."

"I am glad you think so," he answered, gladder still at the warmth in her voice. "It was my mother's," he added.

She paused at this. "And my mother's, before that."

It struck him. Yes, he knew that. He had been told the silk gowns at Kilton, both those worn by Modwynn on feast days, and those laid by for him of his mother's, had been Ælfwyn's gift, hurriedly bundled and stuffed into the packs his mother had taken when she rode off with his injured father.

"How strange that one has returned here, to Four Stones," she mused aloud.

One day all four will be reunited at Kilton, he thought. And Modwynn is sure to leave hers to you in her will; you shall have all four, as once your own mother did...

They were now riding along the palisade wall, and would soon turn in through the opened gate.

The falcon between them moved restlessly on Ashild's wrist. It raised its tail and let loose a short stream of white fluid from its nether regions. The breeze blew a light spatter of it back onto Ashild's blue gown.

"Practical. As you see," she ended with a smile.

Ælfwyn sat in the yellow Sun of her garden. The line of beech trees she had planted years ago as saplings had grown, shielding the small space from the stable yard and busy workings of the hall yard. Shorter, shrubbier growth of white-flowered bedstraw formed a hedge low enough for those exiting the hall's side door to see one standing or seated within her enclosure. Yet it was still a private place for her and her daughters and sisters, laid out by her own hand, the flowers and herbs tended to by herself and her youngest sister Eanflad. No one else entered there unbidden, and even Hrald only came in when asked by his mother or sisters to do so. It was a woman's space, a haven of spicily sweet red roses, nodding bluebells, and the deep pink blossoms of corncockle, the seeds of which she had collected from the meadows, and sown.

She lifted her eyes from the small Psalter and let them fall on these last pink and reaching flowers. Charming they were, yet their charm was short-lived; she was looking now at several empty stems which yesterday had spread their tender and open-petalled faces to the Sun. It was like a lesson from the psalms she had just been reading, on the awe-full brevity of youth and beauty and life itself. But look, she reminded herself: new blossoms, of a fresher pink, had opened in their stead.

The thickness of the beeches prevented her from seeing her son and daughter with their guests ride in, hunting hawks in hand, and they did not see her. She could hear the drifting noise of the hall's various work yards, but clearer to her ears was the droning of honeybees rising from the red roses edging the walkway nearest to her table.

Someone had been invited to join her there, and until he arrived she would delight in the little volume. On every third or fourth page the text was enlivened with painted scenes set in scrolling flowered borders. Within these borders lived shepherds, their flocks resting at their feet; and men holding spears looking at the setting Sun. Purple hills arose over fanciful buildings, and springs bubbled up in dry fields. She wondered over these, and the mastery of brain and hand it took to conceive and paint them. The psalms pleased her just as much, neat rows of rounded writing, small, artful in their own way, symbols bearing to those who could read them the words of God and the ancient King, David.

Surely the gift of writing was one of the greatest God had ever bestowed. Even in the faith of the Old Gods, it was All-Father, Woden, who suffered for the skill of writing, and then gave that gift to man. It was Ceric's mother who had first taught her to write, and after that she had spent years improving her hand under the tutelage of both her priest Wilgot and Abbess Sigewif. But nothing she could ever do with quill and ink could approach the artfulness of the Psalter. Mindful of scratching the silver covers, she had brought a small cushion from her bower house on which it lay perched. She again bent her head over the lines of lettering, tiny but crisply formed.

She glanced up to see Raedwulf approaching on the path from the hall's side door. She rose slightly, and with lifted hand, beckoning him in.

"My lady," he greeted her. He held in his right hand a narrow sleeve of linen, no wider than two finger's width, and in length slightly longer than his hand.

"The second portion of Ælfred's gift to you." He was smiling down at her as he presented it, which deepened the slight cleft in his chin. "May it add to the usefulness of the first."

She gestured him to the bench at her side, a smile of anticipation on her lips. Her fingers found the opening flap of the linen tube, and slid the contents out into her other hand.

It was a wand of gold, fine and narrow. Attached to it at one end was a gemmed piece, almost like a brooch, but without any pin. The frame of it was gold, and upon its face, in enamel-work, was the image of a flower, like unto a white lily on a dark blue background. She turned it in her hand. The back was plain, but not unworked, for tiny balls of gold, no larger than the head of a pin, had been set all over in minute but riotous interlacing. She gasped, without meaning to, at the sheer beauty of the thing, and at the skill lavished thereon.

"It is a pointer, an æstal, to help point out the words of your Psalter. Or of any book," he added.

"Of books this is our first," she told him once more. "I have had letters, and charters sent to me, and now thanks to Ælfred we have a book. And this precious thing. An – æstal."

He made a slight movement with his own hand, suggesting she should use it. Holding the golden wand by the gemmed end, she moved the point of it across the lines of David's song her book lay open to.

"I see – I see how useful this will be," she told him, her excitement in her voice.

"It stops the eye long enough at any word so that the reader can grasp it, before going on to the next," he offered.

"Yes, that exactly. It will help the children with their reading. And me as well."

Her fingertip had caught the feel of something beneath its pad. She took the æstal in both hands and raised the edge of the round end to her face. "There is writing here," she told him.

"The King's own mark. It says 'Ælfred ordered me to be made'.

"Made for you," he ended.

Her eyes shone, making them a richer blue. "How can I thank him. How can I thank you?"

A moment passed as he regarded her. "Telling him of your happiness will be thanks enough."

"It is a great happiness. Ceric coming, and now these rich gifts –" she moved the pointer over the row of letters again.

They sat a while in silence, him watching her delight as she turned the pages and sometimes lowered the æstal to any words which caught her eye. She felt almost a child, exulting in a gift, and watched by those older who took gentle pleasure in her joy.

"Raedwulf," she said at length, placing the æstal down, and seeing how well the slender rod served to mark her place, "you mentioned last night that the King meant to thank me for Oundle, and so sent you with these gifts. And your daughter is wed to Worr, and now lives at Kilton, which ties you too to that place. Ælfred is Ceric's god-father. I know these things. But – is there more?

"I ask because – because Ceric has eighteen years, and Ashild is nearing that." She could not say any more than this, and in fact surprised herself by saying as much. It had been Ashild's prompting, her fears about Ceric's own gift to her, that led her to say this.

She was looking at him, her eyes wide and blue, her lips upturned in question. He let his gaze rest on her a moment before he answered.

"Lady, of Ælfred's gifts to you, I do not know."

He gave a slow exhalation of breath, as if he himself had considered just this question. He seemed sincere in his uncertainty, and she could not help but believe him.

"Ælfred has given many rich gifts, this I think you know. Besides St Peter's Pence, that gift of treasure he has sent nearly every year to Rome to our Holy Father, he has ordered made such gifts as he has sent to you. Bishops, and other great benefactors have received them."

"Bishops," she echoed, not deigning to consider herself near their rank in importance. She scarce thought of herself as a great benefactor, but Raedwulf had insisted last night that she was. And Abbess Sigewif had herself called her that, she must admit.

"About the young people," Raedwulf went on, "I cannot say. I do not know Ceric of Kilton well, and he has not confided in me his plans for his future. Nor do I think has he to Worr, who would I think, tell me something of such import."

Ælfwyn felt she must say the next, as difficult as it was to broach. Here, and in private, was the only way it could be said. She drew a quiet breath, and spoke as slowly as she could, fearful the words might tumble out and sound even worse.

"So you are not here – Ceric is not here – to sue for my daughter's hand?"

She felt an almost giddy lightheadedness now it was out, as if she had asked a suitor about her own prospects. Still, that is what parents must do at times, ask the direct question.

He seemed neither startled nor amused, which is what she most feared. He shook his head.

"It was not my charge, no." He kept looking at her, then went on, "Though in confidence I tell you Modwynn, Lady of Kilton, made clear to me that she would more than welcome such a match for her grandson."

Her face lit. "I am so glad," she told him, with true warmth. "You see, Ceric is the first-born of my closest friend. She and I have been apart for many years; Fate has separated, but not divided us. It was always her wish, and mine too, that our children might find love and happiness together."

The eyes he had kept on her rapt face had lowered by the end of her speech. She felt a flush of embarrassment now, and almost wondered if her cheek had reddened.

It was not that.

His eyes rose to her, and kept her in a steady gaze, one mild, not piercing.

"You do not know who I am," he said.

The heart within her breast seemed to tighten, and she heard herself catch her own breath. Yet she did not know the meaning of his words. Then he made it clear.

"I rode with Ælfred once, to Cirenceaster. Another rode with us. Gyric of Kilton."

All the air had been pressed out of her; her next breath was a shallow gasp.

"My nurse, Burginde…she marked you last night, but could not recall where once she had seen you…"

"At the hall of Ælfsige of Cirenceaster," he answered. "My people were of Defenas, and I joined Ælfred from there. We rode to Kilton, where Gyric joined us, then on to your hall."

"Forgive me…I have no memory of you…"

She found it hard even to say this much. Many young men had arrived with Ælfred. She stared at his face, imagining it then.

"There is nothing to forgive." His words were as mild as his gaze.

He looked a little away from her now, across the garden at some unknown point. "And no reason to recall me. Gyric was there. You saw each other."

His eyes were still steady on whatever he fixed upon. "You saw no one else."

"Yes," she answered, in a whisper. "We saw no one else." She had lowered her head.

"We spent three nights at your hall," he went on. "On the last, our going-away feast, you wore the gown your daughter wore last night."

Her head had further dropped, almost upon her breast. He was looking at her now, saw her eyes were closed.

He gave his head a shake, went on.

"I did not know Gyric well, had only met him then," he told her. "When the Danes set upon us I saw him take the dragon banner from Ælfred's hand. Ælfred had been waving it, shouting, urging us on. A group of Danes marked it. I watched Gyric take the banner, realised why. After that, I was too occupied to know what had happened. When we finally regrouped a number of us were gone. Gyric was one of them.

"There were more attacks. More pitched battles. I heard at length that Gyric had been returned to Kilton. And that you had been wed to the Dane Yrling, and come here."

A pause. It was as if he were distilling their entire lives into a few lines, everything boiled off but the most powerful facts, the essence of their actions on this Earth.

"I wed," he recounted. "A fine woman. She was of Defenas. She died in childbed, but left me Wilgyfu, our daughter.

"Ælfred named me bailiff seven years ago. The King's justice has kept me busy. And he has entrusted me to carry certain gifts from time to time. I was not surprised when he called me to Witanceaster to undertake an errand. What surprised me was to whom.

"Though I have no answers for your daughter, let me say how glad I have been to once again look upon your face."

He was gazing at her now.

Her hand rose to her brow, her fingertips resting lightly there. Ælfwyn of Cirenceaster, he had called her, when he saw her. Her flower was faded, yet his naming her that had stirred something in her breast.

A honeybee, laden with golden pollen, stole her eyes from his, tracing a jagged path in the still air over her closed Psalter. Sweetness, and stings, she thought.

They sat in silence. She had dropped her hand, and now both framed the book on the little cushion. Her chin, like her eyes, were downcast.

Her guest was standing, and spoke in lowered tones. "I will leave you with Ælfred's gifts," he told her, and withdrew.

After a time she stood, took up the Psalter, and went into her bower house. She locked the book and pointer away. Then she stood in the centre of the small house. Her eye fell on the shelf that held the polished disc of silver she used to look at herself.

She moved to it, took it up. It showed her the narrowness of her face. The blue eyes, still clear, had fine lines around them, and a few such lines surrounded her mouth, with its still-pink lips. Her flaxen hair was lighter than it had ever been at her hair line and temples, before it vanished under her head-wrap. She knew that brightness was due to a tiny number of strands now paling to white.

Ælfwyn of Cirenceaster. She lowered the disc, set it back upon its shelf.

Chapter the Fifth: Silver Hammer

RAEDWULF of Defenas did not return to the hall of Four Stones, or the weaving room at the end of the creaking stairs which had been given over to him. Ælfwyn and Burginde had made the narrow loft as comfortable as they could, leaving the small table well supplied with cressets should he need more light. But the looms fixed against the walls named it a work-room, an active one at that. The women of the place, perhaps his hostess herself, would have need to stand at those looms, or to take up the waiting spindles, clustered atop baskets of carded wool.

He wanted the sky above his head. To return to a room would only concentrate his thoughts, and this he did not want. He went to the stable and asked for his horse, which stood drowsing with the others in the nearby paddock. The man in charge of the place, Mul, was quick about it. Raedwulf pulled himself into his saddle and headed through the hall yard and out the opened gates. The village was small enough that he was soon in open country.

He had said more than he intended to the Lady of Four Stones. It was his role to be guarded in speech, and he had let down his guard, even if he had done nothing more than inform her they had before met. Her spoken response confirmed he had left no impress on her mind; her unspoken response proved the depth of her bond with the lost Gyric. The seriousness with which she had taken it had carried him also back to the moment, allowed him to live it once more, as she was doing. He had felt dangerously close to revealing more than he should. He reassured himself that wrapped in her memories she was not aware of his own reactions.

He turned his thoughts to the lady's daughter. On this topic he had left even more unsaid to her mother. He had not told her, when relating his conversation with the Lady Modwynn, that she had spent some little time with him considering a match between Kilton and Four Stones.

He recalled his meeting with that lady, seated alone with her at the table in the hall of Kilton. He could see that the possibility of such a match had been something that for years had been in her grandson's background. Not until Ceric had chosen his gift for Ashild had it come to the forefront in her mind. She did not wish him to wed at so young an age, but realised others would also pursue the daughter of Four Stones. If Ashild and her mother would have him, she would do what she could to secure the boy's happiness.

But her thoughts on the matter could not stop there; there was much else to consider, and he had admired her candid openness in discussing the possibilities with him. Perhaps Ceric would not prove agreeable to the eldest daughter of Four Stones, her mother and their advisors. Yes, he was Ceric of Kilton. But she would bring an immense amount of treasure to any man she wed. Ceric would not be Lord of Kilton. First born, he would yet be second at the place. Ashild was one who could command a man who was, or would be, first.

Thus, she told the bailiff, if the maid and her people sought ties to Kilton and Wessex, her younger grandson, Edwin, could be named. He was four years younger, but another two years would see him near sixteen. If she would wait that long, the match could be made.

It was not easy for Modwynn to contemplate this option, let alone discuss it with Raedwulf. She loved Ceric and wanted his happiness, and believed that he had decided Ashild was his choice. She would do all she could to help secure the girl for him when the time came. But she must also place the interests of Kilton, and of Wessex, above those of her own, or even Ceric's, heart. A union between Kilton and Four Stones would be of the greatest significance in assuring the continuation of the Peace. This marriage of the young of two strongholds, Saxon and Dane, would further tie the two kingdoms together. Marriage between foes was ever the surest way to prevent future bloodshed.

There was a younger maid of Four Stones, Modwynn knew, one of ten or eleven years, and thus more suited to Edwin in age. Four years at least would be needed before she could be wed. Ælfred and Wessex may not have that much time; the better option for Edwin was the elder girl, if that is what Four Stones sought. She would not, she told Raedwulf, expect Ceric, denied the elder, to wed the younger, nor would it be the most strategic match for either. It would doubly bind two houses in two kingdoms, but eliminate the possibility of an advantageous union within their own borders. She concluded by expressing the confidence of her position: If Ashild could not be had by either youth at Kilton, she would find suitable maids in Wessex for both.

He had been impressed with the breadth of her vision, the sweep of her considerations. The bailiff would be able to observe the young people, but need not do more than that. The choice, she stressed, must first be made by Ceric. He had not seen Ashild for four years. If she still proved pleasing to him, Modwynn trusted that this visit would soon be followed by a second, at which a formal offer would be presented. Perhaps Raedwulf could be persuaded to make the journey a second time, if that were the case.

The meadows surrounding Raedwulf were receding into woods, and he did not wish to come upon a watch-man. He slowed his horse.

A return to Four Stones, he thought. No, he did not think this a charge he would again undertake.

He recalled Ælfwyn's spoken wish to him, that Ashild and Ceric might find love and happiness together. The pairing of words held meaning: one could find love, yet miss the chance at happiness with the beloved. It had happened to Ælfwyn. It had happened, as well, to him.

The next day was the Sabbath. Four Stones, as great as it was, had no church nor chapel. Ælfwyn had put much treasure to the building of the stone church at Oundle, where it would benefit its large community of nuns and brothers. Here at Four Stones she had had raised a stone preaching cross, which stood firmly anchored in the grassy sward before the palisade, off to one side of the gates. There both hall and village gathered every week to hear Wilgot preach. The family of Four Stones would then join the priest back in his timber house, where private devotions followed, including the receiving of Communion.

Ceric had been raised in a most devout hall, and was used from boyhood to attending divine service. The stone chapel at Kilton was in many ways a favourite place. He knew by heart its cool gray walls, tall pedestals upon which painted wooden statues of blue-eyed St Ninnoc and St Mary looked down, and the altar with its white linen, and silver candlesticks and cup. Perhaps the floor at Kilton's church was most impressive to Ceric, for beneath a huge slab of polished grey stone lay his grandsire's mortal remains. He had ever felt close to Godwulf standing at that slab, and since he had been given the great man's weapons this bond was heightened.

Now, on the plank floor of the humble house of Wilgot he thought of Kilton, and its chapel. He stood behind Ashild during the simple Mass, kneeling and rising each time Wilgot rang his tiny brass bell. He was flanked by Hrald and Worr; the bailiff stood with Asberg and Asberg's wife Inga. Ashild's mother and sisters and aunt stood next Ashild, as did Burginde. They knelt and rose almost as one.

Outside, speaking to all, Wilgot had told of the Warrior Christ, that bold but gentle chieftain of men's souls, who died, as great Kings do, for his people's sake. Now to this much smaller group of worshipers Wilgot spoke in the Holy Tongue of Rome, most of which Ceric did not understand word for word, but discerned the meaning. He knew the priest spoke of the Resurrection and the Life.

Ceric's hand went to his chest, touched the golden cross that lay beneath his tunic. His father had died wearing that cross, one brought from Rome and given by Ælfred himself. Incense was pouring forth from a small bronze censer, a scented haze in the air. It made his eyes smart, but he had ever liked the smell, one that served to transport his senses. His hand pressed harder against the cross of gold, his finger-tip resting on the smooth red garnet at its centre.

His head filled with the smoking incense, the soft droning of the priest, and the power of his own alive and strong and vital self. He felt the line between Godwulf and Gyric, leading to, and anchoring, him. Gold from two men, sire and grand-sire, gold heavenly and earthly: golden cross, and golden-hilted sword.

He knew his father to be good, and his grand-sire to be great. A prayer came to his lips, that he be both.

That night in the hall Raedwulf asked that he might be allowed to stay a further day. His horse would be well rested by the third day; he had gauged his fitness during his afternoon's ride.

"So soon," Ælfwyn had replied.

He did not know if it was surprise or disappointment he heard.

Ceric had not named the length of time he meant to stay. Hrald had pressed him to make it all the rest of the Summer, almost two months, but Ceric had shaken his head, albeit with a laugh. All expected at least a one month's stay, after so long a journey; but none, even perhaps Ceric, knew for certain.

"Of course. You will have many demands awaiting you at Defenas," Ælfwyn continued, in assent to Raedwulf.

A serving man was holding a platter of beef boiled with bayberries before them, and he forked some of the shredded meat onto his salver. They ate from single salvers; only those wed shared a larger one.

He wondered for a moment when she had surrendered that doubled salver. He knew little of her second marriage, that to the Jarl of South Lindisse, save that it was a union of war-time necessity. Yet the reports he had heard on Sidroc had been in the main approving. He had seen the man twice, at the blood-oath swearing by Guthrum to Ælfred, and then again at Guthrum's surrender. The Dane had been known as a formidable warrior, but all of Guthrum's best men had been so; one did not win and hold such a keep as this with words.

Had she given up the marriage-salver soon after Sidroc's disappearance, or waited the legal requirement, and on the fifth anniversary at last relinquished it? Then there was the oddity of Sidroc's living with the woman who was Ceric's mother. And of his having killed Godwin of Kilton. There were nuances he could not hope to understand, and were not his to encompass. He knew but the barest outline of events.

The serving man had moved off. "Demands there are, always," he answered, aware that, rested as his horse might be, some weariness showed in his words. "But I have delivered Ælfred's gifts, discharged that duty." He looked at her and did not keep himself from smiling.

"As pleasant as it was, I must make my start for Wessex."

She glanced to the table at which sat the thegns. "We will make sure you are well-provisioned. You will take one or two thegns with you?"

"None," he told her. "They are Ceric's men. I need none of my own. I bear a safe-conduct from Ælfred, just as he does, but I expect my return to be met with the same ease as our coming."

He read the concern in her face at this, though she answered with a single word. "Alone…?"

He only nodded in answer. Well, she thought, he had faced grave dangers in his life. Riding alone in peace time through a kingdom of the Danes would mean little.

"Will you…stop at Kilton before you return home?" She felt some boldness in asking it, as if she expected him to tell her what report he would take back to Ceric's grandmother. She was not unaware that she herself would be included in the telling.

He was again watching her face closely, and began to smile. "I will," he confessed. "My daughter and small grandsons are there."

She smiled too. "Then stopping there will be the greatest of pleasures," she nodded.

"But yes," he went on. "I must stop at Kilton to speak to Lady Modwynn." He glanced across his hostess at where Ceric sat next to Hrald. "Though I can tell her little about her grandson's prospects."

Ælfwyn found her eyes following those of Raedwulf, before looking down at her own plate.

"Yes. I am sorry. Ashild has not confided in me." Her eyes rose to his. "Perhaps if you could stay longer…" her words trailed off, abashed at how it sounded. She decided to make of it a jest. "If you could stay longer, you would spare yourself the dangers of the road, and we could all learn more," she said, and let herself smile.

The danger is in my staying, not my going, he thought. But he too smiled at her words.

At the end of the meal Wilgot got up to tell the story of the workers in the vineyards. The priest was less than middle height, and had grown stout over the years at Four Stones, but his voice was one which could command the hall when needed.

He told a tale from the Holy Book almost every night, and had, Ælfwyn thought, much added to his skill in doing so, making much of what was sometimes little, giving colourful voice to characters who were only described in the briefest of terms. He could even draw laughter from the tales when necessary, which Ælfwyn admired for her hall's sake; she did not think much laughter lay within the originals.

Wilgot had greeted the arrival of the Psalter with nearly as much joy as she. Raedwulf had been with her when she displayed it to the priest, before they sat at meat. It was clear by the prelate's tone of voice that the volume represented an answered prayer: his. But Raedwulf had taken no little pains in pointing out the book and its precious æstal were a gift from the King to Ælfwyn, and not the priest of Four Stones.

She felt a surge of gratitude towards the bailiff for this, and for the way he had done it, making it seem that the greater glory was due the priest, for the capacity with reading the Lady of Four Stones had acquired since his arrival there. The gift, he assured them both, was almost a personal commendation of Wilgot's merit by the Abbot of Athelney, under whose care it had been created.

When the meal was over Ælfwyn asked Ashild to join her in her bower garden. Ælfwyn must return later to the kitchen-passage to number and lock up the silver, but a few minutes away in the quiet of her garden would delay no one. They walked together past the white-blossomed bracts of bedstraw; in the dimming light the froth of tiny flowers seemed almost to glow. The light in the sky was now paling as dusk deepened, draining the other flowers of their highest colour within the enclosing hedge.

"Raedwulf will leave, day after tomorrow," she told her daughter.

"O." Ashild blinked, then pulled at the green husk beneath a faded rose, snapping it off. "And Ceric?…I thought he would stay a month…"

"I think he will stay, at least that," Ælfwyn answered. "I know Hrald wants him to."

Ashild nodded. She was now stripping off the wilted petals, which fell limply from her fingertips to the gravel walk. Their perfume had decayed to an almost musky scent.

"And you?" her mother asked. "Do you wish Ceric to stay?"

She did not respond at once. Then, "He is good to hawk with."

Ælfwyn let out a sigh. Ashild's chin snapped up.

"It is the bailiff, is it not?" she claimed. "He has asked you if Ceric and I – he wants to know about us. So he can tell all Kilton."

"Not so, Ashild. He asked nothing of the kind. It was in fact I, who asked him."

"You asked him…?"

"How could I not? You were alarmed at the richness of Ceric's gift. And the gift of the King to me seemed to signal some special favour, beyond any I have earned from my benefactions at Oundle. So I asked Raedwulf."

"And…?"

Her mother pursed her lips. "Ceric, it seems, has said nothing to him, or to anyone, of his intentions." She slowed now. "What the bailiff made clear was Lady Modwynn's welcoming of such a union."

Ashild was shaking her head in rapid movement. All her mother could do was go on.

"I know he has been here only two days. But do you…feel that you…would accept him, should he ask?"

It was a question her own parents had never asked her, a choice she had never been allowed to make. She knew Ashild could not understand how Fate had favoured her, in being granted what had been denied her mother. It was not only the difference of coming of age during a time of peace, instead of war. Ælfwyn had vowed that all her children would be given as much freedom as was possible when it came to time to wed.

Her daughter pondered just a moment. Ceric was blessed with high good looks, was of a house unequalled in Wessex save only by that of its King, and had ever been a warm and good friend to Hrald. His actions and words suggested he felt he had claim upon her, as if Fate had already decreed their union.

She loved her mother, loved Hrald, and knew they wanted this for her. Yet to leave Four Stones, leave Lindisse, leave all she loved behind…

There was affection in her breast for Ceric, and if she stilled herself enough to feel it, attraction too. Yet it was not enough.

She flung the bare rose stem onto the darkening gravel walk, and gave a laugh. "Let his grandmother ask me, for him."

Hrald and Ceric had ridden out the pounded clay road to the valley of horses. It was known as well as the valley of flax, and as they neared it Ceric remembered this, for it was here, at the entrance to the natural plain set between wooded hills, that the tall blue-flowered plant thrived. The morning was bright and dry, and men were at work with scythes, sweeping the sharp arcs of bright metal against the slender plants, just brushing the surface of the dark soil with them, leaving the fibre encased in the green stalks as long as possible. The scythers waded into the centre of the blue-crowned patches, and swept round in circles as they worked outward to the borders. Late nesting ground birds had time to flee to the safety of the margins, and as Hrald and Ceric rode by several nightjars emerged, chirping their complaint.

They wanted to visit the valley for the sheer pleasure of seeing so many fine animals at once; riding and horses had always been a chief enjoyment for them both. And Hrald was hoping he could induce his friend to choose any horse he wanted for the duration of his stay, arguing that as fine as Ceric's black gelding was, it deserved a rest after the long trek eastwards to Four Stones.

A cluster of small crofts had sprung up to one side of the road at the mouth of the valley. They were those of the warrior Danes of the place, now wed and settled to either the women of the village of Four Stones, or their sweethearts that had come across the sea to join them years earlier. The houses were small, but well-made of timber and wattle and daub. Their low roofs bristled with yellowed thatch, and the gable-peaks here and there were crowned with strutting and ruddy-feathered roosters who stretched their necks to call out as the friends passed. Rough-hewn railings penned in the fattening pig that every croft boasted, encircling too the varied fowl houses, and the tended rows of cabbages and turnips and leeks. Past these, and set to one side, was the long house, at which a number of men lived, and whose charge it was to tend and guard the horses. The plain on which they grazed was ringed with woods thick enough to deter their wandering, but the broad area fronted by the flax fields was fenced across, parcelled out into a number of large paddocks.

They reined up first before that which held mares and their this-year's foals. Ceric gave a whistle of admiration. "We should have brought Worr," he said, turning in his saddle as he looked out over the multitude of glossy dams standing cropping the grasses on which their young gambolled and kicked, or lay stretched out, sleeping. The horse-thegn of Kilton would fully appreciate the sight.

Their horses were a great source of wealth to Four Stones, and Hrald had always known this. Apart from their inherent value, they had meant that its warriors could move quickly, either on raids, or to the pitched battles which they had fought. It had been years since those men had thus ridden out, but the herd had steadily been increased.

"We will bring him, tomorrow," Hrald agreed, "and all choose horses and race." He canted his head to the clay road they had ridden on, long and flat, one ideal for giving a good horse his head.

They went at a walk, passing before the horses, at times letting themselves in to one pasture or another to view the animals up close. A few stallions were set apart in single paddocks.

"The bay?" Ceric asked. His eyes were moving from horse to horse, but he need say no more than that to Hrald.

It was Sidroc's great bay stallion Ceric asked after. "He died, at last," Hrald answered. "A year ago. He must have had more than twenty years."

He had sired many of the best horses in the herd. Now Hrald led Ceric to where a group of almost-grown colts grazed. Several of them were dark bays, as was Sidroc's. Hrald pointed to one with a rippling black mane falling over its arched neck. "That is his last colt; I will take him for my own."

Ceric took in the beast, who shook his head with a snort. "He would be my choice, too," he said. "You are training him yourself?"

"Yes, with Gunnulf; he is good with horses, if a little reckless."

Ceric had seen Gunnulf watch them ride away together that morning, and wondered if the young Dane had felt slighted not to have been asked to join the outing. Onund too had been lingering near Gunnulf, and Ceric had seen them talking as they saddled their own horses and left.

"Gunnulf is your friend," Ceric said.

"Yes, of course," Hrald said. "Not – not like you. But a friend."

Ceric nodded. "I know. Not like us," he answered. No other friend could be like Hrald, just as Hrald could have no friend like him.

"Onund has not challenged you to wrestle lately," Ceric now guessed. Hrald was so much bigger that such a match would likely be one-sided from the start.

Hrald laughed. "No. He and Gunnulf wrestle; they are always together."

As they turned their horses' heads they saw a lone rider at the furthest end of the joined paddocks. The horses kept there were not those Hrald and Ceric had stopped before, being a mix of heavy draught and cart-horses, ponies, and any lame or injured who were set to heal amongst them. The rider now dropped from the saddle, and reached up to help a second figure down.

"Ashild," Ceric said, looking to Hrald.

"Picking out a pony for Ealhswith," Hrald agreed.

They moved along outside the wooden fences until they gained the last paddock. Ashild and Ealhswith were standing by the gate together, Ashild pointing out various animals to her little sister. Ceric's eyes fell upon the small herd, then rested on a near-white pony.

"Is that the dappled grey you gave me?" he asked Hrald, seeing in the whitened coat of that little beast the pony that

Hrald had brought to Ceric to ride back to Four Stones when they had first met.

Hrald grinned. "It is. And that is my black," he said, pointing out an even fatter pony, now sprinkled with a few white hairs on muzzle and rump.

Ealhswith was the age now that Ceric had been then; it made sense Ashild would choose from the same mounts they had all ridden.

The two had turned to greet the approaching riders. Ashild gave a smile as she lifted her hand. Little Ealhswith seemed more uncertain.

"The grey pony was mine, for a Summer," Ceric told her after they had swung down. Ealhswith was almost a minikin version of her mother, with straight hair of the palest yellow, a narrow face, and rich blue eyes. Those eyes took Ceric in as he spoke to her, looking gravely up at him.

They were all standing together at the gate, watching the nibbling beasts within move with lowered heads across the grasses. Ceric went on. "He was steady, and never bolted, even when we both got stung by a bee." He laughed at the memory of that.

There was also the black, and two chestnut ponies as well, and the three stood talking over their differing points, asking Ealhswith which she found most pleasing.

"The chestnut, with the blaze," Ealhswith finally said.

Ashild was rummaging through her saddle bag, and produced both an apple and a pony halter from its depths. She handed her sister the halter and lead, but held on to the apple. "Then we will go in, and get acquainted," she said, taking the knife at her side and deftly cutting the fruit into half.

Ceric and Hrald stayed behind as the two sisters entered the paddock. Both the grey and the black pony, guessing a treat might be forthcoming, began ambling towards them. Ealhswith shrank back slightly towards her older sister, but they kept making for the chestnut, Ashild brushing off the two beggars with a pat on the neck. They watched Ashild extend her hand, palm flat before the muzzle of the chestnut, saw the whiskery lips retract and long teeth close around the half apple laying there. Ealhswith's back was to them, but they saw her give a little start. They could just hear the murmur of Ashild's voice, soothing both pony and child. They saw Ashild place the remaining apple half on the stretched and open palm of her sister, and the nodding head of the pony lower over it. The reddish head moved away with another nod. Ealhswith pulled back her hand then, wiping it on her skirts.

Ashild slipped the halter over the chestnut's head, then handed the lead to her sister. They led the pony between them back to where Ceric and Hrald waited.

Once outside the reclosed gate, the two praised Ealhswith for her choice.

"Mul's boys will ride her for a few days, they are your size and age," Ashild was telling her. "Then you and I will ride out together, to gather flowers along the stream banks," she promised.

Hrald had taken the lead from Ealhswith. "I recall this one; she is good and gentle," he was telling her. To prove his point he took the smallest of hops, swinging one leg over the broad back and pulling himself up. His hanging toes nearly brushed the grass they stood upon. Ealhswith could not help but laugh.

He squeezed his knees about the round barrel of the mare, and she moved forward. Hrald checked her and slid off the pony's back. "Now you," he offered to his little sister.

Ealhswith let herself be swung up on the ruddy back, and Hrald led her about.

Ceric and Ashild stood watching by the fence.

"She seems fearful," Ceric said, his eyes upon Ealhswith's fists, which were twisted in the golden mane.

Ashild nodded. "She was bitten, not long ago, by one of my own horses. Ealhswith was standing by his head. Her hair was lying on her shoulder, and he reached out and closed his teeth over it. Not a hard bite; it was fear more than pain. I will help her get over it."

Ceric was thinking on this, that it was sometimes difficult for those spooked by animals to lose their fear, when she spoke again.

"Mother says Raedwulf will leave tomorrow."

"Yes, he told me last night."

Her tone had changed enough that he looked at her closely. She said no more, and he did not know what to follow with.

"He is a good man," he offered. "Worr is wed to his daughter, and though they came to Kilton only at feast-times, they were always welcome company."

Worr had told her this when they were hawking, of the close connection between him and the bailiff. Well, she thought, the portion of the trip concerning Raedwulf had proved a success. He had delivered the King's gift, and now was readying himself to return to Wessex, even without news of their guest's marriage prospects. She remembered her mother's prodding of the night before, and thinking on this caused a sudden spark of ire to flare in her breast. She turned on him with her demand.

"The gown…was it chosen by the Lady Modwynn as a wooing gift?"

His face was a blank, looking at her. He shook his head, a sharp, single gesture. He seemed to hear the first part of her question, but not the closing words.

"No, no. I chose it. I wanted to give you the most precious thing I had, to give to a maid."

He thought of what more he could say, to explain his gift. "It was my mother's, as I told you." Then, a moment later, "There was no one like her. And you are like that, too. Different from her, but like no one else."

The spark of heat she felt ebbed away in the mildness of his response. She waited a moment before she answered.

Ashild had a clear, if girlish memory of Ceridwen, liking her then because her mother loved her, recalling her sadness over the loss of her husband and babe. She remembered too her warmth, something felt even despite the sadness.

"You speak of her as if she were dead." The stiffness had left her shoulders, and her words were calm, unquestioning.

Ceric again shook his head at her words, but gently. "Not dead," he answered, in soft voice. "Not by the grace of God. Just…far away."

Far away, she thought, on an island in the Baltic, with father. And he will not come back. Yet mother does not hate her.

She could not help her next question, any more than she could help her first.

"Did you come here to wed me?"

He was so stunned that he could not at first answer.

"I mean, come to take me away, so that I would be wed to you at Kilton. Bring the bailiff to bargain with Mother and my uncle, set the terms."

Her tone was not one of disdain, despite her words. It seemed a simple, if pointed question.

He opened his mouth, but she went on.

"Did you?"

"I – I do not know. No. I did not," he said, feeling flustered and clumsy.

"So you do not wish to wed me."

"No. I do," he countered, feeling desperate at what she was making him say.

Her look was cool, and her words equally so.

"So you wish to wed a Dane."

He would have laughed if he could; what she was saying sounded almost unreal.

"You are not a Dane," he answered, skirting her charge.

Her head jerked as if he had slapped her.

"I am a Dane. As is my brother. He will be Jarl here, Jarl of a Danish keep in a Danish Kingdom."

"You – you are half Dane. As is Hrald."

"No. I am a Dane. As was my father."

She was watching his unbelieving face.

"Your mother – she was of Mercia, but half-Welsh," she told him. "I know this. Do you then call yourself one quarter part Mercian, one quarter part Welsh, one half of – "

But he had cut her off, and too soon, so eager he was with his answer.

"No," he insisted, with some little vehemence. "I am Saxon. I am of Kilton, a man of Wessex."

"And so I am a Dane," she returned. "And I love this place – Four Stones. More than any of you know. I would not trade it for Kilton, or the richest burh in Angle-land."

"Ashild –" he began.

"You do not know me. Or us." Again, it was not a challenge, though as a statement it was definite.

She had turned away, her eyes on her brother as he led the chestnut pony on which Ealhswith sat. Hrald raised his arm to them, all unknowing.

Ceric stood looking at her back, focusing on the ribband she had knotted at the tail of her braid. He had no ready answer to her charge.

Modwynn told him he was too young to wed, anyway. This thought prompted another. When they had ridden back from hawking she had been proud of her bird taking the biggest prize. Now he wondered: Am I not good enough for her, does she seek a bigger prize? All knew he would be but second at Kilton; in a few short years he would pledge himself to Edwin. There would be war-lords of the Danes she could wed; perhaps even kin to King Guthrum. Ashild knew she could not live her life at Four Stones; it was her duty to wed and go to her husband's hall.

"Ashild," he tried.

It took a moment, but she turned to him. Now that she was looking at him he could not ask her if he were enough. He shifted his eyes down the road.

"I wish I had the luck of your falcon," he said, tilting his head toward the hall and its falcon mews. He paused, wanting to quote her exactly. "You said you have made what it wants, to be what you want. So you are both happy. That is what I wish you would give to me."

"To make what you want, what I want," she repeated.

He knew then it had been the wrong thing to say. He recalled a word his grandmother sometimes used for one with high standards: exacting. Ashild was that, and more. His words ignored what she herself would want.

He began to speak again, but Hrald was near. He had placed the lead in the hand of Ealhswith, who grasped it like a rein, as he held the pony's head at the halter cheek piece. Both were smiling as they came to them.

That evening before the hall gathered Ashild rounded the hedge of white-flowered bedstraw that separated her mother's bower garden from the functions of the work yards. The Sun was lowering in a fading blue sky, and the air carried the spice of mixed mints, rosemary, and lavender. The door to the bower house was open, and Burginde was tipping out the contents of a copper basin of water at the roots of a rose. Herbs had been crushed and added to the wash-water, their dark green leaves slopping out in waves as Burginde tipped it deeper. Ashild ducked her head at her and stepped inside.

Her mother was within, standing in her shift, combing out her long pale hair. Her comb was of nearly-white pear-wood, delicately toothed, perfectly suited for the fine hair it slipped through. That comb now paused, a rill of flaxen hair arcing in its teeth.

How pretty she is, thought Ashild. I am a toad beside her.

Ælfwyn smiled at her eldest. Ealhswith had shown off her new pony when they had returned from the valley, and Ælfwyn had taken pleasure in both daughters' laughter. She was about to speak of this, but a further look at Ashild made her wait. Her daughter had not yet changed her over-gown from her day's activities, which she need do when guests sat at meat with them. Ælfwyn hoped whatever it was would not interfere with either of them dressing. Still, she said nothing, and waited.

Burginde re-entered the house just behind the girl, the empty basin on her hip. She closed the door and looked too at Ashild, and her eyes rolled up to the timbered ceiling; the maid was about to be on about something, that was clear. The nurse set the basin in its corner, wiped her hands, and picked up her spindle.

Ashild had sat down on her mother's bed.

"Tell me of my father," Ashild asked her. A moment passed as she drew a deep breath. "My own father, not Hrald's."

Ælfwyn's lips parted; she was used to Ashild's sudden questions, but this one came without any warning at all. Ashild had, from childhood, been told of Yrling, but had never before asked about him. Ælfwyn lowered her comb. Ashild sat looking at her, her face open, even hopeful.

Ælfwyn took her own steadying breath and began. She spoke slowly, and gave the question the thought it deserved.

"He was, as you know, Sidroc's uncle, but there was not a great number of years between them," she began. Her eyes shifted a moment, in memory.

"When I met him I was frightened of him; he was forbidding. I was your age, no older." The blue eyes returned to her daughter's face. I was the same age as you, she thought; but I was somehow younger.

"He could be fierce and harsh at times," Ælfwyn went on. "But he was never harsh with me. When we were alone he treated me gently. He gave me many gifts, beautiful things, the things I have given at Oundle, for his soul."

She thought what more she could say. "He did things that looked strange to me, he would let his men fight, almost to the death, and not stop them in their fighting."

She had lifted her eyes, and they met those of Burginde. Her returning gaze told Ælfwyn that her nurse recalled the night Yrling had watched Sidroc almost kill his cousin Toki, and had done nothing.

"He was like an eagle," Ashild said. She knew enough of birds of prey to name him thus.

It was apt, and fit his manner too.

"Yes," her mother agreed. "You could say that; he had eyes, and a bearing like that. As I knew him more I understood him better. By the time of his death I had learnt to truly care for him."

"Where…where is he buried?"

Ashild knew her father fell outside the gates of Cirenceaster; she did not know more. Nor did her mother. When Ælfwyn returned to her destroyed home to seek her own father's grave she gave scant thought of anything beyond this.

He was flung into a pit, a vast grave of broken and bloodied Danes, or burnt upon a crude pyre with many others, Ælfwyn was saying to herself.

"He was burnt, with honour, by Sidroc," was what she said to Ashild. It was perhaps the first time she had lied to her daughter, but the truth would be terrible to hear.

Ashild had lowered her chin.

"Is he in Hell?" Ashild asked. Her voice was as soft as a murmur.

Burginde's spindle gave a whirring bump as it hit the floor. She clucked loudly as she squatted to retrieve it, her forehead creased in concern for the girl.

"No, no," said her mother, coming and sitting down next her on the featherbed. She had her arm around her daughter's shoulder, and pulled her to her a moment.

I do not know that, Ælfwyn thought; the Church teaches he is in Hell.

"He died trying to protect your family – your father and mother, and your sisters," Ashild said. "That should count for something in the weighing of souls."

"'Tis true," chimed in Burginde, stepping nearer. "And who knows that the Dane would not have accepted the True Path if his life had not been cut short." Through all these long years the nurse had never stopped referring to Yrling in this way. Her broad brow was now furrowed in thought. She stuck her tongue out, and to one side, as she considered this, then made her decision. "If the final Judging be a Hallmoot, and a just one, such things ought to count."

Ælfwyn gave Ashild a squeeze, and Burginde a grateful look. Their reasoning was perhaps faulty, but she herself had couched the matter this way to Ashild, putting the best face on Yrling's actions.

In truth, Ælfwyn did not know if Yrling would have killed her own father to gain Cirenceaster for himself. He felt he had claim to it, and was in a rage to beat back the competing Dane Healfdene who had arrived before him. Then Godwin of Kilton had appeared, surprising them all, racing across the field of battle calling out Yrling's name…

"What…what makes you think of these things?" Ælfwyn asked. She spoke almost in her daughter's ear, her voice just above a whisper.

But Ashild shook her head. It was something she felt within her breast, this lack, yet she could not name it. Yrling had died before her birth; she had had no man known to her as father save Sidroc. Yet she knew herself to be different from Hrald and Ealhswith, different in looks and temperament, and also in possession of something more. She had a kind of ardent vitality burning within her, making her restless and questioning. She could only name it as her true father's blood; half of what coursed through her body was his.

Ceric and Hrald did not return with Worr to the valley of horses next day. At table that night Ælfwyn suggested that as the bailiff was leaving on the morrow, all who wished should ride with him as far as Oundle.

"It is a pleasant ride, almost due South, and will not take you out of your way; and I would show Ælfred's gifts to Abbess Sigewif before you, so that you might tell him of her joy over them," she told him.

Ceric and Hrald were eager to go, both for the pleasure of the ride, and to join in the send-off. Worr, in his role as

Ceric's man, would of course ride with him; that and for the sake of seeing his father-in-law on his way. But Worr also wished to travel again to Oundle for its own sake. The thegns would go as well, and Hrald would choose a few men to ride with him. The evening ended early, so that all who would make the trek could be fresh at dawn.

Ashild slept in in the house of her aunt and uncle. Beneath her box-bed was a small wooden chest she had not opened for years. That night she lay awake in her alcove until the rest of the house had quieted, then slipped out behind her woollen curtain. She needed no lit cresset to find the chest in the gloom. She pulled it towards her and opened it, her hands sorting through the contents, mostly keepsakes from her childhood. There in one corner she found it, in the small linen pouch it had been given to her in. She drew it from the bag, feeling the silver chain run along her palm, dropping link by link almost like water, or a living thing.

Attached to that chain was an amulet, her father Yrling's hammer of Thor. Squatting on her heels in the dark she slipped the braided chain, cool and heavy, over her neck. Her right hand closed around the hammer. As a gesture it seemed natural, and the thick silver talisman in her hand felt welcoming. She pushed the wooden chest back, and rose and climbed into her bed. She lay there, the hammer on her breast, her hand over it.

Ashild was everyday surrounded by what Yrling had won: Four Stones itself. It was the only home she had known, and she loved with ardent fervour its stone-floored hall, clustered village, and broad and leafy landscapes. This was what Yrling had left to her.

At the same time she had almost nothing of his. His body was burnt in another Kingdom. His weapons had not come back. Her mother had given every jewel from his hand to

Oundle. This one thing remained, the amulet he had worn each day. Her mother had somehow claimed it, and had given it to her while she was yet a small girl, for a remembrance of the father whose face she had never seen.

Lying there she felt something from the warming metal. She knew from Sidroc, him she had called her father, of the guiding spirit that each family shared: the fylgja. The fylgja was a single woman-spirit, dedicated to each member of the same family, and served to guide, to guard, and to advise in time of danger and uncertainty. Heeding one's fylgja could mean the difference between a wise choice or a foolish one, even between life or death. The fylgja was outside us, following closely behind, whispering advice, pointing the way if one would but turn and look. Holding the warm hammer in her hand she felt that if such a spirit could take residence in anything, it would be in that which was precious, and worn over the heart.

She pressed her hand tighter over the talisman, and tried to summon her father's face before her. She knew she shared her true father's fylgja, and was therefore singled out by her. That made all the difference.

"Mjolnir," she whispered, naming the hammer of the God Thor. Mjolnir meant 'miller, crusher', and that dreaded weapon, once flung, always returned to the God's hand. Just as her father's hammer returned to her.

Chapter the Sixth: A Shared Sorrow

IN the morning Ceric stood with Hrald outside the big stable. Hrald had had a few horses brought down from the valley herd, and had persuaded his friend to ride one on the journey to the abbey. The grey morning light was being warmed by the broadening streaks of what promised to be a hot Sun overhead, though the air was still cool enough that the snorted breath of the horses milling in the paddock showed as steam. Ceric picked out a well-fleshed red chestnut with a tapering dark muzzle, and tried him in the turn-out paddock at the stable's side. Hrald too chose a new mount, setting aside his usual bay for another. They jumped down, satisfied with both horses, and began walking back to the hall to collect the packs they would take.

Ashild was standing with Gunnulf not far from the iron-strapped door to the hall. As he neared them Ceric heard they spoke in Norse. Gunnulf was smiling, his blue eyes glinting at her. When he tossed his head it sent his yellow hair back upon his shoulders. He had dropped his saddle bags at his feet as he spoke; Ceric knew Hrald had invited him to join the ride. The Norse Ceric had learnt in Gotland had somewhat receded from his brain, but it was Gunnulf's easy tone and manner with Ashild that made him fix his eyes upon him.

"Hej," Ceric greeted them both. Gunnulf cocked his head at him, but grinned.

Ceric let his eyes drop a moment down to the young Dane's waiting saddle bags, as if to suggest he might now take them up again, but Gunnulf did not.

Ashild was looking at Ceric, a sort of amused half-smile. She had not a horse near her, nor did he see any packs.

"Will you ride in the waggon with your mother and Burginde?" he asked. It surprised him that she would choose this; he well knew that as a girl she had hated the confinement and jolting of any wheeled cart. But then Hrald had told him Ealhswith and Eanflad were going as well; she would have company aplenty.

He glanced past Hrald's shoulder, to where the readied waggon stood. Its team was being harnessed, which to better keep time with the riders, and for the lightness of its human cargo, would be that of two horses.

"I am staying here," she told him, with a slight shake of her head.

Now Hrald touched the shoulder of Gunnulf, leading him off to where their horses stood tied at the paddock rail. Ashild and Ceric watched them as they went, then turned to the other.

"I wish you would come," Ceric answered, his disappointment in his voice. The day promised to be another fine one; he had imagined Ashild riding alongside Hrald and him in the bright Sun. "It would be just as it was that Summer I spent with you, when we rode several times to visit the abbess." Those rides, coupled with the adventure of sleeping in the great monk's hall at Oundle, had been some of Ceric's favourite times of that long stay.

"With Hrald and Mother both away, it is best if I remain," she said.

Her tone was serious enough that he looked at her carefully, to see if any jest lay behind her words. The land was at peace; even given the rumour that Guthrum might be ailing. She could not truly believe that Four Stones lay open to danger, or that her Uncle Asberg could not meet any threat which could, of a sudden, arise. Her blue-grey eyes were placid, but her mouth, set in its slight smile, was firm.

She seemed to read his thought, and revealed this in her answer. "Uncle is a good warrior, or he would not have been named second here," she recounted. "I could wish for no one better at my side in a scrape. But action is one thing. Reasoning is another. Men like Uncle are best when challenged by reason, when someone is near at hand to question their choices."

He was silent, taking both her, and her words, in. At his age Ceric was not used to judging his elders. Ashild knew no such restriction, and had not kept herself from sharing it with him. And he knew, as soon as she had summed him, that she had judged her uncle rightly. Her judgement of herself also gave him pause. He had for an instant to fight back the smile he felt forming at the corners of his mouth, part of him wanting to tease her for holding herself in such esteem. Looking at her face the mirth faded as quickly as it arose. For some reason an image of the Lady of Kilton flashed before him, his grandmother, Modwynn. Perhaps the kernel of her wisdom took root far back, when she was no older than Ashild.

They had held the other's eyes for a long moment. When he nodded, it was enough. He understood, and said just that.

"But I still wish you might be there," he went on. He was smiling now, not at her words, but at a shared memory. "I remember that long table where we sat, copying out our letters, smearing ink."

She let out a little sigh. "The table of many frustrated tears," she said, and gave a low laugh. "Some good it did Sigewif, for all her efforts."

Again he found himself surprised by her words. "But you read," he prompted.

"I read," she allowed. "But I am not good at writing. Hrald is much the better at that. And somehow I always feel reminded of this when I see the good abbess."

There was the sound of voices coming from around the corner of the hall, and they looked to see Ashild's mother approach, a handled wicker basket in each hand. She smiled at them both. Burginde was just behind her, arms laden, heading to the waiting waggon.

"There you are," Ælfwyn said to Ashild. "We are nearly off. Your aunt could have used your help in the kitchen yard, packing up the food gifts," she chided, but gently. Æthelthryth too was staying behind, and between provisioning the party and bringing food to contribute to the abbey's larder it had been a busy morning.

Mother and daughter were loving, and close, Ceric knew this; but now he thought to try to ascertain how fully the elder understood the younger. He did it with a single question.

"Ashild tells me she will not join us to Oundle." He was smiling as he said it, but allowing his disappointment to sound, as well.

Ashild's eyes had narrowed slightly at his words, watching him.

"It is her pleasure to stay, or come," her mother answered, and so lightly that Ceric saw the Lady of Four Stones did not grasp her daughter's concern for the keep's security.

He nodded. He knew something of the maid her own mother did not, and felt the slightest thrill of warmth within him, as if this knowledge somehow brought him closer to Ashild.

"What – what is that necklace you wear," Ælfwyn now asked her daughter, still smiling. The maids of the hall were known to sometimes share their jewellery, just as Ælfwyn had with her own sisters when she was young. "Something new?"

Ceric saw the chain for the first time, one of braided silver. It was tucked inside Ashild's linen shift, but a line of the chain shown at the collar of the white fabric. Over her shift, laying just above where her blue over-gown rose, sat the small golden cross Ashild had ever worn, suspended from its delicately-wrought golden chain.

Ashild looked discomfited for an instant, but pulled at the silver chain, drawing it, and what hung from it, forth.

It was a silver amulet, a hammer of Thor; a large one, a size a man would wear. It was cast of solid silver, and worked over with tiny balls of silver interlacing across the arms of the hammer.

Ceric had seen men, and woman too, of Four Stones wearing both the Christian cross and the hammer of Thor. These Danes had come late to the True Word, and if it gave them comfort to wear both, all one could do was smile. But Ashild had been raised in the True Church.

If he was surprised, her mother was stunned. Her face had paled, and she lowered the two baskets she held.

"Where…"

"In my chest, at Aunt's, where it has always been," Ashild answered. Her words were mild, but her hand had closed about the hammer, as if protecting it. "It is mine, as you told me. Mine to wear."

Ceric was looking back and forth between the two women. Now Ashild answered his look. "The hammer was that of my father, Yrling. He who won Four Stones."

Her mother's lips, which had remained slightly parted, now gently closed. She had never imagined Ashild would place it around her neck, but now she had.

She had asked about her father last night, and then sought the comfort of his amulet. Perhaps it went no further than this. At any rate, there was little she could say now, and before Ceric. She forced a smile, and nodded her head. "Of course," she assented.

Ashild was dropping the amulet back within her shift collar. Her mother was still smiling, but her thoughts had veered. Let us give thanks that Sigewif will not see this, she was thinking. And if Wilgot discovers it, always fussing about heathen idols…

Ælfwyn leant forward and gave her daughter a kiss on her forehead. "We will only be a day or two," she told her. "Keep well."

Ashild returned her kiss. Ceric took up the baskets Ælfwyn had been toting, and Ælfwyn moved off to her waggon, allowing them their own farewell.

Ceric did not know what to say. Ashild had always referred to Hrald's father as her own. Now by this act she had allied herself with Yrling. A moment ago he had felt closer to her than he ever had, without even a touch from her hand. Her placing of the Thor's hammer on her breast placed a barrier between them, almost as if she had donned a ring-tunic. He wanted to ask her more; he wanted to talk to Hrald about it, or even Worr; and he did not want to ride away from her now.

He stood before her, holding her mother's baskets in his hands, feeling foolish and young and lost for words.

"Smear some ink for me," she said. Then with a quick bob of her head she planted a kiss on his brow.

Once underway Ælfwyn was captive to her thoughts. The waggon was open at both ends, with an oiled tarpaulin hanging from four stout uprights, for shade. The morning was dry and reddish dust rose from the feet of the horses which pulled it. Lindisse was always wet, but this Summer had seen a spate of unusually fine weather; they would need rain soon lest the rye and barley begin to suffer. Ælfwyn felt grateful for the thinness of her woollen gown, and the tarpaulin casting her in its coolness. She let her eyes rest on the driver, an older Dane who had been lamed in battle but who served well behind a team of horses or oxen. She sat up front, on the bench just behind him, next to Burginde. Eanflad, Ælfwyn's youngest sister, always preferred to sit looking backwards when travelling by cart or waggon, and so she sat, seemingly content in her quiet. Little Ealhswith clambered between them and the packs of food and clothing resting on the waggon bed. They had rolled through the village, past the fields of spiked barley growing silver in the warmth, and were now out beyond the furthest reaches of the sheep meadows. Ælfwyn could hear the soft singing of Eanflad, and turned to see Ealhswith nestling at her feet, her head in her aunt's lap.

If she had been alone with Burginde she would have told her at once about Ashild, if only to hear the old nurse cluck her tongue and soothe her with a few pithy words. That comfort would have to wait, not only for lack of privacy, but for the fact that Burginde was slumped against the side rail of the waggon, sleeping.

The tarpaulin shielding them from the Sun's glare was of coarsely woven linen, stained grey by the flax oil it had been soaked in, and Ælfwyn raised her eyes to it. Ceric's arrival had brought the joy of seeing him again, of taking pride in his growing manliness, and feeling a share in Hrald's pleasure at having his closest friend at hand. But Ceric's coming had also served to carry her back eighteen years. He was the living link to Ceridwen and their times together, both before and after their arrival at Four Stones. It could not be accident that Ashild had asked about her father, and then the very next morning appeared wearing the Thor's hammer. Ceric had seemingly triggered her curiosity – if that was what it was – in Yrling.

Seeing the amulet again, and so unexpectedly, had affected her in ways that made slight the years' passage. A strange and fearsome Dane had dropped it over her head on the day of their hand-fast. Thereafter he had worn it every day of their brief union.

Ceridwen's returning it to her after his death had told her all she had need to know, all she could bear to consider, about Yrling's end. It would not have been carried to Kilton if it had not been taken as battle-gain. She found herself now squeezing her eyes shut to block the memory of the panicked dread of that time.

And there was more that Ceric had brought with him: The silk gown, once hers, and now returned to her daughter; the bailiff Raedwulf recalling her to her lost home, to the very hour she had first met Gyric.

She turned her head to her right, where Raedwulf and Worr rode side by side. The bailiff's dark hair, which had been neatly combed upon setting out, had through the jostling of the ride separated into those wavy locks she had noted when first she met him. He was talking, and sometimes laughing with Worr, and his air of youthfulness struck her.

She forced her eyes away from them, then closed them once more. She had made this journey to Oundle more times than she could count. She had travelled thence in joy, and in great distress. Oft times while doing so she told herself, One day I shall journey here, and not come back. When Ashild and

Hrald are wed, I will be free to know the peace of the abbey; live as my mother does in its blessed quiet.

A few days in that quiet had always restored her, found her even restive. The demands of the hall, of her children, and of the village could deplete, but also nourish her. She knew herself fairly well, and sometimes wondered if the idea of Oundle was not a greater attraction than Oundle itself.

The jangling of bridles made her open her eyes again. Ceric and Hrald, riding side by side, had moved up from where they had been, behind the waggon. They lifted their hands to her as they passed. Just behind them came Jari, always trailing Hrald. His younger brother Gunnulf had been riding with him, but must have stayed back with the two warriors who brought up the rear.

When they had passed out of earshot of the waggon Ceric looked to his friend. He tried to keep his face from showing what he felt, and tried too to keep his voice low.

"Ashild is wearing a hammer of Thor today," he told him. "That of her father."

Hrald blinked, and narrowed his eyes a moment. Their father did not wear a hammer.

"Yrling's hammer," Ceric corrected.

Now Hrald knew. He looked at Ceric.

"You are sure?"

"She showed it, both to me, and your mother," he answered.

Hrald shook his head. "Why…why would she do such a thing?" He looked forward over his horse's dark ears. "That is sacrilege.

"She cannot mean it," he went on. He studied Ceric's seemingly untroubled face.

"She did it to tease you," Hrald decided. He nodded his head at his own words.

"To see if she could anger you, worry you. It is just like Ashild to do something like that."

Hrald tried to convince himself of this as his thoughts went on. It must have been a shock to his mother. He glanced back over his right shoulder towards the trailing waggon.

Hrald had another thought. "But she still wears her golden cross, right?"

Ceric nodded. "She had both of them on, the cross outside, the hammer in her gown."

Both, like one of the Danes in the keep yard, he thought, but did not say. Some of the Danes even wore them on the same chain.

Hrald studied Ceric's face. "Does this trouble you," he asked. He feared that Ceric might tell him that he must order Ashild to take off the hammer.

"I have thought about it the whole ride," Ceric answered, but with a steady voice. He had, in fact, been picturing bringing Ashild to Kilton as his bride, presenting her to his pious grandmother and aunt. He could not do so with a maid who wore a heathen amulet. Now Hrald's words reassured him. Perhaps Ashild had worn it only to rile him.

He clung to this explanation for the single moment it deserved. Ashild would not play such a petty game. He knew this, and thought too that she had fully seen her mother's troubled brow when she displayed the hammer and named it as her own. Ashild was not unkind, and seeing her mother's brow would have cost her something. Yet she had closed her hand about the hammer.

His fingers went to his brow a moment, touching the spot where Ashild had kissed him. It had been the first touch of her lips, and she had been the one to give it. She was always ahead of him.

They rode on in silence. The Sun was climbing overhead, and large but white clouds rested in the sky. A cooling wind ruffled the ripening grass-heads on either side of the road. No birds sang; the only noise was that of their horses and the creaking waggon, or the infrequent drifting words of one or another of the men.

They both were looking forward now. Trees stood in the distance ahead of them, thickening into a forest, making their path forward disappear in its darkness.

"Will it keep you from marrying her?"

Hrald had rushed it out in his confusion, making his voice rise a pitch higher.

Despite Ceric's thoughts, the question startled him. He tried to laugh.

"You as well? Yesterday at the valley of horses Ashild asked me if I came to wed her."

"I think it is a very good idea," Hrald said at once, and with so much strength that Ceric fastened his eyes on him for an instant.

"I cannot wed yet. I am too young," he countered, glancing down the road.

"But Ashild is not," pressed Hrald.

"She is not yet eighteen." Ceric's tone showed he recognised her to be of more than marriageable age. He brought his eyes back to Hrald. "She will wait for me, will she not?"

It was less question than statement. Hrald did not know what to say; he could not often predict what Ashild would do.

"What did you answer, when she asked if you wanted to wed her?" he asked now.

Ceric breathed out a deep breath. "She asked me – as a simple question – if I had come here to wed her; or rather to take her back to Kilton to wed her. She took me off-guard. I said no, then yes."

"You said yes? What did she say?"

Ceric's green eyes rose upward. "She said, 'So you wish to wed a Dane.'"

"Then what?"

"Not much. She seemed angry. Then you came back, leading Ealhswith on her pony."

They fell into silence. Ceric thought of the question Hrald did not answer, whether Ashild would wait a year or two for him. She must; certainly she would. At least he was sure now that Hrald approved of the match.

As they entered the forest the road narrowed slightly, hemmed in as it was by hazels. They heard a horse moving up behind them, and reined their own to accommodate the rider. It was Gunnulf. He settled in next to Ceric, nearest the edge of the road. He was riding the same restless and half-broken horse he had been on when he cantered up to meet Ceric's party on the road to Four Stones, a red roan who kept tossing its head.

Gunnulf nodded at both, grinning as he patted his horse's damp neck. Gunnulf too looked hot; his brow was glistening. His yellow hair was tangled, and so long it fell far over both shoulders. The roan he was on was not bigger than the chestnut Ceric rode, but Gunnulf, being both taller and broader than Ceric, looked slightly down on him.

"So tell me of your home," the Dane invited. His white teeth showed as he grinned.

Ceric considered how best to describe Kilton. "It is on the sea, in the West," he began.

Gunnulf nodded his head. "Já, I have seen it, on a map," he said.

Ceric found himself shifting his eyes at the Dane. He did not like knowing that so far from its shore, Kilton had been marked out like this, and by one who had once been an enemy. He gave his chin a single nod, tried to dismiss it. He reminded himself that it meant little that this Dane knew where Kilton lay. In the treasure room of Four Stones were maps of Angle-land. Perhaps it had even been Hrald's own mother who had added Kilton to the parchment face of one; she had once gone there. Wilgot the priest had maps as well, one showing as far as the Holy City of Rome.

"It is on a bluff, above the sea. You are then good seamen," Gunnulf prompted.

Ceric had gone sailing often enough in the swift waters beneath Kilton's cliffs, but could not in truth say that many at Kilton relished the perils of the water.

"Our sea is dangerous, with currents and deep tides," he answered.

Gunnulf's grin spread, as if Ceric had just admitted a lack of seamanship. But he moved on with his questioning.

"How many men have you?"

Ceric's dismay was real. At the moment, and with the Peace, Kilton had only five and sixty men, less than half of Four Stone's number.

"Near to seventy," he answered. "Because there is peace," he added.

Gunnulf was proving a skillful and relentless interrogator.

"And the women?" he went on, his grin deepening. "I hear they are pleasing."

Ceric heard Hrald spluttering on his right, but he tried to grin in response. His mind raced; Gunnulf would have been a lad of ten or twelve when his mother was last at Four Stones, and have little memory of her; and he could not have seen another woman of Kilton outside that.

He could not resist. "They are the most beautiful in all of Wessex."

"Good," said Gunnulf with decision. "Then you will marry one of them."

"I have been to Oundle, when I returned from Gotland," Worr was telling his father in law. "To deliver a young serving woman who lived at the hall of Ceric's mother. Lady Ceridwen had asked me to escort her." Worr had almost referred to Sparrow as a serving maid, before he checked himself. He knew Sparrow had been a slave, and no maid remains one long in captivity.

Worr had never spoken to Raedwulf about his few days on Gotland. The older man knew but the skeletal facts of its outcome, and understood the younger's reluctance to speak more of that trial. Now they were nearing the tall wooden palings that surrounded the grounds, Worr spoke about the devout young woman he had brought to the abbess, and of his hope that Sparrow was well.

The broad gate was open, giving the party a clear view of the squat church of grey stone that sat in the centre of the enclosed grounds. On one side stood the timber hall in which the majority of nuns slept and lived, with a row of smaller and conjoined private cells beyond it, including that in which Abbess Sigewif slept. The other side held the men's hall, for the smaller number of monks and brothers. Set off beyond this was the house in which the two priests lived, those who offered up the holy sacrament of the Mass twice a day in the cool recesses of the stone sanctuary. Behind the church was a garden of herbs, fruit trees, and flowers, divided down the middle by a wooden fence, making each half private, that of the nuns to themselves, and that of the brothers, to their own devising.

The inside of the palisade wall sheltered the numerous outbuildings needed by any great hall: barns, fowl-houses, sheds for tools, housing for the lay-folk who lived there and worked side by side with the professed nuns and monks, and whose labour helped the community thrive. Several of these came forward as the party entered; a visit from their chief benefactress was always an occasion.

"Our Holy Mother will be with you shortly," said Mildgyth, who was prioress, and thus second to Sigewif. She had greeted Ælfwyn warmly, and now had shown them all into the great hall. Three novices garbed in pale grey gowns and white head-wraps had carried in basins of water and crisp linen towels. The hall was cool and dim after the heat of the road, and the water they rinsed their hands in bracingly cold, as well-water ever is.

Sigewif entered from a side door, her large, dark-robed person blocking the light for a moment, then showing sharply outlined in the afternoon rays. As she neared, the cross of walrus ivory on her breast stood out the brighter against the charcoal-hued wool of her gown. She crossed with her characteristic briskness over to where Ælfwyn and Burginde stood, with Ealhswith and Eanflad next them.

All bowed to her. Kisses were exchanged amongst the women, and welcome given to all the abbey's guests, with especial fervour for the well-remembered Ceric. The horse-thegn of Kilton also warranted a warm glance from the abbess's grey eyes.

Raedwulf took a moment to assess her; she had the noble bearing of her dead-king brother. Edmund, as King of East Anglia, had been shot full of arrows by marauding Danes, then beheaded. A wolf had guarded Edmund's head, letting no heathen near it, resting the night with it between his outstretched paws, and would surrender it only at dawn to a group of monks.

The slain king had been regarded as a saint shortly thereafter, seen as a Christian martyr cruelly felled by the heathen horde. Sigewif had been his youngest sibling, and made of such stuff that if she had been a man she might have been named King. Of her courage there was certainly no doubt. She had rebuilt Oundle during the most perilous times, won the respect of the conquering Danes, and now governed this doubled foundation, leading nuns and monks both.

"Your kinship to your sainted brother displays itself, in your learning and in your works," Raedwulf told her. It was no idle praise; those in power at Witanceaster and throughout Wessex knew the achievements of the abbess.

She smiled, moving a large and well-formed hand as if to damp down his words. As her brother's fame grew, some claimed the miracle of healing from praying near where his body lay. She had sometimes herself spoken to him in private devotion, not in prayer, but in plea for counsel. Yet the flesh and blood memory of her older brother never left her.

"I knew Edmund as a King, as a brother, and before that as a play-mate," she returned.

Ale had been brought, with cups for all. One of the shy and silent novices poured it out, foaming and brown, into the curving pottery cups. Its savour was such that the bailiff made compliment, as did Worr.

Sigewif glanced at the ewer, then spoke into the novice's ear before turning back. "I think perhaps you would like to meet the brewer," she told her guests. Ælfwyn could not suppress a smile at this.

The novice returned, bringing another with her. It was Sparrow.

She was still small and brown, and marked with that quickness which had given her her name. The angles of the bones of her face remained sharp, but there was a new expressiveness to her, the eyes calmer, the lips more readily bowing into a smile. After dipping her head, hands clasped, to the abbess she went to Ælfwyn, curtsying deeply to the woman who had acted as her sponsor, smiling her welcome at her sister and children. Then she saw Worr.

She beamed at him, and then without warning was wiping tears from her eyes, those of joy. Nearly five years had passed since they had sailed together on three long voyages to reach Lindisse, and Oundle. Worr had treated her as a little sister, taught her her first words of the speech of Angle-land, and surrendered her to the abbess with well-wishes. He was now smiling back at her.

"Bova, I think you recall," Sigewif was saying. She had long ago restored Sparrow's given name to her, that of an early saint of Frankland.

Having Worr before her made fresh the day he had appeared, travel-weary but good-spirited, with the child. Sigewif had watched the girl fall upon her knees before her. She had laughed and raised her to her feet, lifting the tear-streaked face by the chin. The young thegn had been telling his story the while, but the girl's face and glittering eyes were all Sigewif needed. She smiled and gestured her to stand. The girl clung to her outstretched hand, covering it in kisses. All Sigewif could do was soothe her with a few words. Then the girl unclasped her right fist and held out something precious: a coin of pure gold. With her gestures she bid Sigewif accept it, almost forcing it into her hand, as Worr explained that the Lady Ceridwen had provided the girl's dower-fee so that she might be well cared for in her old age.

It was a huge dowry sum, one a King's daughter might bring. It would, for one thing, assure her a cell of her own; she would not sleep in an alcove in the women's hall like the poorer nuns and novices. And the abbess was soon aware that the safety of a closed door meant much to the girl. When she had learnt enough of the speech of Angle-land, Bova told her why, came to her after Lauds one morning with tear-streaked face after having ridden a fearsome night-mare. Cradled in the abbess's arms she poured out the abuse she had suffered at the hands of many men, her sobs choking her words. She felt deep shame at what had befallen her, and utterly unworthy to take a place amongst so many women whom she already regarded as holy.

Sigewif's response surprised her. She listened with calm face, her eyes as mild as if hearing a small child confess some minor fault. When Bova had cried herself dry the abbess took both her small hands in her own large and firm ones. "You are as unsullied as a new-born babe," she assured the girl. "In the eyes of God you are as pure and as loved as any infant ever was. You have only to prove worthy of that love, by the love you give to Him, and his Blessed Mother."

Bova lifted her head, and with eyes shining from more than her tears went on with her morning. Her vocation was clear to the abbess, and soon she professed as a novitiate. She was treated as any novice; it was best for her as she learnt the order and the place. Bova spent time working in the fields, gardens, kitchen, and barns, getting to know the sisters and serving folk. It was in the brew-house where her true talent had been revealed. Ale was drunk by all, and every day, yet brewing was such a temperamental art that the quality of the ale could vary widely week by week. The abbey's brewster had been an elderly nun, whose failing eyesight and faltering hands had caused much waste in spoiled ale. Bova was sent to aid her mainly in the lifting and carrying of crocks and the tending of yeast-twigs. The girl's time spent with Rannveig at the brew-house on Gotland served her well, and soon the crocks in the brewing shed were filled with ale of such savour that the old nun was content to drowse in a corner while Bova ground, measured, and stirred. No novice was perhaps more modest than she, but knowing her skill was valued gave her a deep feeling of belonging.

Bova was looking at them all, and now seemed to recognise Ceric. She glanced at the abbess, who nodded her consent, bidding her speak.

"You are Mistress's son," she said, her voice almost lisping in its softness. "It was Mistress, and Tindr, who named me for the little bird." She was smiling at this memory, and cupped her hands, as if to indicate a nest. "Please, when you see her again tell her I am well, ever grateful to her, and that I remember them all in my prayers each night."

See her again, thought Ceric. I would that were not so difficult. Still, he smiled back, and nodded.

She looked to Hrald. "Perhaps one day you and Hrald will return to the island with a monk or priest, and bring to them the Word of God." She gazed so pointedly at first one, and then the other, that they looked to each other.

Father is heathen, Hrald was thinking, and happy in his belief. And Ceric's mother too. They have heard the Word of God, and turned their backs on Him. It is terrible to know I will never see him in life, and worse to know that after death we will be eternally apart…

The two youths locked eyes for a moment, unable and unwilling to explain, sealing their shared knowledge with a simple nod between them.

After the young brewster returned to her shed, Ælfred's psalm book was displayed and remarked over by the abbess. A simple meal was taken by her guests, and the hour of parting for one of them neared. Raedwulf's well-watered horse stood in the yard awaiting the bailiff; the others would remain the night at Oundle.

They were now all within the chamber Sigewif used as writing room. Ceric had his palm flat upon the worn surface of the table at which he and Hrald and Ashild had copied out their letters, and was thinking of Ashild's words of the morning. He thought he knew what she had meant about being in Sigewif's presence; the abbess had a way of looking at you that made you think she almost read your thoughts.

"Bailiff Raedwulf. A walk in our garden would refresh you before you start on your way," Sigewif offered. She had noted the man's expression as he had watched the Lady of Four Stones turn the pages of the Psalter, and guessed he had need to speak to her. Time was short, but she could give the place.

She looked across the table to her benefactress. "Lady Ælfwyn knows its contents as well as I, and will be your guide." Her face bore the same slight smile it often wore, but there was a subtle pointedness in her directive, which made both named rise.

"I will see you by the gate," Worr told his father in law.

The two made their way through the hall and out the side door to the garden. A few nuns and novices worked there, squatting and bending amongst the beds, pulling weeds or gathering herbs for cooking or the Simples chest. But they were intent on their work, moving silently between the bordered plants. The Sun had passed its highest point, the air was still and warm, and flowers reaching from the green mass of foliage shook from the prying attentions of hovering bees.

"I thank you for riding with me this far," Raedwulf said. A cloud was passing overhead, at times muting the colours of the flowers and herbs, then moving on to restore their full and Sun-lit brilliance. "Though it is easy to see Oundle's many attractions," he added, tilting his head across the garden and its blossoms to the stone church.

"You are more than welcome," she returned. "No man should come so far without meeting a woman such as Sigewif." She bent down to pinch a sprig of costmary where it grew at her feet. He watched as she crushed the tender leaves between her palms, releasing its sweet and minty odour.

As she opened her hands a ray of light struck them, as if she held the Sun there.

He could have spoken of the abbess here, adding his praise to that of hers, or made slight of his long journey by reminding her it was Ælfred's business he rode on. But standing there and looking upon her pleasantries failed him.

She had dropped her hands, those hands which had held the Sun.

He would say one thing more, and did so, quietly. It was to merely, and once again, call her by her name.

"Ælfwyn of Cirenceaster," he said.

He would allow himself no more than this. Greeting her in her hall upon his arrival, all he could do was bow his head and utter these words, when he had wanted to go down on one knee before her. This, despite the heat, the dust in his throat, the sudden and pressing need he felt to present the King's gift; to be not he himself standing before her, but an unknown messenger on an impersonal errand.

Her steps had slowed, and now she stopped. She could not move, and only felt the dryness of her mouth.

"Nothing can recall those early days to us," she said, her voice just above a whisper.

Now he must say it.

"You are wrong, my lady." He turned to her, his steady eyes fixed upon her pale blue ones. "Your very face recalls it. I have only to look at you and be two and twenty once again."

He let out the breath he had almost been holding, releasing it with his words.

She turned her face now, away from his mild eyes which searched her own.

She thought of the afternoon in her garden, of how after he had left her she had gone within her bower house and beheld her face in her disc of polished silver. She had seen Ælfwyn as she was now. Today, in another garden, she felt he held a disc of magic in his hand, one that showed her herself, and him, too, but as they were.

To be desired for her own sake, not because she brought treasure to a conquering Dane, or because later another Danish war chief had needed her to run his hall…

It was hard to compass. She thought on the day she had first seen Gyric. Her eye had fallen on one fair-haired, and he had returned her look. Another set of eyes, under darker hair, also looked her way; these she had not seen. If Raedwulf's eye had found hers first…He survived that battle unscathed, and many more after that, it seemed. He was of good family.

She stopped herself. It mattered not. Her father and grandsire too had made up their minds. She would go to Yrling. She would never have been given the chance to know happiness with Raedwulf.

She forced herself into the present day, looked at him. "Why – why tell me this now?" It was barely a question, more a wonderment.

"Perhaps to be free of it." He shook his head at himself in correction. "No. Something the wise say: A shared sorrow is a lessened sorrow. Perhaps that." He laughed the slightest bit at his own words.

"Yes," she nodded. "It all has been a great sorrow." She lifted her head, but away from him. "Not that good has not come from it. My children. This place, Oundle. The blessings of peace. And I know I had my own share in drawing good from the evil of our times. I cannot gainsay that."

He was quick to answer her, though his voice was low and kind. "Once more you underestimate your role. Yours has been the steadying hand here in Lindisse, through all manner of upheaval, through war and then the long process of rebuilding during the Peace. Through the two Danes you wed. Through the time you have been alone, holding Four Stones for your son."

He was looking at those hands as he spoke, long-fingered, slender, unadorned by any rings. His words slowed, and his tone fell even gentler in her ears.

"Let me end by saying, I admire you. And to repeat what I have before told you: how glad I have been to look upon your face once more."

She turned back to him at this, and her lips parted, but she could not speak. She felt rooted to the spot. He took one long look.

He left her then. She remained in the garden, did not wave to him as he rode off.

She stayed upon the graveled paths, pacing as slowly as if she were at prayer. This is but a fresh sorrow, she thought. Learning now that my life could have been with you, in Defenas...

A shared sorrow is not lessened; not for me. It is deepened.

Chapter the Seventh: A Tale Written by Two

RAEDWULF was four days out when he was stopped. He had hewn to the same roads and pathways he had travelled with the men of Kilton, picking up the track shortly after he headed West from Oundle. Travelling alone and with a fast horse beneath him he had made good time.

He heard the whistle before he saw the men. Its shrillness turned his head across the dry grassland. He saw three horses and three men, resting near the bank of the meandering stream he and his horse had stopped to drink at not long ago at an earlier bend. Two of the men were already pulling themselves back into their saddles; the third still had his fingers to his mouth. Raedwulf reined his horse in and waited.

Three Danes, all young. They bore their long knives at their sides, and each carried a spear, but none had swords. They had come of age in a time of peace, giving them neither the opportunity to pick one up off the battlefield, nor to win enough silver to trade to a weapon-smith to forge one. No matter, thought Raedwulf. One can die just as swiftly from a spear-thrust.

His own weapons were on full display, bright-hilted sword in its brown leather baldric; a seax with a blue lapis-stone in its pommel-tip spanning his belly; light throwing spear lashed to his saddle; round, blue-and-white painted shield hung on his back. His helmet was in his far-side saddle bag. He trusted he would not need it.

He raised his hand to them as they neared. He had the chance to set the tone of their discourse by speaking first, and took it.

"I greet you in the name of Ælfred, King of Wessex, and ride here by consent of Guthrum, King of East Anglia."

His tone was firm and even, the safe-conduct already in his hand.

The three eyed him. He had spoken slowly, and as clearly as he could. Up close he saw that one was no more than Ceric's age, the other two closer to Worr's. The two elder might be brothers, with the same light brown hair and deep blue eyes. The younger had short-cropped yellow hair, and was leaning forward over his saddle bow. The youngest shot a look at the others before returning his eyes to the bailiff.

Raedwulf's own eyes told him much. Their clothing was worn, their horses a notch better than nags. Raedwulf knew they were even then gauging the worth of his own. He found himself squeezing his knees the smallest amount, felt the firm leather under the wool of his leggings. His horse responded by lifting his head, and Raedwulf stilled him with his rein. His mount could out-run those of the Danes, but could not outrun a thrown spear.

"Whose men are you?" he tried next, giving them the courtesy of considering them trained warriors.

They looked at each other, and one of the brown-haired brothers spoke. "We are Hord's men," he said. "And you are on Hord's land."

"Of that I am aware," Raedwulf answered. He had never heard of Hord, one of many petty war-lords who had claimed tracts of Anglia. He extended the tube of hardened leather. "I bear a letter from Ælfred," he said again, "and travel by leave of your King, Guthrum."

He was pulling out the parchment when the young yellow-haired one spoke.

"Guthrum is dead."

Raedwulf saw the heads of the two older snap round to look at the speaker. He glanced at the young one's face, noted the flashing eyes, but saw too a quiver at the upper lip. He was bluffing.

"Dead," the bailiff scoffed. "Who told you that? I have seen him, not two days ago. We sat at meat and he drank half a cask of mead. He was as hale as I."

All three were watching him. "You could not have come from Headleage in two days," one of the brothers pointed out.

"Nor did I," Raedwulf agreed. "Guthrum was at Snotingaham, on his way back from Jorvik."

He was close to having them, he felt. "I carried Ælfred's news to Guthrum, of the laws concerning trade between our Kingdoms."

Trade between Kingdoms was onerous, demanding witnesses to every transaction, and the requisite that all merchants be prepared to offer up hostages as surety of honest conduct. Laws concerning trade could be of little concern to these three, and the banal nature of his proclaimed mission might shift their interest away from thoughts of mischief.

He had the parchment open now, and nudged his horse closer to those of the brothers.

"This is Guthrum's mark, signed after his demand that I be left unmolested in his Kingdom." He was pointing to a single dark letter, simply the word 'and', suspended in the several lines penned on the creamy parchment. He knew by their squinting faces none of the three could read. They did not spend long looking.

"You go from King to King, and yet alone?" posed the other brother.

"For speed's sake, I do." He re-rolled the safe-conduct, but kept it in hand. "And in every chieftain's land I have been unimpeded. But if you must, take me to Hord. It will delay your King's message to Ælfred, but I think Hord will accept Guthrum's anger."

The two brothers glanced at each other, unwilling to take that upon their heads.

"What if instead we kill you now," the yellow-haired youngster asked.

The rolled lambskin flexed slightly in Raedwulf's fist.

He dropped his eyes a moment to the darkness of his horse's mane, then raised them to face the grin on the youngster's face.

"If you do that I will miss meeting with my brethren, awaiting me in two days' time. In just a few days Ælfred will learn of my disappearance, and Guthrum too. And that it happened on Hord's lands."

He turned in his saddle and slipped the leathern tube in his near-side saddle bag.

"Then there is the matter of my horse. You would need to explain how you came by it. My weapons too, which Guthrum marked well at our feasting. You could of course carry all to Hord as tribute to your chieftain. But when Guthrum and his men come asking why I vanished on his lands, horse and weapons both must be hidden. He will order a search. It would all be – awkward."

The silence that followed was marked only by Raedwulf's steady gaze at the three.

"Give us silver and we will let you go," insisted the youngest. It was over, but he did not yet know it.

"I will give you nothing," Raedwulf returned. His hand was on his sword-hilt now. "My death will mean your own. Turn now and ride before I go to Hord myself."

One of the brothers reached his hand towards the rein of the yellow-haired youngster. The youngster scowled, then spat upon the ground beneath his horse's dancing feet. The three turned as Raedwulf stood his horse, watching their dusty retreat.

Once at Kilton Raedwulf's daughter saw him almost at once. A light drizzle was falling, and Wilgyfu, with many of the other women of Kilton, was in the great hall at hand-work, her youngest son in a willow basket at her feet, her older boy romping with the other toddling children. After their kiss and his assurance that Worr was well she took her father's wet wool mantle, and handed him the linen towelling she was hemming so he might dry face and hands. He lifted the boys in turn as she ran to the bower-house to alert Modwynn of his coming. Father and daughter would have the night to visit; first he must attend to duty.

Holding his wet mantle over his head he walked past the pleasure-garden. The rain had picked up and was now steady, the afternoon sky leaden in hue yet strangely bright, as that metal is when molten. The sea beyond the garden was active; he heard the booming crash as waves struck the root of the cliff. Rolls of soft grey mist unfurled themselves as they rose from the surface of the water.

The Lady of Kilton welcomed him, pouring out ale into a cup of silver. He had already assured her that the journey to Four Stones with Ceric had gone smoothly.

"And of your return?" They were seated across from each other at the small round table.

He paused a moment. "Other than a beggar asking for silver, all went well."

She smiled at this, knowing it for far more than it sounded.

"And of Ceric's return?" she asked next.

"That I do not know. He seemed unwilling to name a date. One month at least, he told me."

"Unwilling until he learns what he wishes to learn," Modwynn surmised.

"That may be, my lady." His tone was flat enough that she could read nothing into it.

"And of Ashild?"

"She is a maid to be remarked upon."

"As lovely as that?"

"Forgive me. Not exactly that. She is well-formed, pleasing, certainly. Not a beauty to my eye, perhaps. But she possesses – " His eyes had shifted, considering his memory of the maid.

"What?" Modwynn was finally forced to ask.

"Herself. She is self-possessed, to a rare degree in a young woman."

A confident nature would be greatly desired in the next Lady of Kilton. Modwynn nodded her head in approval.

"But not head-strong," she asked.

He let out a breath with a laugh. "I think she is, that. And it is one of her charms. At least in the eyes of Ceric."

"His gift – the golden gown. How was it received?"

"Gratefully, I am sure. She wore it at our welcome feast."

Modwynn paused, considering the fine effect the glowing silk would have by torch light in a crowded hall. She pictured all looking on Ashild in approval, and how her grandson must have regarded her, so richly dressed, and by the gift of his own hand.

"Ceric had told me there is another maid of the hall," she went on, "a small sister."

"Yes, Ealhswith, most charming. A shy and diffident maid, of perhaps ten or twelve years."

Modwynn rose to pour her guest another cup. "Tell me of their mother," she prompted.

His silence lasted long enough that she glanced at him as she finished filling their cups.

"Ashild is unlike her mother," he said at last. "Hrald and Ealhswith more resemble the Lady Ælfwyn."

"Ælfwyn came here when the two children, Ceric and Ashild, were but babes," she recounted. "I recall her beauty, her gentleness, and, I think, her true sense of duty."

"She has changed in none of those things," he said. He was looking off, to where her loom stood against the wall. A length of creamy linen lay stretched there, held by the clay warp-weights that dangled above the floorboards.

"Her mother would welcome Ashild's union with Kilton?"

"That she was clear on. The lady would welcome Ceric as her son-in-law."

Modwynn need not ask if a self-possessed maid of seventeen years would consider waiting two years to wed the far-younger Edwin. Ashild sounded as if she would wait for little. She began to wish she had encouraged Ceric to ask her outright, and had enabled Raedwulf to bargain for the girl while he was there.

"And Ashild – will she wed Ceric?"

"She gave no hint of her feelings to her mother."

Modwynn was silent some time. The rain had steadily increased. A splatter of drops was lashing the glass casements, and the rising wind causing them to rattle uneasily in their frames. Modwynn found her eyes resting on her hands, curving around the base of her cup.

"The maid of Four Stones will have many suitors to choose from," she observed, before looking up. "We will see what Ceric has to say on his return. It may be a tale written only by the two of them."

At Four Stones Ælfwyn presided over a table with one less guest. Not a few men had sat at her side for a night or two, and the King of the Danes, Guthrum, had been one of them. All of them had known her as the lady of that place, had recalled her as Peace-weaver for Yrling, or wife to Sidroc, or mother to Hrald. The guest lately gone was the only one who knew her before her arrival in this conquered land. Now the place at which he had sat at her elbow was restored to Wilgot, the priest. There was nothing for it but to put Raedwulf, and the memories he had briefly kindled, out of her mind.

The demands of each day crowded in, needing as ever to be met: the cooks and butchers and bakers in the kitchen yard to be marshalled, their work overseen, waste avoided, remnants to be parceled out to the poorest of the villagers. For several hours each day she joined the women of the hall at the endless task of cloth-making, spinning, weaving, and sewing, that all might be clothed. There were grudges and jealousies she must discern and avert; and her own and others' children to be taught the rudiments of sums and letters, by her own hand, and for those with promise, by Wilgot too. Her sheep were always a matter of concern and pride to her, and whenever she could she spent time amongst her flocks, and the men and women who cared for them.

There were satisfactions as well: the quiet and sustaining knowledge that Oundle existed, and that her mother knew contentment in her life there as a professed nun. The daily joy and worry of her children as they grew and changed. And the rare pleasure of Ceric's presence, and the memory of his mother, which had never failed to comfort her.

At day's end all returned to the hall where Ælfwyn presided. There was fellowship and feasting awaiting them there, the bronze oil cressets lit and glowing, glinting light from the silver necklets and wrist-cuffs of the men and women moving within, gleaming upon the polished points of the massed spears standing upright, flanking the treasure room door. When the emptied bowls had been cleared away Wilgot would rise, and tell of the works of Christ from the Holy Book; and then – if the ale had opened their throats – one or more of the men might stand and share a well-remembered Saga-tale of the older Gods.

Ceric and Hrald were always together, through every full day. They were walking in the kitchen yard one fore-noon, hearing the shrill whine of the grindstone being turned as a cleaver was being held against it. Ceric had noticed the old man, bald of head and bent of back, who sat before the whirling wheel, spending part of each day grinding and sharpening knives. The screeching came to an end as the man pulled back the honed edge and tested it with the pad of his finger. Then the man looked up over the wheel to where Ceric stood with Hrald. His eyes seemed fixed upon Ceric, and it was not for the first time. Ceric recalled him from the months spent here as a boy, and that the man looked at him then too.

"Who is that old man?" he asked Hrald. "The one who sits all day at his grindstone?"

Hrald looked surprised. "His name is Eomer. He has been here a long time, all his life almost. His wife died a while back, she was the old cook."

"I wonder why he looks at me."

Eomer was indeed still looking upon him. "Let us go and ask him," Hrald laughed.

The old man nodded as they came up to him. On a table to his right was a range of knives and tools he had yet to sharpen, or vessels to polish. His thin lips cracked into a smile.

Ceric did not need to ask, for the man spoke first, and to him.

"You are like your young mother." The man's watery blue eyes were fast upon Ceric's face.

Ceric looked quickly to Hrald; some old men went daft. But Eomer's eyes had shifted now, to a door set at the base of the hall.

"I carried your father out of that hole, put him on a horse."

Ceric felt his chest tighten. He knew this yard was not always one of well-fed and justly ruled folk. He knew too that the folk of the hall had aided his mother when she ran off with the maimed Gyric.

"You helped save my father," he said.

"Aye," Eomer nodded. "But the maid – your mother – she did, most of all."

Ceric did not know what else to say. This kitchen man had carried to safety the son of the great Godwulf of Kilton, taken him from where he had been thrust to die, and helped give him a chance to live. He knew his mother had been a maid of less than sixteen years when it had happened, but it was hard to think of her like that.

He found himself fumbling in his belt, digging at the fat store of coinage there.

Eomer's watery eyes were following him.

"I will take no silver," the old man answered, lifting his hand in refusal. "Seeing you grown a fine man is enough." The old man looked now at the weapon that spanned Ceric's waist. "And seeing you wear with pride the seax of my dead Lord Merewala."

"So it is his seax," Ceric answered. It had been considered such at Kilton, but no one had known for certain. Merewala had been a famed warrior, and his father, the builder of Four Stones.

For answer Eomer nodded. "'Twas Dobbe, my wife, who saved it, took it from my lord's body, kept it hid. When the maid set out she packed it in the kit she carried.

"'Twas those two women, my old wife, and the maid who would be your mother, who made it so."

"My father always wore it," Ceric was able to tell him.

And one day the son I shall have with Ashild will do so, he thought, further bonding these two halls together.

Ceric took full part in the needful activities of Four Stones. Hrald had been for years at the side of his uncle, Asberg, or his mother as they dealt with matters of village and hall. With Ceric at his side even commonplace tasks took on a new savour and interest. They rode out with Asberg to oversee the mending of the long wooden fences that spanned the paddocks penning the beasts at the valley of horses, and attended the yearly tallying of sheep and cattle. They worked with Jari, who had a head for such things, as he led a group of villagers and men in the digging of a new drainage ditch, channeling off the groundwater that yearly turned the common pasture nearest the palisade wall into a bog. Worr and the thegns lent their backs to this as well, and Hrald and Ceric took up spades and worked themselves into a sweat alongside the ranks of cottar folk and warriors striving for a common good.

Over a series of days they rode to the greensward edging the forest by the stream, where men had gathered to undertake the cutting and hauling of the coming year's wood for the making of fire, and for building. Oxcart after oxcart was filled, and the steady and strong beasts hauled bundles of saplings and whole mighty trunks back to the hall yard to be seasoned and sawn. Riding back at the end of one such train put Hrald in mind of earlier wood-gathering.

"All the wood we stacked at Tyrsborg," he remembered aloud.

"Right up to the eaves," Ceric agreed.

"The Northern Lights – how green they were."

They went on, naming things that stood in memory of their time with Hrald's father and Ceric's mother.

"Gunnvor's honey cakes."

"The stags Tindr took; those big harts."

They fell silent for a while. Ceric knew Hrald still had the bow Tindr had made him; he had seen it, with the leathern quiver full of arrows, hanging on the wall of the treasure room. Ceric saw that a few of the arrows were missing, proof that Hrald had used them hunting, or at least lost them shooting after game.

"I have mine too," Ceric had told him, as they grinned at each other. But he had never used it after returning to Kilton.

Hrald's bow and quiver hung by the boy-sized shield Sidroc asked the nearby weapon-smith on the island to make; Ceric still had that made for him, as well. Those shields bore the marks of the boys' avid sparring, facing each other in the stable yard of Tyrsborg.

"The little ones…Yrling and Eirian. I wonder how they are," Hrald hazarded.

Ceric glanced over to Hrald. They were nearly back to the palisade wall. The waggons in front of them had slowed as they climbed the rise around to the front where the broad gates stood.

Ceric only nodded, and looked down at the mane of his horse. It was hard to think of his mother's twinned children, and of her. Now he was older he felt shame at how he had at times spoken to her at Tyrsborg. He had made her cry more than once, and her tears, and the things she wept at, had confused him as well. He regretted most of all his parting from her, telling her he would never see her again, then almost begging her to come with him.

His thoughts returned to the day before that parting, when he had ridden off from Tyrsborg alone. He went along the trading road to his uncle's grave, aware of his mounting anger, knowing with every step of his horse that it would be his final visit there. A bitter taste was rising in his mouth, and he knew he held his reins in clenched hands. When he came to the grave he almost flung himself from the saddle. He felt he must stand there and make some kind of vow, a bloody vow, over the ground that marked the earthly resting place of Godwin of Kilton. But once at the spot, he knew not what to swear. He stood mute, seeing the fresh sprouts of green grass and white wild flowers, looking upon the weather-stained wooden cross he had driven into the stony soil.

Could he swear revenge? For what? The laws of the place made his uncle's killing lawful. He saw with his own eyes, heard with his own ears, that his mother did not want to return to Angle-land, was not in fact being held captive. And he had heard and seen his uncle's killer offer him his life in return for his departure. Godwin would not agree, wanted to fight. Now he was dead and buried far from the haven of home, or even the sanctity of a church or priest. And Ceric's mother was part of his death, the biggest part of it, which only confused him more.

There was no vow he could make, bloody or otherwise. He had dropped to his knees. He bowed his head and tried to pray. He remembered his first visit to the grave and how Hrald had come up beside him and began saying the Lord's Prayer, and wished he had brought Hrald with him.

Now Hrald spoke, breaking into his thoughts. "I will go back, someday," he told Ceric.

Again Ceric said nothing. He could not imagine going back.

"Strike to the chest," Jari was urging. "My heart is open to you."

He was speaking to Ceric, who was facing him with raised sword and shield. They were standing on a grassy patch not far from the Place of Offering, sparring. Ceric and Hrald had wanted to try their weapons and their skill, and had been joined in the effort by Jari, Worr, and a number of others.

As the days of Ceric's stay at Four Stones stretched into a fortnight, Worr took note of signs of restlessness amongst the thegns of Kilton. The five he had chosen for the trip had been carefully selected; good fighters, all, but steady and cool-headed ones. All were wed, with not only wives but young children at home, and all were devout in their Christian faith. The last thing Worr wished to face was friction arising from entanglements with any women of Four Stones.

The troop had been a congenial one on the road, and the rest afforded by the first few days after arriving had been welcome. Now after many days away from Kilton and the demands of everyday life they were become restive. A bout of friendly sparring amongst themselves and the lead men of the place would expend energy. And Worr wanted to see for himself the skill of the men of Four Stones, and how his own ability, and that of his men, would measure up. Charged as he was with Ceric's welfare he also wanted to witness the lad's efforts, and guard against injury.

The sparring was held much as it would have been at Kilton: a more practiced warrior against a younger, so that the latter might learn; blunt-ended staffs instead of iron-tipped spears; sword blades sheathed in narrow casings of thick leather. A sleeveless leathern tunic, such as those worn under a ring tunic, for body protection. War-hammers and the Dane's deadly battle-axe, the skeggox, were laid aside in such sparring. For the heat, no helmets would be worn, thus no blows to the head or neck allowed. One could be battered and bruised, but no blood drawn, with such precautions.

What was new to Worr, and Ceric too, was who they faced. Worr had fought Danes at Godwin's side throughout Wessex and at Kilton, and had killed not a few. Now he faced them in a friendly contest. Three-fingered Jari was the most interesting of them.

Hrald had sparred with the left-handed Jari many times. Ceric had never faced such a swordsman, but Jari was generous in his schooling. He had lost the first two gripping fingers of his right hand when he was but twenty, hacked off above the knuckles by a Saxon sword. With a larger grip inside his shield boss he could still hold his shield with his maimed hand, and the power in his right arm made the shield itself a weapon. He was by force become left handed, and had proven a most capable warrior that way.

"You do not expect to face a sword held in the left; it surprises you. That is my first advantage," he told Ceric. At this point he spoke the tongue of Angle-land well, but still with the lilted tang of the Danes. "There are few of us and so I will disturb your thinking. I will spring for your right side before you know how to gauge me. If I miss you then we will be face to face, straight on, no offset to our shields such as you are used to."

Ceric had seen this at once, that Jari moved in ways he did not expect. It was discomfiting. They traded blows to the other's shield. Jari was big enough that Ceric must use his compact quickness as a way to gain ground.

After a few more slashes Ceric found his own sword almost resting above that of Jari, who with a sudden up-cut wrenched it from Ceric's hand. The gold-covered hilt flashed in the Sun as it lifted overhead. Ceric took a deep breath and recovered it from where it lay in the grass. If it were battle he would likely be dead now, his opponent having knocked away his shield to make one final thrust through his body.

Jari lowered his shield and waited for Ceric to rejoin him. His grin was not unkind. "Many men will scramble to pick that up on the field," he noted. He resumed his stance before Ceric.

"But your advantage, if you see it, is that the left hand is the heart hand. I must hold my shield away from my heart to strike. Your blow can pierce my heart, not just my chest."

Ceric nodded, and after several more feints and parries both lowered their swords.

"Now if you face a Tyr-hand you will know what to do," Jari ended, referring to the one-handed God. "Note that he is left-handed. Protect your right side. Go for his heart."

Worr was standing by, watching Ceric's bout, as were the others. Worr had already faced Jari, and thought their match a draw; Worr had fought left-handed men in the past. One such, who lived in memory, could fight with either hand. A Tyr-handed Dane had stunned him by dropping his broken shield to the ground and taking his sword in his right hand to attack with renewed vigour as he worked his way to the shield of a fallen man nearby. It had been at the Twelfth Night attack at Kilton, and if an arrow from a Kilton archer had not found its way to the Dane's chest Worr's surprise might have cost him his life. Jari was right about that.

The five thegns were now taking turns, pairing off with this or that Dane, sometimes fighting shield-to-shield, two or three to a side. Ceric and Hrald joined in, as did Gunnulf. Ceric and Hrald fought side by side, against Gunnulf and his friend Onund. Gunnulf would not engage Ceric, dodging his approaches, hair flying, teeth gleaming. It felt a slight to Ceric, and angered him.

Gunnulf now turned to where Worr had stepped in, and hacked at his raised shield. This angered Ceric the more, that Worr was worthy of engagement, but not him. Worr saw this, in Ceric's hard eyes and gritted teeth. Amidst the grunts and laboured breathing there had been laughter too, and Worr did not want the mood to sour. Worr lunged at Gunnulf, whacked his shield up and away to his right, and with slightly more force than needed rapped the young Dane with the flat of his sword on the back of the left shoulder, pitching him forward and to the ground. Gunnulf rolled over with his shield, and leapt up to his feet.

The others, Danes and Saxons alike, met him with laughter, his older brother Jari most heartily. Ceric alone did not join in, knowing Worr's act for what it was. He would have liked to have put Gunnulf in his place himself. Hrald and Onund and the rest made light of it, and Gunnulf, after a look at the smiling Worr standing before him with lowered shield and sword, had to laugh.

When all were winded they stopped in their sparring. Their linen tunics were soaked from sweat, and they pulled off the sleeveless leathern tunics they had worn over them. They had brought no small cask of ale with them to slake their thirst, and all the water-skins were empty, or nearly so. The men began to pick up their shields where they had dropped them in the grass, and make their way back to the hall for refreshment. Hrald and Ceric still lay sprawled on the ground, telling the others they would soon be along; the afternoon was far progressed, and the time to gather for the evening meal not far off.

"Worr is a good fighter," Hrald praised, as he and Ceric looked after the retreating band. "As able as Jari."

Ceric agreed. "We will be glad to have them at our sides." The day might not be far off when more than sparring was required, and this they knew. "Jari is heavier, and has, as he showed me, an advantage in his sword-hand."

"They have fought many men, and learnt something from each one," Hrald added.

Ceric rolled from his back to his stomach. "Gunnulf learned not to fight with Worr," he said, at which they both laughed.

A little time went by. Whirring insects rose and fell about them. Hrald had pulled a stem of grass from its green sheath and was nibbling on the sweet white tip of it. The grass and the ground it sprung from was warm in the afternoon Sun, but a freshening breeze, cooling to their heated brows, was setting in.

"I was thinking of what your father said." Ceric's voice was low.

Hrald turned his head to him, but Ceric's face was looking straight ahead. The golden cross about his neck was hanging down, almost touching the grass he lay upon.

"About every man having their own style of fighting. About how when we are young we must try to use our speed, try to watch men and see how they fight, spot their weaknesses. Like what Jari just told me."

Hrald did not think he had forgotten more than a word of what his father Sidroc had said while acquainting the boys to the warrior's art. Now he knew Ceric had not, either.

Ceric got to his knees, stood up. Hrald rose too. They pulled their leathern tunics back on, and took up their discarded shields. Hrald's was black and red, like his father's, but with the black colour brushed on in two wedges, meeting at the central boss, on a red background. Ceric's shield was half-yellow, half-blue. Their sword baldrics lay off where the rest of the men had laid theirs; with the leathern sleeves slipped over their sword blades, they could not sheath them until the thick sleeves had been removed. They stood facing each other, the protective guards still upon their swords.

They had fought side-by-side, shield-to-shield in their practice. Now Hrald lifted his sword and playfully gave a tap to that which his friend held. Ceric laughed, but nodded. He looked at Hrald, nearly a full hand's length taller than he, as tall as Jari. No matter. He would have to fight men of all sizes, and one of the things he had always heard was that quickness could undercut size. Hrald's father had said it too, and he was one of the tallest men Ceric had ever met.

They pulled their shields into position before their bodies, the round expanses covering the vital torso. Their eyes locked, and they nodded. Then they began.

Hrald's heavy eyebrows almost touched as he focused his gaze on the movements of his opponent. Ceric struck first, a hit to the outside edge of Hrald's shield, which Hrald quickly returned. Another blow followed by Ceric, an attempt to get inside Hrald's briefly opened shield. It was rebuffed with a solid movement from Hrald's strong shield arm, its large and pointed boss propelled directly at Ceric's chest. Hrald used his friend's momentary step back to rain blows upon his iron-rimmed round, trying to force it aside with uppercuts. But Ceric held his ground, and even found himself forcing Hrald to turn with his own movements; he was now facing up the path towards the hall, which Hrald had been facing as they began.

They went on, at times snorting or calling, as they traded sword-thrusts. The swords, sheathed as they were, could not do more than dent the faces of their shields, marring them with shallow gashes, but the weapons still hit forcefully, with dull thuds. Going for the iron rim was more effective, trying to knock the shield away and open the torso to a touch.

Both were now soaked anew, and Hrald about to call a draw. He gave one more slice towards the rim of Ceric's shield. It hit, knocking the shield to the left, continuing on into the top of Ceric's upper arm.

He yelled.

Hrald watched Ceric drop his shield to the ground, and saw the golden-hilted sword fall too. His freed left hand rose to cover his right arm just below the shoulder. Ceric's face was twisted in pain, and blood began to run from between the fingers clapped over his arm.

Hrald looked at his sword. The heavy leathern sheath still covered the blade, all except near the tip. There it had split, riven apart by the blows Hrald had delivered to Ceric's iron shield rim. He had cut his friend, and badly.

The sword dropped from Hrald's hand as if it had burnt him. He shook his left hand free of his own shield, and sprang to Ceric's side.

They had been speaking of what his father had taught them of fighting. Now he remembered another, far earlier instruction, given to them both not far from where they stood. The Lord of Four Stones had taken them as small boys to witness a duel here. When it had been settled Sidroc had privately mocked the men for fighting. Then he had parted the beard on his face and shown the boys the scar he bore. Never draw your blades against each other, he had warned them. Yet they had done so, and not a rock's throw from where the warning had been given.

Ceric's hand was clenched over his bleeding arm, his dark tunic showing darker under his fingers, the cloth glistening with wetness. "It is nothing," he told Hrald, though the blood was welling between his fingers.

"Let me see," Hrald said. His shoulders had slumped, and despite the sweat on his brow he felt cold, even light-headed.

Ceric lifted his hand away from his rent tunic. The cut lay across the meatiest part of the muscle, a slice through the skin angling upwards. Hrald looked at it, then at his friend's face, teeth gritted with pain. Ceric's bloodied left hand rose to hold the wound again.

Hrald jerked off his leathern tunic, stripped off his linen one. Before Ceric could call out he had his knife in his left hand. He thrust the blade of it hard against the upper part of his bare right arm. He made his own stifled yell as the blade sliced through the muscle there.

He stepped before Ceric, facing him, bodies offset. Ceric dropped his hand away from his wound.

"Stand still," Hrald said. He stood shoulder to shoulder with Ceric, pressing his bleeding arm against that of his friend.

They stood that way a long moment, leaning their shoulders together. Hrald pulled back, his own arm red and dripping.

"Now we are brothers through our blood," he told Ceric.

Both their hands had returned to hold their wounded arms. Ceric nodded, a near-smile working at the corners of his mouth. He craned his neck to try to see the cut better.

"Will it need to be sewn?" he asked.

"I do not know," Hrald could only answer.

"Yours, too," Ceric added, looking to Hrald's bloodied hand. "Can your mother do it?"

Hrald shook his head at the question. "I would rather ask Burginde; she is skilled in such things." He struggled back into his linen tunic, and looked at his own arm. His white sleeve was rapidly turning red.

"Your tunic is dark. If we bind the wounds with that, the blood will show less," he reasoned. They had to enter the kitchen yard and try to find Burginde without undue attention.

He helped Ceric pull off his leathern tunic, and then his linen one. This they sliced into lengths, and bound each other's right arms. Ceric put his leathern tunic back on over his bare chest.

They rinsed their hands with what was left of their water, and picked up their shields and swords. The stinging pain in their arms had begun to change to a deeper, steady throbbing.

Both felt it, but Hrald felt sick as well. For a moment he had had to consider the response of his mother; Ceric had put him in mind of it when he asked if she could sew up their wounds. He could not think of that now, nor could he think of Worr or Jari and what they would say. All he knew was that he had sliced into the sword-arm of his best friend, a wound deep enough to drip blood upon the grass they walked over, a wound if it grew hot and green could kill Ceric. Wounding himself in no way made up for it.

They went straight to the edge of the kitchen yard, busy with folk making up the coming meal. One of Jari's young daughters was near, and Hrald called her over, bidding her fetch Burginde. The girl's eyes rounded at their bloodied sleeves, and she was off. Soon Burginde appeared from out the hall's door, hustling towards them. They watched Ashild step out after, face untroubled, her arms full of linens. Her eyes were caught by Burginde's haste, followed her progress, and then rose to where the friends waited. She dropped her linens on a nearby table and reached the two just after Burginde did.

They were standing side by side, their shields now at their feet, their swords in their left hands. The right arm of Hrald's white tunic was red with his blood, seeping from under the dark linen tied round the arm near the shoulder. Ceric's bare right arm was similarly wrapped, and blood ran down his arm and dripped from his elbow. It was clear his dark blue tunic had been used to bandage both wounds.

"What happened?" Ashild demanded.

Both began to answer, but Ceric spoke first, saying only, "We were sparring."

"Ach," Burginde answered, hand raising to her forehead in a solid smack. "Come, come," she ordered, gesturing the friends into the kitchen yard. Hrald shook his head.

"Then here," Ashild said, shoving open the door to the storage hut they stood near. Within were casks and chests to sit upon, and with the door open there would be enough light.

Burginde turned to Ashild. "The Simples chest – we will need it," she told her.

"Woad?"

"Woad too," agreed Burginde.

Ashild nodded and ran. Her mother kept a supply of healing herbs in the small Simples chest in her bower house, and fresh woad grew in her herb garden. She knew Ælfwyn was in the treasure room in the hall; she had just come from there; the bower house should be empty. Ashild took the box of Simples where it sat next to her mother's clothes chest, snatched up her mother's sharp shears, and ran back into the garden. There was the woad, a dye-stuff valued for staunching bleeding. She ripped a handful into her fist. Then she thought of her mother's sewing goods; she had a few needles wrought of steel. She went back and ransacked the basket, plucking the needles and the linen they were stuck into from the neatly-ordered bone bobbins of thread. She tucked a few things into the Simples chest and with it under her arm made for the storage hut, stopping to pull a length of linen from the pile she had set down.

When she got inside she saw Burginde had gotten Hrald and Ceric each a cup of ale. They would need something stronger, she was sure; later she would try to get them mead. Right now their pale faces and dry lips said they needed drink of any sort.

They were seated side by side on the lid of a barley bin, the sweet and malty grain smell strong about them. Ashild was nearly stifled by it, and by the racing of her own heart, which felt too large for her chest. The storage hut was windowless and dim, save for the sharp shaft of light pouring through the doorway.

Now that the Simples were here, Burginde began unwrapping the linen around Hrald's arm. Ashild did the same for Ceric. The bloodied tunic strips dropped to the wooden boards of the hut. Burginde was muttering oaths, and Ashild's dismay was clear in her sharp release of breath.

Burginde straightened up. "I will get water," she said, and left.

Ashild looked at both bloody wounds. Ceric's was bad, but Hrald's deeper and broader.

"Yours is much the worse," she told her brother. She turned to Ceric, her look no less than a glare. His lips parted, as if he would answer her, but then pressed closed again. He could say nothing.

She looked at Hrald. Tall as he was, he was her younger brother, and to see him in pain was almost to suffer it herself. "You cut yourselves this badly, sparring?"

Again Ceric spoke first. "Our blades broke through the leather guards on our swords."

Her brow furrowed with disbelief.

"Both – at the same time?" Without waiting for their answer, she went to where her brother's sword lay, resting on the top of a cask. The tightly fitted leather sheath was laced firmly up the flat face of the sword, over the shallow depression of the fuller, wrapping the edges of the sharp blade in thick, unbroken leather. But there at the top of the blade she saw it. Repeated blows had forced the steel through the hardened leather.

She picked up Ceric's sword, laying next it. The leathern casing was intact. Her head lifted.

She looked at Hrald, reached for his side, and closed her hand over the dark grip of the knife hanging at his hip. It felt damp in her grasp, and she opened her hand. A small amount of blood lay there. Then she knew.

Her eyes went first to Ceric, next to Hrald. Their faces were glistening with sweat but pale beneath it. They stared back at her. All three were wordless.

She nodded her head the slightest bit. She drew Hrald's knife out, and they watched as she used it to rip open the tip of the leathern casing on Ceric's sword so their tale could be believed.

"Thank you," her brother told her.

She knew why he had done it, hurt himself because he had hurt his friend, but it troubled her still. And Ceric had tried to cover for him, tried to take the blame himself. But Hrald was speaking again.

"Do not tell mother we got cut." His voice made clear his plea.

"I will not tell her," she returned, and allowed some heat to shade her answer. "You will be the one to tell her. I have never told tales and never will, you know that. Besides, do you think you could hide such a wound? Your arm will be stiff and sore for days. You will have to show the wound to her." She looked to Ceric. "Yours too."

Burginde was back, a large basin of water in her hands, which she set down next to the friends.

Ashild was cutting the linen she had brought into lengths, silently bemoaning its loss for such a foolish reason. Burginde was not so restrained. "'Twas your dear lamb of a mother wove that linen," she lamented. The women washed away the drying blood so they might see the true extent of the cuts.

"It clots well, the bleeding slows. But they are too broad. They must be sewn," Burginde judged, turning her head to Ashild.

Ashild swallowed, trying to push back her fear. She took the cup of ale from her brother's left hand and swallowed a sip; her mouth felt dry as dust.

The older woman now looked at Hrald. "Poor Jari," she fretted, clucking her teeth. "For years he shadows you night and day, and then this."

She watched Hrald wince the deeper at her words, then went on in a brighter tone. "Still, if friends such as you hurt themselves this bad, he will be proud of what you will do to a foe."

Ashild was turning to the Simples chest. "Mother has steel needles; I brought them," she said, to which Burginde nodded her approval. Bone needles were thicker, and would make a larger hole as they pierced the skin. They were also prone to break. Ashild took linen thread from the chest, scraped it along the lump of beeswax there, and threaded up both needles; she knew Burginde's eyes would not allow her to do so quickly. She gave one threaded needle to Burginde, and left the second stuck in a piece of linen. She would let Burginde do any stitching.

Ceric spoke to Ashild. She had shown her willingness to cover for them, but he could feel she was angry, and upset as well. Yet he would risk asking a service of her.

"If it must be sewn, will you not be the one to do it," he said.

"I am not a good needle-woman," she returned.

But her mother's old nurse had decided for her. "This one for you," she said, tilting her head at Ceric's wound. "I will work on Hrald's; it is worse."

She had no choice.

"My seams are never straight, I warn you," she told Ceric. She could not help a slight and rueful smile as she said it. She slipped a leathern thimble over her finger, so she might protect it as she pushed the needle.

They set to work. Ashild never had cause to sew a wound before. It was horrible to hold the needle and pinch the flesh closer so she could puncture it with its sharp point. She wondered why Ceric did not flinch every time she did so.

Finally she stopped in her work and asked. "Does not the needle pain you?" She was halfway up the trackway of her lacing; five stiches in, five more, she reckoned, to go.

He was looking straight ahead. "I hardly feel it, for the pain of the wound," he assured her. "I think I feel the drawing of your thread through; it is strange."

"I am glad to hear this," she said, her voice almost a whisper. She turned to look at Hrald. Burginde was still bent over her work. Hrald had dropped his head back against the wall the grain bin rested against. His eyes were closed, and his jaw clenched in pain.

Ashild turned back to Ceric's wound, made her next stab through his flesh. Hrald had hurt Ceric, given him a cut that would mark his sword arm for the rest of his days. Then he had gone on to hurt himself, even more so. Either wound, or both, could fester, and either friend, or both, die. And she stood before Ceric, who thought he loved her, as she drove needle and thread through his skin, trying to seal a wound her own brother had driven.

The wound now felt like one mass of searing heat to Ceric. He closed his eyes, then opened them at a sound. He turned his head to look at Ashild. The gaze of her blue-grey eyes was steady on her work. Tears flowed from those eyes, sparkling as they ran to her chin. He watched her a moment, almost in wonder. He lifted his left hand to her face, and she turned it to him. The pad of his thumb wiped the tears as they welled from her right eye.

Their eyes met, hers wet with tears, his glazed with pain. She bit her lip and turned her face back to her stitching.

Ashild is weeping for me, Ceric thought. She cries for Hrald too, I know this; but her tears are flowing for me as well, and for what she is doing. My arm feels as if it were on fire, but she is holding it with tenderness. She is touching me, as a wife would.

The pain, and his thirst, and the thought of this made him feel faint. He closed his eyes and lay his head back against the wall as Hrald had done.

He did not know when she finished. He opened his eyes to the touch of a hand upon his brow. Ashild was standing before him, holding a bronze cup in her hand. After what he had been thinking the gentleness of her tone no longer surprised him.

"Drink this, Ceric, it is mead."

He took it in his left hand and looked over at his shoulder. His arm had been wrapped in strips of linen; he had not felt it happen.

He wanted to take a sip of the rich mead and then pass the cup to her so she might drink from it too, as a man did with his bride at their wedding-feast. He lifted the cup, the honeyed sharpness of the aroma rising upward. The sweet strength of it filled his mouth, a savour deeper and more enlivening than any mead he had ever tasted. His eyes closed a moment, holding the flavour, relishing the gesture. Then he opened them, moved the cup away from his own lips and towards Ashild.

But she had left him. She had moved over to his side where Hrald sat.

Ceric straightened himself and saw that Burginde was still bent over Hrald's arm, laying green bracts of some herb over the sewn gash, then binding it with linen.

Ashild wrung out a piece of cloth in the basin and wiped her brother's face. His skin looked white, and was cool and damp to her touch. He opened his eyes to her.

"Hrald," she told him, "here is mead."

He smiled, which gave her heart. His voice, though, was almost a croak. "Mead?"

Mead was both costly and potent, and their mother and aunt alone held the keys to the storeroom where it was kept waiting by in small crocks. She smiled back. "I have my ways," she said, teasingly. In fact she had gotten her busy aunt to hand her the entire set of keys from the keeper at her waist by claiming she must fetch a silver salver for her mother. She had poured out a quantity of mead into an ewer before returning the keys to Æthelthryth. Then she had stopped in the hall, rifled through Ceric's saddle bags for a tunic, and taken one of Hrald's, as well.

Neither friend could lift his right arm without crying out in pain, and the women struggled to dress them.

"You will never be able to eat," Ashild proclaimed, now both were on their feet.

"We will be Tyr-hands tonight, like Jari," Hrald answered, trying to jest despite his furrowed brow. After two deep gulps of mead his head felt fuzzy, and his painful arm as though it were further away from his body.

"At least let us get mother, and Worr too," Ashild urged, "so you might tell them now, and not in the noise of the hall."

Hrald and Ceric exchanged looks. There was nothing for it; Ashild was right. Better to tell them now and have it over with.

Burginde, clucking all the while, was moving around them, balling up the bloodied remains of their tunics, ordering the contents of the Simples chest, and finally tipping out the reddened basin water into the dust outside. A few drops of blood flecked her gown, and Ashild's right sleeve at the wrist hem also showed red. "You fetch them; 'twer always a better liar than me," she told Ashild.

Chapter the Eighth: Not So Easily Bought

FATE favoured them. The Lady of Four Stones and the horse-thegn of Kilton did not make the friends show their wounds that night, trusting the word of Burginde and Ashild as to their nature. Hrald and Ceric took their place at table, trying to master their pain and make light of it. But both Ælfwyn and Worr insisted on being there when the wounds were re-dressed the following day. Then they saw the true extent of the gashes, worse than either the young men or the women who had helped them had let on.

Ælfwyn gasped, her hand lifting to her mouth as she pulled back the final turn on her son's bandage. She steeled herself with a deep breath, and flicked away the woad leaves clotting the wound. Ælfwyn had seen sword wounds and spear cuts aplenty in her first years at Four Stones, but seeing her own son's arm riven in this way was a fresh and heart-rending moment. She allowed herself no tears, though, instead praising Burginde for her stitch-work. Ashild was there too, unwrapping Ceric's arm, and Ælfwyn and Worr turned now to it. The edges of both gashes were clean, but swollen, the trackways of the linen stitching straining against the risen flesh. A clear yellowish liquid had dried about the wounds, and no fresh blood flowed.

"I will rinse them with betony water; Wilfrede the dyer taught me that, years ago," Ælfwyn finally said.

The horse-thegn of Kilton had watched silently. He now spoke his thanks to Burginde and Ashild. "May we always have as able healers as you."

He canted his head at Hrald, and then at Ceric. Men did get hurt in training, and these two had been amongst them.

"Better first blood at the hands of a friend, than an enemy," he noted.

Ceric nodded back, meeting Worr's half-grin with one of his own. But after a moment Hrald looked away, the guilt of self-reproach all he could feel.

Two days had passed since then. The fiery sting of pain had steadily subsided, though using their arms, or even trying to lift them, hurt.

"I wish I could see it," Ceric said of his wound.

They were alone in the treasure room, and had unwrapped the fresh linen which Burginde had just replaced. He had tried to twist his neck and pull the shoulder towards him, only to occasion more pain. Hrald thought a moment, then fetched a polished silver disc from a shelf by the bed. It was the shelf that his father had kept his small belongings on, and now which he used too. Hrald had just begun to shave his face once a week, and the reflecting silver disc was his.

"Here," he said, holding it up and away from his friend's arm. The gash was as long as a finger. Hrald could barely look at it, but understood why Ceric wanted to.

Ceric saw the way the slash angled upwards, and saw too the cross-laced path of Ashild's stitching. The white linen thread she had used was brown with dried blood. He took a good look, then nodded.

"Now yours," he said, taking the disc from Hrald's left hand.

Ceric had not seen Hrald's wound before, and now paused a moment before he lifted the disc into Hrald's view. His own wound was a clean slice. The one Hrald had given himself was more a jagged rip, longer and broader than that marring his own arm. Ceric could not keep a low whistle from sounding under his breath.

Hrald looked at the reflection in the shimmering metal. Then his lids dropped over his eyes.

"You could have just pricked your finger," Ceric said about Hrald's act, and the mingling of their blood. It sounded a jest, but he did not mean it as one. The wound was ugly and far worse than his own.

Hrald nodded, tried to smile. He had not reminded Ceric of the warning his father had given them as boys, but it had sounded in his ears every night as he tried to fall into sleep, knowing that Ceric too was in pain.

"At least Worr was right," Ceric said now, beginning to bind Hrald's arm back up. "Better first blood by a friend than an enemy."

"Remember setting snares with Tindr?" Hrald asked.

"Já," answered Ceric, falling without noticing it into Norse. The jostling of riding pained them, and so they often walked, as they were today by the stream which ran behind Four Stones.

"I remember it well." He looked to the forest on either side, where he and Hrald had spent so much time at play the Summer he had spent at Four Stones. "Did you ever set them here?"

"Já, I did, at first," Hrald said, brushing the tops of the tall grasses they walked through with a stick held in his left hand. "I like being in the woods alone. And building them made me think of Tindr showing us how to do it – all the days we spent with him." The hand that held the stick fell still, and he too looked towards the trees. "But coming home with one hare – not much to feed a hall with."

Ceric laughed. A week had passed since their wounding, and though their arms were sore and tight, the burning throbbing they had known was but a dark memory.

As they went on they found they were not alone. Two maids, perhaps not older than Hrald, were sitting a little distance ahead on a fallen tree trunk at the water's edge. Their backs were to them, their shoes and stockings scattered on the ground where they had been pulled off. Now both maids rose, and hiking up their skirts above their knees, began to walk about in the cool water.

Ceric paused, grinning as he watched them, and Hrald too stopped. The maids spoke to each other, sometimes laughing and stomping their feet to splash the other. One held her gown bunched so high that they saw much of the backs of her white thighs.

The friends moved closer, and one of them stepped on a dry tree branch, causing it to crackle. The maids whirled round. One scrambled to the grassy bank. The second flushed red and dropped her skirts where she stood. The light blue of the hem deepened in hue about her as the water soaked it.

"Hrald," said the one on the bank. She was smiling brightly at him. Both maids were daughters of the men of the hall; Ceric had marked them before this.

Hrald had coloured slightly too, and returned the maid's greeting. The one still standing in the stream composed herself enough to ask how both their arms were healing.

"I heard you hit each other with the skeggox," posed the one on dry land. "Is that true?"

The friends laughed their denial, and went on.

"Comely maids," said Ceric, when they had passed out of earshot. "The one on the grass likes you."

Hrald scoffed, but it put him in mind of a question to his older friend.

"Have you had a woman?"

Ceric took it in stride. "Not yet. You?"

"O – no." Hrald felt his face warm. His thoughts had certainly been much occupied with the subject. "Mother and Wilgot preach to me about remaining chaste."

Ceric had heard the same, and nodded.

Now Hrald laughed, and went on.

"In Spring a serving woman, one of the younger ones, showed her bottom to me," he admitted. "I was in the treasure room, and she slipped in, which is forbidden anyway. She said nothing, just smiled, then turned and pulled up her gown. I almost laughed, but I think she meant it. I just stood there, and then Burginde walked in and saw; she howled like a cat. She slapped the woman's face, and then marched her out by the ear."

Ceric gave a short laugh at this. "I reckon that many will wish to be first with the young lord of the place," he teased. They were both quiet for a moment, then Ceric spoke again.

"I will, when I get home," he said. "When I wed Ashild I want to know what I am doing."

Hrald did not know what to say to this, except to nod in agreement.

After a short space he asked, "So you will wed her?"

"I have always meant to wed her." Ceric was certain of that. He felt she was already promised to him, already almost his wife. A feeling flooded into his breast, an echo of what he had felt when she had sewn up his arm, that she was touching him as a wife would.

"I think you should speak to her," Hrald said.

His tone was uneasy enough that Ceric slowed. Surely she knew his desire; he had already told her. Then he thought of something else.

"Is there another she would have – other than me?" he asked his friend. "I know you will give her much treasure to bring with her, but I will meet any bride-price you set."

Before Hrald could answer Ceric spoke again.

"Guthrum has sons, I know. If he dies soon..." He could not quite bring himself to say it, to ask if Ashild would chose him over one who might be the new King of the Danes.

Hrald shook his head. "Asberg says he has sons enough, but none worthy to be King."

"Have you seen them?"

"Three of the sons, yes. They have been here."

"Do they know Ashild?"

"Of course."

"But you do not think she would choose one of them?"

Hrald tried to laugh. "And I do not know if they would choose her." Hrald looked about him, shook his head. "Ashild can be – contrary. She sometimes turns from even what she herself wants."

"Why?" Ceric demanded, trying to understand. "Why would a maid do that? She can have nearly anything she wants."

"She is hard on herself. And she is…restless." He gave another short laugh. "Mother says she should have been a boy."

It made little sense to Ceric, and yet bothered him.

"I will ask her. Ask her to wed me," he decided. "Modwynn told me to wait, but I feel sure she wants Ashild for me. As I do."

Hrald invited his sister to join him and Ceric for a walk next day. Their route took them along the pounded clay road leading to the valley of horses, but ended much earlier, at the groves of fruit trees shading one side of the road. The apples were still green and hard, but the plums were ripening, and two or three small boys stood ready with handfuls of pebbles to deter the sharp beaks of passing birds. The groves were cool and pleasant to walk in, and Hrald soon absented himself for his friend's sake, taking his own meandering path through the trees.

Ashild saw this, noting her brother's studied withdrawal. She felt a curious amusement, paired with a flutter of discomfort. Ceric wished to be alone with her, and Hrald knew it. There was ease in the friendship between the three of them, and something deeper too since the day of the sparring. She had discerned their secret, one she joined fully into when she slit the guard protecting Ceric's sword blade. Her actions had made her worthy of their trust. But it was more than this. Today she felt she knew what Ceric would say, and thought she was ready for it.

They had brushed under some low hanging apple boughs, palming the firm globes in their hands, and now stood by sturdy plum trees. The fruit on several was already dusky with ripeness. Ceric plucked one, and then another, offering the first to her.

"One day we will eat from a shared plate," he declared, after they had licked the sweet juices running from their fingers. The tart yielding of the plums' flesh seemed a happy harbinger just then, spurring him on. "And Modwynn gave me two silver cups. One shall be yours."

"A shared plate. A silver cup. I am not so easily bought." But she was smiling as she said it.

"You may name your price, Ashild. It will be met. I have told Hrald that."

His voice was light, but he was far from jesting. They had paused in their walking, their shoulders almost touching. Eating the fruit with her, standing this close, and alone with her, sparked his desire. He would kiss her if he could, hold her against his body, if even for a moment.

But she had resumed her walking, passing on the other side of the plum tree from him. "So to you it is as simple as that?"

"Why should it not be?" he wanted to know, all honesty in his voice. "That morning at the valley of horses you said I did not know you. But all my life I have known you." He had joined up with her again, and lifted his hand in question. "Our folk have been connected a long time, since before we were born."

She stopped, turned to him. The sweetness in her mouth felt of a sudden cloying. "Connected how? Through shed blood and forced marriage, the way all such bonds are made. Look at my own mother. And my real father – my blood-father – died even before I was born, warring in Wessex. He never saw me, nor me him. He did not even know about me. He was killed before he could."

Her voice had risen in the telling, though she kept her eyes steady.

"I know this," Ceric answered, his tone low.

She looked at him now, seeing more in his face than his simple words expressed.

"Cursed be he who took him from me, from mother, from all he had won here," she ended.

"He is beyond your curses," was all Ceric could say.

Now she stopped. "You know his murderer is dead?"

Ceric nodded, just once. Too much had been spoken for silence now.

"It was my uncle, Godwin, who killed him."

Her face looked blank, her lips parted as if stilled while trying to speak.

"Godwin of Kilton killed Yrling," she repeated. "My father."

"Yes. Godwin did it because of my father, his brother Gyric. It was in vengeance for what had happened to him."

She was blinking, taking it in. She had been told but half the tale. Her hand had lifted, and she pulled the silver hammer out of her shift.

"Mother said he died fighting at her home, trying to win it from other Danes who had lessor claim to it."

He nodded assent. "Yrling was there at Cirenceaster, fighting, just as she told you. But Godwin was looking for all involved in the blinding of my father. He found him fighting outside the walls of Cirenceaster, and killed him."

She swung around to face him. He saw her knuckles had gone white, clasping the hammer of Thor.

"Then you have brought disaster to me!"

"It was not me, Ashild," he said, stung at her words. He would have reached to take her other hand, was not the gulf between them growing wider by the moment. She was leaning back from him, as if he were a serpent or some odious thing. But he must go on, try to make her understand.

"My uncle sought vengeance against those who had hurt my father. He knew my father had been brought here to Four Stones; my mother told him these things when she and my father arrived at Kilton. Godwin found and killed the Dane Hingvar who burnt out my father's eyes. Then he learned Yrling was in Wessex, at your mother's home…"

"His Thor's hammer," she said, still holding it. "Godwin took it as proof of his death…"

He only nodded. He did not know what more he could say.

She let the hammer drop upon her breast, obscuring the much smaller cross of gold that hung there. Her hands dropped to her sides, and he saw her fingers curl, almost into fists.

"Your mother. Your uncle. How much have we suffered here at Four Stones because of them?"

Now he reached across the void, grasped her forearm, and pulled her close.

"Ashild. Stop. Godwin was avenging his pledged man. His brother. And my mother – despite how she lives now, Lady Ælfwyn loves her as a sister, and that love is fully returned.

"Hrald and I – we are as brothers. He means as much to me as Edwin. More, maybe. And you – I do not think I need to tell you what you mean."

Her face and voice both challenged him, but not harshly.

"What do I mean?"

His grandmother's words came back to him as he stood there in her bower house, the yellow gown in his hands.

"You are my choice."

The quietness of her voice did not deflect the power of her answer.

"You are not mine."

It felt a hard and deadening blow between his breastbone. He let go her arm. She stepped back from him.

She had made herself almost gasp by saying it. She wished to twist his words, fling them back at him, and she did. But staring at him she felt her heart turn. It was not Ceric she did not want. It was Kilton, and all Kilton meant.

"Was I ever your choice?" he asked. He was shaking his head as if trying to make sense of it. "You taunted me, out by the valley of horses, but did not say No. Was it what I told you here, about your father's death, that makes you say it now?"

Anger at herself, at him, at deeds done long ago and finally understood welled up within her. Her chin thrust into the air. Rebellion rang in her answer.

"Our mothers saw us playing as babes and assumed we would one day love each other. Hrald was born a boy. It is assumed he will rule South Lindisse as Jarl. You bring me that gown, rich enough to serve as a queen's morning-gift. You assume I will be honoured to leave my home for Kilton, be the perfect Peace-weaver between us. You are all making plans based on what you have assumed.

"Now I hear it was your uncle who killed my blood-father, just as I have known that it is your mother who has kept Sidroc from returning to my mother."

And to Hrald and me, she wanted to cry out; but she bit her lip to keep that pain from pouring forth.

She stared at him, eyes like clouds pushed to the point of storm.

"Our folk are bound together, you said. They are, but in sorrow and loss."

She turned away now; she could not stand before him looking at his open and pained face and tousled hair. Her brow felt hot and her hands as cold as if they lay in spring-water.

She must order her thoughts, narrow them to one thing only: How could he believe she could go to the hall where her father's killer once ruled as lord? True, this had been the fate of other maids; it was, she knew, almost the fate of the daughter of Merewala, who ended her own life here at Four Stones rather than be the captive bride of the conqueror. That he had been Yrling, her own father, only muddied everything in her mind.

Her cool and numb hands had lifted to her face. She held them pressed to her flushed temples. The pounding of the blood beneath her fingertips filled her head.

Ceric did not know what more to say. The waters had closed over his head, and quickly; he was out of his depth, and felt her swimming strongly, and away, from him. He knew she must learn the truth one day, and wagered it was best coming from him. And she had turned away.

"Ashild," he pleaded. "Say you will be my wife."

It took a moment, but she turned to him. He saw that water glittered in her eyes, though no tears had yet stained her face.

"What are you asking?" she said, a question with no answer. "It will never work. Godwin, the Lord of Kilton killed Yrling. Sidroc, the Lord of Four Stones, killed Godwin. An alliance between enemies – yes. The healing of those wounds – never."

He swallowed the rising lump in his throat, and found himself nodding, despite his desire to disprove her. "Only if – only if you will not allow it to," he promised.

But she was shaking her head at him.

"Is there anyone else," he wanted to know. Perhaps her reluctance ran even deeper; perhaps Hrald did not know all. "Some other man who you would choose?"

It took courage to ask, and he saw her acknowledgement of that in her face.

"No other, Ceric." Her voice had softened, as had her eyes.

"Já," she corrected herself now, pointed in her use of the Norse. "Hrald. He needs me."

She brushed her hands against her brimming eyes, straightened herself.

Hrald, he thought. Hrald would have his uncle and all their men around him. Guthrum had approved him; as long as he lived that would stand as well. There were only two women who could be of importance in Hrald's future: his mother, to guide him until he became a man, and the woman he would wed, in the treasure she would bring him, and in how well she would run his hall. This was Ashild thinking too highly of herself.

They looked at the other a long moment, distrait defiance in her face, hurt wonder in his. Then she began walking.

He fell in beside her, recounting in his mind what each of them had said. He would not give her up as easily as this. Her pride was something he would learn to work around; it was part of her, and he could value it for the courage she drew from it. And she knew the truth now, both about her father, and about his desiring of her.

He felt a way stood open for him. Ashild's role was to make the best marriage she could for her brother's sake, and her folk. Why should it not be him? Once her anger had cooled she would come round to seeing the rightness of his choice. And he felt his suit would be upheld by all Ashild cared for and trusted here, just as he had felt his grandmother's unspoken approval. He would not worry about the hammer around her neck; that would come right too.

They walked for some time before she glanced over at him. She was surprised to see a slight smile on his lips, as if he were recalling some special jest.

"Why do you smile?" she found herself asking. She felt far from any mirth.

He shook his head, but answered. "I was thinking of when you cursed me."

Her mouth opened, and she gave a small laugh. She nodded.

"You had followed Hrald and me out along the stream bed," he remembered. "We were throwing rocks, looking for frogs, building dams in the water. Then you were there, wanting to join us. We took off, running as fast as we could. You ran after. I recall your skirts were wet and you tied them up about your knees so you could run the better."

He watched her nose wrinkle at this unseemly detail.

"Still, we could not free ourselves of you. We took to the woods, dodging through trees, following a deer-track. Still you came, but we were too fast. Hrald with his long legs was in front. I heard you call out, turned to see you had fallen in a tangle of brambles."

Her eyes were steady on his face now.

"I watched you stand. You wiped your face – you were fighting tears. It was the only time I saw you cry.

"You stood there, your two fists outthrust towards me, thumbs pointed straight at me.

'I curse you, Ceric, I curse you,' you called. Then you spoke again."

A moment passed, of shared remembrance. It was all fresh again. Her hot tears, Ceric and her brother running deeper into the dark woods, away from her. She broke the silence with her question.

"Do you recall my curse?"

He shook his head. "I do not know; you spoke that part of it in Norse."

"I will tell you. My curse was: That you should lose your way."

Their eyes had locked. It was he who looked down.

"Well," Ceric said, to lighten the mood, "I may never be as good at tracking as Worr, but I have always returned home."

"And so you shall," she said, trying to join his effort. "And home is Kilton."

There followed two days of rain, most welcome in the Summer dryness, rain which refreshed the limp stalks of barley in the village fields, and the drooping flowers of the bower garden. On the third morning of it Hrald and Ceric sat facing each other at a trestle table in the hall. The game of tæfl was set up on a scored wooden board between them, and they moved the smooth stone pieces across the squares, capturing the other's men. Worr and the thegns were ranged about this and a second table, playing as well, both at tæfl and at dice. Asberg and Jari joined them, winning their share of the silver the men played for. The others in the hall were mainly women, driven indoors by the rain. Most stood spinning wool, pulling the combed fleece from out of a mass of fluffy roving on their shoulders or caught in wood distaffs. Others sat winding up the spun thread into balls of cream, grey or black. A few young ones dodged about in play of their own, chasing each other around the timber uprights holding the roof beams, and playing jumping games upon the red and white stone floor.

Despite the rain the three hall doors were open to admit light. Hrald and Ceric sat next that opposite the great horse barn. They heard a man's sharp whistle and a moment later the jangling of horse-hardware, then the churning of hooves in muddy ground. Their heads turned to see several horseman, two on horses so badly lathered that the rain left streaks on their necks and chests. Mul the stableman and his two sons were already out from the barn, reaching for the horses' heads. The riders jumped off their mounts and made for the open door.

All the men within the hall were on their feet to meet them, and the women, though their fingers did not slow, looked over to the door. Two young men, not of Four Stones, came first, followed by Gunnulf and two others also serving as watch-guards that day. Both of the visitors were armed in the way of warriors, and both were tall and well-knit. The elder was not more than five-and-twenty, the second perhaps a little over Hrald's age.

All five men were drenched, and shook off their dripping mantles as they came. An attentive serving women untied her apron and handed it to them so they might wipe their hands and faces, while another vanished down the passage to the kitchen yard.

"Thorfast," said Hrald, coming to greet the young man in the lead.

Thorfast held a smoothed stick in his hand, and did not put it down as he embraced Hrald. Asberg and Jari were just behind Hrald, their eyes wide as they waited.

"I have news from Headleage," the visitor said, nodding at Hrald, and at his uncle. Ceric was now standing at Hrald's right arm.

Thorfast glanced at Ceric, questioning, uncertain if he could speak.

"This is Ceric of Kilton. My friend. You may speak before him."

The young man looked to the second he had ridden with, then spoke. "Our uncle, Guthrum, is dead."

Guthrum, King of the Danes, was dead. There was silence. Heads turned, eyes meeting for a moment before shifting to the next man. Worr and Gunnulf, Asberg and Jari, the thegns and Ceric.

Hrald raised his right hand to his forehead, and crossed himself, a twinge of hidden pain in every movement of his arm. He reopened his eyes.

"Go and fetch my mother," he told the serving woman who had returned with ale.

The men stood there hearing the creaking of the side stairs leading from the weaving room. The Lady of Four Stones soon crossed to them, Burginde at her side, and Ashild also.

Ælfwyn took in the group of men, her face paling as she approached.

"Thorfast. We bid you welcome," she said. She could not keep the tremor from her voice, but her hands were gently clasped before her.

"My uncle is dead, Lady," he answered.

Her lips parted.

Thorfast saw who she stood with. "Ashild," he said. Their friendship was made clear to Ceric by Thorfast's look.

Ashild's brow was creased. "I grieve for you," she told him. She made a gesture of comfort with her hands, the slightest motion towards him. Ceric felt it, a rush of jealous warmth swelling in his breast.

"Where was he buried," Asberg asked now, and all turned to him.

"At Headleage, two days ago." Thorfast again looked to his younger brother. "We were there," he avowed, his tone signifying that Guthrum truly was dead.

Buried and not burnt, thought Ceric; Guthrum took his Christian vows with more gravity than we assumed. Or was it example to Ælfred, that he should honour the Peace, as Guthrum honoured his adopted faith? He looked to Worr, but the thegn's eyes were locked upon Thorfast.

Hrald asked that which all were thinking. "What will happen now?"

"I cannot say," Thorfast said. "The lands Guthrum held in his own right have been divided as he asked, between his sons and nephews. The Kingdom…it is not known who will come forward to claim it."

The spectre of war between the dead Dane's sons, and nephews, and the many chieftains Guthrum had unified, could be as close as Thorfast was to them.

Ælfwyn spoke. "Let us get you dry clothing while your food bags are being filled."

"I thank you, Lady. But we cannot stay." Thorfast held up the stick gripped in his fist. Though darkened with wet, those closest to him could see the knife-marks it bore.

"You must make your mark, Hrald, to show you and Four Stones have heard this news."

Hrald took it, moved to the table, drew his knife. The stick already bore the carvings of three war-chiefs, men or the sons of men who had wrested this corner of Anglia from the Saxons. Now, scarcely more than a lad, he would add his own. He cut in the rune Hagel ᚺ, and then with the point, his name in the letters of the speech of Angle-land: HRALD.

He stood up and handed the stick back to Thorfast.

"Your horses – we will give you fresh ones," he said.

Thorfast nodded. "I thank you. We will not kill them in the riding; we have only two stops more before we turn for Headleage. By then all of us who rode should be back." He and his brother were already wrapping themselves in their wet mantles. "I will send word when I can."

The men of Four Stones filed out into the stable yard after the two. Worr and the thegns remained in the hall, their concern creasing their brows. Ceric went with Hrald, but held back a space from him, lest Thorfast should wish to speak in private. The rain had lessened to a drizzle, but the grey sky was over-clouded in scudding billows, with that tang in the damp air that foretold another drenching to come. Inside the open doors of the barn Mul and his boys were transferring the kit and trappings of Thorfast and his brother to two fresh horses.

Ceric watched Thorfast lace the telling-stick into one of his saddle bags. Both visitors swung up, as did Gunnulf and the two Danes he had arrived with. Thorfast and his brother said something in Norse to Hrald and Asberg and Jari, a few words only. Then they were off, the messengers to the next keep, Gunnulf and his brethren back to their post. Ælfwyn stood looking after them from the side doorway, and Asberg and Jari went to her, signaling to Hrald they would wait for him in the hall.

Ceric now joined Hrald where he stood just within the stable. The smell of horses and damp hay and wet leather hung about them. One of the many tortoiseshell barn cats slunk into view, only to vanish, scrabbling in a pile of bedding straw after a mouse. Ceric's eyes followed the line of stalls into the gloom of the stable's far and murky end; nothing was clear. He turned back to Hrald to find Ashild hurrying across the muddy ground to them.

The three traded glances. Ceric could read the worry on Hrald's face, and thought he must look the same. Ashild could not keep her brow from pinching.

None of them spoke. Then Ceric broke the silence.

"I should leave."

Ashild answered first. "Nothing has happened yet."

Ceric gave a shake of his head. "There are six of us. Only six."

Hrald's eyes had gone from his sister to his friend. Now he spoke. "I will ride with you, take my best men. We will serve as escort to the Wessex border."

Ashild was quick in her reaction. "You cannot go," she told her brother. "Send an escort, já. But you must stay here. You must."

Hrald let out a breath, saw the rightness in her urging. "Já," he conceded. Four Stones must not be left without its heir. All the Jarls and smaller chieftains were vulnerable now, and would stay at their seats of power, watching and protecting. He spoke now to Ceric.

"Four Stones has many men. But other jarls have as many. If a group of war-chiefs, or Guthrum's sons, band together…"

Hrald's voice trailed off, as his thoughts had. He could not speak of this now, of Guthrum's Kingdom dissolving, of having to fight off other Danes, or even Ælfred and his own son Edward, should they wish to try and claim all in the disorder which might follow.

They entered the hall to see the thegns already at work packing up their kit. Worr stood with Asberg and Jari, their heads together. A look from Asberg bid the three approach.

"The stone road-ways will have men upon them, likely as not," Asberg was telling Worr. He spoke of the straight roads built long ago by the Caesars, the fastest way to return to Wessex. "Best to take a northerly track. It will be longer, but you will meet fewer travelling upon them."

Hrald stepped a little forward. "You are six," he told Worr. "We will send six with you, as escort to the border of Anglia." He spoke with decision; they were his men to send.

Asberg and Jari looked at him, nodding their approval. Hrald had given his first command.

"Ælfred will hear of your help," Worr promised. He canted his head to the thegns working behind them, bidding Ceric do the same.

Ashild knew her mother would be already in the kitchen yard, seeing to their provisioning. She would go and tell them that a troop of twelve would soon ride.

Hrald turned with Ceric to where his packs were stowed. Their abandoned game sat upon the table; Hrald had been winning. He looked up to see his absent father's shield hanging on the wall, by the raven banner embroidered by his mother.

It was mid-afternoon when the riders set off, six men of Kilton, six of Four Stones. A cloud-burst had cleared the skies, leaving only a fine mist in the air, but the number of horses tethered by lines outside the horse barn had churned the soil into fetlock-deep mud. Hrald had forced two extra horses upon

Ceric, two of his best. He had meant to give his friend a young bay stallion in thanks for the ring-shirt Ceric had given him. Now at parting he pressed the reins of a second mount into Ceric's hands as well, a strong, arched-necked chestnut gelding loaded with food-packs. They need take as much provender as they could carry, he reasoned. It would speed their way, and keep them from having to show themselves unnecessarily.

Gunnulf and Onund had asked to be part of the escort, but with Asberg and Jari's help Hrald named only older and experienced fighters, chosen for their knowledge of the terrain and of the men they might come across. The safe passage of the godson of the King of Wessex must be assured; Four Stones must not fail in that, even beyond the borderlands of South Lindisse.

They left in the same haste in which they prepared. Hrald knew Ceric had asked to see Wilgot, and after that short visit to the priest's small house Ceric had placed a slip of parchment in Hrald's hand. "Give this to Ashild after I leave," he bid Hrald.

Back in the treasure room Hrald helped his friend roll and stuff things into his packs. They were emptier now.

"The ring-shirt," began Hrald, wishing to say something fitting in thanks for such a gift. It was laid carefully by in the chest next the store of fine swords.

"Do not get it dented," Ceric answered.

Hrald's dark lashes fell over his blue eyes. "Yours, either," he returned.

He would have liked to say something more, felt he must at least speak about Ashild. One day she would journey to Kilton; Hrald felt certain of that. After that he might never see her again. He would need to be happy in the knowledge she was there, protected and rich, the wife of Ceric of Kilton.

"Kilton," Hrald said instead. Ceric looked up at him over the saddle bag he was stuffing.

Hrald shook his head. "Nothing. I will never see it, that is all."

He could not imagine how he could travel thence, not when his father had killed the Lord of the place. His father's act would shadow him, always, at Kilton and perhaps throughout Wessex.

Ceric's hand had stopped in mid-air, the tunic he was holding hovering for a moment before being thrust into the leathern pack. He would not be Lord of Kilton; he could not make Hrald welcome.

He gave his head a shake, spoke with firmness.

"I will be back, for Ashild. And to see you."

Hrald helped him with his sword-baldric; their healing arms still pained them in the lifting.

"The sword of Godwulf," Hrald repeated, watching Ceric position the scabbard, the brilliant gold of the blade's hilt gleaming against the darkness of his clothing.

"One day it will be called the sword of Ceric," his friend predicted.

Ceric nodded, then grinned.

Once back in the body of the hall, ale was passed. Wilgot moved amongst the departing men, blessing each of them. The Lady of Four Stones did not try to hide her tears as she embraced Ceric. Ashild stood at her side, grave-faced, trying to smile. She gave Ceric her hand; in the crowded hall he could hope for no more than this.

"Be well," she bid him.

He gave her hand a squeeze, studying her face. He felt the warmth of her fingers in his own, those fingers which had pushed the steel needle through his flesh as her tears fell.

As they rode off, both Ceric and Worr turned in their saddles to look back. Worr waved his thanks once more, hand raised in the air. Ceric only stared, eyes fixed at Ashild and her mother and on Hrald, standing so much taller than both.

Hrald did not wait to give his sister the parchment. He gestured her into the treasure room. "A letter from Ceric," he said, lifting his hand to the single small square lying upon the sword chest. He moved to the door to leave her alone with it.

"Stay," she said. "He is friend to both of us. You shall hear what he says." Her eyes fell on the blank back of the creamy parchment. She made another decision. "Mother too. I will keep no secrets from her."

Hrald drew a deep breath. The damp warmth of the rains made the room feel airless. He was not sure he wanted to hear what Ceric had written. He wished at that moment to walk alone through the wet grass along the stream bed, or even wander off into the cool and dripping woods. But Ashild had left the room, to return a moment later with their mother. Ælfwyn took up her place next Hrald.

Ashild held the parchment square and began reading it aloud. Ceric's lettering was small and even, strongly-formed, that of a man of learning.

"MY ASHILD

I will return for you in two years, bringing great treasure with me. Your bride-price will be met. Modwynn is old; she will welcome you and give you the keys to Kilton. You shall be Lady there. It will be years before Edwin is wed; you will hold the keys until he does.

You must say Yes.

CERIC OF KILTON"

She lowered the square of parchment, but kept her eyes upon it. *My Ashild*, he had named her.

"You will say yes," Hrald echoed, all his hope in his words. His face felt damp and hot, and he feared her answer.

Ashild lifted her face to him. Her eyes moved to her mother and saw the tears, now freely flowing down her face. Ashild knew they were rooted in joy, not sorrow.

"The farthest coast of Wessex," Ashild said to both of them. "Do you truly wish me as far away as that?" Her voice sounded as if it already came from a distance.

Ælfwyn was nodding her head. "If you can know love with Ceric, I would happily see you there," she whispered.

A circle, one thought broken forever, would somehow close if that should happen, Ælfwyn thought. Gyric could not bring her home to Kilton, but his son Ceric could do so with Ashild.

Ashild looked at them as they watched her, Hrald strong and tall and yet so tenderly young, her mother with all her beauty and goodness. They desired this for her, these two who loved her more than any other. She dropped her hand, but did not surrender what it grasped. She felt her own breath, felt the hammer of Thor resting between her breasts, reminding her of who she was. A woman. A Dane. Her father's daughter. And her mother's.

"Two years," she began. In a life as short as hers it was a vast span. "I will promise you this," she vowed, gazing on their searching faces. "I will wed no one else in these two years."

Chapter the Ninth: Firelight

Island of Gotland

MID-SUMMER and its fire and feast always saw the folk of Tyrsborg travelling to the horse farm of Tindr's cousin, Ragnfast. He and his wife Estrid had taken over the farm from Rapp, Ragnfast's father. Rapp had had the good fortune to long ago wed a maid whose father owned a number of horses, and who had inherited both beasts and land when her father died. Rapp was the older brother of Tindr's mother Rannveig, the brewster from the trading road, so the bonds ran deep and long.

Each high Summer, to celebrate the longest day in the wheel of the year, Sidroc and Ceridwen and their household had walked or ridden or jostled along in an ox-cart to reach Ragnfast's farm. The day began before noon, with the men and boys laying wood and charcoal for the huge fire to come. The gathered women busied themselves about the trestle tables which had been carried out under the pear trees, unpacking the baskets they had carried from their own farms or town-homes. These bore loaves of bread, trays of oaten cakes, crocks of sweet butter, meat pasties, salted fish paste, boiled eggs, pickled walnuts, and jugs of homemade mead. Early beans and fresh greens enlivened their offerings, as did small baskets of carefully plucked wild strawberries, and jam made from the dusky blue clusters of salmbär, those prized berries found only on the island, springing on slender vines from the limestone rocks.

Rapp's wife, Ragnfast's mother, still lived, but was now bed-fast, suffering from a wasting illness, so that her daughter-in-law Estrid acted as hostess to all. She and Ragnfast laid a fine table, carrying on the tradition set by his parents. There was, as always, a whole roasted lamb. As the numbers of friends grew, and the trestle tables stretched longer under the trees, a whole goat was added to this, as well as a hearty stew of fresh herring made up from a brimming bushel of fat and shining fish.

Coming from Tyrsborg on horseback were Ceridwen on her odd-coloured dun mare, and Sidroc on his black stallion. Their twinned children Eirian and Yrling rode alongside, each on their short-legged ponies. They rode on the forest path, while a different group took the meadow-way. An ox-cart, borrowed for the day, bore Rannveig and two deep brown crocks of her famed ale, and one of the last remaining deer haunches from her smokehouse. The driver of the cart was her son, Tindr, he whose skill at bow and arrow kept both Rannveig and the folk of Tyrsborg in deer meat. Also in the waggon were the sister-cooks, Gunnvor from Tyrsborg and Gudfrid from the brew-house, and Helga, Tyrsborg's serving woman.

Another woman was there, one dressed unlike any of the women-folk of Gotland. She was of the Sámi, and like her people, attired herself in the carefully dressed skins of deer. Šeará still had the tunic and leggings of ren-deer she had come to Gotland wearing four years ago. These were laid away, as precious things, in the small forest house she shared with her husband Tindr.

She wore today one of the tunics and leggings she had made herself from the hides of the red deer Tindr felled to feed them. His young wife had herself scraped the hides free of fat and flesh, slowly and by her own hand, using a bone scraper she had fashioned from a deer shoulder-bone. The hides she so treated were softer and more supple than any Tindr had ever seen or felt.

The care she gave to her work meant no thin places flawed the hide, where impatience or steel scraper had dug too deep. He had watched her many times as she worked, the smooth bone tool grasped in her white hand, the hide stretched before her in a frame she wove of willow withies. Deer, he called his wife, and gestured it with his hands, for Tindr, being deaf, had no spoken speech. He knew her by the great deer she had arrived at Tyrsborg driving, and by that running forest beast who she, with her narrow, fine-boned face, resembled.

Tindr smiled over at Deer as she walked by the oxen. Their little son had grown restless sitting within, and she had taken him out to walk alongside her for a stretch. The boy too was dressed all in deer-skin, a small set of soft napped hide leggings and tunic made by his mother.

The boy was lagging behind now, his legs tiring in the tall grasses. Šeará scooped him up in her arms and braced him against her hip, but he was too big to carry for long. Tindr halted the waggon, gestured to her that she take the reins, and he carry the boy.

As Šeará settled herself next to her mother-in-law on the waggon-board she watched Tindr swing their boy up over his head and upon his shoulders. She heard Juoksa's crowing laugh, and knew that his father felt it, for he laughed back with his short braying honk, like that of a goose.

Rannveig laughed as well. The Sámi woman nodded, smiling at her, and gave the oxen rein a little shake. Before Juoksa was born, Rannveig had helped her welcome the Sámi Goddesses into her forest home. Šeará asked Máttaráhkká, the mother-Goddess, that the babe might come hale and strong into the world, and if that was not to be, that the spirit of the dead child be taken into the care of Juksáhká and Sáráhkká, the daughter-Goddesses who protected unborn boys and girls.

Together with Rannveig and Ceridwen Šeará poured out offerings of honey and milk beneath the floor boards of the round forest house she and Tindr had built. The Sámi woman had made offering the first night she and Tindr slept there, inviting the Goddesses to abide with her, so far from her Northland home. Now with the coming babe the offerings must be renewed, and protection sought, especially from Sáráhkká, who guided child-birth. The three women had gone about the small house, pulling up floor boards so that the liquids would dribble directly on the welcoming Earth beneath, listening attentively as Šeará sang, in a tongue so unlike their own, her fluting invitation to the Goddesses.

One late Spring dawn she awoke with the pangs that told her the coming of her child was near. Tindr ran through the still-dark forest path to Tyrsborg. He was back at her side as quickly as he could come, finding Deer standing in the middle of their house, clinging to the rafter-pole which held up the roof. Her face was already damp with pain, but she smiled as he came to her, placing his arm about her thin shoulders. He watched her shudder with each pang, him feeling a fear that she did not let herself show.

Tindr had not been privy to the many tales of young wives who suffered and died in child-bed, but he had stood and watched when the body of his friend Ring's wife was laid upon the pyre at the place of burial. She had not been able to bring forth their child, and died trying to do so. As Tindr held his trembling wife by the shoulders he would not allow himself to dwell on that image. Deer would not be taken from him; the Lady, the Goddess Freyja, had given her to him.

Bright Hair and Scar, whom he had awakened, came soon after, and gestured to him that his Nenna was on her way. Bright Hair came to Deer and kissed her, and then began to shift the bedding and deer hides upon the floor, and unfold lengths of linen she had carried in a deep basket. Deer was still holding to the rafter pole, and as he watched her slender form buckle with each pang he knew some sound escaped her lips.

Then his Nenna was there, with Good Food, the woman who cooked for her, and Scar was leading him out of the house.

The Sun came up, lighting the glade in which his house sat, ringed by white-barked birches in nearly full leaf. Good Food was busy at the cook-fire, warming water, boiling broth, and forcing loaves and cheese upon him and Scar. Nenna had earlier brought a crock of ale, and both he and Scar drank from it, dipping pottery cups into the frothing brown depths. Then Scar signaled that they work at Tindr's wood pile, splitting cut lengths with spike and axe. It was good work to do, demanding attention and aim, and they stood opposite each other, setting up and striking with firm blows the seasoned wood. Soon they both were sweating, beads of it forming on their foreheads and upper lips, and darkening the linen of their tunics at chest and underarm. Even given the work Tindr sometimes saw Scar's eyes shift over to the house. He wondered if Deer was crying out, but as often as he paused in his swing, watching Scar's face, Scar would shake his head, urge him to go on, and himself deliver another blow to the oak or ash awaiting him on the splitting-stump.

Sidroc knew the best thing a new father could do to aid his wife was to himself split, rend, and open up wood or soil; to cleave wood, or till furrows. It was like the bronze keys women dropped upon the floor, unlocking the coming babe from its mother's womb, or the ritual unbraiding and unbinding of hair and sash that his own wife had told him about when their two were born. And, he reflected with a wry smile, it kept the man out of the way of the women going about the work within, and kept the mind and body busy, unable to dwell on the ordeal his wife underwent, or the risk of her bleeding to death as she brought forth new life.

Both men watched Gudfrid go back and forth into the house, carrying food and drink. At times they stopped to rest in their wood-splitting, and sat on the bench by the small table Tindr had built not long ago, now that fine weather was come again. They drank more ale as the Sun climbed over their heads. Then Gudfrid came out, hands empty, but her mouth smiling.

Tindr saw Good Food's lips move, and then Scar was slapping him across the shoulders and grinning. Good Food gestured, Come, and Tindr left Scar and went with her.

The house was dim after the brightness of noon in the glade. The air had a sharp smell, like that of blood and slaughtered beasts, and also the faint tang of sweet herbs or hay.

Deer lay before him, on their bed of feather cushions. Her hide tunic was off, and on her bare breast lay a tiny, glistening creature. Bright Hair and Nenna were on either side of her, beaming down at Deer, and now turning to face him. Bright Hair stood and made way for him.

He knelt at her side. Her eyes were lowered, looking at the pale head of their babe. The little one's fists were tightly curled, but its mouth was open, and seeking. He watched Deer pull the babe further up on her breast, saw the tiny mouth reach for and close around the swollen nipple there.

Now her eyes lifted to his. She smiled at him. He saw the tears in her eyes, and knew his own were wet as well. He reached and touched her lips with his fingers. Then he moved his finger to the head of the babe. The hair there was like fine fur, and he stroked the tiny head as it suckled.

Nenna was at his side now, clasping him, and he felt her laughter even before he looked to her. They turned back to Deer. The little head had shifted, and the small mouth bowed open, like a yawn. He saw Deer laugh, and watched her take both hands and lift the babe up, showing it to him.

A boy. He had a son.

Later that day Deer slept. Scar and Bright Hair had gone home, as had Good Food, but Nenna had stayed, and was out by the cook-fire making their supper. Deer had never learnt to like ale, and the sweet taste of cow's milk had surprised her; Tindr had seen that long ago in her face. But she liked milk thickened from long-standing, the way Nenna's cook made, and liked as well the cheeses from it. Good Food had brought much with her, and now his mother had a fish stew simmering. Nenna brought them food and drink, and urged them both to rest. When Tindr carried their emptied bowls out, he saw his mother sitting at the little table by the cook fire, eyes closed, a smile on her own face. When he came back in, Deer was fast asleep.

The boy had been washed and swaddled and lay tucked up next to his mother. Tindr sat by the bed on a low stool, watching them both in wonder. When Deer opened her eyes he moved to her, and lay down next her, the little bundle between them. The babe's eyes were closed fast. They spent some time looking down at his round face.

Tindr touched the child's face again, at the brow, gently so as to not wake him. What, he asked, tapping now at his own temple.

Šeará smiled. She nodded at Tindr. Her own name for her husband was Wolf Eyes, for the blue-white eyes that marked both Tindr, and that most formidable of hunters. She looked past Tindr, pointed to his bow which hung on the wall. He stood and brought it to the bed.

Šeará touched the bow, then touched their son's face. "Juoksa," she said aloud. "Bow." She smiled again at Wolf Eyes. "A name for the son of a great hunter."

She watched Tindr make the sign he used when he wanted her to speak aloud, his fingers curled under his lower lip, then unfurling.

"Juoksa", she said again, as he placed the tips of his fingers on her lips, feeling them round and then stretch open at the name.

She repeated the name, his fingers now laying on her throat, so he might feel it there. He looked at the tiny face, looked at his bow. He nodded, then lowered his head in joy.

Once at Ragnfast and Estrid's farm the two groups from Tyrsborg joined up. Ceridwen and Sidroc and the children were there first, and had time to greet their hosts, admire the wealth of foodstuffs already upon the table, and walk from group to group, renewing acquaintance with rarely-seen family and friends of the farm. When the ox-cart wheeled into view, Eirian and Yrling ran to it. Little Juoksa was nearly a brother to them, and they took him off to where a group of children played under the pear trees. The heavy ale crocks remained in the cart bed, so that those thirsty might help themselves, but after Rannveig and Gudfrid and Gunnvor unpacked the smoked meat and pottery cups they had brought, the two lowing oxen were led off to a meadow. Gunnvor had baked four score of her small honey cakes, and these too were added to that bounty heaped upon the tables.

Sidroc and Tindr joined Ragnfast and the rest of the able-bodied men, heaving and sliding the last of the logs into place for the great fire which would be later kindled. Ceridwen stopped a while with Ragnfast's ailing mother, who, unable to walk, had been carried out on a litter and sat propped up on cushions to partake of the festivities. Her own daughters, and her old friend and neighbour Thorvi, Estrid's mother, sat with her.

The Sun, shining down from a sky of purest blue, crept overhead. All gathered about the base of the great fire. In a day as long and bright as this one would be, they recalled that after today the Sun would slowly die, leading them into Winter's darkness. But this noon was a time to salute the good and life-bringing Sun, to thank its warmth that made crops grow, gave comfort to all beasts, and made full and happy the hearts of men. Even as the Sun began to diminish, it drew the grain in the fields and the vegetables in the ground to spread and flourish, and end in rich harvest.

"We cannot live without the Sun," Rapp reminded them, "and as it dies, it gives us life."

The fire was lit, the oil-soaked rushes thrust into its heart catching.

The dancing began. There was, as always, a man who plucked a harp, and a woman who beat time with a goat-skin drum and wooden mallet covered in the same. Two pair of brass hand cymbals added their bright and clashing chimes to this, played by two women, cousins to Ragnfast. And for many of the dances, Rapp, Ragnfast's father, sang, and sang too when even the most lively of the young people had collapsed, laughing, in the meadow grasses, far from the fire's heat, unable to take another step.

All who could walk danced, at least the first few dances. There was a freeing joy in joining hands, circling round the base of the blaze, turning to and then away from it, and then as the line broke into twos or fours or sixes, taking as partner loved one or stranger, old man or young child, and moving to and then away from the others. The throbbing of the harp strings, steady beating of the drum, and the clash of the brazen cymbals rose and fell in the dancers' ears, just as their own panting laughter did. Even the laughter would end, and those young folk determined to be the last to drop would sway as they clasped moist hands.

Tyrsborg was not broad enough a hall for indoor dancing at the Winter's Night feasts, and its mistress relished any chance to so move with the man she loved. When Sidroc took her hand and led her to the circle of fire the smile on her lips reached into her heart. To feel her hand in his, the strength of his wrist and arm guiding her, to see his head thrown back in laughter and his brow damp, as hers was, with their movement, and to have all this, surrounded as she was by those she knew and loved, seemed feast enough, before a single crumb had passed her lips. At one point he lifted her in the air, swinging her by her waist about him. All others dancing passed before her in a whirl. Her gaze was fast upon the dark blue of his eyes, his brown hair flung wide above his shoulders.

When they stepped away to slake their thirst from Rannveig's great crocks they looked on those still moving. Tindr and Šeará had danced but briefly, but Tindr liked to see the others do so. Now they stood with other young parents, watching the smaller revelers. Eirian and Yrling and many other children had circled all the youngest, and little Juoksa stood there, holding hands with another toddling child, pumping his feet up and down and laughing.

It was after the feast, when all were gathered once more about the fire, that something strange happened. The benches which had flanked the trestle tables had been dragged around the fire, now burning low but hot. Cups of ale and of mead too were filled and refilled, and folk sat talking to one another, at times rising to visit with some friend, not seen for the past year, at another bench. The sky was still bright but the quality of light had changed; the brilliant Sun shifting and throwing sharp and dark shadows from the backs of men and trees and buildings.

Ceridwen sat with Eirian at her side; Sidroc was off speaking with Rapp and Ragnfast. A woman, who she had noticed after the dancing had stopped, moved around the far side of the fire, and now walked to where she sat. Ceridwen saw she was not of Gotland; the woman's gown and jewellery told her that, just as her own told the same about her. This woman coming to her looked like those of the large trading post of the Prus, that which she and Sidroc had stopped at years earlier. It was on the southern edge of the Baltic, and had been a place ruled by a powerful leader called a knez, and the place too where she had met a priest from Mercia, and an old silk-gowned spice merchant, who had told her she would one day have two daughters. This woman now stood before her sole daughter, Eirian.

The woman was of middle-age, no more, and had dark, red-tinged curling hair. She wore a long-sleeved gown of green, a green so deep to be nearly black. She had a wealth of slender, shining gold about her neck and wrists, in the form of narrow linked chains. Her head wrap was bright red, that shade of a cockscomb, a colour that swore against the dark ruddy hair it only partially confined. The eyes were dark and sharp, but moved slowly over Eirian. The girl sat up under this scrutiny, ready with a smile, but uncertain by the woman's look if it would be welcome. Ceridwen found herself placing her hand in her daughter's lap, to reassure her.

"You," the woman said, addressing the girl. The voice had the same accent Ceridwen remembered in the land of the Prus, even in this one word of Norse. "You will travel far."

"Someday I will go with father to the South, and see where the grind stones are made," Eirian returned. She smiled uncertainly, as if hoping she had said the right thing.

The woman did not laugh at this, and went on as if the child had been silent. "You will travel far," she said again, as if considering her own words. "Far from this island, and live among those strange to you, even as your mother does."

"I am not amongst those strange to me," her mother protested. She had lifted her extended hand from Eirian's lap, as if to ward off this woman's words. "This land may not be the place of my birth, but it is home to me, and its folk are my friends."

The Prus woman's eyes had dropped to Ceridwen's wrist. Upon it sat the silver disc bracelet that her husband had fastened there on their first night on Gotland.

"The bracelet," the Prus woman said, pointing now at it with her finger. She looked back into Eirian's uplifted face. "You will wear it, take it from here. Take it to your grave."

Ceridwen stood up. The Prus woman was just her height, and she found herself looking into her eyes. She did not know what to say, but she need not say anything, as the woman gave a nod of her head, and left them.

Eirian's eyes were full of questions, which her mother tried to soothe. Estrid had witnessed part of the exchange and now came over to her.

"Who…who is that woman," Ceridwen asked. "Is she of the Prus?" The woman had returned to a bench on the far side of the fire, and was almost out of sight, her red head-wrap only visible.

Estrid's eyes followed Ceridwen's. "She is mother to a woman of the Prus that one of Ragnfast's distant cousins wed, and brought here. She is visiting them; we have never seen her before." Estrid's eyes returned to her friend's face. "What did she say to you?"

"She spoke to Eirian, telling her she would leave," Ceridwen repeated. She paused before she went on. "Leave Gotland."

She did not say more; this alone was too terrible to countenance, that one she loved would leave this haven of peace and safety.

"Perhaps she is granted second sight," wondered Estrid aloud. Her eyes had flitted back through the waving air over the fire, to where the Prus woman sat alone. She was fearful of such folk; sorrow could come from learning things out of turn.

"Já, perhaps she is," Ceridwen answered, feeling chilled despite the fire's warmth. Not, I hope, the evil eye, she said within herself.

Estrid must make response to her friend's distress. She looked down at Eirian, put her hands on the girl's shoulders. "That is not true, Eirian," she soothed. "You would not leave us."

Estrid was called away then, but not before giving Ceridwen a squeeze of her hand.

"Will you really give me your bracelet, Mother?" Eirian asked. Her face showed her bewilderment of it all.

Ceridwen's hand had gone to her wrist, and she felt the silver disc beneath her holding palm. It was Sidroc's pledge-sign to her, and she would die wearing it. He had taken it from the body of Saxon thegn he had killed, then given it to her at the keep of Four Stones in thanks for her searching his fetid wound. She had left it behind with Ælfwyn when she rode off with Gyric, and Sidroc had worn the bracelet himself for ten long years, before he could at last claim her as his own the night of their arrival here on Gotland.

She would be laid on her pyre wearing it, so that in Freyja's hall she would come before her husband wearing that which had adorned her wrist in life.

Now she had been told that Eirian would wear the bracelet, and take it to her grave. A grave could mean a heathen or a Christian burial; that of ashes, or of the body itself.

Still holding her hand over the silver disc she answered her daughter. The bracelet had almost a life of its own. It had a life before it had come to Sidroc, and then to her, and perchance would have a life after her own had ended.

"I do not know, my bright one. If it should be worn by any, I would have it worn by you."

Silver Hammer, Golden Cross

Part Two: War

Chapter the Tenth: Fire in the Sky

The Year 892

ÆLFRED, King of Wessex, pushed back from his writing table. His shoulders ached, and his neck was stiff from bending over his manuscript. His eyes too were blurred, the result of fixing them upon his work through the unsteady light of the guttering tapers ringing his desk. They had burnt low in their copper bases; dawn would be no more than two hours away. He lifted his fingertips to his eyes, pressing against them so that the darkness showing under his closed lids turned to a shrouded red. He let out a breath, stood. He knew the skin around his eyes was lined, creased with a fine netting caused by war, worry, and the simple passage of years. If his work forging the Latin of the wise-man Boethius into the tongue of the Saxons added to the lines, it was a price worth paying.

He crossed to the door. He was not in his hall, but rather in the house he had given to Asser, his Welsh priest. It was Asser who had schooled him enough in the Holy Tongue of Rome that he might turn his free hours to these scholarly labours. The King slid back the iron bar and pushed out into the night air. The Welshman's small house was surrounded by other timber buildings, and all were enclosed by the great palisade wall of oaken planks encircling the fortress of Witanceaster. Ælfred's face lifted in the dark, up and far beyond the palings.

It was still there, the great and long-haired star, that was called in Latin cometa. It was so much brighter than the wandering stars that its brilliance rivalled the Moon. He studied it again, his tired eyes filling with the splendour of its light. It was not golden in hue, such as a taper flame or a heaped wood-fire would show, but a pure and crystalline white, dazzling to behold. For a fortnight he had watched it grow. It would fade, he knew, perhaps even quicker than it had appeared and commanded the night heavens. Until then he would take his full of it.

When it had first showed itself, not long after the rapidly-shortening nights following Easter, it was greeted with wonder amongst his folk. The star was small, yet strikingly bright, with a tail of light streaming back, as long hair does from a wind-blown head. As it grew in size, fed by some unseen fire, fear had spread. Asser had preached calm; all was in the hand of God, and the world not due to end for one hundred years. Such stars had been seen before, heralds of good, such as that which had hung over the stable in which the Christ Child lay.

Ælfred himself had ordered those disturbed by the star not to gaze upon it. Some women, got with babes, stayed within doors all night, shuttering windows against any stray star-light, lest their wombs be turned before their time. The random madman or two, ready to rave at oddities, clawed at their faces and tore their hair. The priest was wrong, they cried, the world would go down in fire, and soon. Asser himself spent time seated in the gloom, bronze stylus in hand, sketching the thing in a wax tablet, so that he might one day commit it to ink.

Tonight the King looked at the cometa alone. Whether it be herald of good or ill, it held beauty. His thoughts filled his head, just as the white light of the star filled his eyes. If portent of evil, there was much to foreshadow it. Guthrum's death had fractured any sense of surety regarding the vast portion of the island under Danelaw. He thought of his son Eadward, riding even now from Saxon burh to burh, exhorting the lords thereof, gauging the readiness of each keep's men to fight. He rode thus as son of Rex Anglorum – lord of all Angles and Saxons not under Danish rule.

Ælfred shifted where he stood, put one booted foot upon a squared stone used as measuring-base. When he became a King he was one of four Anglo-Saxon monarchs of four Anglo-Saxon Kingdoms. His own brother-in-law, Burgred, King of Mercia, had been driven out. Now he alone stood, the rest of Angle-land ceded to the Danes. His hair of golden brown had paled with age. The bowel ailment which had sapped his strength in youth has become less frequent with the years; God had blessed him with a malady to keep him humble, yet spared him from debility, allowing him to reign. His life as King had been a never-ending round of out-thinking and out-maneuvering a foe greater, yet not more determined, than he. Ever on the move from hall to hall, shire to shire, showing himself to his people, strengthening the bonds between crown and Saxon war-chiefs. Always building new burhs a day's walk from where the most scattered of his folk lived, so that they might reach shelter during attack.

In the stolen hours of night he laboured to bring the hard-won wisdom of the ancients into his own tongue, so that other men could find there the same comforts he had found. Preserving and extending the beauty of poetry was near as vital as those of the tenets of philosophy and law. *The love of Wisdom must be as strong as bodily love,* he believed. *Thou must put thy bare body towards it, if thou wilt experience it.* Ruling, war, and study; all demanded effort. He was now three and forty, and growing weary. He had a worthy son, but he could himself not yet rest.

This great star recalled to his mind the three Irish monks who had been brought to Witanceaster last year. They had set to sea in their round ox-hide boat, a coracle like unto a tiny island itself, a boat without oars, trusting God to guide them where they would be most needed. They had landed in

Wessex. Their unlikely arrival was not perhaps unlike that of the cometa. He hoped this flaming star would prove as benign.

The star was as bright at Four Stones as it was in Wessex. In the keep at Lindisse men furtively sought the place of Offering and made sacrifice. Some did so in shame, falling back upon their old Gods, creeping at dusk to spill the blood of rooster or goose to show Thor his mighty hammer might be needed still to smash this star to harmless sparks. Others were open, even brazen, dragging goats to the overgrown trench and burying their knives into the beasts' throats. The wooden figure of one-eyed Odin had crumbled to a shapeless shaft; these men bellowed now their promises to rebuild it.

More were steadfast in their new Christian faith. Wilgot offered special prayers. It was true Christ's birth was heralded by such a star – its reappearance could mean his second coming, and the end of the world, he pondered aloud. He would exhort repentance and fasting, threaten those who soiled their hands with heathen sacrifice the punishment of being dispelled from the Church. Not until Sigewif sent word from Oundle that the cometa had been met there with songs of praise for the glories of Heaven did the priest of Four Stones relent in his doom-saying.

One near-dawn three stood alone in the bower garden at Four Stones, gazing up at the star.

"It is beautiful," Hrald said, breaking their silence. His eyes were fastened upon it, and he felt his whole being drawn towards the ball of light.

"Perhaps it is the souls of Earth's beloved dead, returning to show themselves to us," mused Ælfwyn. Her voice was soft, and grave, as a prayer.

Both her older children answered her, a caught breath from Hrald, a soft exclamation from Ashild.

"If that is so," her daughter whispered, "how kind the Fates that snip men's lives soon."

"Begu," murmured Ceric.

She turned in her sleep, her face covered by a tangle of fine, curling yellow hair.

"I must leave now. But the great star will be there. Come look at it with me."

She smiled and took his outstretched hand. He was already dressed; she felt it a kindness to wake her before he left. She pulled her mantle from the wooden peg that held it. It was lined with the pelts of martin Ceric had brought her, just as they had earlier drunk from two fine bronze cups, also gifts of his hand.

One cresset still burned upon her low table, and as soon as he unbolted her door the star could be seen, guiding them as they made their way the few steps to her wattle fence. Freed from the thick overhang of her thatched roof they could look at open sky.

They held their faces up to the star, saying nothing. Ceric thought of the distance spanning him and that shining torch; greater than he could number, or conceive. Yet the star was here too, part of his night.

It shines on Four Stones, he thought of a sudden. His lashes dropped over his eyes a moment, thinking of one who might be looking up at that bright orb as he was. Then Begu clasped his arm with her hand, bringing him back to Kilton.

He covered that hand with his own, gave it a squeeze, and took his leave. His horse ambled through the darkness; the path was smooth. Soon, even in the dimness, he could make out the forms of houses sitting in other crofts. There was no need for haste, or pretence of secrecy. For several months now he had spent a night or two a week in the house where Begu lived. No one spoke of it, but he felt certain that all who might care must know of it. He was discreet, leaving Kilton's great hall after it had quieted, rising silently and making his way to the paddock where waited his horse. He returned, without fail, before cock-crow. The hours between were given up to the delights to be found in a woman's bed.

It was Worr who had brought him to Begu. But it had been Modwynn, Lady of Kilton, who had spoken to Worr.

When her grandson had returned from Lindisse he had told her he meant to claim Ashild of Four Stones as his wife. She did not hide her warm approval, but bid him keep the news private until he could return to fetch her. Anglia was in uncertain state, and travel there would likely entail not only a large train of thegns, but the help of both Ælfred and whatever war-lord might emerge as most powerful amongst the Danes. The fact that no open fighting had yet taken place in Anglia reassured Wessex that the Peace would be still honoured. Still, claiming the maid would take time and care in preparation.

This decided, Ceric felt Ashild to be his. That certainty gave a destination to his near future, a goal he had sought now within grasp. It committed him and freed him at the same time. Thinking of Ashild, of their first wedded night together, spurred him to think of other women. He would not, clumsily, and with reddened cheek, lead his bride to the bed in the bower house that would be given over to him. The thought of Ashild, trying to still her smile, lips pressed together to keep from laughing, was enough to move him to action. He had told her brother he would have a woman when he returned to Kilton. Once home he determined to act.

Ceric had long been raised to understand that the sisters and daughters of Kilton's thegns were in a class unto themselves. Their brothers and fathers were the pledged men of the Lord of Kilton. He and his brother Edwin would treat them with the respect due such a bond. Marriage between them and the daughters of even the richest and most esteemed of the warriors was highly unlikely, and in the case of the hall of Kilton, with but two male heirs, impossible. As winsome and comely as many of the maids were, they were destined for the sons of other thegns, both here at Kilton, and in other burhs. Ceric and his brother would seek brides from amongst the great families of Wessex, and in Ceric's case, the Kingdom of Anglia.

But in the village of Kilton, there were maids in plenty. Ceric had seen them, and sometimes played amongst them, since he had been a toddling boy. After he returned from his long Summer at Four Stones, at the age of nine, he spent less time with the village children. His uncle, Godwin, had kept him much at his side, and his training at arms was begun. And he had returned a sad and sober child, grieving the loss of his mother. Yet as the years wore on the maids were there, smiling up at him when he rode by on his pony, and then his horse; bringing him freshly-plucked green bracts at the Mid-Summer festival, even taking his hand and dancing with him through the heat blasting from the huge fire. He saw their bodies grow and thicken into those of blooming womanhood, breasts ripening under thin woollen gowns, hips defined by a sash pulled snugly around supple waists.

At this deep harvest time, on St Mathew's Day, was held a gathering festival. Apple picking was at its height, and pears too were heaped up in abundance, withy baskets of them sticky from their running juices. It was custom that the cooks of the hall serve a meal to all the village, to honour, and thank their labours for the year, and to celebrate this final harvesting. Hand-carts and ox-carts were rolled out through Kilton's great gates, laden with casks of foaming ale, cauldrons of herb-scented barley browis, meat and fowl pies encased in buttered pastry, baskets of newly-gathered walnuts, and numberless loaves of crusty wheaten bread, kneaded from flour of a fineness the villagers rarely knew. This bounty was unpacked on trestle tables set fast by the orchards on the red clay road to the keep. Under boughs heavy with clustered fruit, all gathered to eat their fill.

The family and thegns of Kilton came on horseback and by waggon to join in, and sat where they would amongst those whose sweat had brought to bear all the good things they had eaten this past year, and sat as well with the careful shepherds, men and women both, who watched over the flocks whose spun fleece adorned their bodies. Dunnere the priest was there, and any passing monk or lay-brother whose path had brought him near the place. Thus those who fought, those who tilled, and those who prayed sat down together to feast.

Modwynn always made much of this occasion, sitting at first at one table, then the next, as the food was ladled out, so that she might speak with as many of her folk as she could, taking a this-year's babe into her ready arms, as she had last year's; asking after the health of any man or woman too old or feeble to sit thus at meat; consoling those who had lost parent or child in the preceding year. Edgyth, her daughter-in-law, did the same, and both women were loved for it. The young men of the hall of Kilton sat likewise, moving from trestle to trestle. Edwin was but thirteen and shy, which the deference given him as the future Lord of Kilton only deepened. Ceric relished the day.

All were in high spirits. The harvest had been good, the day a fine one, and he was flush with the richness that happy possibility provides. He wore a new linen tunic, embellished by his aunt with coloured thread-work at neck and hem, and circling the hem of each sleeve as well. The linen was that green which made his own eyes the deeper, and his coppery hair more golden. The thread-work Edgyth had lavished was in richer green, and a blue so deep to be almost midnight. Accustomed as he was to darker clothing he felt a brilliant bird, and was surprised at how it further heightened his mood.

As he moved from table to table, Ceric found not a few village maids hastily making way for him, and had to hide his laughter at one, who by her vigorous movement unwittingly pushed a younger sister off the end of her bench.

His aunt saw it too, and had to stifle her own smile, both at the maid's action and the handsome form of her nephew who had occasioned it. Edgyth was glad Ceric accepted the green tunic; he wore too often the drab hues Godwin had favoured as he grew older. She had in fact taken the tunic from her dead husband's clothes chest. He had never worn it; it had not been finished at his death, and she had amended it to fit Ceric's form. She had two wooden chests of fine clothing, awaiting Ceric and Edwin when they grew large enough.

Her steady grey eyes went to Edwin, sitting at another table in the tunic of sky-blue she had sewn for his slight form. This too she had spent days over, joining with fine needle and tiny stitches each seam, drawing coloured threads in a riot of spirals and running hounds and stags upon the hem. There was satisfaction in such work, and in the care invested in the making of something of beauty to clothe the body of a loved one. Modwynn, who she admired more than any mortal man or woman, had taught her to see her needle-work this way, as a gift of time and love beyond value. Whether swaddling blanket or binding sheet, all cloth bore the stamp of those who spun the thread, wove the fabric, cut and sewed the finished item. For a learned woman needle-craft was but another expression of art and love. In her sorrowful widow-hood

Edgyth had embraced this. Her Latin was as good as that of Dunnere, her hand at writing, better. She had learnt the skill of herbal healing amongst the famed nuns at Glastonburh, so that here at Kilton her leech-craft was unequalled. But it was this most womanly of arts that gave her deepest pleasure.

Modwynn, Lady of Kilton, rose from where she sat. She and Edgyth and Edwin would soon take their leave, allow the groaning trestles and the casks of ale sitting at the end of each to make gay the party until well after dusk. Ceric, she thought, would choose to remain; he was standing now himself, laughing with a group of maids and youths, some of the village, some of the hall. She saw his eye shift from the young man he jested with to follow the passage of a pretty brown-haired village girl as she strolled before them.

Modwynn looked to Cadmar, seated at another table, who nodded back. The faithful warrior-monk would stay until Ceric turned for the hall. She looked then to Worr, seated with his young wife Wilgyfu, one son suckling in her arms, the second wobbling on chubby legs round the trunks of the pear trees. Worr rose and came to her, and Modwynn asked that he absent himself a short while to escort her and Edgyth and Edwin back within the palisade of Kilton.

Once within the gates she spoke in private to the horse-thegn. She had seen Worr watching Ceric as well, and did not stay her concern.

"Worr," she began. Her voice was as calm and low as it ever was, but carried with it the strength of its import. "Ceric must avoid entangling himself with any village maid." She paused, a moment only, before correcting herself. "Or rather – the potential results of such entanglements."

The horse-thegn's open face changed not at her words. He gave but a nod, and a word of assent. She had no need to say more.

On one certain day each Winter, an old woman of the village would creep into the hall. She would look into the face of Modwynn, and stay unblinking while the Lady of Kilton placed three coins of silver into her withered palm. This aged woman was the mother of a girl long dead, whose new-born babe had also died. The horse-thegn of Kilton had seen this woman, and knew her story.

Worr returned to the fruit groves, drank and ate more, all the time enjoying the company of his wife and sons. After a time he stood and signalled to Ceric. Waggons were loading, carting now-empty baskets, pans and pots. He put his family on one of them, then went to Ceric. He had drunk not a little ale, and was not happy when Worr told him they must go; the young were about to kindle a fire at the far end of the apple trees, and he would join in. Worr shook his head, and Ceric followed him back to Kilton.

In the morning, after all within the hall had broken their fast, Worr spoke to Ceric. "Ride with me," he said.

Ceric looked his question to his friend, who gave but a nod of his head in answer. They took their horses from the yard paddock and set off. Their path led through the village, then branched off, away from the main road where the St Matthew's Feast had been held.

Ceric just waited. The day was another fine one, cool enough this morning for a mantle, but the Sun lifting overhead foretold a day of almost Summer warmth. They had passed one of the common wheat fields when Worr spoke again.

"Do not touch the village girls, Ceric," was what he said.

Ceric was so surprised his mouth opened, but he did not answer. He turned his head away, looking down the trackway their horses walked upon.

"Your uncle had a son, at your age," Worr told him.

Ceric jerked his chin back to Worr. He knew Godwin had not wed until he was in his twenties.

"A natural son, with a young woman of the village," Worr went on.

He was stunned. He had a cousin he had never met? But no.

"The babe died, and the mother too," Worr explained. "So it came to nought."

Ceric tried to take it in. Godwin had had a true heir, one of his own flesh and blood. But the boy had died.

"That is why it is important to think before acting in these matters," Worr summed.

He was not done.

"I know you would not risk it with a thegn's daughter. But do not demean yourself with a cottar girl. No good can come of it."

Ceric's head was filled with what he had been told about his uncle, and filled too with the warning issued by Worr.

Ceric swallowed. A hawfinch flitted over the leaning spikes of chaff left after the wheat-harvest, rising and falling with its straggling waves.

"It is simple for you," he returned. "You have a wife."

Worr gave out with a sound of assent. Then he spoke again.

"There is a woman you can safely see. We are going there now, you can look at her. If she is pleasing, you can choose to see her."

"What woman?"

"Her name is Begu. You will have seen her at times, but she does not come often to the greater village. She is not of Kilton; she came here from further up the coast. Her husband used to fish there. The farm that is now hers fell to him, and he brought her here."

"What happened to him?"

"He cut himself a few Summers back with a scythe. The wound went green and he died."

"Why is it safe for me to – see her? Is she old?"

Worr allowed himself a short laugh. "Of her years I do not know; she looks almost a maid, and is as comely as you might wish." He considered a moment. "But she is barren. That is why she is safe."

The far side of the wheat fields held more crofts, and the furthest hamlet of the village of Kilton. They passed by a few folk working in the warm morning light, women scrubbing laundry, men prising turnips from dark soil. A common well stood on the trackway before one of the crofts, a wooden bucket lashed to a nearby post, with a long handled copper dipper ready upon a flat stone.

They moved on, turning to the left and the last small croft there. Ceric heard the woman Begu before he saw her. A female voice, high-pitched, sweet, melodious, drifted in song from around the back of the small house.

They stood their horses and just listened. Then she appeared, her apron held up in her hand. She had been gathering eggs from the tiny fowl-house, and the newly freed hens were scratching about in the shorn grasses on which she stood.

Her song died on her lips. She looked at Worr, knew him, and smiled. It took her a moment longer to know Ceric for who he was.

She dropped her head, bent her knees beneath her ruddy gown in a curtsy.

Worr swung down from his horse, staying Ceric with a movement of his hand. He crossed to where she stood. Ceric looked down on them from his saddle, taking her in.

She did indeed look a maid; Worr was right in that. She was slender, and not tall. Her hair was lying in tousling pale yellow waves upon her shoulders; not long, but striking in its curl. Her head wrap was the slightest, a mere band of white linen, and set off her hair the more. He thought her eyes must be blue, with such colouring. He wanted to find out.

Begu had glanced up at him once as she stood with Worr, that is all. Then Worr came back and pulled himself on his horse. Ceric looked at where the woman stood, watching them, her hand still cradling her eggs. Her chin was slightly lowered, but she gave a half-smile and a nod as he looked down at her. Then Worr was turning his horse, and his turned as well.

Worr's eyes were straight upon the trackway before them.

"You may come tonight, to see her," he said.

"Tonight."

"If you like."

Ceric's mouth felt dry.

"And bring her silver," he hazarded.

"A small sum of silver, yes."

"Have you – seen her?"

Worr gave another short laugh. "Twice," he allowed. "I was not always wed."

He looked now to Ceric's face, saw the mix of excitement and fear.

"She will make all easy for you," he assured. "Go slowly with her, let her show you the way."

There was just enough Moon that night for Ceric to make his way back to the end of the pounded trackway to her house. He slipped off his horse and led it behind the wattle-and-daub walls of her small dwelling, fixing the reins to his saddle, then tying a lead about the beast's neck so it might browse. Then he moved back to her door.

All was dark. Light was costly, and he did not expect to see the glow of cressets coming from within, glinting from a crack in the shutter covering the single window. He drew closer to the door, feeling the pounding of his heart, grown large in his chest. The window was just to his left, and now between the warped wood of its shutter he saw the smallest amount of light. He tapped on the rough planks of the door.

She opened it. He stepped within, and she closed it behind him, sliding a wooden board into an iron brace across its breadth. Now inside, he saw two cressets burning, sitting on a low table. A stool with three legs stood near, with a bed, heaped with cushions, on the other side of the table.

He saw an almost fully charged spindle lying on the table, anchored by a thin thread to a fluffy mass of wool roving. She had been spinning when he had knocked. This knowledge almost startled him; this homeliest of duties making her as it did, almost like any other woman he had met.

She was fully dressed, but in a different gown than that she wore during the day; in the low light he could not tell if it was light green or yellow.

He tried to smile. She smiled too, almost shyly, and again dropped her curtsy.

He wished she would speak. He said the first thing that came into his mind.

"Your voice – it is a beautiful one. I heard you before I saw you."

Again, she ducked her head. "I thank you, Lord Ceric," she answered.

"I will not be Lord," he corrected. "Please to call me Ceric."

She gave a nod of agreement. He kept looking at her. "And you are – Begu."

It was dim in the room, but she did indeed look truly a maid. Standing this near her he saw he was more than a full hand's length taller. She was slender as a reed, delicately boned, the skin of her face parchment-pale and fine. Her tumble of light yellow curls, resting just below her shoulders, struck him as almost wondrous, a nimbus for a saint. He caught himself at that, remembering what she was, but went on admiring it just the same. It was entirely unbound, with not even the slight strip of linen she had tied around it this morning. He wondered what such hair would feel like, crisp or soft; wished to grasp it in his hand. The lack of light denied his finding out the colour of her eyes; she would tell him.

He could not recall having seen her before. She seemed altogether fey, not of the world. Despite her spindle, she was not like any other woman.

He saw her eyes had been following his, reading perhaps his thoughts. Now she spoke again.

"Please to have some ale," she invited. She had bent to a squat earthen jug that sat upon the table, poured out ale into two thick-walled pottery cups. She made a slight gesture to the bed. There was but the one stool, and nowhere else to sit. He placed himself on the edge of her bed, sinking in slightly on the featherbed beneath the wool coverlet. She sat next him, and handed him a cup. Her fingers were each as slender as his little finger.

He took a deep draught into his mouth, too much. He almost choked, his throat was so tight. He struggled not to sputter out the ale, but a few flying drops escaped his lips. He felt a hot-faced fool.

She waited for him to compose himself, then stood. He stood too, uncertain if he were somehow being dismissed.

Instead she reached her arms towards him. He took her up in his own, pressed her into his chest. She felt so small in his arms, and he thought he was feeling the rapid beat of her own heart as well, as he held her. She lifted her face to his.

They kissed just once, and he knew his lips met hers too hard.

She only smiled, and began to undress him. She started with the leathern belt from which hung his seax, reaching to the brass buckle at the side of his waist, pulling the beautiful weapon off, laying it on the table by her spindle. Next she worked the buckle of his broad belt, which held the small purse in which the silver meant for her waited; and which held too the second pouch which bore flint and iron. She dropped down to the floor, unfastened the toggle on the ankle of his boots, and pulled them off with his stockings.

She took his tunic from him then, grasping it at its hem, a smile lighting her face for a moment as he bent towards her so she could reach to draw it over his head. Nothing was left but his leggings.

Her fingers went to his waist, found the toggle, and the few laces. He thought he might erupt as her hands grasped the waistband and pulled the leggings down, to free him. He reached towards her, wanting to press her once more, and far more urgently, against his hungering body. But she had once again dropped down, lifting his feet out of the leggings. She let the leggings lie where they fell, and rose to him.

He stood naked before her, wearing nothing but his golden cross against his bare chest. She regarded him a long moment, her face kindly, and almost radiant, in the soft light. She reached and touched that cross, her finger lightly falling upon the red garnet set in its heart. He burned to feel her hands on his flesh.

Her action, her touching of his cross, stayed him; he heard Worr telling him, Go slowly with her.

He began with her sash. There were no keys, or other goods attached to it, just a ribband-like length of cloth with some kind of thread-work. He dropped it upon the cushions at the foot of her bed.

He knelt at her feet. She wore upon them night-shoes of beaten felt, and no stockings. He pulled the woollen slippers from her feet, saw them as fine and delicate as her fingers.

Her gown. He had taken up the hem of her skirts in his hand when he finished with her shoes, and now gathered the mass of fabric in handfuls as he rose. She lifted her arms and he drew it off, a pool of dusty hue fallen behind her. Only her shift remained, of white linen, and bright even in the low light. It was sleeveless, with broad straps of linen reaching over her shoulders. He could see the tips of her nipples raised against the thin cloth.

He pulled off her shift. He could not look at her naked body for more than a moment; he must have it pressed against his own.

Their mouths met. His hand ran up her back between the sharpness of her shoulder blades, pressing her more fully to him. The other traced the line of slender hip to slenderer waist, then up between their bodies to her small and firm breast.

They sank upon the cushions of her bed. She yielded her body to him with modest grace, a slight smile ready on her lips when he betrayed his awkwardness, and full ardour in response to his desire.

Begu slept. But after this first coupling, Ceric could not sleep. He lay awake at her side, looking at her pale and perfect form.

Perfect but for one fact, he reminded himself: she could bear no child. But this was the very lack that allowed him into her bed. He kept on with his gaze, from slender white ankles, up the sweep of her legs and the small tuft of golden curls there where they met; up her belly, rising and falling with the slightness of her breathing, to the small yet tender pink-tipped breasts.

He returned his gaze to her face. After a time he fell to stroking her hair as it lay spilling over the linen sheet her head rested on. Despite the wave it was soft to his fingers, almost as soft as the white skin which felt like new silk beneath the callouses of his hands. She awakened, lids lifting slowly over drowsy eyes. She smiled at him, propped on his elbow, twirling a strand of her floss-like hair round his finger. In another moment he had moved closer to her, brought his mouth to hers. After their kiss she pressed his shoulder down to the featherbed with her own hand, forcing him on his back. That gentle smile once more, as she swung her leg over his hips.

At night's end he knew he must leave. Dawn must surely be near, for he had heard the first notes of the lark's call. As he picked up his belt he remembered the silver within. It felt an ugly thing to hand it to her, yet he did not know how to give it. She was sitting now upon the bed, and had donned her discarded shift. He took the silver from his purse and laid it, quietly as he could, upon one corner of her table, a small stack of whole coinage. He finished dressing, turned, and smiled again at her. To thank her seemed also wrong, and in his uncertainty he said nothing. He could not keep from reaching his hand to her, and she took and held it for a warm moment. Then he was outside in the cool dawn, finding his horse, heading to his hall through the gloom of a day not yet begun.

He did not see Worr until late in the morning. The horse-thegn stood with Cadmar at the workshop where spear-shafts were fitted with their iron tips, sorting through sheaves of smoothed shafts meant for light throwing, and heavy battle-spears. Ceric moved to join them, face lowered, but with firm step. Worr caught his eye in a short but meaningful glance. Ceric felt his cheek warm, his only answer.

Tired as he was he moved through the hours half-dazed. He had gone to Begu with the thought of seeing her once, and no more. But every spare moment of that day his thoughts returned to her, and oddly, returned also to Ashild. Each caress he received from Begu kindled his imagination, considering those he would receive from, and give to, Ashild. It confused, and excited him the more.

By the end of the day he determined he must see Begu again, and that night. He lay down in his alcove without undressing, awaiting the time when a hush would overspread the expanse of the hall. He replayed in his mind what they had done the night past, and despite his exhaustion found himself near panting with anticipation for more. Lying on his back he thought he saw Ashild's face above him, pictured her darker hair falling down over her larger breasts as she straddled him as Begu had.

When he awoke it was past dawn. He had slept and missed his chance. His only solace was that he had not told Begu he would come again so soon.

That night he did not miss his chance. The small house was dark, and it took her a moment to rise from her bed. He puts his lips to the crack in the window shutter and called out her name. She opened, leading him into a darkness which she soon banished, lighting the two cressets with a straw brought to flame from the coals of her small fire pit.

In the weeks that followed, that pit would blaze, as leaves fell to the tired ground and Winter neared. He brought her more silver coins to begin, then found gifts that might give comfort or delight. He could not give her anything that had been his mother's, but with silver he could buy and then bestow upon her small furs, ribbands of silk, a sack of goose-down, tapers of fragrant bees' wax, cups and plates of bronze. He had the comb-maker, a woman of much skill, carve a pear-wood comb, its teeth wide-set to allow for Begu's curls, its back bearing the incised design of doves trailing garlands of ivy.

One night she complained of a rat, and he too had heard the low rustling at the wall-skirting. He returned in broad day, a lidded woven basket strapped to the cantle of his saddle. Within was a half-grown kitten a stable boy had caught for him. The day was cold and grey-skied, and she was within when he reined up. He did not enter her house, just passed the basket and its mewling contents into her hands at her threshold. Her surprise at seeing him thus could hardly have been greater.

As she looked up into his smiling face he could finally gauge the hue of her eyes. They were blue, as he had supposed; that blue of near-dusk after a clear day. Those eyes now laughed along with her voice. Much as he wished to stay, he quickly mounted and left, but not without raising his hand to her in salute. Gaining the croft of her nearest neighbour he saw a man at work, smoothing the planed edges of a new hoe-handle. The man did him the courtesy of not seeing him; keeping his eyes intent on the draw-knife in his fist. Ceric knew her neighbours marked his comings and goings; they could hardly do else. Once or twice he had come upon the early risers amongst them as they stumbled out into the dimness of their crofts. They always ducked their heads, hastily and away from him, preserving his privacy.

For Ceric was of the hall of Kilton, and their own, as they were his. And Begu herself was not despised. She was a quiet and otherwise decent woman, unlike those women trolling the streets of the great trading towns like Lundenwic. There whores reddened their cheeks and lips with berry-juice, and walked unashamed and with roving eyes through crowds of men.

Moreover it was understood that she was somehow also of Kilton; it was the thegns of the hall who visited her, not the sons and husbands of the villagers. If she was not warmly received by the women with whom she drew water from the well, neither was she shunned. If she had surplus produce, she shared it freely with the others in her hamlet, as did they with her. When one of her sheep suffered from the dropsy, she could knock unafraid on another's door and ask her husband to help. Begu had in fact never been within the palisade gates of the great hall. She had come to Kilton years after the Danish threat had forced all within for safety. Yet her connection to the warriors who lived there was understood.

Near Martinmas Ceric arrived at her house, well wrapped against the blowing cold in his thick wool mantle. The sky was black as pitch, yet swimming with stars. In the dark he could not make out the form standing by her wattle fence until he neared. It was a horse. It nickered, softly, as his own approached, and his horse gave an answering snort.

He pulled his rein up short. Another man was there.

He knew he made a sound, a sort of strangled gasp. He felt his chest had fallen into his lap. He squinted towards the shuttered window, and closed door. He scanned the outline of the house, one he thought almost his own. A small curl of smoke rose up through her roof's smoke hole, bearing the scent of apple-wood.

He drew nearer the horse to see if it was one he knew, but did not get off his own for fear of next finding himself pounding down her door.

In the dark he could tell nothing of the beast. He must go, he told himself, and finally he did.

In the day he noticed the thegns' faces more than he usually did, and spent some little time in the yard paddocks, looking over their mounts. There were nearly a hundred horses at Kilton, and thirty or more just now in the stable yard. He could not mark them all, unlike Worr, who could. He watched with mounting anger the browsing heads move across the tufted grasses, and again forced himself away.

That night he came earlier than was his wont to her door. The fire blazed in her fire-pit, as if she knew he would come. The smile with which she ever greeted him faded as he entered; his clouded face spoke even before he opened his mouth.

"You must not do that. Let other men come to you."

She dropped her hands, which had been reaching to take his mantle. She still took it, digging her fingers into its cold softness.

He had said nothing of this before. Now she almost feared he might strike her. Still, she must speak the truth. She did so, her voice as caringly light as she could make it.

"You must not become – possessive. It would be all for nought."

She found herself looking down at the expanse of wool she held clutched in her hands. "I can never be more to you than what I have been. There is no future, here."

He could not, at first, answer this. In the past few weeks he had already begun to think of how he would tell her, in Spring, that he was leaving to fetch his bride, and after that he would never again visit.

But the heat of jealousy was on his brow.

"We have now," he countered. "And for now, you are my woman. No other man is to touch you."

He meant it as an order, but as she stood watching his face she saw water come into his eyes. He was in pain, just as she had known pain.

After they had finished in their love-making, Ceric again lay awake at her side as she slept. He found himself placing his hand across her flat belly, spanning the narrow distance between the points of her hip bones. With his hand there, his thoughts strayed to Ashild's more generous hips, and the children they would bring.

The cressets had burnt low, and he was grateful for the dark. He blinked his eyes and a tear rolled from one. Everything was tumbling in his breast. He felt his desire for Ashild, burning like a torch whose oil was never consumed, and yearned for the coming day he would bring her as wife to Kilton.

He felt his desire for a woman, and how he had acted upon that desire, and felt shame. The woman had a name, Begu, she who lay before him now, who had given him much for the trifles he had carried to her.

He had wanted the one to make him a better man for the other. He knew for the first time the sinfulness of his dealings with this village woman. Before he left for Four Stones he would kneel before Dunnere and confess it all, be shriven of his sin.

He lifted his hand from where it lay, and took up the gold cross about his neck hanging against his bare chest. He closed his fist around it, hard.

Ashild will be the making of me, he thought.

Chapter the Eleventh: Disturbance

THERE was still a full month or more of Summer when Ceric rode away from Four Stones. A fortnight after he left, another visitor arrived. Thorfast came to see Hrald, spending two days at Four Stones. He brought back with him the horses he had been lent, but their return was but a pretence for his visit. By the will of his uncle, Guthrum, Thorfast had been granted the keep directly North of Four Stones. The name of hall and lands was Turcesig. His younger brother Haward would take charge of the hall to the East of this, in which they had been raised by their now-dead father. Joined with their smaller lands, it made a considerable holding. Thorfast was four-and-twenty, and he and his brother now in charge of almost two hundred men.

Thorfast rode with forty warriors at his back, an impressive display of his new estate. This would have been but idle show if the lines of succession in East Anglia were clear. They were not. Thorfast had reason for caution. He was one of several direct heirs, and there were five or more war-chiefs with no blood-claim, but powerful enough to plot seizure of large tracts of the land. Beyond the borders of Anglia was the wily Ælfred, who had proven in the past impossible to kill. The King of Wessex had a son, Eadward, now close to Thorfast's age, one said to have the prowess of his father. Considering these threats before he rode, forty men behind him did not seem unwarranted.

Thorfast, and his own father before him, had ever been friendly to Four Stones, the elder to Yrling and then Sidroc, the younger to Hrald and his kin. This short stay was meant to reaffirm the friendship. It would allow Thorfast to speak of the uncertain state of things with Hrald and his uncle, and gauge the sway of their leaning if sudden action might be required to assert and maintain control. It also allowed Thorfast to be again near Ashild.

He had wed once, and early, but his wife had sickened and died shortly after rising from child-bed. He was left with a daughter, now five years of age. After this he had been in no rush to wed again. Time could greatly improve his prospects, allowing him to command a daughter of the richest halls in Anglia – or even Wessex, should he chose to deal with the Saxons for a wife. Ashild of Four Stones was one maid he would be glad to have.

He would not speak to Asberg of this, though as her uncle the man would have much to say in bargaining her bride-price. Instead he asked Hrald, when the two sat at meat on the second night.

"Ashild," he began, naming her abruptly enough that Hrald snapped to attention. Thorfast had turned his eyes from where she sat at the woman's table, chatting while she ate with her little sister and the old nurse. Hrald's guest was looking directly at him now.

"As my wife she would be but a day's ride from Four Stones."

Hrald scarce knew what to say; it seemed not a proposal, rather a statement of fact. And his guest did not seem to jest. Hrald had not ever considered Thorfast in this way. Thorfast was one of several young men of his own standing who had filled the hall at Four Stones at Yule feasts or Mid-Summer celebrations, just as Hrald had filled theirs. Hrald knew he was older, and had been wed. He had long known Thorfast's family was of the best; his mother had been sister to Guthrum.

He was silent long enough that Thorfast was forced to speak again.

"If I made offer, would you accept," he wanted to know.

"I – I cannot say," Hrald answered. Even before Ceric's visit he thought of his sister as destined for his best friend, and Kilton. Yet her voice had caught, that day Ceric left, when she asked her mother and him if they truly wished her as far away as the coast of Wessex.

Thorfast searched Hrald's uncertain face. He had known Ashild and Hrald since they were babes, and been seen often enough by them to be a constant in their lives.

Hrald watched as Thorfast turned his head and again looked on Ashild.

"Together, we would have our own army," Thorfast said.

It was stunning, as a thought, but it was true. Four Stones paired with the two halls that Thorfast and Haward now commanded would yield a vast army of warriors, almost four hundreds of men.

Hrald looked to his Uncle Asberg, deep in converse with Thorfast's chief man.

Hrald's throat felt tight and he feared his attempt to speak. Hrald was taller than Thorfast, but a full nine years his junior. The great Guthrum's nephew was speaking to him as an equal, as more than an equal, as one who had the power to grant what Thorfast wanted. Hrald feared a misstep, and wished his uncle was hearing what he was. Then he checked the thought. Ashild would not easily be wed to any chosen for her; she must have her own pick, or at least be made to feel she had say about whose bed she would find herself in. Asberg might seize upon the chance to strengthen Four Stones through such a match. It was good that Thorfast had told him this alone.

"I will take Ashild," Thorfast went on with a smile, inclining his head to where she sat, unaware of what they spoke. "And later Haward will wed Ealhswith. We will be doubly bound." He raised his cup to his lips. "I only wish I had a sister to give to you."

Hrald's fingers curled around the base of his own cup. He had no answer for any of this.

"I will not speak to her yet," his guest was ending. "But do not wed her to anyone else. On a fast horse I am even less than a day away, should you need to send to me."

Jari's older cousin, a warrior of Yrling's, lived now at the edge of the forest growing up on either side of the stream than ran behind Four Stones. He had married a woman of Lindisse, a member of three families, all kin, who were the charcoal-burners of that place. He had lived amongst them practicing that craft since peace had come to Four Stones under Sidroc. He was thus kin to Gunnulf, and Gunnulf went with Hrald when he rode out to their mounds to provide part-payment for the charcoal smoking thereunder. It was a few days after Thorfast left, a hot and bright afternoon.

Firewood was used in vast amounts at the hall and its kitchen yard and workshops, but charcoal was prized. It was smoked long, and carefully charred in deep ricks, sealed under cut turves of sod laid above and around the stacks of wood. The blackened result was hard and long-burning, perfect to smoke meats and warm braziers. The charcoal burners of necessity need dwell at the forest's edge. Living so far from Four Stones they did not strictly enjoy the protection of the hall, but were a vital part of it. Hrald rode with a bag plump with silver to pay them for their efforts.

They arrived to find the men of the place labouring all at one mound. The strips of sod enveloping the smoking mass beneath were oftentimes checked for dryness, and water cast upon them so they remained pliable. Likewise the air holes at the base of the mounds would be tested to ascertain that the fire smouldering at its heart still burned. This fire had faltered for lack of air. One of the ricks had shifted, blocking the flow, and Hrald and Gunnulf found themselves standing in a billow of dark grey smoke as the men pushed and prodded the ricks back into line.

The fire was re-lighted by an oil-soaked torch flung into its base. The sod covering was replaced, and Gunnulf's cousin and the others now could pause and take ale with their young guests.

Payment delivered, Hrald and Gunnulf remounted their horses to head back. The smoke from the faulty fire had been intense, and both had been glad for the throat-clearing ale that had followed.

Halfway back to the keep they stopped to water their horses. The stream deepened and broadened in several places; here was one of them. The Sun was hot overhead and they could rinse their faces and refill their water skins. They dropped off their mounts and as the animals lowered their necks to the water, Hrald and Gunnulf went to it as well.

Hrald unbuckled his knife belt and stripped off his tunic so he could splash face and chest.

"I stink of smoke," he told Gunnulf, flinging his tunic on a bush.

"You stink anyway," grinned Gunnulf, pulling off his own.

Hrald's dark hair was not held in plaits that day, but loose upon his shoulders. He knelt in the springy grass at the pool's edge and flung handfuls of the cool water upon his heated body.

After they had drunk Hrald fell back into the grasses, his wet hair cool and clinging. A few clouds swam in the sky, and he could hear the chirping of insects, but it was too late in the Summer for much bird song. He was staring into the void of the blue sky, thinking about the stars hidden in that light.

He flinched slightly at a touch. It was Gunnulf's finger, tracing the line of the scar on Hrald's upper arm. He had been aware that his friend had laid down next him. He turned his head back to the sky.

"He hurt you," Gunnulf said in quiet discovery, his finger still upon the scar.

Hrald was looking up, but his lids had slightly lowered over his eyes. His friend's finger ran slowly back the length of the scar.

Gunnulf spoke again, his voice soft, softer than Hrald had ever heard him use.

"I would not have been so careless."

Hrald closed his eyes. They felt dazzled by the Sun, and he was bewildered by the way Gunnulf sounded. Like all except his sister, Gunnulf thought his wound to have been caused by Ceric. But it was his tone, rather than his words, that discomfited him.

He felt Gunnulf's hand move, come to rest flat upon his chest. It lay almost over his heart, the fingers curling slightly over the muscle of his breast. Hrald's eyes were closed tight now, and he felt his heart beneath Gunnulf's hand begin to race.

Gunnulf moved his hand, gently stroking down Hrald's chest. He had never been caressed before. Though he felt his breath catch in his throat, he could not move. Gunnulf had brought his face closer to Hrald's head, was now murmuring softly, and wordlessly, near his ear. The hand which stroked him had all the strength and firmness of a warrior's, but moved across his chest with calm assurance. He felt that hand, felt his own body respond in its growing hardness, felt his confusion. He felt his fear.

He sat up, his action driving Gunnulf a hand's length away. A wind-storm was forming in Hrald's brain; he could barely form words.

"You – you are my friend." It was almost an accusation, a troubled one.

Gunnulf looked up at him, his face open, his eyes fixed on Hrald's face, but soft. He laid his hand over Hrald's wrist, closed his fingers slightly about it.

"I could be more than that."

A kind of panic filled Hrald's chest. He drew his hand away, and so roughly than Gunnulf was repelled back.

"What…what…" he stammered, not able to manage more. Then a thought came to him. "You and Onund…"

Gunnulf and Onund. They were much together, choosing to ride patrol in tandem, sharing food and drink, their arms draped about the other; nothing that he had not done himself with Gunnulf or others. But he knew the difference, now. He stared at his friend.

This – this was taboo. The Holy Book of Rome declared it an abomination. It was forbidden as well, he had been told, amongst warriors honouring the Old Gods. Men were killed for such things.

Hrald jumped to his feet. He was almost panting in his eagerness to get away.

Fear was now in Gunnulf's blue eyes. He rose as well, took a step near him. His chest heaved, as if he too found it hard to breathe just now. He reached out his hand, but did not try to touch him. Gunnulf's fear sounded in his voice, his words an urgent command.

"Hrald. Do not betray me."

Hrald could do no more than nod his head: I will not betray you. He grabbed his tunic and belt, made for his horse. He kicked the beast so hard it leapt into the air before charging for the palisade walls.

Inside the yard he rode his winded horse right inside the dimness of the great doubled stable doors. He threw himself off, letting one of Mul's boys take and cool the beast. The boy had never seen Hrald treat a horse thus, and slipped out with the young stallion into the paddock with no more than a duck of his chin.

Hrald found himself at one of the drawing wells, that closest to the buildings of the kitchen yard. He pulled the wooden bucket up, sloshed out most of what it held, then tipped the rest back towards his opened mouth. He let the bucket fall back in, hearing the loud splash, even seeing a few droplets rise up against the grey stone walls of the shaft.

He raised his eyes from the hole. Not far away stood Milburga, the serving woman who had bared her bottom to him months earlier. She had a rung-neck capon in each hand, having just cornered them in the fowl house and brought them out and killed them. She gripped them by their scaly legs, their brown wings falling down from their lifeless bodies.

He was not looking at her, but at some point through and beyond the serving woman. She saw his face and shook her hands free of the capons' feet, dropping them upon a small table top made from a single round of a tree trunk.

She was before him in an instant.

"Come with me, Master Hrald. There is something I must show you."

She led him to one of the grain sheds; the very shed in which his wound, and that of Ceric's, had been dressed. No one was about just then, but the door was wide open.

Once they were both within she turned to him. She smiled as with both hands she pulled up her gown, far above her round hips, almost to her breasts, showing off her naked body.

He shut the door, and fell upon her.

It was dark, and rushed, and utterly without tenderness. The stink of the fowl house rising off her body filled his nostrils, and that of his own sweat. They lay upon the rough and grain-dusty planks, his knees between her spread legs, his frantic and confused desire driving him there. It was over, almost as quickly as it began, in an explosion of sensation. He drew back from her, angry and depleted. She tried to hang on his neck, cooing nonsense at him. He pushed away, ordered his clothing. In the dark he found his belt and the tiny pouch hid within, plucked out a piece of silver and thrust it at her. Then he pulled open the door and was gone.

Burginde came walking through the yard past the fowl houses, carrying a salver heavy with broth and bread up to

Ælfwyn in their weaving room. She saw the abandoned fowl carcasses and scowled. That hussy Milburga oftentimes did such things; she would ask at the cooking rings who had been sent to fetch the capons.

As she entered the side door of the hall she saw Hrald at the door of the treasure room. She paused, seeing with what force he turned the key in the lock. She caught but a glimpse of his face before he vanished within.

She took the bread and broth up. Ælfwyn stood at her loom, a length of creamy linen growing under her weaving-sword. Ashild and her Aunt Eanflad stood together at another, working jointly as a broad piece of heavy wool built up beneath their fingers, Ashild smartening up the selvedges as her aunt swept the shuttle through the tautness of the warp. Ealhswith was gazing out the window, drop spindle in hand.

"Back in one moment," she promised, though only Ælfwyn noted she spoke through gritted teeth.

Burginde asked of the two head cooks, and learned they were in fact waiting for Milburga and the capons. The nurse clucked to herself, then turned back to the fowl houses. There was the woman now, standing by the little round table, her back to the prostrate birds and the approaching Burginde. She was looking down at something in her hand.

She startled when Burginde appeared.

"What have you in your hand?" she demanded, as Milburga had closed it in a fast fist as soon as she became aware of her.

"Show me," Burginde ordered.

She opened her fingers, showing the whole piece of silver in her palm.

Burginde took a great gulp of air. She looked at the woman's face, recalled Hrald's haste.

She snatched the coin from Milburga's hand, and gave her a smack across the cheek. Then she pulled her around to the back of the fowl house, out of view of those crossing the kitchen yard.

Once alone with Milburga, the nurse's fury knew no bounds.

"You filthy tart! He may look a man in body, but he is a boy at heart. Have you no shame?"

"He – he…" sputtered the serving woman.

"He nothing!" howled Burginde. "You threw yourself at Master, as sure as day is day he would never waste his seed on one such as you."

Milburga stood there, eyes bugging from her head, rocking back and forth on her heels.

"Give me my silver back," she pleaded.

For answer Burginde slapped her again, leaving a reddened cheek. "Your silver! It was never your silver!"

The woman was truly afright now; Burginde had more than twice her years, but there was real strength in her arms and hands. All knew she was beloved of the Lady of Four Stones, and had her ear as no one else. Milburga stood before the nurse and began to blubber.

Burginde would have none of it, but let her anger spew forth.

"You wicked-hearted whore! You cry for the silver and nothing more, and take triumph in what you have done. I should wring your neck like the fatted fowl you are. If you so much as look at Master Hrald again I will have you cast from this hall. Out into the village you will go, with nothing more than what you wear upon your back. You will be forced to beg, and I will make sure all decent woman know of your lewdness. See how they will like that!"

Milburga's hands now rose to her face. Tears streaked her crimson cheeks, and her nose ran as she snuffled.

Burginde could not bear to look at the woman any longer. "Go back to your work now," she ordered. "If my Lady hears of this, I will do worse than cast you out!"

Back in the hall Burginde made straight for the iron-strapped door of the treasure room. She tapped on its wooden planks, and brought her mouth close to the lock-edge.

"Master Hrald, you open this door to me," she hissed.

It took a moment, but the door opened. She stepped inside.

Hrald's face looked flushed and ashen, at once and the same time. She stood before him, looking up at his furrowed brow. She opened her fist before him, showing him the coin.

"You dropped this, down a trash pit," she told him.

His eyes closed, and his chin turned away.

"Does Mother know?"

"She does not, nor will she ever, if that hussy understood me."

He bowed his head. Burginde placed the silver on the edge of the nearest chest, and went on.

"She be a bad enough woman without turning her into a whore. Go tell Wilgot what you have been doing. You'll not sit at table with your mother until then."

He yearned to tell her the whole story, and could not. He must protect Gunnulf; no one could know. His lips were dry and he licked them, trying to buy time to order his thoughts.

"You need say nothing," she went on. "Go to Wilgot now. And take him that coin, for the village poor."

She was ready to go. Hrald seemed unable to speak, or even look her in the eye. She loved him almost as a son, had been the one to swaddle him, took turns rocking him when he cried from teething-pains, watched him suffer with the loss of his father. She would say one more thing, and did so, quietly.

"With your wife – a maid that you love – 'twill be the sweetest joy you have ever known."

She touched his hand with her own, and turned and left.

The door to the priest's house was open. Before he approached the threshold Hrald heard the sound of pounding from within. His figure filled the door frame, making Wilgot look up from where he stood at his work table over a thick wooden bowl. Wilgot's slightly stooped back made his girth look the plumper, and his dark cassock was bunched at the waist where his cross hung. A mallet was in the priest's hands, as he was crushing oak galls for the making of ink.

"I…have known a woman," was what Hrald said.

Wilgot blinked. He wiped his hands, gestured Hrald to sit. The priest crossed himself, then sat as well, his face turned away from Hrald, his head lowered.

"What kind of woman?"

"One of the serving women."

Wilgot paused a moment before going on.

"Was force used?"

Hrald made a sound, an exhalation of breath. "No, no. She…"

But the priest was nodding his head. "I see.

"Are you truly contrite?"

"I am." Hrald could answer no other way; there had been so little enjoyment in the encounter.

Wilgot went on, mumbling, having Hrald repeat prayers with him. Hrald gave him the piece of silver, asked that it be given to the poor as an offering. At last he released him.

He left Wilgot's door, only to see Gunnulf walking with Onund and two other men, heading to the hall; it was nearly time to sup. Gunnulf slowed, said something to Onund, dropped back to join Hrald.

Gunnulf's head tilted towards the priest's house. Hrald looked at him steadily, seeing the fear behind Gunnulf's eyes.

"Nai," he told his friend. "I was there for something else. No one will know. Ever."

But Hrald remained troubled. In the morning he announced he would go to Oundle for a few days' stay. He had once or twice made the journey without his mother; all knew he enjoyed the hushed nature of the place, and he had since boyhood looked forward to a day or two living amongst the monks, a few of whom were great favourites with him. And, he told his mother, he felt moved to make a donation to the abbey, in his own name.

This would be the first such he had given.

"Would you not have me there, to see the pleasure in Sigewif's face?" Ælfwyn asked.

She was proud of his decision to do so, and wished to join him.

"I would rather she see it was from me," he countered.

Ælfwyn considered this. Hrald was thoughtful, like his father. He had given some time to his decision, both to go, and to take a gift. It was a man's act, and she would let him take it.

She kissed him. He had seemed almost unwell the night before; now she knew it was his thinking on this that had caused it.

He reasoned that he need only ten men with him; unlike Thorfast he would not ride heading a long train. As he told her and his uncle, "I am not kin to Guthrum, and have no need to look over my shoulder at another heir."

He need not ask Ashild if she would accompany him; he had understood long ago that one or the other of them must always be at Four Stones. She would not leave, if he must, and the obverse was true. Their hall, filled as it was with warriors, was too important to be left unwatched by the children of Four Stones. As he gathered his kit he reflected that no one else saw that; no one realised this unspoken pact between him and his older sister.

At any other time Gunnulf would of course have ridden with Hrald; they were fast friends. But this time Gunnulf did not step forward, begin at once to gather his trappings. He heard Hrald was going and asked Asberg for the patrol by the valley of horses.

Hrald rode side by side with Jari the whole of the dusty trail, the chosen ten behind them. He was glad to get away from Four Stones, and glad for Jari's stoic company. He was not heading to Oundle to have time to think, or make decision. There was nothing to decide. Two things had happened, in rapid report, and he must live with them.

He winced every time he thought of the risk Gunnulf had taken. Another man might have killed him, then and there, and faced no penalty for doing so once he had spoken. Ceric would always be his closest friend, but Gunnulf, near at hand, was one he had gladly spent his hours with. He had tamed, and raced horses with Gunnulf; beat, and been beaten by him in wrestling; laughed and gamed with him. They sparred together, for years now, and he felt Gunnulf as good as any untested fighter; he took risks, just as he did on horseback; but he was fast and daring in his blows.

That Gunnulf had wanted him in that way shocked him. It had taken that same daring, a kind of wild courage, for Gunnulf to show him that want. That courage, and what lay behind it, made him shudder, just as the thought of Gunnulf burning in Hell made him shudder.

Jari was riding just next to Hrald, watchful as ever. Hrald could not imagine Jari knew this of his younger brother. He let himself wonder for a moment what Jari might do if he found out. He could not guess, and he did not like to think of it.

As far as the woman, the sickness he felt at that was one he tried to shrug off. Burginde was right; when he wed, the knowledge of his wife's body would be a sweetness he could finally taste. He would have almost his pick of the comeliest, and richest, maids in Anglia; Asberg and Jari and any number of other men had told him so, and he knew from watching the faces of the newly-wed men about the keep of the pleasures to come.

Wilgot had absolved him, given him penance and told him to sin no more. As much as he felt the urgings of his body he would keep away from Milburga and her like, at least as long as he could. He could wed in a year or two and then those urgings would be met.

He had brought to the foundation at Oundle a small wooden chest filled with two hundred pieces of silver. Sigewif received it with the dignity she accorded every gift, large or small. She clasped Hrald's hand; he was always surprised at how large a hand hers was, and what strength lay in it. As she did, her eyes, grey and clear as water drops, searched his face. He thought his own would be forced away, but they were not. He could hold her gaze. She did not challenge him. She read whatever she read in his face, accepted it, acknowledged him.

"Use it as you will," he told her. He knew many gifts came with special requests appended; he would put no conditions on his.

The abbess thought a moment. Her nuns and novitiates had come with sums of silver, whatever their families could afford. It had been set aside, sometimes at birth, as dower-fee, and though at Oundle they wed Christ and not a man it had been planned for all their lives. Most of the monks had no such start. Nearly all the wealth of the place was held on the female side. Two hundred silver pieces would assure every monk there comfort in their final years.

She told him this. He listened with care. It held meaning to be used this way, made his gift more valuable and real.

Later that day he asked that he might see Bova. This meant as well the granting of speech to her. Sigewif consented. Bova would be at her brewing shed after Sext, or mid-day prayer.

He had on past visits asked Sparrow to tell him of his father, wishing to fill in those years before he and Ceric had landed with Godwin of Kilton. She had been fearful of Sidroc a long time; it was easier for her to speak of the Lady Ceridwen, she who had redeemed and fed and clothed her, or of Tindr, who had led her out of the forest.

Today he did not ask Sparrow for any stories. He had been thinking of his father on the ride to the abbey, wondering what he would have done at his age. He could not guess, but for the sake of all at Tyrsborg he wanted to spend time with she who had lived there.

He found her standing under the roof of the open-walled brewing shed, a doubled row of brown-glazed crocks lined up on the sturdy work table. She was stirring one of them with a wooden paddle. The height of the lip of the crock meant she need stand on a low stool to reach with her spoon.

"I am brewster now," she said, brown eyes darting up over her shy smile. "Sister is content to sit and help sort the brewing herbs." She turned her head to the square table sitting under the roof of the shed. The old nun sat doing just that, a green and grey mass of leafy stems before her.

Bova handed him a pottery cup, bid him dip and taste that which she had just finished. It was brewed with fermented rowan berries, deep and ruddy, a favourite brew for Hrald, and he praised it.

They spoke a few moments more. He had taken his leave when he turned back.

"Bova," he asked. "Will you pray for me."

Her lips parted slightly, but she nodded her head. "I will pray for you, Hrald, and all whom you love."

The third day he left. Hrald had lived three days with the monks of Oundle, rising when they did, eating and working with them. As honoured guest he sat at meat with Sigewif in the woman's hall his first night, but other than that his hours were spent amongst the men. Except for the oft-imposed silence it was much like a hall of warriors in some ways.

They were no more than an hour gone from Oundle, moving at an easy walk, when a cloud of dust ahead of them proclaimed fast-moving horses' hooves. Such haste meant only ill tidings, and Hrald's small troop reined up as they readied themselves. He had not his new ring-tunic with him, none of the men did; but they all had helmets, and pulled them from their saddle-bags. Hrald's had been gift of his uncle, and this was the first time he had donned it with any expectation of need.

They slung their shields round to their chests, untied their throwing spears, and transferred the reins into their left hands. Jari, as a Tyr-hand, stayed at Hrald's near side, and ordered the ten with them to form two lines of five in front and behind. Then they waited, blocking the road, their horses dancing beneath them in sudden anticipation.

It was a single rider.

He slowed his canter only a little as he neared, which told them he was friendly. He wore no helmet, given his speed, but had a spear at the ready. He pulled up before them, his horse's hind legs folding under its haunches as it lurched to a stop.

"Hrald of Four Stones," called the rider. "The Gods and Jesus Christ are with me. I ride to Oundle, and then to Four Stones, to see you."

They knew the man. It was a messenger from Agmund, Guthrum's eldest son, who ruled the southern-most reaches of Anglia. This messenger had once been to Four Stones, a warrior in Agmund's train.

Hrald pulled off his helmet.

"Agmund sends you greeting," went on the man, nearly as winded as his horse. "Danes from Frankland have landed at Apulder, two hundred fifty ships of them. They have horses and are making camp there."

Apulder was across the southern border, in Wessex, a direct insult to that Kingdom, and threat to Anglia.

Two hundred fifty ships, the men of Four Stones were thinking. The waters would be dotted with their long-ships. Such a fleet was unheard of; it meant the joining of many war-chiefs together. With that number they could only be glad these strange Danes carried their horses with them, thus limiting the number of warriors to crowd their decks.

Being raised inland and in a time of relative peace, Hrald had never seen a single war-ship. He knew from drawings and the words of the men of their beauty, and their speed. His head quickly filled with an image of the onslaught. The image formed had little to do with the word Beauty.

"Who leads them?" demanded Jari.

"That we have not yet learned. But they have found little plunder along the coasts of Frankland, and now try their hands here. And they are heathen."

The man had given a nod of his head, as if towards the abbey that lay at the end of the road.

All raiders knew the treasure that lay within the walls of churches, convents and monasteries. Only the halls of the richest war-lords could compete with the silver, gems, and even gold that Christians harboured. And Hrald had just further enriched one such holy place with silver of his own.

"What news of Ælfred?" Hrald asked.

"He is in the West, from what we know, but by now his riders would have come to him."

Jari looked to Hrald, then nodded his head at Agmund's man. The King would find this fresh affront to be just that, an outrage to his well-tended borders. Yet Ælfred rarely acted recklessly; he would watch and wait as he gathered his men. A sufficient force under his command might drive him in an attempt to reclaim all that had been given over to the Danes. Suddenly there were two threats to the Peace.

"Agmund has our thanks," Jari said.

Hrald had been doing quick reckoning in his head. The place they had just left must be protected. "Stay," he told the messenger, "and nine of us will ride with you to Oundle."

He turned to the men he led, chose the best rider amongst them "You, Aki, ride back to Four Stones. Tell them what we have heard. The rest of you return to Oundle. Jari and I ride now for Thorfast; he may know more. Either way we will send word back to Oundle within three days."

Jari was looking at the nine who would remain. "Set and keep watch, three at a time. There are men enough there to help you, and some of the monks are warriors still beneath their cassocks."

Hrald and Jari were in fact the first to bring the news to Thorfast. He was at his new holdings at Turcesig, and listened with careful attention.

"Two hundred fifty ships," he repeated, as they sat over ale in his timber hall. Women had been weaving and spinning within, and had been shooed out so that the three were now alone. The doors were opened for brightness, but as Hrald lifted his face to the heavy timber rafters the roof was lost in gloom.

The hall was large, and fine by any standards, high ceilinged, thickly thatched, pocketed with sleeping alcoves along much of both long sides, and with a fire-pit ringed with square-cut stones. Thorfast's younger brother Haward was at the keep they had grown up in; Thorfast at this grander one which Guthrum had left him in his will. Once on Thorfast's lands Hrald and Jari had been met by a mounted patrol of five men and escorted to their young war-chief. They rode through palisade gates into a keep of full alertness, men actively sparring, honing blades, flinging spears at gashed wooden targets. Once Asberg heard the news Four Stones would be much the same.

"Who will come forward to lead them?" their host wondered aloud. Of his cousins, Guthrum's sons, he did not think even the eldest, Agmund, could amass enough men and treasure to take command.

The three sat, discussing this, Hrald wishing Asberg were with him.

A serving woman poured out more ale, and Thorfast reflected on how this landing would shape his life in this new hall. News of such great import served to compress time itself; since his uncle's death he, and all war-chiefs, had been preparing for possible action; now this seemed inevitable. Things which he had planned for the future would be required to be undertaken, now.

Silence had fallen upon the three of them, each deep in their own thoughts. Thorfast broke it with a quiet declaration.

"I would have Ashild for my wife," he said. He was looking straight at Hrald.

Jari made a sound of surprise, but of approval, too. It was sudden by any reckoning, and the maid's uncle and mother were not present to hear this.

Hrald gave a slow exhalation of breath.

"She has been spoken for."

Thorfast's brow furrowed in puzzlement. Then he made his guess.

"That Saxon."

"Já. My friend. Ceric of Kilton."

Hrald felt that Ashild was nearly at his elbow. He could almost feel her anger at being so discussed.

"You cannot throw away her value like that," Thorfast countered. "What good will she do you, buried away in Wessex?"

Hrald had recoiled at this, snapped his head back, and was staring at him. It was a misstep, Thorfast knew; the rashness of his words had given offence. He had forgot how young Hrald was.

"Ceric of Kilton is godson to Ælfred," Hrald was telling him. "He wears a golden cross from Rome, gift from the King to Ceric's father, who fought shield-to-shield with him. Ashild will go to a burh known throughout Wessex for its treasure."

Thorfast was not sure he could offer the same bride-price as could be summoned from such a place. He thought on what little he recalled of the Saxon youth, well-knit, able-looking enough, and not a man a maid would scorn.

"And Ceric will be Lord of Kilton," Thorfast considered.

Hrald paused a moment before answering.

"He will not," he admitted. "He has a younger brother, adopted by the Lord of Kilton, who will fill that seat."

The door was not closed after all. Thorfast wedged it open.

"Would you have your sister be second in that place? Ashild is proud. She will want, and deserves, to be first, to be Lady of the keep she goes to."

Jari had made a small grunt of assent. If Ashild was anything, she was proud.

Hrald floundered, looking left and right as if for answers. Ashild had never said to Ceric or to anyone, that she would wed him. Yet Hrald knew she had true affection for Ceric; how could she not, with all the time they had spent together, and the love between their mothers.

Thorfast was speaking again.

"And she would be here in Lindisse, close to Four Stones and all that matters to her."

Hrald's chin lowered at this. He knew more than anyone how she loved her homeland and folk. The thought of sending her so far away to Kilton had been his only pang in surrendering her to Ceric.

Thorfast would not relent. He dropped his voice. "Soon all of Angle-land could become Danelaw. Would you have her taken as booty when Kilton falls?"

Hrald stood up. "Kilton will not fall. The Peace will hold. And Ashild will not wed anyone but whom she wants."

Thorfast stood as well, hand outstretched in calming gesture. "Hrald. We are friends of old." He lifted both hands, opening them in entreaty. His eyes were steady on his guest. "If Ashild is not destined for another, give me leave to speak to her."

Destined for another. Hrald had no idea where Ashild's Fate lay.

Jari was looking at him expectantly, eager for him to agree to so reasonable an offer. And he himself must admit that to deny his sister the chance to be courted by Thorfast did her a disservice.

He was thinking on this when the piping voice of a child sounded. A girl of about five years scampered out of the passageway to the table, laughing as she ran to her father. Thorfast bent to pet the child's round cheek, then gestured her back to the care of the out-of-breath serving woman who had followed her in.

Hrald watched the child be led away, then answered.

"You may speak to Ashild," he said.

After his guests had ridden off Thorfast pondered all he had heard. He and Haward would soon be fighting someone, either defending their lands from these Danes come from Frankland, or joining with them to ride against Wessex. It was not what he wanted but at least now he had men enough to have a voice in what came next. Hrald as an ally would vastly strengthen his hand.

As for Hrald's sister, he had seen women he liked better in the face, but she was comely enough, and she had spirit, which he valued. And when he looked at Ashild, he saw not only her person, but the two hundred warriors of Four Stones.

Chapter the Twelfth: Few Choices

The Island of Gotland

HUNDREDS of leagues from Lindisse, in the near middle of the Baltic Sea, the brewster Rannveig stood before the long wooden table against the wall of her brew-shed, wiping pottery cups. It was just past noon, hours before she would be serving, but five Danes had come in, flush with silver, and she had seated them and brought the ewer of mead they had asked for.

She knew they were Danes the moment they opened their mouths; their Norse told her. But one of the five she looked at with special care. He wore his knife across his belly, suspended lengthwise from a belt, instead of on his hip. Only one man wore his knife thus, Sidroc the Dane, and she knew the knife this new Dane bore to be that called a seax, and the work of Saxons.

After the first ewer of mead had vanished down their throats they dropped a small pile of silver into her palm. She carried it back to her scales and shook it into the measuring bowl. The silver was mostly pieces of coin, but one whole piece was there. She picked it up and looked at it, and knew it for what it was. Ceridwen had several of such coins, and when Rannveig came across a newly-minted one she saved it for her, for it bore the countenance of the great Ælfred, King of Wessex. Ceridwen knew this king; he had once been hers.

They had asked for food, as well as more drink, and she moved into the passageway and out past her brewing shed to ask Gudfrid to feed them. Then she headed up the steep hill to Tyrsborg.

Sidroc was stacking firewood against the outside wall of the hall with her son, Tindr. Her boy smiled at her, and Sidroc nodded down at her from his perch atop the tightly packed cords.

"I have Danes, at the brew-house," she told him.

He shoved the cut piece he had been holding into place, and jumped down to her. Sweat beaded his brow and his dark hair was plastered against his temples, making the grey streak by his left ear slightly darker than it was. Over the years she had made it a habit to tell him whenever any he might take interest in appeared at her tables. Danes were foremost in Sidroc's line of interest.

"What manner of men are they?"

Rannveig had summed them, and quickly. "Warriors. Young. Cocky with silver. Including this." Here she handed Sidroc the piece with the side-portrait of Ælfred.

He turned it in his hand, feeling the raised edges of the King's crown, the line of his nose and chin. He handed it back to her.

She had more to say.

"And one – one wears a seax."

His chin jerked up at this. It was almost proof of a Dane having fought in Angle-land.

"You have never seen them before?"

"Never. And I know from their talk it is their first time on the island. Their ship dropped them here for the day, I think, while it sailed further North. Their captain has trading dealings somewhere up the coast. They were not needed and asked to wait here."

"Happy the man who can chose drinking over dealing," Sidroc observed.

"I will be down, and soon," he told Rannveig.

She gave her son another smile, then turned and left.

Tindr had been watching his mother, and Sidroc, with his usual care. Sidroc faced him, pointed to Tindr, to himself, then to his eye. He gestured a sword at his side. We are going to see some warriors, he was telling him.

Tindr grasped it. He made a move with both hands, signing the pulling back of a bow string. Should I get my bow, he asked. But Scar shook his head. Just come with me.

Ceridwen saw the departing Rannveig from her front door, which she had pulled open. Eirian and Yrling were off playing with Deer and Tindr's small boy, and she had thought to prune the rampant growth of her grape vine, now that fruiting was over. She went to her friend.

Rannveig nodded towards the sea. "There are Danes at the brew-house. Your own is coming to look at them." She wished it to sound a light jest, but she herself felt concern. Before she made her way back she told Ceridwen what she had told Sidroc.

The Mistress of Tyrsborg put down her pruning-hook and walked over the grassy way to the cooking rings. Their cook Gunnvor always had a cauldron of water warming, and Sidroc stood at a basin on one of her work-tables, where he had just finished washing hands, face, and chest. He toweled himself dry, his dark blue eyes crinkling in the easy smile that he almost always greeted his wife with. He picked up his discarded work tunic and met her as he crossed to the side door of their hall.

She followed him into the treasure room, watched as he pulled on one of his best linen tunics. He took his comb from the shelf and ran it through his hair. Then he knelt on the floor, pulled aside her precious plush weaving which lay before the bed, pried up a broad floor board. Under it, for the sake of fire, lay a flat stone, which he also moved. His fingers angled around and pulled up something bright, which he clapped on his right wrist. It was a cuff of gold, cunningly wrought of many hammered, overlapping scales, like unto the scales of a fish or dragon.

He replaced all and stood as he buckled on his seax. He did not usually so array himself when he sought out Rannveig's customers. She knew he had reason, perhaps the fact that the Danes he went to meet had been to Angle-land.

"Rannveig said there were five of them," she found herself saying. Her eyes flitted to his sword belt, hanging where it always was, on the wall by their bed. He had made no move towards it.

He nodded. "She did," he agreed.

He looked ready to leave.

"I will come too," she suggested, "come in through the passage way, stand with Rannveig as if I am of the place."

"You will not," he said, as simply as that. "I will not have their heads turned by gawking at you."

She let a dismissive laugh escape from her lips. She had three-and-thirty years.

He looked at her. She wore that day a gown of indeterminate hue, not quite blue nor green, a happy accident of dyeing. Its colour made her green eyes a deeper, stiller shade. Her hair spilled out from her white head-wrap onto the sleeves and bodice of the gown, thick tresses the shade of bright and burnished gold. If she lacked the freshness of a maid, she had won through years of life and loss and the children she had borne the warm and vibrant ripeness of a woman greatly loved.

He found himself grinning at her.

"You will stay here, until I am back."

He tucked the pouch that held his silver into his belt, got Tindr, and left.

Walking down the hill he noted the roughness of the Baltic. Sailing season would soon be over; even the fishermen in their stable, broad-beamed craft would haul up soon. But sometimes one must stretch the season. His own captain, Runulv, sailed only early in the year, often in wind and waves matching or exceeding those of Fall. These five Danes may have landed on Gotland now, but likely as not more sailing lay ahead of them.

The day was warm enough that Rannveig had the awnings to the sea rolled up. When he opened the door he saw the Danes, still alone in their eating and drinking. It would be hours before any from the trading road came in. They had their war-kit with them but no packs; it was true they would be picked up and returned to their ship soon. Their round shields stood propped up against the wall behind them, along with five heavy spears. They all looked up as he walked in, and kept watching as his retainer followed him in. Sidroc motioned to Tindr to stay by the table where his mother stood. He approached the men.

They were, he gauged, all of about five-and-twenty years, at their peak in quickness if not yet in strength. Two of them had swords he judged as good ones, including he who wore the seax. They were finishing their meal, and broken loaves and an empty pot of the savoury fish-paste Gudfrid made from salted herring told it had been enjoyed. Just now three of them were again lifting their mead-cups to their lips, and looked at Sidroc over the rims as he reached their table.

"Brothers," he said.

They took him in, five pair of light eyes raking up and down upon his person. He was tall, lean yet powerfully built, and rich. The cuff of gold was heavy, and the valued work of the Rus, thought one of the men. And he bore a seax with a silver-wrapped hilt. Whether this tall Dane had traded, or raided, for such things, they must admit he wore them well. And there was that scar.

One made way on the bench for him. Sidroc inclined his head to Rannveig, watching all with the discreetness of her calling, bidding her bring another ewer of mead. He took his place at their table.

Sidroc's eye fastened on the one bearing the seax.

In response the strange Dane spoke, nodding his head at that Sidroc wore.

"Your seax," the young Dane asked.

"From a Saxon war-lord I dropped at Readingas."

They had heard of that battle, but had been boys when it had been fought.

He did not ask in return, and the other Dane did not offer. His was not nearly as fine, and he had in fact cut it off the body of a man already dead.

Sidroc let his glance fall again to the man's weapon. "That Saxon you killed was a good warrior," he praised.

The bearer of that weapon cocked his head at this.

Sidroc made a slight gesture to his own seax, and went on. "It is a tribute to a dead opponent to wear his weapons," he noted. "Proof he was worthy of your attention."

The other Dane gave a short and scoffing laugh. "I never think of the dead," he claimed.

Sidroc looked at him. "You will," he promised.

Rannveig brought the fresh ewer to the table, with a cup for Sidroc. Sidroc filled his cup and pushed the ewer to the Dane across from him, who nodded his thanks.

The one with the seax spoke again. "Mine is from Basingas."

So he was thinking of the dead man, after all.

These men were too young to have fought at the famed pitched battle there, Sidroc knew. He would hazard a guess at some other, smaller, and much more recent action fought there in Wessex.

"That skirmish," he nodded.

"Já. Last Summer," agreed the Dane, refilling his cup.

The ewer made another pass around the table. Despite the food they had eaten these Danes were well on their way to being drunk. Sidroc took care to pour himself out equal measure to what they filled their cups with, but had no fear of dulling his wits. He had fifteen years more experience in holding his drink. He called for another ewer, which Rannveig carried over. One of the Danes asked about the treasure on his wrist, and was lauded by its wearer with the assurance that it was indeed the famed gold-work of the Rus.

"The Svear have it all," complained one, thinking of those distant lands. "Nothing left for us."

"Like Frankland," agreed another. "All the easy takings are claimed."

They were half-drunk, had full bellies, and sitting on an island far from any war. He would risk a direct question.

"Will the winds take you home, or back to Angle-land," he asked.

"Angle-land, to join the army already there."

It was the one with the seax that answered. Sidroc leant forward slightly on his elbows, showing his interest, bidding him go on.

"We are throwing in with Haesten. He has eighty ships; even more. He landed just after a fleet four times that size put ashore in Wessex. Most are come from raiding Frankland, but no one of their leaders is strong enough to take command, none but Haesten. Now that Guthrum is dead Haesten will be chief of all, and soon, King of Anglia. After that all of Angle-land will be his."

"Ours," corrected one of them. He was grinning like a milk-fed cat.

Sidroc had just heard a great deal. A new Danish army was somehow lately encamped in Angle-land; and Guthrum, who had been his own King and war-lord, was dead. And these Danes he drank with had, a year ago, already fought at least one skirmish there, on Saxon soil.

He knew his eyes had shifted at this news, but he had kept himself from otherwise showing surprise. Deep in their cups as these men were, they may not have noticed. Of Haesten he knew plenty, but not this.

His mind turned these facts, extracting as much as he could. None of Guthrum's many heirs ruled all Anglia; that was clear. New Danes, seemingly having given up on Frankland, had landed. A war-lord with a big enough army could make his move, hoping for aid from those long-settled there.

He thought on Haesten. He would have no less than fifty years now, but was renowned still as a warrior. He had once been one of Guthrum's chief men, just as Sidroc himself had been. But Haesten had a hard time accepting orders, and soon left to try his hand in Frankland, taking his men with him. There he had fought many battles, and had with his own hand killed the famed Frankish warrior Rutpert. Haesten had been back and forth between Dane-mark and Frankland since then. Now he was ready for his biggest quarry yet, and seemingly had the men and ships to back him.

The Dane with the seax had been studying Sidroc. "You should come with us."

It took Sidroc a moment to answer. "Perhaps I will."

He roused himself. He glanced over to where Tindr stood, watching patiently, his mother still at work, needlessly, he knew, wiping and re-wiping the same cups, unwilling to leave. Sidroc began to rise. He had got what he wanted; far more.

One of the Danes was fumbling in his belt, and a clatter of hack-silver spilled out on the table. Two walrus-ivory dice rolled out as well.

"Stay for one game," slurred the Dane, eyeing Sidroc's cuff of gold. "Our ship is not here yet."

Sidroc considered the five of them.

"I have never had much luck at dice. But I will play with you..."

Once back at Tyrsborg Sidroc did not return to stacking wood. Having taken most of the Danes' silver, he had dropped it into the weighing bowl of Rannveig's scale in thanks. He walked slowly up the hill, Tindr at his side. He was oft times grateful for Tindr's silence, as he was now.

His head was buzzing enough from the mead he had drunk that his first stop was at his own well. He downed a full dipperful of the cold water, then dashed some on his brow. He gestured to Tindr to go back to the wood pile. He went into the hall.

Ceridwen was in the kitchen yard with Gunnvor. Their serving woman, Helga, was back with Eirian and Yrling, and when they saw Tindr they ran to him, asking him to help them saddle their ponies. The Mistress of Tyrsborg saw Tindr had come back, and went to look for her husband.

She found him in the treasure room. He stood in the middle of the room, a sharp shaft of afternoon Sun striking the floorboards before him. It was the only window, and the corners of the room were dim, save for near the door, opened to the hall. She could not tell what he was looking at.

She moved a little deeper into the room, and he turned to her.

"Guthrum is dead. Many Danes have landed in Angle-land. They have come from Frankland, given up on taking more from there. Haesten will lead them."

Her lips opened, but she did not speak. The gravity of his tone said far more than those few words.

"Landed where?" she was finally able to ask.

"I do not know. In the South, most likely; somewhere in Wessex. Ælfred is cautious. There is less risk in landing in his kingdom than in any of the Danelaw."

"What...what will happen?"

"Haesten will count on the Danes already in Anglia and Mercia to join him."

He watched his wife put her hand to her mouth.

"Join him against Ælfred and Wessex?"

She answered herself a moment later. "With Guthrum dead, the Peace no longer need be honoured."

He nodded.

Her brain swam, grasping the vastness of this threat. In her mind's eye flashed Ælfwyn, gone to Danish lands before that Peace, and ever a part of it. Next she saw Ælfwyn and Sidroc's son, Hrald, whom she loved, thrust into command before his years. The faces of his sisters rose before her.

Then with an awful-ness that clenched her throat, she thought of the response to this threat. Her son Ceric, old enough now to fight shield-to-shield with Ælfred's troops. Her second son, Edwin, heir to all the richness that was Kilton...

"What – what of those Danish keeps which would honour the Peace – such as Four Stones?"

He took so long to answer that she was forced to speak.

"Will there be a choice for them?"

"War allows few choices."

Chapter the Thirteenth: There Will Be War

ÆLFRED, ever on the move throughout his Kingdom of Wessex, was brought news of the invading Danes from one of his many fast-riding messengers. He was far in the West; had been in fact as far as Kilton. Apulder, named for its wealth of wild apple trees, was where the ships had landed, one of the Eastern-most points of Angle-land. The King had begun another of his many forts there, on the banks of the River Rother. The men so working were surprised by the sight of the multitude of dark ships oaring swiftly up the water. The Danes began to land, killing the men as they stood to defend their work, scattering the rest as more and more ships beached. Enough men lived to watch from a distance as the landing party took over what they had begun. They saw the intruders start in at once to enlarge the fortification.

The news was deeply disturbing, but no shock. Guthrum's death had left the Danelaw without a strong hand to rule as over-King. At the same time Frankland, having been the repeated target of Danish attacks, was now resisting with a strength that the Danes had never met there. The channel waters were choppy and full of danger, but the greater gain now lay back in Angle-land. Ælfred saw that and planned to refute it. It was late Fall, the days cool and growing short, but clear and dry. This mass of Danes surely meant to over-Winter here in Wessex.

Then word came of a second force which had landed. His riders had spotted no less than four score war-ships now at Middeltun. The strange Danes had swiftly beached, killed the King's men who had gone to meet them, and began digging themselves in. Though a third the number of the ships that had landed further South at Apulder, this fleet now at Middeltun gave Ælfred more concern.

Apulder was wild and open country, with little in the way of either folk or treasure. An enemy encampment at Middeltun was by far the greater threat, for it sat at the very mouth of the Thames. Up that vast river was easy sailing to the richness of the great trading centre of Lundenwic. And Lundenwic was under the command of Ælfred's own son-in-law Æthelred of Mercia, the powerful ealdorman wed to the King's capable daughter Æthelflaed.

His distance from both invading forces demanded time to go and meet them. Time was the King's friend. Time granted the opportunity to think, and thinking was something Ælfred excelled at.

He would ride to Middeltun first, meet the war-lord who had been bold enough to draw his dragon ships up so near to his own family's holdings.

He arrived at that encampment with a considerable force, one hundred fifty men, all mounted. For speed's sake only thegns on their horses stood with him; the spearmen and archers and sling-men – foot-men all – who made up the bulk of his true army were left behind. He did not mean to engage, only to impress.

He halted his men on a shallow rise above the growing fortress. Beyond that were the broad waters leading into the Thames, swelling now at the sea-tide. If the Danes swarming below at their work, digging ditches, hauling tree trunks, sawing timber, paused in their labours and happened to look their way, they saw a blank grass-covered field. Seemingly a moment later the sky above that field was punctured by the silhouettes of a mounted army.

Ælfred held his men steady, knowing that below the frantic activity of building had been replaced by the frantic activity of arming. He could make out the scrambling figures, hear the winding of a horn. He held his men.

His line of thegns was made the more impressive by the banners they carried. Every twentieth man had a pole attached upright from his saddle cantle, and every pole held a pennon bearing the golden dragon of Wessex, Ælfred's standard. It was a display for a great festival day, or one of thanksgiving; in battle one banner was consecrated and kept close to the King at all times as he directed the action behind the shield-wall. If that shield wall should be broken the banner stayed with him, held by a young man, waving it in both hands to mark the King still lived, even though the King himself be thrusting with sword or spear against the foe he found himself face-to-face with.

Other banners were there in the line of mounted men. Ælfred was flanked by large white pennons, marked with a red cross made of strips of coloured fabric; the cross Christ was crucified on. These sprang from the saddles of the two priests, each mounted on an ass, that rode on either side of the King.

The King held his line long enough to judge that all below were now staring up at him. It was time to go and meet whoever led them.

He gave a word, and five moved forward. Ælfred touched his heels to the flank of his chestnut stallion, a beast as golden as the dragon which was his symbol. The two priests on their dusky asses ambled forward, the beasts unperturbed by the fluttering white flags bearing Christ's cross. One warrior rode next, fully armed and clad in a ring-tunic, whose saddle held a dragon pennon. The fifth was the King's serving-man. These last two each led another horse, laden with treasure.

The five, detached from the force behind them, walked forward at a steady pace, riding with a composed confidence that made the men they approached narrow their eyes. Chief amongst those watching was Haesten. He had enough time to send his wife and two young sons onto one of the ships that bobbed gently on the incoming tide. Not all his fleet had been beached; a few were always kept in water, a prudent provision in the past.

He was not surprised that a few days after his landing Ælfred already knew of his arrival. What narrowed his eyes was the King himself riding, with no more than four men, right into the heart of his building-works. The King of Wessex, riding almost alone. The Danish war-lord appreciated this boldness. It showed him too, a certain respect being paid; that once Ælfred saw who he dealt with, he would be acknowledged as a King in his own right.

Before the five left the long line of thegns, the elder of the two priests blessed Ælfred, stamping with his thumb a drop of holy oil on the King's brow, mouthing a hushed and fervent prayer that if he were soon to meet death, God would take mercy on the soul of the monarch. The younger priest did the same with the chosen warrior, and the King's man-servant. Then the two priests exchanged blessings. The warrior was older, hardened, but not indifferent to death. His name was Raedwulf, and he was bailiff of Defenas. He had before been at Ælfred's side in moves as brash as this one. If one day the King miscalculated, he would sell his own life dear protecting that of Ælfred. The priests, completely unarmed, calmed themselves with the knowledge that an end at the hands of the heathen horde was a martyr's death. Only the man-servant, young and with toddling children back at Witanceaster, trembled.

Standing before the ditch being dug, Haesten made his decision. He would ride out and meet Ælfred, five men to five men. He called for his two eldest sons, and two able warriors. They swung into their saddles and started. A group of disbelieving Danes who had been stopped in their digging-work began calling and hooting after him, urging a reception at the end of a spear. Haesten turned his head back to the unruly and with his look quelled their racket.

He moved steadily towards the King's party, his horse tossing his head up and down as if to acknowledge their guests. He and his sons and his two picked warriors had donned ring-shirts, had shields on their backs, helmets on their heads, and spears in hand. Haesten grew close enough to see Ælfred bore none of that. The King was garbed as if for a feast. His tunic was of golden hued wool, from which glinted threads of true gold at hem and sleeves. His mantle of deep blue was lined with fur of such thickness that it must be mink from the furthest Northern climes. On his brow lay a broad golden circlet, mark of Kingship. And other than a sword of magnificence he wore no weapons.

Haesten let a low oath escape his lips. He had been bested in this first contest.

They were only two horse-lengths away when they all halted.

"I am Ælfred, King of Wessex," the King told the Danes.

Haesten pulled off his helmet. The King spent a moment staring at the man's face. The hair was grey, as was the short beard. But he had little doubt who it was.

"I am Haesten," said he.

The King spent the next two days within the nascent fort. He began by presenting Haesten with a footed silver goblet studded with lapis stones. The Dane, in his rough encampment, found himself ordering food and drink, calling for another tent to be raised, changing his leggings for a pair less soiled. Ælfred learnt that Haesten had brought his newest wife and young boys with him, unspoken proof of the war-chief's intention to stay. It gave him pause. Yet he could build on this, Ælfred knew.

First he must discuss a point of justice. He did so after his small party had dined with the Dane and a few of his chief men. The King had brought several jugs of choice wine in his baggage, which had supplemented the modest fare Haesten could provide. After their repast the King and Haesten sat alone within the tent which had been pulled up for him.

"You have killed my men," Ælfred noted, referring to those who had fallen when Haesten's ships had beached. "Under the laws which Guthrum and I approved, the wergild of Saxons and Danes is the same. These were King's men, so their wergild is doubled. They leave wives and children."

Haesten considered. The audacity of the King in coming essentially alone and unarmed still played in his head; this man fascinated him. It was like gaming with a man in rags who nonetheless pulled from his belt a nugget of gold.

"I will give you silver," the Dane conceded.

It was a small triumph to Ælfred, but a triumph nonetheless. Haesten was recognising and adhering to the law.

More than once during their first hours together the Dane had been seized with the desire to lay hands upon the King. His ransom would be treasure unimaginable, and his killing throw all of Wessex into disorder. But Haesten had planned his moves with care, and had reason for measured action. To be repulsed now would be disaster. He and his army were newly landed, in the act of throwing up their long houses, had as yet secured no additional lands. The supplies they had carried with them were carefully rationed. Wessex was too rich and powerful to allow an outrage committed upon its King. Ælfred was beloved and the thirst for revenge would only be quenched in his own blood. A return to Frankland was no option, and his line of enemies ran deep and broad in his Danish homeland. He must make his mark here or not at all.

On the second day came the greater concession. Early in the day the King sent his serving man to invite Haesten to break his fast with Ælfred in his tent. The Dane thus found himself a guest in his own encampment. Also present were the two gowned priests, and Ælfred's lone warrior. The serving man drew forth a series of delicacies and laid them before the five men. Tiny roast fowl were there, brined in sharp and flavourful verjuice. He added to this pots of goats' cheese which had been pounded with herbs, unknown to the Dane and delicious; and boiled goose eggs pickled in some liquid unto mead, both sweet and savoury. The tiny fowl, the huge eggs, the cheese rendered green by the cress and purslane – all added an unexpected, even unworldly touch to the meal, one which Haesten, accustomed to the traveller's fare of salted fish and stale loaves could not but be affected by.

The small fowl required a restrained touch; Haesten found himself watching the King eat his. Ælfred was quietly aware of this. Once the Peace had been made with Guthrum, that Dane began patterning his reign after that of the King of Wessex, even to coining silver pieces with Guthrum's image on them, modeled after those of Ælfred. Such coinage was unheard of amongst the Danes, to whom silver coins meant no more than hack-silver. Ælfred had seen first-hand the power of imitation.

Raedwulf, sitting at the end of the table, took it all in, his eyes steady, his movements slow and controlled. The Danish war-lord had taken his measure when they all sat at meat the prior night. Haesten's eyes had raked over him, gauging the brawn of his shoulders, noting the value of the seax spanning his belly, seeing too the strands of grey in Raedwulf's hair. Haesten's own was wholly grey, and the bailiff of Defenas knew that the Dane understood he had been chosen to ride with the King not only for his prowess but his hard-won experience.

After they had supped the King drew forth a golden neck-chain, and set it upon the table before his guest.

"No metal is purer than gold, and no word greater than the Word of God," he said.

Ælfred began explaining, then expounding, the Christian faith. All that I have has come from God, he stressed, but far greater than any Kingdom will be the Kingdom of God.

Haesten knew much of Christians, and had killed not a few monks; their temples held treasure. He knew Guthrum had submitted to baptism as part of the Peace. He knew he would do no such thing.

But Ælfred surprised him yet again, by proposing baptism not for him, but for his two young boys. Ælfred himself would stand as sponsor to the older boy. Beyond this he offered, by proxy, his son-in-law Æthelred of Mercia, he who governed Lundenwic, as sponsor for the younger son.

Haesten suddenly had the prospect of the two richest men in Wessex acting on behalf of his youngest sons. To hide his interest he sat as still as he could, elbow upon the table, stroking his beard. He gave, at last, the smallest nod of his chin. The King turned to the priests, the elder of which, round-faced and jovial by nature, chimed in with a homily on the favour to be won and succour to be enjoyed as a Follower of Christ.

Haesten had kept his eyes from resting on the chain of braided gold, yet it was always there. If the King was profligate with his gold Haesten would be there to accept it. The children were brought, without their mother, boys of six and seven years. While they waited the priests had been busy readying basin and a crisp linen towel. The dutiful children were kindly received, then sprinkled from a flask of holy water drawn from the sacred well at Witanceaster, and blessed and anointed. The neck-chain, having fulfilled its purpose, left in the hands of the boys' father.

"There is a bond between us now," the King told Haesten before he rode off. "I have sworn in the eyes of God to take interest in your sons. Of your doings in Anglia I can make no demands, but of my own Kingdom I do. And that is that Wessex is left unmolested."

Haesten's fingers stroked his beard. He nodded. The chiefs of Angle-land valued the lives of men. He offered six as hostages to prove Wessex would be left alone, two of which he stressed to the King were young cousins, and thus his own kin. Ælfred accepted them, swore they would be well treated, and returned when appropriate.

At no time during his stay did the King inquire as to Haesten's intentions. He would not be served in prompting the man to lie, and besides, he felt that at this early date the Dane himself did not truly know. His choices were limited enough. Ælfred could imagine Haesten's best men fanning out throughout the countryside, announcing their chief's arrival, taking the measure of each Danish chieftain as they came upon them. Later Haesten himself would ride out, bidding them join him. Even those long-settled and content might be tempted. Young hot-heads who had missed the carving up of Mercia and Anglia would be spoiling for their share.

Ælfred had made his point, demonstrating to Haesten a few of the benefits to be enjoyed by accepting the King's boon. Friendship with the King of Wessex and with Æthelred of Mercia offered protections to the former, and gain to Haesten.

By the time Ælfred and his party rode back to his waiting men he felt he had gained much. Foremost was a glimpse into the nature of his new opponent. He had known but few facts about Haesten prior to this meeting. Now he added what he had directly experienced to what he had heard. This was a man of great prowess who found himself in a shrinking world. All knew Haesten had killed Rutpert, one of the most celebrated warriors in Frankland. That Rutpert's son had gone on to become King of the Franks had not made Haesten more welcome in that land. Haesten had no kingly blood; he was not kin to Guthrum. But he had ranged all along the coasts beyond the vast holdings of Cordoba, pillaging as he went, as far South and East as Pisa. All he had won had been grasped by his strong hand. And he was one who in battle the bear-spirit could enter, could fight almost out of his head with berserk fury, driving himself to extreme acts of ferocity.

In battle Ælfred himself had felt a similar spirit fill his breast; his chronicler, recording his deeds to inspire men, had compared him to a wild boar. But to Ælfred it was the Holy Spirit which had filled him, lifting him to feats of unthought-of strength and boldness.

When the five rejoined the thegns camped upon the hill slope, one young warrior in particular went to meet Raedwulf, eager to embrace the older man in grateful welcome, eager to hear of all that had transpired. Camp was struck and the entire army turned their backs on Middeltun, and the gaping mouth of the Thames beyond it. As they rode away Raedwulf looked back at the bustle of Haesten's building and wall-raising.

"We will come here again, Ceric," he told his young companion.

Ashild looked down into her blistered palm. Two fluid-filled sacs were rising under the pinkness of her skin, one at the root of her pointing finger, and one, even larger, in the centre of her hand. Her right arm ached and her shoulder had begun to burn. Still, she kept on. She had nailed an old shield to the trunk of an elm, and walked towards it to recover the second of the spears she had just flung. One spear lay a man's length from the base of the tree, the other off to the left.

She was beyond the old place of Offering, away from the path leading to the stream that ran behind Four Stones. She had come here three days running, to a place unfrequented, where she might learn to kill a man.

Throwing an iron-tipped wooden-shafted spear with anything like power proved to be far more difficult than it looked. As she reached down to pick up the first spear, the pain in her shoulder made her bite her lip. Her palm felt so hot she knew the blisters were soon to burst if she closed her hand around the shaft a few more times. What was worse is that she was no better at hitting her target on this third afternoon than she had been on the first. Her frustration mingled with her mounting anger at the weakness of her own body.

She stood holding one of the spears; just bearing its weight caused pain in her tired arm at this point. She knew Sidroc had always cut a shallow groove in his spear shaft to mark the balance point, but holding the thing aloft, shifting it up and down in her hand, she had no idea how to find where that balance point was.

She put the butt end of it down in the dried grass, and with her other hand pushed her hair away from her face. It was held in a plait, but much had worked its way loose. Her brow was damp, despite the cool greyness of the day. She raised her eyes to the elm tree and what she had fixed there. The shield had once been painted in two nested rings of red and yellow, and looked to her like a mocking, open eye. She took her sash from off her waist and wrapped it twice about her blistered palm, then flung the spear again.

She missed. She let out a short cry of anger, staring after the failed throw. Then she whirled at the sound of a horse's snort. It was Hrald, standing behind her on his bay. He grinned down at her, his laughter dying at the look on her face. He got off his horse.

He began to ask a question, then checked himself. It was all too clear what she was trying to do.

He came up to her. Her face was lowered, and he wondered if she wept. He reached out and took her right hand, unwrapped the sash she had used to protect it. The large blister had popped, soaking the blue wool with a darkened, wet spot. He dropped her hand.

His voice was low, even solemn.

"I know what you are trying to do. But why?"

The round chin lifted. "There will be war," she told him.

Hrald began to speak, to counter her assertion, but it died in his throat. He too feared war was near at hand.

Ashild went on, her eyes bright, her words strong. "I would protect myself. Mother, Ealhswith. And Aunts Æthelthryth and Eanflad – "

She stopped there. They both knew their aunts had been ravished as girls by invaders. Their grandmother, now a nun at Oundle, had suffered the same violation.

Hrald was looking from tree to her. "But a spear…"

"I will not stand by, cowering, with only a knife to fight with." This was a retort, and she let her anger show in it.

He nodded. He could not but take her seriously.

He looked at her, as if sizing her up. She was smaller than any of the men of Four Stones, but not smaller than some of their sons, who were training.

"If you throw from a run you will have more power behind it," he said. "You are fast, and your speed will help propel your throw." He looked around again, as if finding answers for her in the straggly bushes. "Let go the idea of throwing a spear, to start. Holding it in two hands, fighting man-to-man, you can do real damage with your quickness; cripple a man."

She let out a breath. He was neither chiding nor shaming her. He wanted to help.

He went towards the tree and reclaimed the thrown spear. He came back to her and hefted it in one large hand.

"And you need a smaller, lighter spear, one sized for your height and weight." He smiled. "This one suits Jari, or me."

"Will you have some made for me?"

He paused a moment, then nodded his assent. She could not go to the weapon-smith and ask such a thing.

He passed the spear to her, saw the pain in her face just taking it from him. "Let me teach you," he urged. "First you must wait until your hand heals."

She nodded in return. She dare not admit how her shoulder ached.

They stood together a moment. It was cold and the wind picking up. From overhead in the elm came the cawing of a rook, sounding cold itself.

"I was looking for you," he told her.

She turned her eyes back to him.

He must get it out, and did so quickly.

"Thorfast asked leave to come see you. He wants you as his wife."

"Ugh," she grunted. She flung the spear at the tree; it hit the rim of the shield with a dull clang before falling to the ground on one side.

"A glancing blow. That is good," said her brother, trying to praise. She had thrown it with fury, and all he could do was keep talking.

"Do not be angry. I allowed it, out of respect for you. I would not say Yes or No for you; you know that."

She tossed her head back, then rolled her shoulders. She was older than Hrald, and she was being the child to his adult.

"I thank you," she said. She gave him a fierce hug before they both turned to retrieve the spears.

When Thorfast arrived to see Ashild, he had only ten men at his back. All at Four Stones knew the numbers he could command to ride with him. There was no need for show, and just then he judged, no need for caution. He and Hrald had riders enough all through their lands to warn of sudden approach. Coming with few men made him seem the abler, he thought; showed his confidence and courage. And the feeding and housing of a few men and horses eased the burden on his host.

He had sent a rider ahead, to tell Hrald he would arrive by sunset next day. By this point all the family knew it as a courting-call.

"Ach! Hold still and let me comb it out," Burginde was urging. She was standing over Ashild, whose head was bent over a copper basin on the table in Ælfwyn's bower house. The hair-washing was almost complete, and while Ashild's hair floated loose in the lavender-scented water was the easiest time for the nurse to address the knots and tangles.

"Make haste; my back is breaking," grumbled the object of her ministrations. Ashild had been nearly growling with first impatience, and now discomfort. Still bent almost double, she stamped one foot. At last allowed up, Burginde wrapped the soaking head in a towel. Ashild snatched the wooden comb from the nurse's hands; she would not suffer through Burginde's combing it dry.

"Mind you comb it through," Burginde warned. "I'll not have you thrummy-headed as an unshorn ewe!"

Ashild's mother looked up from the pile of gowns lying on her bed. The small fire-pit had been heaped with charcoal, and Ashild neared it. The maid wore nothing but her shift, and Ælfwyn could see she was chilled; the fine hairs on her arms standing. She stepped forward with a mantle to wrap her in.

"The red, or the blue? Or perhaps the green?" her mother wanted to know, tilting her head to the wealth of choices hiding the coverlet.

It was not easy for her mother, Ashild knew this, and anyone hearing the quiet tones of Ælfwyn's voice would know it too. There was no trace of excitement in it, no happy anticipation for the sake of her offspring. And Ashild was uncertain enough about the visit to echo her mother's concern.

"It matters little," she answered, but with no tartness. "He is not coming here for me. He is coming for Four Stone's sake, and his own."

Burginde was in the act of wringing out the washing-cloths she had used, the still-warm water dribbling back into the basin beneath her strong hands.

"Not here for you! Then dress me up in one of them, and let us see if it matters!"

Mother and daughter both had to smile at her. Turning back to Ælfwyn, Ashild watched the corners of her mother's beautiful mouth relax. Despite the heaviness in Ælfwyn's heart she worked to keep her mood light. Ashild saw her now turn slightly away from her daughter's gaze.

"Choose that which gives you most pleasure," she advised, opening her hand to the gowns.

Ælfwyn retreated a few steps, watching her cloaked daughter yank the comb through her wet hair. She picked up a stool and brought it close to the fire-ring's heat.

"Let me," she softly offered, taking the comb from Ashild's hand. The girl sat before her, and Ælfwyn plucked out bits of dried lavender flowers from the water-darkened hair. A few minutes passed in silence as she gently combed, drawing the damp hair over her daughter's shoulders.

"This choice must be yours, Ashild," came her mother's voice near her ear. "I will not ask you to turn one way, or another."

Standing behind her as she was, she could not see the tears well in her daughter's eyes.

Much had already been spoken. A few days earlier Asberg had asked Ælfwyn for a word. He and Jari had followed her into the treasure room. They all knew that Thorfast would be coming, and would hope for immediate answer.

The three of them stood, the subject too grave to admit sitting. Two men wanted Ashild as wife. One meant union with Wessex, and its King, through Ceric; the second the strengthening of the alliance between Thorfast and Four Stones.

They had not gone deep into the matter when Ælfwyn looked about her. "I will bring Ashild," she declared. "We will not speak of her life without her present."

She returned from the upstairs weaving room with her daughter. Since Hrald had told her of Thorfast's suit Ashild had spent much time turning the matter in her mind. Now her uncle and Hrald's body-guard weighed in.

"Thorfast is nephew to our dead King," Asberg pointed out. "If he proves able, he could be King himself." He paused a moment to look directly at his niece. "And you, his Queen."

Ashild a Queen. All were silent. What Asberg said was true, but the obstacles to such an outcome were many.

"Guthrum still has sons," Ælfwyn said. "Thorfast would have them to overcome, or to convince join him."

Jari was nodding his head. "Then there is Haesten, and after Haesten, his own sons, to consider," he countered. "If he truly has the forces we have heard, Haesten could try to take all of Anglia." His head turned to look at each before him. "Even beyond."

This meant war on a scale that had not been seen before.

Ælfwyn could not countenance that now. "If Ashild chooses Ceric, that means Ælfred himself is tied to us. He has been the greatest of Kings, and always honoured the Peace. The reward for our honouring what he and Guthrum created will be his favour."

Ashild looked from face to face, each with their own concerns, known expectations, and private fears. It was dizzying. She could be a Queen. Or an abject captive. Or soon dead. And possibly anything she did would make no difference.

In the silence that followed Ælfwyn had bethought her something else. "Thorfast is no Christian; he has not been baptised. Thus it would be left to Ashild to persuade him to conversion, and to assure their children were raised in the light of God's Truth. This is a task which perhaps she does not wish to take on."

She watched her daughter's eyes widen, perhaps less at the reminder of her suitor's heathen state than at the freighted role of bringing Christianity to Turcesig.

Ashild found herself speaking. "Why is Hrald not here? He will be Jarl, he should be here."

Her elders had meant to discuss Ashild's future amongst themselves. Ælfwyn had expanded the circle by insisting Ashild be present. But her brother, destined to rule all of South Lindisse, was absent.

Ælfwyn was the one to answer. "He is still young."

Ashild gave her head a single shake.

"He is older than you know."

Much was discussed that day, nothing determined. Hrald was brought and listened quietly. Ashild too said nothing; she did not need to. She knew both her mother and brother wished her to wed Ceric. What she felt about the second heir of Kilton seemed almost beside the point now. It was easier to picture happiness with Ceric than it was to picture happiness at Kilton. If he could come and live with her here at Four Stones as he had when they were but children she thought she find joy in being his wife. But the man could not be parted from the place.

Her hair was dry, her mother's hands smoothing it down her back.

"I will wear the red gown," she told her mother.

Thorfast rode through the palisade gates bringing an exceptional gift. He came first, leading by a tie-rope a pure white horse. It was a stallion, bearing the thick arched neck, heavily-muscled haunches, and long mane and tail that marked it as a worthy stud. Upon its back was girthed a saddle of wood and leather, the leather inset with silver medallions, the wood of the cantle rimed with silver braiding. The bridle on the noble creature's head and the long reins were fashioned of green-dyed leather. The head and cheek-piece of the bridle were again studded with lozenges of stamped silver.

The ten men he rode with came next, but all eyes were upon Thorfast and the prize he led. The family of Four Stones were gathered to greet him, but even those working in the yard at their varied tasks stopped in their labours and whistled in exclamation at the sight at the snow-white stallion.

"Look what he brings you," muttered Asberg into Hrald's ear. "A worthy brother-in-law, and brother-in-arms."

Once off his horse Thorfast handed the lead to the stallion to one of his men. He came to Hrald, who had stepped forward to meet him. They embraced each other, as they ever had. He then passed to Asberg, who greeted him warmly.

"Lady Ælfwyn," Thorfast said next. He was smiling, and nodded his head to her as she dipped her own in welcome.

Ælfwyn saw he had made no little effort. He was as finely dressed as for a Twelfth Night feast, in a dark green woollen tunic embellished with thread-work in yellow and blue. For a man with no wife nor mother, he had skilled women at hand to so adorn his clothing. His mantle was of a rich and mellow brown, lined with dark fur such as otter. His short boots were new, and of a deep brown, the toggles fixing them about the ankles small chunks of squared amber.

He now stood before Ashild, gowned in red, with a mantle of thick blue wool over her shoulders. He was smiling, and she could not help but smile as well, despite the awkwardness of standing there before him with all eyes upon them. But he took it lightly, and she would try to match his ease. She dipped her head. He inclined his own, and said only, "Ashild."

It was the way he spoke it. He had used her name countless times in the past; they had seen each other at many feasts and gatherings. There was gravity in how he used it now, gravity and purpose. She found herself casting her eyes down.

When she lifted them she saw him turn back to his men, take the tie-rope to the stallion. Thorfast was again smiling at Hrald. But he walked past her brother. Ashild stood as their guest came back to her, the huge beast at his shoulder. She could hear the soft snorting breath of the stallion as he stopped.

"My gift to you, Ashild," Thorfast told her. He extended the tie-rope to her.

She had never beheld a creature of such magnificence. And Thorfast, who wished to wed her, now gave it to her.

She showed her startle, there was no way she could not. The white stallion would have been a remarkable gift for her brother, and beyond; one worthy of a great war-chief or a King. And women did not ride stallions. Those who rode at all rode geldings or the less testy of the mares. She felt her cheek flame, despite her efforts to control the warmth rushing to her face. She became aware of the undercurrent of surprised murmuring from those in the yard watching. It stirred her to action. She took a breath. With all eyes upon them she had no choice but to accept it.

She said what had come to mind when he first rode through the gates with it.

"I have never seen a more beautiful horse."

His face, which had been held in a look of expectant confidence, creased into a smile.

Yet she had not lifted her hand in acceptance. Still smiling he reached his own to hers. She responded, and took the tie-rope into her own hand.

The party was then welcomed into the hall with ale. There was still an hour or more before the evening meal would gather all together. Thorfast and his men would sleep in the second hall, and after they had stowed their packs Hrald and Asberg and Jari took Thorfast out to the falcon mews, to view the birds before dusk sent the raptors to early sleep. In the morning they would hawk together.

Ashild found herself out by the paddock attached to the lead-roofed horse stable. Mul had already freed the stallion from its bridle and saddle, ever remarking on the beast's soundness and value. They stood together now, watching his massive form glow even brighter in the dimming light of dusk. Mul would be up early, and ride the newcomer first, just to ascertain its manners; he would not risk the young Lady of Four Stones on an untried beast, regardless of her skill as rider. But this he kept to himself; no need to raise the hackles on a filly as spirited as she.

"There is no reckoning his worth, Lady," Mul told her, as they watched the fine, dark-muzzled head lower to the stubble.

And no way to gauge what will happen, Ashild thought in response.

At the feast that night Ashild, gowned in her dress of red wool, sat, as she ever did, at the women's table. She was aware at times of Thorfast's eyes upon her, as he sat next Hrald. She saw her mother smile at her guest, gracious as always. She knew Hrald laughed and jested with Thorfast as if his visit was of no special consequence. She also saw her brother seemingly recollect why Thorfast was really there, saw his young brow cloud as he looked over at her. She smiled her reassurance at him, one she did not herself feel.

As she lay awake in bed that night images filled her mind. The great stallion browsed in the paddock in the little moonlight; a prize with her name on it. It still surprised her. It was compliment to her skill as a rider, and acknowledgement of her true interests. It showed Thorfast had thought long on what to offer her, an honour itself. But there was as well a kind of cunning in the thought behind this gift. Thorfast meant to flatter her by it, to underscore what she thought of herself. She saw that.

The image of rustling, shimmering silk next entered her brain, a golden pile lying safe in a chest in her mother's bower house. Ceric had brought her a gown, to delight and adorn a woman. A silken gown, that would also give him pleasure to see her in. Wearing it, she felt older, more stately. And she could not forget how his face changed when he looked at her; he looked a man. There was a difference in these two gifts, and not a small one, she felt.

She lay there, waiting for sleep. She shifted, and the heavy silver hammer of Thor slid between her breasts. It sometimes hurt her in her sleep, digging into her tender flesh. Yet she could not take it off, as she did the small golden cross each night. She closed her hand over it instead, feeling the rounded metal edges of the hammer-shape through the roughness of her palm.

In the morning she was invited to join her brother and his guest at hawking. Mul had the new stallion ready-saddled, and as he busied himself with Hrald's and Thorfast's mounts Ashild placed her hands upon the beast. Its slightly snorting breath and the warmness of its muscles told her something. She looked to Mul, as his head appeared over the saddle on Hrald's horse he was cinching.

"You have run him," she accused, with a smile.

"That I have Lady," he confessed. "He be fit for you. Mind his strength, though."

Mul loves me, she thought, wants no harm to come to me, just as he loves his boys. She had at times in her young life known she was cared for by those who served her at Four Stones. This morning Mul's small gesture of concern filled her chest with a wave of aching gratitude.

There were two mounting blocks by the stable wall, and with the stallion she need use the higher of them; he was that much bigger than her mares and geldings. She was already mounted and riding the animal about the paddock when Hrald and Thorfast joined her. They opened the gate for her, grinning, and she trotted out and held her horse as they swung up themselves. She felt her face warm once again at Thorfast's smile, and was glad when they started for the falcon house.

Once again she took the female falcon to her wrist. It was now fully trained, and when the three of them reached the fields flanking the stream it easily knocked a fat and fluttering partridge back onto the ground. Hrald's hawk too downed a bird, but they stayed long before that Thorfast carried made a strike. It flit after a lurching starling, only to be distracted by a ruddy-coated squirrel that leapt suddenly within view. It closed its talons on neither. At last it made a kill of one of the many blackbirds that sprang from the tattered grasses.

They rode back, their cheeks reddened with the cold and fresh air. The wicker basket at the side of Hrald's saddle carried the prey each had taken. Ashild found herself between the two men, their horses walking at an easy pace. On hers she was as tall as she had ever been. They spoke little; now that the hunt was over she felt lost for anything to say.

At last Thorfast spoke.

"He goes well?" he asked, indicating the stallion she rode.

"Very well," she agreed. "And steady, too, when your bird dipped low after the squirrel."

Thorfast's own horse had shied at that, and he nodded his head. A moment passed, one during which she knew he was still looking at her.

"Steady is good," he noted.

Unspoken was the rest of his thought, she knew: that he was also steady. Or perhaps she. At that moment she felt many things, but not steady.

She was glad when he turned his face again towards the palisade they neared. He would be here a day more perhaps, and would expect an answer. She did not know what it would be.

She felt she did not truly know Thorfast, had not the months of living and playing together with him as she had with Ceric. She had seen him more often in recent years than earlier ones. It was Hrald who knew him better, had hunted with him, spent time at weapon-play.

If Thorfast had not the striking colouring and good looks of Ceric, he had manliness, and was a full four-and-twenty. He was not so tall as Hrald, few men were; but he walked and moved with sureness. His brow was broad, the eyebrow ridge prominent, the nose large but straight, the jaw well-defined, his teeth even and white. His hair was like her own, a honey brown, lightened with a few pale streaks. Of his eyes she was not so sure; even being as close as she had been to him when he handed her the lead to the stallion, she had not looked long enough to judge. If he was not a man a maid would secretly gaze after, he was also not one whose looks could be disparaged.

They returned the falcons to their mews, and handed their yield over to a plump and smiling cook in the kitchen yard. Mul was at the stable to meet them, and held her stallion as she lowered her foot to the block she had used.

"I will be wanted in the weaving room," she told them. It was not strictly true; all knew this was a visit unlike any others, and the day would not unwind like others either. But she took her leave, just the same.

Ealhswith ran to her when she walked within. "Next time you will let me come, and ride him too," she pleaded. Ashild gave her a squeeze.

"You may sit on the saddle before me. Next time," she promised.

Their mother was not there, only her Aunt Eanflad, working soundlessly at her loom. Ashild guessed the demands of another feast that night had called her mother away from her spinning and weaving.

In fact, the Lady of Four Stones was in the treasure room. That morning Thorfast had asked that he might speak with her and Hrald and his uncle on their return from the field, and they were ready for him. It was cold in the room, and three braziers of pierced brass had been filled with glowing charcoals and brought in to warm the place. If they did, perhaps none within the room were aware; their heightened alertness alone warmed them.

The four of them sat at the small table in the centre of the room, Burginde on a stool off by the long-neglected bed. Four cups of silver stood upon the table, with a carved silver ewer of ale. Ælfwyn poured out first for Thorfast, then for her son, and then for Asberg and herself. The handle of the ewer was wonderfully formed, a crane turning its long beak back over its body. It had grown slightly worn under Ælfwyn's touch over the years, and its smoothness helped calm her.

Their guest needed no prompting to begin.

"I am aware another seeks Ashild's hand. But he is away in Wessex. I am ready to act, and now.

"You know that Guthrum has given me Turcesig, and its nearly one hundred twenty men, and all the livestock attached to it. Haward my brother has our family hall, and the eighty good men there. Our rents from our father's lands we have divided, two shares to Haward's one, as I am older. These rents bring me nearly one hundred pounds of silver a year, and the rents from Turcesig more than double this."

Asberg was nodding his head; it was a great sum. And Thorfast had no mother nor sister. However Thorfast ended up, Ashild would begin married life as the lady of a considerable hall.

As if he had read her uncle's mind, Thorfast went on. "You will agree Ashild will come to a hall of both comfort, and safety."

"She comes from such, and will go to nothing less," returned Asberg. He took another draught of ale, awaiting Thorfast's next words. He had to admire their guest. Most men his age had fathers or uncles to bargain with, and for them, when it came to the buying of a wife. Thorfast must do so unsupported, and did it well. Asberg recalled he had been married once before, and felt that counted in his favour; he knew how to treat a woman.

Thorfast drew breath before his next words. "If you will, in respect, name her bride-price, we may see how it can be met."

Hrald had sat silent, holding the footed stem of his silver cup loosely in his hand. Now Thorfast had made formal offer, as quickly as that. He found himself blinking his eyes. He looked to his mother, saw the slightly parted lips, her concern written plainly on her face. Too little had been said to proceed to the question of bride-price. And Thorfast had not yet spoken to Ashild.

Hrald must speak, and he did.

"Ashild – she has not yet accepted you," he said. Thorfast's confidence that she would, or that her objections would be overruled, troubled him, and it showed in his voice. But Hrald knew enough maids had no choice in this matter.

Thorfast took it without insult. "She accepted the stallion, which, I need not say, will be hers whether or not she consents."

This was true; a gift was a gift. Yet it was also true that a rich gift demanded another in return. Hrald and Asberg had already chosen the fine pattern-welded sword that Thorfast must be presented with.

Ælfwyn would speak now; all three men had done so, and she could without boldness enter in. She had been watching her guest with care. There was much of Thorfast that reminded her of Yrling; his directness, for one thing. Thorfast was more polished, to be certain. But looking on, and listening to him felt a faint echo of being in the presence of Ashild's father.

Her voice was as low and gentle as it ever was to Thorfast's ear; only Hrald and Asberg could detect the subtle strength behind its mild tone.

"Your gift was well-chosen to delight Ashild," she told her guest. "But there are considerations we have not yet touched upon."

Thorfast's eyebrows raised slightly at this.

"You have not been baptised, Thorfast. Our faith is important to us."

"O, but Lady, I was, as a boy," he returned.

His tone was such that made it clear his relief at so slight an objection. If he is a believer, thought the Lady of Four

Stones, he wears it but lightly. She had never seen in him, nor at his father's hall, even a hint of true observance.

Ælfwyn let his answer stand unchallenged. She went on, slowly, but in the same low tone. "Hrald's father Sidroc was part of the Peace that Guthrum made with Ælfred. That Peace has endured over long years, and Four Stones has thrived. As Guthrum thrived. And now, his nephew."

Hrald was watching his mother's face, and knew the courage it took for her to broach this. He did not want to make her ask the question which must be asked. He looked Thorfast in the eye.

"Will you honour the Peace, Thorfast?" he asked.

Asberg was enough taken aback to make a small sound of surprise. Thorfast gave a short shake of his head, but was ready with his answer.

"Guthrum is dead. Haesten has landed, ready to unify a great force. Surely he will strike in the Spring, or Summer at the latest. The time is now for us to join together, Four Stones and Turcesig. Together we can gather even more men – Agmund and other of my cousins – and either defeat Haesten, or share with him in the spoils of all Wessex, and all Angle-land."

It was much to hear. Even Asberg found himself leaning back from the table, as if to slow the words and their meaning.

Hrald was trying to shape his next question when Thorfast spoke again.

"There will be war, either with Haesten if we do not join him, or Wessex if Ælfred decides to strike while we are in disarray."

"The King of Wessex will not break his own Peace," Hrald protested.

"That Peace was made with my dead uncle," Thorfast reminded.

But Hrald's father was not dead, and he would recall Thorfast to this fact.

"The Peace was made also by my father. I will not break what he signed in blood."

This was said with enough force that all looked at him. Burginde, perched on her stool, winding wool thread, made a soft sound of assent, then shifted in her seat. She felt a flush of pride at Hrald's words, one she knew his mother shared.

Hrald's declaration proved a spur to Asberg's thoughts. Sidroc had been gone for a decade. He and Jari had upheld the trust that Sidroc had placed in them, keeping Four Stones for his son. But Sidroc the man was grown distant in his recollection. Only Hrald had recent memory of him, and that now several years old. Asberg had never been a match for Sidroc's powers of thought, and this he knew. He could not imagine how he would react to the new conditions they all found themselves in. Sidroc ever kept his word, yet was as shrewd as any. If he found need to change direction, he did so. And when pushed he could be ruthless. If he felt wronged, he would not fail to exact the utmost for the offense. Asberg had stood and watched as Sidroc had killed his own cousin, Toki.

Asberg had sometimes wondered if during that contest the faltering Toki could not have been offered quarter. But Toki did not ask, and Sidroc did not offer. They had both witnessed the slaying of their uncle, Yrling, at the hands of Godwin of Kilton. Asberg had been there too. But Sidroc had run after the man, determined to inflect what damage he could on the rapidly departing Lord of Kilton and his men. Toki had watched and fled for his horse, calling those near him to follow him in his claim for Four Stones.

The enmity between cousins ran deeper still, back to their contest for the chestnut-haired maid that had arrived with Ælfwyn; back before that to the knife-slash to Sidroc's face Toki had inflicted. Yet Asberg had seen Sidroc burn Toki's battered body with great honour, piling it with treasure, and seen too him make sacrifice to Odin on behalf of his dead cousin. Asberg could not hope to guess how a man of such conflicts would decide the matter before them.

Hrald's uncle broke the silence himself.

"We speak of war, but none can say if and when it may come. Ælfred may make a new Peace with Haesten; if that be so, Haesten will honour the Danelaw but come sniffing round to see which of the Danish keeps he can quietly overtake."

Thorfast was quick to leap on this waggon. "All the more reason why Four Stones and Turcesig be joined through marriage. I will tell you what I told Hrald: together we are an army of our own."

Ælfwyn could hold her tongue no longer. "Far better my daughter was away in Wessex, safe at Kilton!"

Thorfast snapped his head back at this, "Safe, Lady? Think you any place in Wessex will be safe if we cannot resist Haesten?"

He had spoken with more heat than he had meant. Even so, it must be said. He felt Ashild slipping away from him before he had ever asked her for her hand.

He tried another tack.

"Guthrum has daughters; my cousins. Three are yet unwed, and comely." He said this coolly, a simple recounting of fact. He alone knew the additional fact: Guthrum had left them nothing in his will. They could be married off for the sake of their blood, but their brothers would need to produce suitable dowries.

Thorfast too had choices; his hosts sitting down with him knew that. Yet all at that table knew Ashild would bring great treasure to her husband. The pride of Four Stones demanded it, and securing Ashild's place in her new home depended upon it.

Ælfwyn took a quiet and calming breath. She stood, and dipped the silver ewer over each waiting cup. She knew the bartering for a bride sometimes ended in bad feelings, even in blows. She would not do a disservice to her own daughter by muddying the waters before the bottom could be seen. As she filled Thorfast's cup, she smiled on him.

He lifted the cup to his lips, taking a mouthful of the good ale within, savouring it. He lowered his hand to the age-smoothed surface of the table, but kept it coiled round the cup.

"Have I leave to speak to Ashild," he asked.

It was voiced not to one, but to all of them.

"I do not even ask to know what her dowry will be. I will ask for her hand without knowing it."

This was so striking an offer as to be met with silence. Thorfast would enter blindly into his suit without knowing what Ashild would bring him. He went on, in firm assurance.

"My bride-price for her will be her weight in silver."

From behind her Ælfwyn heard Burginde gasp. She herself could not speak. The sum was so great, the gauging of it so bald.

Asberg let a low whistle escape his lips. Ælfwyn looked to him, looked past her brother-in -law to her son. She could not tell if Hrald had taken offense, or was merely stunned at the amount Thorfast offered.

A long moment went by, in which Ælfwyn's eyes were set on Thorfast. He was indeed like Yrling, in his boldness. And she recognised with a sobering pang that Ashild was far more like Thorfast than she was like Ceric.

Hrald straightened himself where he sat, and looked too at his guest.

"If she accepts you, she will arrive at Turcesig with fifty of our best horses," answered her brother.

Chapter the Fourteenth: The Bride-price, and the Bride

THE four at that small table were now all standing.

"Burginde, please to bring Ashild," asked Ælfwyn.

Burginde's knees unfolded, and creaked upright. She left her wool-ball on the wolf-skin spread covering the bed, and disappeared out the door.

Asberg was studying Thorfast's face, looking for signs of strain. The man was notably cool considering the trial he was under, and Asberg must admit it.

Asberg's eyes now went to his nephew. Hrald looked as uneasy as any who had ever pledged a vast treasure. Nearly a quarter of their horses would follow Ashild if she made the short journey to Turcesig. Hrald's bold offer was almost a challenge, and in any other instance Asberg would have protested so great a dowry. But Thorfast proposed nothing less than a single defence to be formed between Four Stones and Turcesig. And the bride-price he offered was something out of the Sagas, like unto a price offered for a Goddess. There was more than a touch of magic in his naming this Ashild's value to him. His thoughts strayed for a moment to what Wilgot the priest would say of such an offer; he would rail against it a heathen thing, he guessed.

Ælfwyn was holding the silver ewer in her hands. Its cool substance helped ground her own flitting thoughts. In a few moments her daughter's future might be decided, and by Ashild herself. She tried to take comfort in that one fact.

Burginde returned, Ashild in tow. The nurse resumed her stool, and again took up her wool-winding, eyes cast down at her work building up the ball of thread.

Ashild neared the table, then paused. All were looking at her; the air felt charged as if lightning were about to strike. Thorfast was nearest her, and she let her eyes meet his, bowing her head for an instant in greeting. Her eyes next sought her mother, who smiled at her, with lips pressed firmly together. Next she looked at Hrald.

His arms hung at his sides, his palms turned slightly towards her and open. He stood upright, yet there was a slackness about him, an uncertainty that showed not only in his stance but in the single furrow on his young brow. If they had been arguing her bride-price it should be Thorfast who looked so. She saw Hrald's eyes fasten on her face, and sensed the stress and pressure her brother bore for her sake.

Her uncle began to speak, just as Hrald too opened his mouth. Asberg yielded to his nephew. Despite the way her brother looked to her, Ashild could not but note the firmness in Hrald's voice.

"Thorfast has offered a great sum as your bride-price. If you accept him fifty head of horses will follow you to his hall."

Ashild lifted her chin higher at this news, and needed a moment to take it in. A maid's bride-price was set by her kin. Had Thorfast offered his own sum before they had named her price? And had Hrald truly agreed to send fifty of their horses with her? How great was the treasure Thorfast offered to make Hrald answer it in this way?

She knew Hrald did not want this marriage. Yet the discussion of terms was far advanced, with sums that seemed to have been accepted by both sides.

She stood biting her lower lip, watching her brother as he looked at her.

Her mother's soft voice now sounded. "We will leave you," she said, with a forced but tender smile at her daughter.

Ashild came to the table, where her mother kissed her brow.

"Take this," Ælfwyn told her, pressing her silver cup into her daughter's hand. Ælfwyn glanced to where Burginde sat, stolidly winding her wool. "Burginde will attend you."

The nurse settled herself more deeply on her cushion as her mistress, Hrald, and Asberg filed out. Before she lowered her eyes again Burginde gave a long and piercing look at the prospective couple as they stood, standing by the table. She had no reason to dislike Thorfast, other than the fact that Ælfwyn was intent on her daughter becoming the wife of Ceric of Kilton. And having Ashild near at hand would save them much of the heartbreak of separation. Being privy to Thorfast's appeal would allow her to more fully judge the man. Not that Ashild, strong-headed as she was, would take much heed of her opinion.

At the closing of the door all three were aware of the silence of the treasure room.

Ashild put down the cup. Thorfast cast a single glance at Burginde's lowered head, then spoke.

"I would like to wed you," he told Ashild, as simply as that.

She considered his choice of words. No pretty flights of fancy to frame his statement. Not even, Will you be my wife, but: I would like to wed you. It was almost as if he said, I would like Four Stones and its men to join me.

That was marriage of course, the joining of houses great or small, goods and treasure exchanged, pooled, and built upon. A maid was but a tool in this exchange. Yet she would have liked for him to have spoken differently.

He went on, not with ardency, but with sureness, one made seemly by his low tone of voice, and the apparent sincerity of his words.

"Your brother and uncle approve the price I have set upon you. Hrald himself told you the handsome dowry he places. Yet he insists the choice be yours.

"It is only right that that be so. You are the daughter of a great war-chief, and can command the attention of many men." The briefest of pauses, as he looked on her. "Men who find you as pleasing as I do."

This was handsomely said; simply, and without flattery. She felt a bit of warmth rushing to her cheek. Perhaps he did want her for herself.

Thorfast took a step closer to her. He moved enough so that when she looked at him, his torso blocked the old nurse sitting by the bed. It gave an illusion of the privacy they did not have.

It was closer than he had perhaps ever been to her, save for once having taken her hand at a Mid-Summer's-fire dance a few years ago. He was glad now when she lifted her head and looked him fully in the face.

He had never before noticed the colour of her eyes, a deep grey-blue, like the sheen of an oiled blade caught in uncertain light. His eyes traced the line of her face, as if seeing it anew. He let his gaze drop down her person.

His first wife had been a beauty, a fragile one. Ashild looked as if she could withstand the rigours of childbearing, and more. She had a certain attraction, and he was not today immune to it. She was unaffected, handy, and seemingly without fear; her way with the stallion he had just given her proved that.

An image came to him. He recalled last Winter at a Yule feast, watching her down an ox-horn full of mead in a single draught. She thought no one watching as she stood in the shadows, echoing the action of the rowdy men at their drinking contest. When she pulled the horn away from her lips she looked quietly satisfied, and surprised both, that she could do it. Her secret action had been caught by his eye, and it had excited him.

His thoughts strayed to picturing her as bed-mate; with these qualities and her innate lustiness she could prove a willing, even eager partner. He had to force the smile from his lips, considering this.

He thought then to take her hand, and reached for it. He lifted it in his own, felt the crinkled roll of dry skin in her palm. It made him open her hand as he held it. She had had a bad burn or blister, that was clear. He was going to remark on it when she closed her fist and drew the hand away. She did not wish to speak of it.

He would return to his quest.

"In the custom of your mother's people, all that I give to you will remain yours," he assured her. "If we should decide to part, or I die, my gifts to you are yours. And your dowry will be returned."

This was news indeed. Thorfast was a Dane, with no blood of Angle-land in his veins. She had assumed that if she wed a Dane here in Anglia she and her kin would abide by the traditions of Danish marriage-law. Other than no longer taking more than one wife, the men of the Danelaw had insisted on keeping the favourable terms of their homeland. Treasure sent with a bride to her new home remained in her husband's family, save those goods marked as strictly household items. Here he offered her the same broad protections the women of Wessex enjoyed.

"And it is time Siggerith had a mother." Ashild knew of his little daughter, a sweet slip of a girl she had seen at past gatherings. It touched her that he mentioned her now.

He saw this, saw her lips soften. Though she be a maid and young, he knew she was quick-witted. He felt certain she understood the breadth of his offer, the generosity of his terms.

Ashild's eyes had dropped to the table, and her mother's favourite silver ewer there. The gleaming ewer, the solid table, everything about her seemed more real and vivid, more demanding and worthy of her attention. She noticed, and almost wondered at, her calm. The quiet of the room, the lowness of his voice, the knowledge that Burginde was with her, yet out of sight, all must be serving her as she considered his words. Even the knowledge that the choice was hers to make gave her strength.

It was all here, at her fingertips: a chance for her to stay near Four Stones and her folk. A man known to her and her kin, and with whom she felt she could know ease. One whose liberality seemed beyond doubt, who had fashioned his offer to meet and overcome every objection she or her family might have. A man who might even be King…

She could extend her hand back to Thorfast, and he would grasp it.

She brought her palms together instead, then let the fingers of her right hand fold over that healing skin in her palm, reminder of the deep and painful blister she had caused herself flinging a spear. Her need to be able to defend herself rose anew in her breast.

He had spent these few moments studying her face. She had, as yet, said nothing, and was, he knew, weighing all in her mind as she listened.

He dropped his voice still lower. "What…what keeps you from accepting my offer? Your kin and I have come to terms."

She seemed moved to speak, but stayed herself. He filled the silence with another question.

"Seeing you handle the stallion while we hawked makes me think we are well suited. Do you not agree?"

This opened her mouth. She had in fact not thanked him for the gift. She had had no choice but to accept it; to have refused such treasure in public view would have been an insult. But she was fully aware of how her acceptance of the horse implicated her.

"The stallion is magnificent. But I wish you had not brought him to me."

Having said this she did not know what more she could say. She saw his surprise, and did not wish to voice aloud her fear that his gift had been chosen almost to ensnare her.

She thought of Hrald's face and stance when she had walked in, Hrald who loved her, Hrald who also loved Ceric. Both Hrald and her mother desired her for Ceric, even though it meant her perhaps never seeing them again.

As unseemly as it was, she must tell him he was not alone in pursuing her.

"There is another who seeks my hand."

Thorfast was ready. "Ceric of Kilton. He whom I saw when I rode here with news of Guthrum's death."

So Hrald, or her mother, had told him. She nodded, gave herself time to take a breath. "We do not yet know what his terms will be. But he has told Hrald it will be great treasure. For Hrald's sake, and the sake of Four Stones, I must wait for that. I must wait, before I decide."

He saw his advantage, and would press it.

"For Hrald's sake," he repeated. "If you love your brother and your home, you will wed me. There is no better way to aid Hrald."

Her chin had lifted at his words, but he saw the acknowledgement flash in her eyes.

He met her look with new urgency in his voice.

"You are no common woman, Ashild. You seek to strengthen Hrald, protect Four Stones. Your heart is here. Would you allow yourself to be thrown away in Wessex? And why? A boyhood bond between your brother and a man who will not even be Lord of Kilton. As my wife you will be Lady of Turcesig, from the first day you come to me.

"Think you who I am, Ashild. Kingship runs in my blood. My uncle, Guthrum, conquered half this great land, became King. Guthrum was nephew to King Horic, King of all Dane-mark. Fate works in threes. If Turcesig and Four Stones join as one, little can stop us. We can meet any threat from Haesten. Even defeat Ælfred, if it comes to that."

She recoiled. He had spoken in some haste, and could not now recall those last words.

She drew herself up, stiffened before him. "We have a Peace with Ælfred, with Wessex. He has been too great a warrior to defeat, all Danes have seen this. My mother is of his land." She recollected herself, then went on. "I have my mother's blood, am of Wessex too…"

"Do not think on Ælfred," he urged, silently cursing himself for having named the King in the first place. "Think of Haesten, biding his time in the South, plotting how he will carve up Anglia, so much to those who join him. And death or slavery to those who oppose him."

Ashild heard a small sound behind him, Burginde stifling herself. It helped quell the fear rising in her breast, one that had closed her throat. She forced a breath out between lips that were nearly clenched. And he put so much on her head; it was not fair. She let her anger rise, beating back her fear.

"We must wait for Ceric to return," she found herself saying. "I must wait for that."

He had lost. His eyes darted into the darker corners of the room. He shrugged his shoulders with a discernable sigh. He would salvage what he could; they must part friends so that her mind stayed open.

"I will wait for you, Ashild," he conceded. "And I will tell Hrald and Asberg that in addition to what I have already offered, all that Ceric of Kilton brings to win you, I will match."

He saw her lip tremble then, whether through fear or strain he could not tell.

"For Hrald's sake, as well as your own, I will wait for your answer," he repeated.

She stood clutching her hands before her, her shoulders pinched. He saw the tremour in her lip extend to her entire body.

He could not leave her like this. He gestured to the table, and the ale cup her mother had pressed into her hand.

"Will you drink with me, Ashild, to seal that promise?"

She reached for it, a thing of wrought silver studded with garnets below the smooth rim, the stones as red and round as drops of blood. She passed it to him, watched as he took a sip.

He handed her the cup. "In friendship," he promised.

She nodded, held the cup to her lip. The ale was Four Stones' best, rich and almost creamy. She let it fill her mouth before she swallowed.

"In friendship," she answered, her voice hovering above a whisper. Their eyes met a moment, and she felt the water come into her own as she looked at him. This was a man whose tie to Four Stones could indeed mean more than anything, or anyone, else.

When he left the room Burginde was still rising to her feet when Ashild flung herself into her arms, weeping.

Chapter the Fifteenth: The Summons

Kilton and Four Stones

EDWIN OF KILTON stood before his King. He was a Winter's child, and it fell his fifteenth birthday. Ælfred sat before him in the great carved oak chair that had been Godwulf's, the grandsire Edwin had never known. Next him, in her own chair, sat the aged Modwynn, Godwulf's widow, Lady of Kilton.

Ceric stood off to one side, his aunt, Edgyth at his left, Worr at his right. Their heads turned now at the approach of the warrior-monk Cadmar, walking with measured step from the treasure room, bearing in his arms the weapons that the King of Wessex would now bestow upon Edwin.

It was almost five years since Ceric had received his own weapons. Though Ælfred was Ceric's godfather he had not been there to watch Ceric receive them, but away riding from burh to burh, as he almost always was. It was meet and right that the King be here today, and he had, all knew, taken pains to be so. Edwin was not his god-child, but Edwin would be Lord of Kilton. Ælfred presenting him with a sword, and naming him such, would make it so.

Ceric found his hand rising to his sword-hilt, recalling Modwynn passing the precious thing to him. Godwulf's sword was his, and he was Godwulf's heir through it, as well as through his blood. The fact that the sword had been given long ago by Ælfred's father to Godwulf tightened the bond between sword, monarch, and he who now wore it.

As Cadmar moved closer Ceric looked to his younger brother, eyes fixed on the massive form approaching him. He felt pride for Edwin's sake, and if he searched his heart, also a touch of envy. But Edwin was so good and true a brother that that baser emotion could be brushed aside. Ceric knew Edwin admired him, patterned himself after him. As a boy Edwin had watched with eager eyes all Ceric did, a sometimes onerous burden to the older brother. And in fact just a short time ago Edwin had seemed a child to him. Now he looked almost a man. He was already nearly as tall as Ceric, and the breadth of his shoulders foretold that once he filled out, he would be bigger. His hair was the same coppery-gold, his eyes a similar green. But the face differed. Folk had always told Ceric he favoured his mother. He had little memory of their maimed father's looks, but felt Edwin must favour him.

Worr, standing at Ceric's side, also considered Edwin. His eyes travelled to what Cadmar bore in his arms, the seax and sword of Godwin of Kilton. It had been Worr who had received the dead lord's weapons first, far away on a Baltic island, and it was his sacred trust to carry them back to Kilton, awaiting this very day.

"He has a son," the scarred Dane had told Worr, as he surrendered the treasure of steel to him.

The words were sounding again in Worr's ear as he looked back to Edwin. A son by adoption, all knew; the son of the Lady Ceridwen and Gyric, Godwin's younger brother.

Yet studying Edwin's young face, Worr saw how he resembled his uncle Godwin, as if the Lord of Kilton had been his true father. This sudden thought jolted him, so much that he found himself trying to dismiss it before it could take hold in his mind.

It was no good. Once again he was back at the Dane's hall, sitting in the hot sunlight, looking into a barn at a bloodied pile of straw on which his Lord's body lay. He had heard that which forced him to ask the widow of Gyric a question he dreaded the answer to. Yes, she had told him. Godwin had entered her bed. For four nights, during the most dire part of the struggle to contain the Danes.

He found himself reckoning backwards the years, gauging if it were possible that Edwin was in fact the natural son of Godwin. It was only his warrior's strength of will that stopped him. He forced himself to look to Godwin's widow, Edgyth, the gentlest and most learned of women. She revered the memory of her dead husband, and that also of her former sister-in-law, whom she had taken joy in knowing was in fact alive and safe. Edgyth, a famed healer, was of fragile health herself. A betrayal of this degree might kill her.

And who or what did such speculation serve? It could not be proved, and could only cause pain to the living. Ceric appeared to feel both pride and protection towards Edwin; accepted the fact that Edwin and not he had been given over to be heir. Ceric did not need proof of Edwin's claim, to honour it.

Cadmar had stopped now before the King, and dropped on one knee. He passed the sword and seax into the King's lap, and withdrew.

All eyes were upon the King, save Modwynn's, which shone on her younger grandson. At a nod from her Edwin stepped forward.

Ælfred spoke.

"Edwin, come now and take up the arms of Godwin, Lord of Kilton, and with them his hall and men. May you bear them with honour in service to Christ, service to Wessex, and service to your King."

Weapons were passed from King to the new Lord. Edwin bowed his head, and clutched the bright things to his breast. Modwynn's eyes were glittering, but she raised them to look at Ceric. He nodded back at her. Of all there perhaps she knew best the stirrings within him, brotherly pride and envy mingled.

Edwin now received the King's embrace, and that of Modwynn. Next he turned to Ceric, and it was Ceric he asked to help arm him. The thegns of the hall encircled them, cheering when Ceric stepped away and Edwin stood alone, resplendent in his war-kit.

"How like your uncle you have grown," Ælfred told Edwin later, toasting cups of mead together, joined by Kilton's most trusted men. "I almost feel that Godwin himself stands before me."

Ælfred was at Kilton only two full days. Ceric had seen the King on and off through Fall and Winter, including the long but fast ride to Middeltun to meet Haesten. It was during those months that Ceric first joined in the defence of Wessex. He was gone two months, riding off with Worr and his pledged men, to serve mostly under command of Eadward, the King's son. He had seen no action during that time, but they had twice, near the Anglian border, come upon signs of marauding Danes, come over to despoil two hamlets that lay at the edge of Wessex. As second at Kilton Ceric would continue to ride with the Prince, while Edwin would soon take his place at the side of the King with the other lords of great burhs.

On the third day at Kilton Ceric and his thegns would leave with the King, riding with him as far as Cirenceaster, and then split off to again join Eadward. While the King remained with them Ceric begged a moment of his time. With Modwynn present the three met in the treasure room, joined by Raedwulf, the bailiff of Defenas, who was traveling with the King.

"My King, I would wed Ashild of Four Stones, and ask your blessing upon that union, and permission to fetch her as soon as my tour of duty with Eadward, Prince, has ended."

Ælfred had been prepared to hear this, through private converse with Ceric's grandmother the night before, and had been thinking on both request and response. He was of course aware of his godson's long connection with Four Stones. The King's own gift of the illuminated Psalter to the girl's mother was intended not only as response to that lady's benefactions to the religious foundation at Oundle, but to endorse any prospective marriage between the halls. The King's benevolent expression remained unchanged as Ceric made his petition. Both he and his grandmother were surprised by his answer.

"I will bless your union, but I cannot allow your travel across Kingdoms."

The King had been sitting well back from the table, his long fingers steepled together, as he listened to Ceric. He now dropped his hands and leant forward towards his hosts.

"I said 'Kingdoms,'" he went on, "but in truth there is but one Kingdom now, and that is Wessex. East Anglia has no King. No son of Guthrum has proved strong enough to take his father's mantle, none of the many war-lords who signed the Peace have gathered allies enough to make a move to unify. Now that Haesten – whose ambitions are without bounds – has landed, his wiles and repute will likely find him leader of the great force of restless Danes ever-crowding the Eastern shores. They number those beyond even his own encampment. And despite his vow to me, his men have repeatedly ridden into Wessex, and raided our border villages."

It was further proof of the malleable quality of Danish vows. Haesten had accepted the King's gifts of gold and silver, and offered up hostages of his own in bond. A lesser King would have sent the heads of those hostages back to Haesten now, in answer to his duplicity.

Ælfred turned from the greater dilemma to the smaller. He shifted his gaze to address Ceric alone.

"The ride to Four Stones will entail your travel with much riches from Kilton, and a large troop of men to guard it. This is travel through a land in which the Peace and its many laws are no longer honoured. Then you must return with the maid, bearing her dowry, a second treasure."

The King looked fully at his godson. "I cannot risk it. I cannot risk you."

Ceric was speechless. He had spoken long with Worr and Cadmar about the venture, had together considered its dangers, had determined that with precautions it could be done. He looked now to Raedwulf, who he had hoped would join him. He understood now why Raedwulf had said little last night at Edwin's symbel when he had asked him for his company, and to stand with him as the bride-price was named.

Threat of full-scale war must be near indeed for Ælfred to so forbid a quest that would strengthen Kilton, and Wessex. The King watched Ceric's eyes go to Raedwulf in entreaty.

The bailiff cleared his throat.

"May I propose, my Lord, an alternate. Ceric of Kilton and his men place themselves in undue risk by riding across Anglia. But Ashild of Four Stones could ride in relative safety with a troop of her own men, right to the Wessex border, where they could be met by Ceric."

All were looking at Raedwulf now. It was his role in life to search out solutions, and he may have struck upon another.

Ceric was almost rising from his seat in his keenness to have the monarch endorse this plan. He restrained himself, looking hopefully from Raedwulf's face to the King.

As Ælfred considered, Ceric's mind raced ahead. He would be denied the pleasure of seeing Hrald, as he knew Hrald must stay at Four Stones, but other than that the plan seemed ideal. The men who delivered Ashild would ride back to Four Stones with her bride-price. He began to wonder who would do the bargaining on her part; her uncle, Asberg, of course…

Ælfred was ready with his answer. "Write your letter to the maid's kin. Have it ready when we ride tomorrow. I will be heading near the border-lands myself, and know a priest who will carry it to Four Stones in Lindisse."

A priest, thought the King, who was eager for martyrdom.

Less than a month later this same prelate, denied easy entry into Heaven, found himself and the young monk who accompanied him surrounded by the out-riders of Four Stones. They had been stopped six times by various patrols as they made their way across Anglia, but each time, having proved through rough search they carried no silver, had been allowed to progress on their way. Both were gowned in wool cassocks and bore the large crosses about their waists that proclaimed them men of Christ. If those crosses had been of silver and not wood they may have been relieved of them along their path. But the warriors who had stopped and questioned were Christian enough not to harm those in Holy Orders, at least not without hope of material gain.

It was Gunnulf and Onund and two others who spotted them, patrolling as they did the road from the West. The day was one of early Spring, of chill and grey-skies, with a fine mist in the air that almost obscured the steam from their horses' breath. The two strangers were each mounted on grey asses, which despite their diminutive size moved smartly enough along the wet and lightly sticky clay road.

Once he had overcome his consternation at being once again ridden at, spears pointing, the priest, whose name was Tatwine, expressed his gratitude to the warriors who now would lead them to their destination. At the same time he heaved a sigh. His instructions were to ride with the large body of men who would be summoned by the contents of the letter he bore, and enjoy their protection on his return to Wessex. His chances of being called to Heaven while fulfilling an errand asked him by the King were dwindling.

The patrol flanked the two men and rode to the palisade gates. Gunnulf shrugged off the aid of the watch-men nearer to the hall; the strangers were unarmed, and could be of little importance. Perhaps there would not even be a greeting-ale passed once they gained the hall; he did not know. Wilgot the priest would be glad to see more like him. Perhaps the letter the elder one told him he bore in his shoulder-pack was for him.

Still, when they arrived Gunnulf and Onund would complete their duty. The stable-man Mul appeared, his face wreathed in a smile at the two visitors, and ducked his head at them as he led their still-frisking asses to the stable for a rub-down. Mul told them Hrald and Asberg were not about the yard, and had not ridden out; perchance they were within the hall.

They were indeed in the treasure room. The door was closed, as it ever was, but the women about the hall standing at looms or spinning told Gunnulf so. Gunnulf knocked, calling out his own name.

Asberg opened. Gunnulf had the other two from the patrol wait outside, and with Onund and the men of God entered. Within that room of treasure they saw a long trestle table that had been carried inside, now laden with weaponry. Hrald turned from where he stood at the table, a sword in one hand, and gestured the four enter. Both he and Asberg were surprised at who Gunnulf escorted.

"Ælfred, King of Wessex sends you God's greeting, and his own," the priest began. "I am Tatwine, humble priest and servant of Christ. At Ælfred's bidding I bear a letter from his godson, Ceric of Kilton, for Hrald of Four Stones."

"I am Hrald," answered he. Tatwine was already fumbling in his pack. He withdrew a hardened tube of leather and passed into Hrald's hand.

"I thank you, Father," Hrald said. The round case was a new one, smooth and uncracked, the leather dyed madder-red.

Hrald looked to Gunnulf, who stood eyeing the wealth of swords and knives on the trestle. Onund, slightly behind Gunnulf, was craning his neck at the display.

Hrald nodded his dismissal at them. Despite their long friendship it was sometimes hard to look at Gunnulf, and seeing him with Onund was even harder. Here they stood next to two in Holy Orders. Hrald found himself glancing down at the floorboards for their sake.

A short time later Hrald sat with his mother, his older sister, and with Asberg at the small table in the treasure room. Their cassocked guests were having ale and loaves in the house of Wilgot, resting on cushions which had been brought for their further comfort.

Ashild had been called from the depths of the great stable, where she watched over one of her favourite mares, who was restlessly close to giving birth. It was the horse's first foaling, and though Mul kept assuring her all was progressing as it should, the mare's pacing and occasional snorting breaths kept her on edge. Now was come a missive from Ceric. Letters only came with great news, either good or ill.

Hrald pulled the furled parchment from the leathern tube. He straightened it in his hands, letting his eye drop upon it a moment. Then he began to read aloud.

"TO HRALD OF FOUR STONES

> My brother. Know that my King forbids my coming to Lindisse to claim your sister. Ælfred in his graciousness allows and endorses my union with Ashild, but judges the risks of travelling to Four Stones to be too great. Know that the Bailiff of Defenas, in aiding the union of our two halls, has proposed that Ashild travel to the Wessex border. There, at Bryeg, I will meet her and her party on St Elgiva's Day. Under the friendship and protection of Kilton and the King they will come to Kilton, where any terms you set for your sister's bride-price will be met. I know you cannot ride to bring her yourself, and this is a sorrow to me. Yet I rejoice in the thought of soon making Ashild my wife. She will be received with all honour by Modwynn, Lady of Kilton, and by Ælfred himself.
>
> I await Asberg and your party at Bryeg, on St Elgiva's Day. I convey my warm wishes and true friendship to your gracious mother, Lady Ælfwyn of Four Stones, and to little Ealhswith.

Silver Hammer, Golden Cross

Know I will see you again, Hrald.

CERIC OF KILTON"

Hrald lowered the letter, laid it down upon the table. Ceric had written it himself; he would know his friend's hand anywhere. The letters were small, round, thickly black with well-made ink. The hand was sure, the letters well-formed, but without artifice. He had lined the parchment but lightly, faint scratches showing on the creamy surface, and kept the many lines of his message straight and true upon them. If a man could be known from his letter, this told the truth of Ceric.

He cannot come, Hrald was thinking. He looked to Ashild, sitting opposite him. Her hair was mussed, and the apron she had covered her gown with was soiled with dark splotches. She carried the smell of the stable and her beloved horses with her. Her head was lowered, and he saw her eyebrows, a shade darker than her hair, knit together.

Ashild felt as if her heart was slowing in her breast. She had told Thorfast that she must wait for Ceric's return. Now he could not come, and instead sent for her. St Elgiva's Day was two months from now. Ceric could not know another had made active suit for her hand. He could not know how important his presence was, nor how Thorfast had challenged his bride-price offer by declaring his would always exceed it. She was forced to choose between one far, and one near. Going to Kilton meant giving deep joy to Hrald and to her mother. It also meant such a vast distance between her and her kin that she might never see them, and all she loved about Four Stones, again.

Thorfast was near, rich, and wanted her. She could not forget his insistence that the best way to aid Hrald was to make alliance through marriage with Turcesig. Yet if it was hard to see herself at Kilton, it was easier to see herself with Ceric. He had of old loved her, she knew, or at least had always assumed they would wed; it was part of the way he saw the world. She knew this. And her wedding him would forever bind the families, in a way that she knew both Hrald and her mother yearned for. They could not have Ceric and Kilton, but she could.

She felt utterly lost. If she could but see Ceric again, she felt she could decide. Seeing him would make all the difference. Now she was denied that.

Ælfwyn too was looking at her daughter. The letter seemed almost Heaven-sent. In it Ceric could declare the King's blessing on Ashild's entering into the hall of Kilton, as well as his own clear and public offer to meet any bride-price. His assurance that Modwynn, the revered Lady of Four Stones would welcome Ashild touched her more deeply than any could know. If the Fates had been kinder Modwynn would have been her own mother-in-law. Ælfwyn had been denied that, but thinking on how that great lady would receive, aid, and foster Ashild was like a balm smoothed over a raw wound.

Something else about the letter had moved her, had caused a small spark to flare in her breast. He – Raedwulf of Defenas – wanted this, had posed the solution. He was her ally. Ceric had named him, specially, because of this; Raedwulf was his ally too. The bailiff's first loyalty was to King, of course, but then to Kilton. And somehow, by extension, to her.

Asberg was not looking at Ashild's lowered head, but instead into the face of his nephew. After speaking alone with Ashild, Thorfast had stressed to her brother and uncle that he would extend his bride-price offer to meet anything the hall of Kilton would pay. What the girl had said to him to make him offer such was beyond her uncle's ken, but he had said it. Pride drove men to extremes, he had seen that many times. But more than treasure was at stake here.

They had heard enough from various riders to know Haesten was poised to strike. He had Wintered his army on the inlets of Apulder and Middeltun, and had been largely undeterred by the King of Wessex's near presence. It was not one that Ælfred could maintain for any length of time with real continuity; every three months brought a change of men, as those who had served were sent back to care for kin and cattle.

Asberg had ridden out himself a few times to seek news, speaking with the Danes who ruled to the South and West, speaking also to a younger son of Guthrum's. Nothing he had seen or heard gave him confidence the Peace with Wessex would last. Few trusted Haesten, but joining with him might prove the wisest choice, either that or banding together to repel him entirely. None of the war-chiefs would commit, one way or the other, just as Four Stones had stayed, watchful, but waiting.

Asberg's eyes now shifted back to his niece, head downcast. He shared with her her discomfort about the prior contact between Kilton and Four Stones. There was something almost uncanny in the bonds, and the bloodshed, between the two, bloodshed that extended back many years. War ever made strange bedfellows, but he himself felt it would be hard for the daughter of Four Stones to take up a new life amongst a hall in which the man who had killed her father was so honoured. And she had been raised by Sidroc – would not the folk there look at her and recall this, and recall also it was Sidroc's hand that felled Godwin?

Thorfast was young and bold, with the blood of Danish kings running through him. And Thorfast was right: together Turcesig and Four Stones made an army. If asked in private, he would counsel the maid to stay in Lindisse, wed Thorfast.

It was Ælfwyn who broke their silence.

"What will you have, my daughter," she asked, leaning forward to lay her hand over Ashild's. "How shall you answer Ceric's letter?"

Ashild's head lifted. "I will not go," she proclaimed, though her mouth was trembling. She looked into her mother's face, into that of Hrald, and then at her uncle. "I will not leave you, not yet. Thorfast too must wait." Her mind was whirling, yet she found words.

"Ælfred thinks there will be war. A union either way could harm us here. I must have time."

She said next what she had felt for years, useless conjecture though it was. "If I were a man, I could stay here at Four Stones all my life." It pained her the greater that she was Yrling's offspring, he who had won Four Stones in the first place.

It was no bitter jest; her mother and brother heard the sorrow behind it. Hrald made a movement of his shoulders, and tried to smile. "If you were a man, you would be Jarl. You are older than me."

"Yet God marked you to be a woman," her mother observed. Her tone was mild, yet not without a hint of rue for her daughter's just complaint. "He has some work for you, some task perhaps equally great to what a man may accomplish."

Ashild's head dropped forward, as if to ward off these words.

Hrald spoke again, and was now unable to hide the hurt in his voice. "What…what will we tell Ceric…?" His large hands had turned towards the slip of parchment, awaiting answer.

His sister said the only thing she could. “The truth,” she pressed. “We must not be rushed. We shall write it together, you and I.”

None at that small table were content with this, least of all she who had spoken. Three sets of eyes turned to her.

“Forgive me, all of you,” she pleaded. “I must do what I think is best. I must have time.”

Her mother saw a strong maid close to breaking, and this too was what Hrald saw. Asberg saw the strain in the girl’s face, but saw too the resolve. She was cast from the same mould as Yrling, that was certain.

A tapping was heard at the door, followed by Mul’s voice sounding at the box-lock. “Lady Ashild,” he summoned. “Your mare. The foal is coming.”

Hrald had joined his sister in the stable. The place was dim, and thick with the warm smell of horses, and the odour of birth. The tiny colt was now standing on wobbling legs, and had found its mother’s teat. The mare was charcoal-black, her son the same, now that his mother’s tongue had washed him.

The foal’s coming had taken longer than most, the mare growing more and more restless as she circled her box stall, head tossing. When the first pair of minute hooves had appeared Ashild had clapped her hands in relief, and Mul’s eyes had crinkled above his deep grin. After the foal dropped to the straw they let the new mother begin the washing process, poking and prodding the little one as she warmed it. Once it stood and had its first suckle they both entered the stall, Mul going to the mare’s head to soothe her, while Ashild took the chance to run her hands all over the wet foal’s small body, squatting down to clasp it in her embrace, stroking the fine little face, slipping her fingers lightly into the flaring nostrils so that the creature might know her scent. It was the first step in gentling a horse, and one of the most vital.

Now she stood with her brother outside the stall, looking in on this new member of Four Stone's herd. They had spent some time speaking of the foal and his handsome mother, and were both grateful to have their minds so occupied. The dusk had deepened in the stable, and soon the hall would be gathering to sup.

Before Hrald turned to leave her he would ask one thing.

"Those priests. The letter. We must write it soon."

She nodded. "In the morning, if you like. Though they will welcome the rest of a day or two before they are sent back."

"I will give them escort," Hrald said. "We can spare three men to ride with them to the border."

This was a great distance, but hearing the tales the men of cloth had told about having been apprehended so many times in Anglia made up his mind. It should take no more than three heavily armed warriors of Four Stones to make certain they arrived back in Wessex with the answering letter. They would be on their own from there, having to cross Wessex to reach Kilton, but any of Ælfred's men would aid them.

Hrald's eyes were trained on the black foal, now folding its legs to fall upon the straw. He watched his sister's face, looking on the young creature, and saw the joy she gleant from her horses. He thought of the huge white stallion, outside in the paddock, that Thorfast had brought her, and thought too of the fifty horses he had pledged if she chose him.

Ashild too was thinking of Thorfast. She looked up at her brother and asked a question.

"What – what was the bride-price you set for me?"

She watched Hrald swallow, the knob in his throat slightly moving. She knew he had set her dowry at fifty of Four Stone's best horses, but did not yet know what Hrald had asked in return.

"I did not set it. Thorfast made offer. It was a price so great, we could say nothing."

Her lips had parted, but her question remained, there in her dark eyes.

"It was your weight in silver," he admitted.

Her breath sounded through her lips.

It was a huge sum, but it was not only that. There was about it a crudeness that shook her. Brides were bought, yes, but to be bought by the hundred-weight seemed akin to selling her soul. Her mind flashed on how her mother must have received this offer. But her mother had depths of strength she had only guessed at.

Another came to her mind: Yrling. It was like a ploy her own father might have played. And Ælfwyn had come to care for Yrling, in the end.

She made herself smile.

"My weight in silver?"

She had tried, and failed, to playfully repeat the terms.

He could not bear the pain in those light words. "Ashild," he said, and put his hand on her arm.

She met his eyes, but could not answer.

"I am sorry," he said. "Mother and I...we want you to wed Ceric. You know how I feel about him, what we have shared. He is my best friend." He lifted his hand, and looked now back into the stall. "And in Wessex you will be safe."

She could hear in the rasp of his voice, how much he wished to believe this last.

But she had made at least half of her decision, and would tell him, and now.

"That is why I cannot go."

In the late morning of the next day Hrald and Ashild seated themselves at the long table where Wilgot did his writing. The Lady of Four Stones had invited her priest and the two visitors to her bower garden for refreshment. The priest was now taking Tatwine and the monk on a tour of the healing herbs that flourished under the Lady's care.

Lying before Hrald and Ashild on Wilgot's table was a piece of lambskin parchment, which the priest had ready-ruled, his faint pin-scratches marking lines to be inked upon. The table was well-lit, with three bronze oil cressets, easy to position where the letter-writer needed them. There was a small pot of freshly made ink, smelling darkly of the gall it contained. There were as well a number of goose-quills, trimmed but for the final cut, making the ink-bearing point finer or blunter, as the writer preferred. A scraper, sharp as any razor, lay nearby, its blade sheltering in a split piece of wood. It would only be needed if a drop of errant ink should spoil a word, or the writer decide on a new arrangement of expression.

Hrald began.

CERIC, MY BROTHER, MY FRIEND

You look for Ashild and receive nought but this letter, and the regard of all at Four Stones. I pray that time will find me sending happier news. I look forward to our soon meeting, and with peace between our lands. Until then you will be riding, I think, with Ælfred or his son, and know you will win your way to his right hand. I rejoice that Worr is ever at your side.

I embrace you.

HRALD OF FOUR STONES

When Hrald had finished writing, he spent a moment reading what he had put down. It said so little, but Ashild must write the important part. He slid the letter to his sister. She paused, letting the ink dry, reading it herself. She felt more restive than usual, and not able to focus on Hrald's few words. A dull ache was in the small of her back; her Moon-flow would soon be coming.

She had already trimmed a quill with the final cut, making it short, giving her the broad stroke she liked. She rolled the stiff point of the feather in her hand and thought.

She did not know who other than Ceric would read this letter. Perhaps he might keep it wholly to himself, or perhaps it might be passed amongst the family of Kilton. She had not forgotten the greeting on the letter he had left for her: My Ashild.

She decided to begin as if all might see it. She dipped her quill-point in the pot of ink.

CERIC OF KILTON

All at Four Stones are grateful for your esteem, and the beneficence of Ælfred, great King of Wessex.

– She stopped and looked at this; it was so formal that Ceric would think she had dictated an outline to a trained scribe. She glanced at the two lines and checked that thought; no scribe would write so poorly as she. She had some confidence in her spelling, but her letters looked crude next to Hrald's large and well-formed ones. She lowered her head again over the parchment.

I cannot leave Four Stones. Your King himself knows the unsettled nature of our Kingdoms.

– And I will not let Hrald send fifty of our horses with me, far from Four Stones where they may be sorely needed, she told herself. She had not asked Hrald what he intended to settle as her dowry, but feared he would name that which he had set if she accepted Thorfast. She was not now willing for any such treasure to leave her home.

The danger is too great to all I love. I cannot now leave.

– She had drawn a circle around those she loved, and Ceric was not within it. She looked at that line again. To scrape it out would be a lie, yet it was not the full truth. She felt the stirrings of affection for Ceric, had missed him since he had left, desired his company with her and Hrald, just as she had desired his company when they were young. She did not know how to say this, and let the line stand.

Please forgive

ASHILD OF FOUR STONES

She spent so long laboring over these words that Hrald had risen to stretch his long legs, which had been crammed beneath the priest's too-low table. When she raised her head she saw him looking out the single window they had opened to allow light.

"Will this do?" she asked, summoning him over.

He read the few lines. It was so little, yet reading it again he saw it conveyed all of importance. The only thing missing was word of Thorfast, and the suit he pressed; and she could not tell Ceric that. Nor could he. Learning another man was pursuing Ashild would cause Ceric needless pain, a pain that he could not act upon, denied as he was from coming to Lindisse.

"It is good," he said, with no heartiness.

It would, he knew, stun his friend. He could not look forward to how Ceric's face would change while reading what they each had written.

"If you – accept Thorfast, will you write to Ceric again," he now found himself asking.

She grimaced, and he went on, "In friendship, will you tell him?" It was almost a plea.

"You will write him," she deferred. She felt of a sudden chilled, and wanted to go to the weaving room and lie down, with her mother and sister and aunt around her. Burginde would bring her hot broth from the kitchen yard, and rub her back…

"Já, I will write him," she corrected, seeing the pain in her brother's eyes. Refusing Ceric was refusing Hrald; Hrald and her mother both.

Chapter the Sixteenth: The Raven of the Danes

The Year 893

ASHILD cut the length of linen from her loom. It had taken a full week to weave, and before that an entire month to spin for, working at it as much as she could. Her thread was not of the finest; it had ever been full of lumps since girlhood, but she had felt the importance of the entire piece being of her own hands. She had dyed the spun thread a pale blue, using the leaves of woad from her mother's garden.

Her shears snipped through the final warp strings. The piece now measured a full ell, that being the distance of a man's outstretched arm from shoulder to fingertips, but she determined that her woman's arm would serve just as well. She left the weaving room with it and her work-basket, and went across the short passage outside its door to the small drying-room, which they used when the wet of outdoors forbade the hanging of laundry. She had carted a small table up there. She smoothed the linen down upon the surface, pinning each corner with brass pins. Thus made taut, she took a piece of sharpened charcoal in her right hand, and began her design.

It was a raven she drew upon the hand-spun linen, a raven in arrested flight, wings outstretched, beak gaping, claws extended and ready to grasp.

She finished her drawing, released the brass pins. She should hem it first; she could almost hear her mother telling her so. She threaded up a needle with a long strand of the light blue linen, folding the edges over, holding them close in her finger pads as her needle pierced the cloth, giving her a finished edge. She used no thimble for this task. Her hands were hard from riding anyway, and the spear-work she was doing with Hrald had further toughened them.

When both raw edges were hemmed she took a broader-eyed bone needle, and looped a length of black wool through it. She began to outline the raven, starting with the gaping beak. Her drawing was large, the size almost of a real raven. This outline must be firm, her stitches small. So absorbed she became that she scarcely heard her mother and Burginde coming up the stairs. They passed by her closed door and into the weaving room, without suspecting she was within. Each stitch became another step in the outline, each short length of black wool laid down leading her closer to the back of the head, the flaring wing-tip, the breast, the spread talons, the second wing-tip.

Her shoulders hunched and her eyes burned, but she would not stop. She would complete the outline today, so that on the morrow she could begin the work of filling in the body.

She began singing a song to herself, an old tune in the Norse tongue, taught to her by Jari's aged and now-dead mother-in-law, who had taught Ashild the drawing of bind-runes, and those things of magic the old woman thought a clever maid should know. It was she who, when Ashild was but a girl, showed her how to throw a curse, thumbs forward, on any tormenter; the same curse she had thrown at Ceric in the woods as he ran from her. This song however, Ashild had forgot the meaning of. Falling from her lips it sounded half-lullaby, half-lament. She went on, drawing her hand-spun thread over and over through her fabric, the needle rising and then vanishing as it pulled the black line, encircling her raven. Her intent was such it felt an act of devotion, almost an act of prayer.

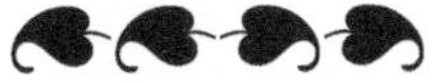

Spring had come, and with it no end to the uncertainty. Haesten had completed his camp at Middeltun. From the mass of men who had landed at Apulder no single leader had emerged, and Haesten took pains to convince the chief men there that he was fittest to head all. Apart from a few supply raids into Wessex he had kept his combined troops close. The Winter had been wet and cold, but now with the breaking of bad weather, movement was to be expected, either West into Wessex or North into Anglia. Yet no riders came to Four Stones with message from the Dane.

Younger men on active patrol at Four Stones were always in training. But those warriors who had fought and won Four Stones with Yrling were older, and farming now, and had not the need to keep up their skills. Now, with the landing of this great force, all of them were actively training, and hard.

The yards within the palisade yielded some room for smaller groups to practice, but with near to two hundred men the greensward without the gates was pressed into service. There in the shadow of the tall stone preaching cross men flung spears at targets thrown up against the wooden walls, and paired off to spar. Villagers looked up from crofts and barley patch to see lines of men run towards each other, spears foremost, or stand shield to shield in steady advance, swords at the ready. This last was not the chosen way of the Danes to fight; they much preferred the quick scramble through woods to surprise and overtake a lightly-guarded target, snatching what they could before retreating. But the warriors of Wessex fought in the way of Angle-land, tightly formed lines of men with shields almost locked, their war-chief behind them, shouting commands and encouragement, the line forming and reforming as men were felled. The pitched battles the Danes had been forced to fight over the past decades had been mostly of this kind.

Near the end of the session today Hrald sheathed his sword and walked to the water barrel. After a long sparring session with three other men he was left breathless, his body as wet from sweat as his mouth was dry. He drank of the cool contents in the copper dipper, his eyes watching the men still at their fighting. Jari was ever in demand as a sparring partner, and Hrald watched him take on two younger men at once, the whole time calling out a mixed stream of admonishing counsel and taunting insults. One had gotten in a touch at Jari's body, but the other Jari had felled with the flat of his sword, giving the older man victory. Asberg had joined in now, relieving the two, to face Jari alone, a change that was met with goading shouts from the men who circled them. Asberg's two young sons stood amongst them; they had been sparring together, though not yet sword-age, and had paused to cheer their father on.

After a few blows were exchanged Hrald saw that Gunnulf too had stopped in his practice to watch his older brother spar with Hrald's uncle.

Hrald found himself looking at his friend, and not at the contest beyond him. He missed Gunnulf. Since the day at the stream when Gunnulf had touched him they had spent no time together. Nor had they chosen to face each other in sparring, as they always had in the past. He did not think anyone else noticed this, none but he and Gunnulf. Now, with the sparring ended between Jari and Asberg, he saw Gunnulf turn and see him. Hrald still stood at the water barrel, and Gunnulf now walked to him, and it.

Gunnulf nodded greeting as he approached, and spurning the dipper, threw handfuls of the water over his own heated face, then lowered his mouth to the sloshing surface and drank deeply.

When Gunnulf straightened up he looked over to where his older brother and Asberg stood jesting as they wiped their brows with their sleeves. His own face was dripping, and he did the same.

"Who would win, in a real fight," posed Gunnulf, his eyes upon them.

"Ah," thought Hrald aloud, and looked back at them. "They are almost matched in strength, and Asberg has faced Jari enough times so that he is not thrown off by the sword in the wrong hand." He narrowed his eyes at the two as they stood together, laughing, and gesturing to each other the blows they had thrown and blocked. "Asberg is, I think, faster. Your brother, stronger."

He kept on, considering the outcome. "If they did not know the other, Jari. He will always have the advantage over an ordinary warrior, with his Tyr-hand."

Gunnulf nodded, and gave out with a grin. "I think so too. Jari."

This was more than they had said to the other for long months. Hrald felt almost at ease again. Then he saw, across the field, Onund stoop to retrieve his dropped sword. Onund looked up and saw the two standing together. Hrald had never understood why Onund watched Gunnulf so carefully, but now he knew.

He turned his back on Onund, turned to face Gunnulf. He did not know how to say the next, but he had thought much on it, and it forced its way past his lips.

"Do you not fear for your soul?"

Gunnulf paused just a moment, then answered the question with one of his own.

"Would it matter, if I did?" His voice was light, almost jesting, the voice of Gunnulf which Hrald knew best.

Hrald did not know how to respond.

"It would matter to me," Hrald told him.

He knew he was more Christian than his friend; it was to be accepted, as Gunnulf was wholly Dane, his aged mother baptised late in life, his older brother Jari fully a man when he received that sacrament. Gunnulf himself was a boy when he was sprinkled and blessed, but Hrald had been baptised soon after his birth, and had had much instruction from Wilgot and from Oundle. He knew his friend's faith did not run as deeply as his own.

"I fear for you," Hrald told him. "Not only after death, but here." He turned his eyes to sweep the men before them in the field, at rest, or still at sparring. Hrald dreaded what might happen if Gunnulf and Onund were discovered.

Gunnulf turned his head, looked away at trees now coming into leaf, then back to Hrald's searching face. "It is a form of brotherhood. Just a different form."

There was no reckless daring in Gunnulf's answer, and in his now-grave tone no challenge, no excuse. Hrald found himself looking at his friend's face, found himself nodding.

The men of Four Stones were not alone in their training. A woman also spent hours at her spear-work, with her brother Hrald to guide her. Ashild's two spears were kept in the hall, in the iron hoops filled with such weapons, flanking the great dragon banner on the wall. When they could break away from their other duties Hrald would pull those two short spears from the scores of larger shafts they stood amongst.

They met at the same stand of elm trees at which Hrald had first discovered her, shoulder-sore and angry in her own attempts. Now Ashild could throw a spear a respectable distance, and with good aim. Hrald had had to replace her old target shield twice, so often had she struck it. She could do even better at a run, but her skirts often bound her legs, hampering her actions.

One morning when they worked there they heard the nicker of a third horse. They looked up to see their Uncle Asberg. Ashild had a spear in her hand, poised above her shoulder, and his surprise at seeing her so made his mouth open.

"Throw," Hrald told her, and she did. Asberg watched the spear sail through the air, hitting solidly enough into the shield hung in the tree that she must go to it and pull it out.

He got off his horse. "A fair throw, my girl," he praised. He was looking from her to Hrald, nodding his head, taking it in without question or explanation.

"Have you had her spar with you yet," he asked his nephew.

Ashild's surprise was as great as her brother's. He shook his head. "Only to throw at a target, which she can now do." He gestured to the many punctures in the face of the hanging shield.

Her uncle was looking her up and down. "You are not smaller than Abi," he decided, naming his younger son, who had thirteen years. "And can therefore wield a spear with equal vigour," he judged.

Asberg was known as one of the better spears-men at Four Stones, and he now stood assessing her as a spears-man in her own right. She would have kissed him, had he not been so intent about her efforts.

"You cannot always throw; at times you will be forced to hold your spear and thrust," he began. "Two-handed is best; there is more than twice the strength behind your spear point, as you can use both arms and your whole body weight. A shield lends protection, já, but for those of lesser strength, use both hands on the spear."

He took the shield from the tree and feinted before her, moving left and right, calling out instruction. Hrald, standing at the side, wore a grin so broad that Ashild had need to turn away from him, lest he break her focus. Asberg was not a small man, but he moved nimbly enough to tire her, and kept the shield before him in almost constant motion.

"The calf or foot; strike out there," he told her. She jerked her spear at his booted left foot, making him jump back. "Even if you do not make a hit, you can force a man to lose balance, even fall." They went on some little time, Hrald too joining in, serving as living target for her thrusts.

"And," finished her uncle, mopping his brow, "remember a man has four sides to him. Strike where you can – foot, back of leg, the side at the waist, a high blow to the head. Do what is needful to make your hit."

A week later Ashild, seated the women's table, raised her eyes to where Hrald sat. The meal was drawing to a close, and she had already told him she wished to see him after, in the treasure room. There were but three keys to this room, that held by her mother, her uncle, and now by Hrald. As many times as she had been within that room, she knew she was but a visitor there. When Hrald took a wife he and his bride would sleep there, their babes be rocked in the cradle still within, the same in which she and Hrald had slept.

She looked at Hrald, gazing down with a thoughtful face into his plate. She did not think the dried, stewed pears warranted his expression. He was looking at one thing and seeing another, the way she remembered Sidroc often doing.

Her eyes lifted beyond Hrald's head to the large round disc of Sidroc's shield. The red and black spiral of its painted face issued from the iron boss in the centre of the shield, and flowed outward to the iron rim. She well recalled the day her brother was made to lift that shield over his head until all in the hall saw him, all acknowledged him. It was a man's shield, that of a great warrior, and he was asked to hold it aloft and then place it aside.

Her eyes shifted next over Hrald's left shoulder, and the broad banner of a raven in flight over distant fields. Her mother and Burginde had made that, while she and Hrald where still small children. She had memory of seeing her and Sidroc seated before it, just as she now looked at her mother, head lowered, in converse with Wilgot the priest. Ashild knew her mother had made the banner to replace an old charcoal drawing of a raven which one of Yrling's men had scrawled upon the wall there. She had once lifted the heavy fabric of the banner, and thought she still could discern the raven on the time-darkened plank wall. Like much from the time of her real father, an echo remained.

When the hall began to break up she rose, bending first to take up the linen pouch under her bench. She met Hrald at the door; he had the iron key already in the box-lock. She had taken up a cresset in her other hand and followed him in. She laid the wavering cresset on the square table and pulled the contents out of the linen pouch.

He was watching her, with expectant curiosity. His mother and Burginde made all his clothes, and he thought Ashild resented every hour spent standing with spindle or at a loom. Yet it was clear it was fabric she had brought.

He saw a splotch of dark against a light background. She unfurled it fully, holding it before her.

"A battle pennon," she was saying. "A flag so that your men always know where you are." She lifted it a bit higher against herself. "And that you live."

He took it in. The raven on the large banner in the hall flew over grasslands, looking down. This one faced the viewer as a raptor would, wings outspread, talons reaching. The gape of the curved beak was as threatening as any eagle's.

"You made this for me?"

There was more than a touch of wonder in his question. All war-chiefs of renown went with pennons into battle. The warriors of Angle-land especially used them, marked with that device that held meaning to the man or his family, as Ælfred of Wessex flew the golden dragon. It was a sign of state, yes, but served vital purpose during war. The battle-flag would always be kept near to the war-chief whose device it featured.

In the disarray of hand-to-hand combat there was dire need that his men always know where their chief was, not only to defend him if his immediate body-guard was faltering, but so all might know that he still lived. It heartened warriors to see the pennon fluttering against the sky, oftentimes held and waved by a man, who, unable to defend himself, might be cut down in this service. The flag would be snatched up by another, giving reassurance to those who battled on. The battle-flag was a source of identity and pride. Likewise, no disgrace was greater than having the pennon taken by the enemy.

Hrald had reached out and touched the raven figure as she held it. She could see his amaze, perhaps less for her handiwork than for the meaning of the thing itself. She felt a quiet sense of pride, watching his fingertip run over the wool body of the raven. It would have been far faster to cut the raven shape out of dark fabric and sew it upon the field of blue. But that had not been her goal. There was power in every stitch, every inch of dark wool that she herself had spun, piercing the blue linen cloth that she had woven, filling in her design, interweaving as she had sung her song. Her spell.

He was looking down into her eyes.

"I thank you."

He felt unable to say more.

"There is a sleeve, here, to slip over the pole," she told him, showing the narrow margin she had folded over and sewn.

He began to smile, went to one of the spears resting against the wall. He turned it in his hand, slipped the sleeve over the butt end of it, lifting the raven banner in the air over their heads. The shadow it cast on the wall from the cresset's flicker was as large, and as full of life, as a real raven.

She took the flag from him, waved it over his head. They both laughed.

She lowered the spear shaft, and he pulled the pennon off, holding it before him a moment to admire it once more. Then he laid it upon the wooden chest that held the ring-tunic Ceric had brought him. Hung above it was the bow and quiver Tindr had fashioned, and the boy-sized round shield given by his father at Tyrsborg.

In the morning the Lady of Four Stones came into the treasure room. As she neared the table she saw something new upon the weapons chest by the wall. She looked down on the raven pennon, knew it for the battle-flag it was. Her hands went to it.

Ashild. She would know her daughter's weaving anywhere. But she marvelled at the thread-work, the power of the great bird. As she held it tears crowded her eyes, thinking of she who had made it, and he who would stand, sword drawn, beneath it.

Chapter the Seventeenth: You Are The First

Wessex

NEAR the end of Spring, Ceric was back at Kilton. He and Worr and their twenty thegns had ridden with Eadward, both directly East through Wessex and also to the North. Ælfred had set his greatest force of men between both enemy camps at Middeltun and Apulder, preventing the Danes from mass attack of Wessex. His army lay encamped for months, informed by steady reports by his outriders, and where travel by horseback was made impossible by the thickness of forest, by swift runners. Even so, small bodies of Danes got through, striking at villages for supplies, driving off livestock, carrying off grain, and killing all folk who resisted, leaving a wake of misery and hunger behind them.

Eadward's charge was to intercept these small raiding parties, and when that was not possible, to visit the despoiled villages. His father's system of a fortified burh within a day's walk of any larger settlement allowed for many to seek shelter if word of marauders was received in time. But it was now both planting and lambing time, and cottars were loath to leave their fields and flocks. The garrisons were built to shelter both folk and their beasts, but lambing ewes could not be forced to walk the day to reach them.

Beyond the forays into Wessex for supplies, Ælfred had learnt from his riders that Danes long-settled in Northumbria and parts of Anglia had agreed to throw in with those newly arrived. And Haesten had indeed emerged as the newcomers' leader; his fame as a warrior in Frankland and his earlier exploits here in Angle-land and elsewhere assured that his authority and skill was acknowledged.

It was during this second tour with Eadward that Ceric saw action. He had before witnessed the aftermath of Danish attacks on the villages they rode through. Now he would be part of one. Half a day's ride from the Wessex border a breathless runner on a pounded clay road had come upon Eadward and the forty men he led. He was a youth from a small trev of ten crofts, now seeking aid from a fortified burh still an hour or two away. A flurry of mounted Danes had appeared that morning at his small settlement, rushing into their midst brandishing spears, leaping from horses to grapple with terrified folk who tried to drive their pig or cow into the nearby fields where it would be harder to catch. The boy had fled, and no Dane had ridden after. Eadward listened, and they gave the boy drink and took him up upon one of their horses, so he might lead them back to the trev.

Arriving at the plundered village they found the wretchedness that all such attacks provoke: trampled wattle fences, upended fowl houses, stunned and grieving folk milling about the four that lay dead, wailing children sent after the few wandering hens or sheep that remained. The stammering survivors clustered around the still-mounted Prince and his men. Ceric and Worr were foremost, and had begun to swing down off their horses. Then, from the edge of the common pasturage, a second group of horseman appeared, come from a distant track leading to the wood.

A few of the folk shrieked, so that Ceric's horse nearly bolted. He and Worr regained their saddles, and all warriors turned to face the new arrivals. These horseman betrayed themselves at once, yanking their horses' heads back towards whence they had come as soon as they spotted the warriors led by Eadward.

Ceric was already urging his horse forward; it took Worr reaching for his reins and turning his own horse to block that of Ceric's to awaken him to the need to await orders. All eyes were fastened on those who now were crowding the track into the forest, pressing their horses back into the trees. There were no more than six or seven of them; the folk had numbered no less than a score who had just been through. This was yet another group of Danes.

"My Lord," called one of the village men. "That path opens up to the pasture further on. If you ride in the field you can catch them from there."

Eadward made his decision, his horse wheeling beneath him. "Give chase," he ordered, kicking at his horse's barrel. The cowering villagers were left behind as they raced across the pasture, Eadward at their head.

A gallop across the field and along the tree line brought them to the opening the cottar had told of. Eadward dismounted, gathered his men about him. He and a few strode over, entered the trees at the opening, looking up and down the narrow track.

They hurried back to where the rest waited. Eadward's eye roved over the faces before him.

"Twenty of you, stay with the horses. Keep them quiet and out of sight. There were seven of them; sixteen of us will enter the wood and wait for them. Eight of my own men, eight from Kilton.

"The track is little more than a deer-path. There will be no room for shields; and you will need both hands. If they are riding, it will be single file; if they are pulling their horses, it will be the same. Pair off. Hide along the track, and an extra man at each second pair. At my signal, one man to go for the bridle, the second to pull the man down. Kill them all."

His orders were as simple and decisive as this.

Ceric could feel the quickening of his own breath. His eyes, like those of all the men he stood with, were fixed on Eadward. The man who looked back was of three-and-twenty years, a taller and more robust version of his kingly father, and more than ready to act. Now he called out the names of those of his own men who would join him in the wood, and those who would stay with the horses.

He looked to Ceric, who cast his own eye over his pledged men, and called out the chosen seven, beginning with Worr. He was guided by the eagerness he read in each man's face, that and by their age, choosing those with most experience amongst them. The timbre of his own voice surprised him; he sounded almost hoarse as he named his men. He was more than aware that he might be calling one or more to their deaths.

They donned ring-shirts and helmets, working as quickly as they could. "You take the bridle, Ceric," Worr told him as he re-fastened his sword. "I take the man."

Ceric began to protest, but Worr's next words were an order. "Do as I say, this first time," he countered. The set of Worr's mouth was enough to still Ceric. He nodded agreement.

The chosen sixteen slipped into the wood, ranging themselves along the track, stepping behind trees or brushy growth. Eadward and his partner were the closest to the opening to the pasture, and thus the last the oncoming Danes would reach.

Ceric and Worr were at the mid-point of the range of men; the warriors of Kilton began there and would be at the end of the line of Danes. If the last Danes were straggling and Eadward gave the word before they were near, it would place them in additional danger. As Ceric gripped his unsheathed sword he thought on this. An ambush was nothing that was ever practiced, and in such tight quarters anything could happen. He could grab the bridle or reins with one hand if the horse was near enough. Worr would need both hands to seize the leg or body of the rider and pull him to the forest floor. Ceric could see none of the other men, but Worr was almost at his shoulder, and looked to him. Like his own, Worr's helmet had eye-holes that descended almost like a mask, and a thin strip of steel as a nose-guard. Worr's steady eyes looked back at him beneath that steel as they waited.

It was not long. They began to hear the sweep of boughs and cracking of branches. This was followed by the unmistakable sound of bridle hardware, that jingling of bits that ever announces the nearness of ridden horses. A human voice sounded low; that of a man, doubtless swearing an oath. They were coming as fast as they could, thinking they were being pursued down the track from behind. Ceric stood stock-still, not wanting to cause any rustle, but turned his head at their approach.

He saw the lead man, bending low over his horse's neck to avoid being hit by the overarching branches. If the Dane had helmet or ring-shirt, he had not taken time to put them on. The man's face was to the near side of his horse's neck, the side the thegns of Wessex were ranged along. Ceric saw a mop of dark hair over a face glistening with sweat. The horse too was blowing, unhappy at the narrow path which it was being forced to walk along, and unhappy too at the severely shortened rein it was held at.

The horseman passed. Ceric's heart felt like it was near to exploding in his chest. The second Dane passed, this one also bent low, but with his face off to his horse's right side. He could only hope the man they tackled would be the same, looking away when Worr seized him.

The third man surprised him; he was on foot, holding his horse tightly and leading him. The man's sightlines were thus just at the level where the thegns hid, and Ceric knew he sucked in his breath, seeing this. But the man's gaze was fixed on the rump of the horse before him.

The fourth Dane. He was mounted, again crouched low over his horse's neck. Ceric saw the face, the eyes looking almost straight at the trees behind which he and Worr stood hidden. This should be their man, he reckoned, and his startle would be the less as his face was turned towards the movement they would make as they sprang at him. Like the others, he wore no ring-shirt nor helmet. Like the others, he held no weapons, but used both hands to guide and urge his horse forward.

The fourth man began passing them; Ceric saw the hind legs of the horse lift and fall. Then a yell rang out.

"Ælfred!" screamed that King's son. It came out in two bellows, sounded like a warrant of death.

Ceric sprang, and so did Worr. Golden-hilted sword uplifted in his right hand, Ceric leapt at the head of the horse, a big and raw-boned roan. His left hand snatched at and missed the rein, then lunging deeper closed around the cheek-piece of the bridle. The horse snorted and shied, trying to toss its hard-held head.

Ceric saw the blur of brown that was Worr, tackling the Dane's shoulders with both arms, wrenching him down. The Dane's left foot caught a moment in the stirrup, the man twisting, looking up at them as he hung, howling out an oath. In the time it took him to fall free Worr had his sword out, and plunged it through the man's body.

Horses and men were both screaming; Ceric heard Worr yell as he drove his weapon through the Dane's chest.

Beyond Worr he could see the next two men grappling with their Dane, and see the man be felled by the hacking blows of both. The horse Ceric held was bucking and dancing, turning and crashing into the shrubby growth lining the track, and Ceric turned with it, trying to keep himself out of the way of the hooves. Then Worr yelled at him.

Ceric whirled about. The Dane who had been leading his horse had broken away from the two thegns who had set upon him, leaping to his horse's far side and away. Now he stood, sword drawn, and thrust forward at Ceric.

He was older than Ceric, Worr's age perhaps. His long light brown hair swung freely over his shoulders, and his eyes were a blue that crackled beneath a furrowed brow as he closed in. His upper lip was lifted, showing his teeth. Through his snarl came a hissing stream of oaths.

Ceric's eye was drawn to the sword waving before him, a common piece of metal with a plain iron hilt and grip. And he saw the Dane's eye drop a moment to his own weapon, with its gold hilt and pattern of waving blue steel beaten into the working part of it. Ceric's hand tightened about that gold hilt.

Without a shield there was nothing Ceric could do but attack. The Dane bore no shield either; it was hanging on his frightened horse, now blocking the way of the thegns who had gone after him. Ceric sprang closer, further from the big roan; they were enclosed by the narrowness of the track and the bodies of the two horses.

Ceric had ring-shirt and helmet, the Dane had neither. The protections afforded Ceric also slowed him. And the Dane was battle-hardened; Ceric knew this from one look at the man's face. He had fought and overcome many times in the past.

Ceric swung at the Dane's left arm. The man was taller than he, but protected as he was, he got in close. The Dane leapt back, then quickly forward and to the side, his sword cutting through the air and back towards Ceric's sword arm. Ceric lifted it, hearing the bright steel ring out as the blades met, staggering back a step as he absorbed the force in his opponent's blow. The Dane's blade ran a hand's length down his own as the man's lunge propelled him forward. Then, seeing he had met only steel, the Dane pulled back, rocking on his heels.

At this slight pause Ceric shifted his sword, bringing it closer to his own body. The Dane lurched forward at him, as if he had gained momentum through the act of rocking backwards an instant. Ceric saw a flash of metal, and felt his own sword being wrenched from his grasp. The bright thing fell from his hand as the Dane's blade cut down upon it. He stood, stunned, as the man's sword rose again, aiming for his chest.

He threw himself against the roan horse, causing the beast to whinny, and its hindquarters to swing towards him. The horse's head and front hooves struck out towards the Dane, giving Ceric a chance to snatch at his sword, lying upon the trampled ferns and torn mosses of the path.

He was still in his crouch when he drove forward with it. He caught the Dane first in the right leg with a slash. The man's mouth opened as he dropped to his knees. Ceric was fully standing now, and sunk his sword point with a driving thrust into the belly of the Dane.

He pulled back his weapon. The man pitched slowly forward, face-first onto the softness of the moss. His eyes were rolling up as he fell, and though they paused to look at Ceric, he could read nothing in their look. They seemed to change from bright blue to dull grey as Ceric stood there, panting, over him.

He was aware Worr was now at his side, and the two thegns who had been blocked had pushed their way past the dead man's horse to reach where they stood.

Worr's arm was about his shoulders; he knew that without feeling it. His eyes fell on the tip of Godwulf's sword. It was filmed with blood, the same blood now seeping out from beneath the Dane's body, and darkening the mosses on which he lay.

Ceric let out a breath. He had heard the Dane's oaths at the start of their contest, but everything since had been muffled. Now his ears were filled. Horses were snorting and stamping, and men – men of Wessex – were calling and cheering. His hand was cramping from the tightness of his grasp upon his sword.

Worr was speaking to him.

"Well, and rightly, done," he praised.

Ceric knew he was trembling, and felt it showed.

"He almost killed me," he answered, eyes again on the body before him.

In the pause that followed Ceric turned back to Worr, his stare boring through the iron-rimmed eye protectors of his helmet. Worr's own eyes were bright with what they had both just done.

"But he did not," his friend said, "and nothing else matters. You gave him an opening, drawing back and shifting when you did. But you kept your head and used what you had – a horse – to win out."

There was no time for more; Eadward's voice sounded above all. Ceric found himself bending to wipe his sword tip on the new ferns at the track's edge. He took hold of the roan horse's head. Men were hoisting the bodies of the dead Danes upon their horses, and after the man Worr had felled was slung upon the roan, he helped the two thegns with the body of the one he had killed. They followed the track out into the pasture, out into the brightness of day.

The Danes' horses, freed from the confines of the woodland track, were no less troubled now they were in the open. Each bore the weight of a dead man slung over its saddle. From each man blood streamed, the smell of which made the beasts snort and dance, despite the firmness with which they were held. The thegns of Kilton who had been tasked with taking the walking Dane pressed the reins of the dead man's horse into Ceric's hand; he had made the kill, and those who had dispatched their men walked at the beasts' heads, leading the newly captured animals.

They rejoined their companions in the field, and mounted their own horses. As they approached the trev the folk gathered before them. Eadward was at the head of the troop, one made seven horses larger. Several of the village women were crying, but all looked up to him with grateful faces. The Prince got off his own mount, and gestured to his men to pull the bodies down.

Ceric gave a tug to the back of the Dane he had killed, and the man slid off and hit the ploughed ground. The saddle was slick with blood, and there was blood also along the flank and rear leg of the horse. Much of it had flowed from the killing strike to the body, but some too from the gash in the man's right thigh.

He watched Eadward roll, with his foot, the man he had himself killed, face to the sky. Ceric's man had flopped face up when he fell, one bloody leg bent back behind him, pinned in a way that would have been painful to the living.

Eadward passed in front of the dead, looking on their faces. After he did so, several of the villagers did the same, staring at the men who might have caused them even further harm. They were not those who had killed four of them this morning, but that did not matter. Here were seven less Danes to despoil their folk and foodstuffs, seven fewer to return with their hard-earned grain to the enemy camp.

Eadward turned to his men. "Those of you who killed, strip them and take what you will. But bring me their purses."

The Prince watched his men kneel and take what battle-gain was to be found. Each Dane bore a sword and knife, each had a round shield. All had pins of bronze at the shoulder to fasten the mantles rolled in their saddle-bags, and a few wore necklets or bracelets of silver.

Ceric had never touched a dead man before. When he was a boy and Kilton was attacked he walked through the blood of the dead, but he had never done what he did now, kneel at a man's head, put his hand in the man's neck-opening, against his still-warm chest, to see if he wore a chain of precious metal, pull back the sleeves of his worn tunic to see if any silver cuff sat upon the wrist. His man bore nothing, and his eye was caught at the sight of the Dane's sword hand, strong, calloused, dark hair upon the back of that hand, the hand that might have killed him.

He had no care for the man's short boots nor clothing; he would leave them. But now he must unbuckle the sword and knife belt. One of the thegns had slipped the dead man's sword back into its scabbard. Ceric's hands went to the twinned buckles. All about the man's torso was dark with blood, and Ceric's fingers fumbled and slipped as he worked the buckles and straps. He had to tighten the strap to free it, and the act of doing so caused a fresh issue of blood to ooze forth from the wound. The blow he had driven into the man's belly was straight, his sword withdrawn with no upper or lower thrust. Yet the smell of the warm blood, and the odour of the entrails he had punctured, made him close his eyes for a moment.

He pulled the two belts off, having to lift the man's body a moment to do so. He wiped his bloodied fingers in the crumbling soil he knelt on. The man's purse was next, a small pouch of leather that Ceric snapped by its securing strings from the belt holding the man's leggings.

He stood then, weapons belts in one hand, the tiny purse in the other, and came forward to Eadward, Worr behind him. A small trestle table had been carried to him, and the other men were now standing before it, holding what they claimed as battle-gain, and placing the dead men's purses before their Prince.

Eadward looked at Ceric as he filed before him, nodding at him. The youth had pulled his helmet off, and his coppery-gold hair was being tousled by the steady Spring breezes. Eadward let his eyes meet the green eyes of this scion of Kilton. He knew Ceric was the youngest man there, and thought it likely his first kill.

"The hall of Kilton has done well," Eadward said, glancing behind Ceric to where the dead man lay. Ceric nodded, ducking his head as he placed the dark leather pouch down.

"I thank you, my Lord," he murmured.

He went back to stand with the other thegns. The Dane's weapons were heavy in the hand, and he felt of a sudden weak. He glanced again at the man he had killed, thinking of how his sword had felt in his hand when it had entered the man's body. When he had slashed at the leg he had felt some resistance. But unprotected by even a leathern tunic the belly had yielded almost like a fruit. He forced his eyes up and away, planting his feet more firmly beneath him.

Eadward had emptied the contents of the purses. Some held little save for talismans. There was still silver enough, though, both coins and bits of coins, and hack-silver, pieces of broken jewellery and chopped lengths of silver rod.

He addressed the villagers now. "Bury these men, taking what you wish from them. This silver I leave with you. Divide half of it amongst those of you who lost folk; the other to all who suffered hurt or loss to croft and livestock."

The folk answered this beneficence with muted but earnest thanks. Eadward signaled that his men should ready themselves to ride. The horses and their trappings would be forfeit to him, to add to the store needed to horse the thegns of Wessex. But each man who had killed had the honour of leading the beast so claimed. Ceric turned to the horse who had carried the Dane he had felled. It was a light bay gelding, compact, and well-muscled. As he made secure the horse's reins to the tie-rings of his own saddle he saw the folk of the trev swarm the bodies of the dead. One grasped at the boots of the man he had killed, pulling them free.

He looked away, stooped to pick up the man's weapons, now lying on the trampled furrows they stood on. As he rose he saw a lad was watching him, the same they had come upon running from the trev, and had carried back with them. Ceric had not spoken to the boy, but now gestured him forward. He was of fourteen or fifteen Summers, tall and gangly, his tunic sleeves too short for his growing frame. His hair was dark yellow, and a wisp of yellow fuzz was upon his upper lip.

Ceric wordlessly extended the Dane's weapons to the lad. The boy's lips parted, then closed. He took the weapons in both arms, clasped them to his chest. Those nearest had stopped in their salvaging, watching. The lad did not speak, and Ceric did not wish to. He gave a single nod, then pulled himself into his saddle. The boy stood unmoving, watching him ride off, holding a treasure of iron now his.

"There is no thinking on it," Worr had counselled him, as they rode back to Kilton. "We were given orders. They were just. We followed them."

Ceric did not respond, and Worr saw he was looking rigidly out over his horse's head. The horse Ceric led was a constant reminder of the man he had killed.

"The first one is not easy," Worr finally said. His voice told Ceric that he thought of his own first killing.

"Now it is behind you. And you had rare privilege to do so before the Prince. He regarded you well." A moment more passed. "The next will not be this bad."

Ceric nodded, and looked down into his horse's mane. He lifted one hand to his breast, and touched the gold cross laying there beneath his tunic. Hrald came to his mind; he and Hrald as boys, listening to Sidroc the Dane tell them how to strip a man on the field of battle. Hrald's father had numbered in sequence what to take and how to take it. Doing so on a real foe was as different as listening was from doing.

The act of reaching into the man's tunic stood out in his mind. Plundering the still-warm body had nearly turned his stomach. He pictured a Dane doing the same to him, the hand finding something, grasping his own golden cross, ripping it from his neck, eyes alight at the hidden prize.

When Ceric and his troop returned to Kilton, three months had passed since he had entrusted his letter for Hrald to the King. In a fortnight he would ride to Bryeg to meet Ashild.

There had been a welcome feast at Kilton for those returned, and as none of his men had been lost nor suffered hurt it was undimmed by the lamenting of any woman. Before the feast had even begun all in the hall had heard of the ambush. They knew that eight of Kilton's men had taken direct part, and three of them each killed a Dane. Edwin had heard the story at least twice, once from Ceric, and once again from Worr, and had asked many questions of them both. When all were seated, Edwin raised his cup to those returned, and led all in a toast. He could not keep from grinning as he held his cup to his brother.

After the plates and salvers had been cleared the old scop assumed his stool, harp on his lap, and began to sing, telling of the encounter in the woods. Ceric had always liked the man, Garrulf by name, who had been a part of every early memory of the hall. Now he heard how Garrulf's skill took the rushed ugliness of the ambush and formed from it something heroic and stirring.

Ceric listened, but what Garrulf sang of seemed unreal. Ceric had nothing to show for his action. He had given the man's blades to the boy, and the horse had been claimed by Eadward. He had brought nothing back to Kilton but the story, told haltingly by him, and more fully by Worr and the other thegns. Garrulf the scop made of it a small saga of his own.

Over the years Cadmar the warrior-monk had sat at different places at Kilton's high table. Since Edwin had been named Lord he sat at Edwin's left, with Ceric on his brother's right. Once Garrulf had finished his song, Ceric gestured to

Cadmar that he would like to speak to him once the hall was broken down for the night.

He felt the urge to be alone with the warrior-monk, and to ask of him some counsel. Both Ceric and Edwin slept in the hall with the rest of the unmarried men, and he did not feel it right to ask Modwynn to unlock the treasure room so that he could speak alone with Cadmar; it was not his room, but Edwin's, who now held the other key. And he did not want his brother there.

They lingered as the trestle tables were knocked down, the serving folk had carried off the last of the cups, and Modwynn and Edgyth had locked those of silver away. Then he and Cadmar stepped into the kitchen passageway. A few serving folk might still pass them, but no others. It was dim in the passage, lit from the hall end by the torches still burning and the low glow of the fire-pit, and lit from the other only when the door to the kitchen yard and its cooking rings was pulled open. The dimness reminded Ceric of the small room which the priest Dunnere used for the confession of sins.

They stood side by side, resting their backs against the plank wall. Standing there, Ceric bethought him that it was not much broader than was the wooded track on which the ambush had taken place. Cadmar was huge, one of the biggest men at Kilton; Ceric still felt a boy next him. He saw the monk's curling beard out of the tail of his eye. It had once been wholly black, but now was streaked with silver. One of the monk's eyes twinkled in the low light. It was the expression Ceric always thought of when Cadmar came to mind.

He had no need to recount the killing. Cadmar had heard it from him and Worr earlier, and likely from one or more of the other men as well. Dunnere had already blest and shriven him, and Cadmar was a monk, not a priest. But Ceric felt he must speak.

"The Danes…they never had a chance. We outnumbered them, took them by surprise. We could not even offer them quarter; Eadward had told us to kill them all."

He heard Cadmar take a deep breath. He knew the trouble he felt sounded in his words, and the man was considering. Then came a steady, slow exhale.

"Yet one almost killed you."

Ceric nodded, muttering assent.

"The folk at the trev who were earlier attacked – they had no chance, either," Cadmar offered.

The monk knew this was not enough of an answer. Even though he could have died himself, he knew Ceric thought this first contest to have been an unfair one. Only in extreme cases did Ælfred not offer quarter to Danes; he would not have them slaughtered like wild dogs, and they had value as ransom, even those not of high birth. He had many times exchanged prisoners with Danish war-chiefs. But the heightening tension between the newly arrived Danes and the repeated raiding and destruction of his people made it harder to be merciful. And Eadward was not his father. He had not his father's devoutness, nor his patience. Ceric of Kilton had been exposed to that, first hand. The folk of the injured trev had been watching; Eadward must show them the King's justice and right would be upheld.

There was nothing, as an unlettered man of God, that Cadmar could say; that task was Dunnere's. But he might say something that neither the priest nor Worr had said.

"The Dane you killed – he is now in Asgard. He sits in a hall finer than any he ever knew here on Earth. A shield-maiden of loveliness pours forth mead for him. He fights all day long with his fellows, and at night all wounds are healed, and he feasts. All this for price of a blade to the belly."

Of all Cadmar could have told him, this was the last thing he expected to hear. The monk neither jested nor mocked. Ceric turned in the darkness and faced him.

Cadmar nodded his head at him. "It is true," he assured him. "It is true, because it is what the Dane believed. It is his truth. Just as eternal favour with Jesus Christ is ours."

The big man put his hand on Ceric's shoulder. "You are your father's son, and have done well. And you have done the better for being troubled at this first death."

Chapter the Eighteenth: Two Beds

THE day after their welcome feast Ceric stood in the treasure room. With him were his grandmother, brother Edwin, and Cadmar. It would take three days to reach Bryeg, and before he started he was eager to begin selecting all that he would offer as Ashild's bride-price once she arrived. She would, he gauged, come to Kilton with at least a score of men, including her uncle, and preparation was already under way for the visitors.

Although Cadmar and Modwynn would stand at his side when the bride-price was named, Ceric insisted to both there would be no bargaining; Hrald and Asberg would have earlier agreed on what they would ask, and he had told Hrald and Ashild he would meet their demands.

Both his grandmother and Cadmar nodded their heads in assent. Between friends there were often few or no counter-offers; both families wished for the union, both knew well what the other was likely to offer or provide.

Edwin's eyes widened at this; he did not know these Danes his brother had picked his bride from, and only knew what sharp bargainers they were as a people. But watching Cadmar and his grandmother agree, looking at the firm set of his brother's mouth when he had quietly declared there would be no countering, he found himself nodding too. He let his mind wander to the treasure-trove of that place named Four Stones, packed as he imagined it was with Saxon booty. Whatever this maid brought with her it was likely to be great treasure. He looked at his older brother, standing in the centre of their own treasure room. Edwin did not fully understand what he himself owned, but he knew what Ceric laid claim to was considerable.

Ceric had long been thinking of his offer. He could not present land, the way he could if he were wedding a maid of Wessex. Modwynn had given him her girlhood burh of Sceaftesburh when she gave him his weapons, but he could not divide and offer that expanse of fertile farm and pasturelands; it was too far from Lindisse for the collection of rents. Portable treasure was what was needed, and not horses nor swords, as he knew himself Four Stones abounded in those.

Three thousand, three hundred and thirty three silver pieces had been set aside for him from the store of five thousand his mother had been left by the great Godwulf's will. He had granted to his second daughter-in-law no less than that, and she had asked Ceric's grandmother to divide this treasure between her two sons, two-thirds to Ceric, and one third to Edwin, who would, as Godwin's heir, see a great fortune of his own.

Ceric thus had silver in abundance, and began building his offer with this.

"One thousand pieces of silver," he told his grandmother and Cadmar. This was a most handsome sum, but for such a maid as the young Lady of Four Stones, it was but a start. He had something else, and he went to it now, set aside in a special gem casket.

"And these five gold coins," he added, showing the thin but large glittering discs. They were the only gold coins he owned, and had come to him as a gift at his baptism from his Uncle Godwin.

"What more," he asked his elders. "What else would make a fitting offering?"

They all knew Four Stones was rich in steel and horseflesh. Kilton could tender silver and gold.

Modwynn had no daughter, and had come to the treasure room with one of her own jewel-caskets. During her long marriage to Godwulf the lord had bestowed upon her many ornaments, housed in small caskets of bronze or walrus ivory. She carried one of worked bronze now to her grandson, the box and contents thereof she offered to Four Stones. Edgyth wore no gems, only the simplest of silver pins, and Modwynn had already set aside rich store with which to adorn her new daughter-in-law.

"To secure your bride with," she told Ceric, as she passed the small trove into his hands.

He set it on the table, swallowing at this generosity. She smiled back at him.

Four Stones had no worker in precious metals; they needs must go North to Jorvik for that. Ceric wished to keep all that remained of his mother's adornments for Ashild, but that which Modwynn readily surrendered made a glittering and precious display. Within were silver brooches, circular pins, bracelets and finger rings, all beautifully-wrought, and some bearing bright gems. All were fit to one day adorn Hrald's own wife. She had even brought forth a golden bracelet for a man, something Godwulf had carried off from an old conflict. Ceric picked it up now, imagining Hrald angling it over his strong wrist, and wearing it henceforth.

Edwin's eyes were nearly popping from his head, and even Cadmar looked his amaze at the wealth of metal now lying upon the table. And the one thousand coins of silver had not yet been counted out and added to it.

Ceric considered it all soberly, even anxiously. "It is enough," he finally judged. He looked into Modwynn's face, and then to Cadmar. "If it is not, I will add more coinage to it."

Edwin almost laughed. "You could wed a queen with this," he said. "What will she bring you in return?"

Ceric had thought much on this as well. He could not know for sure, but named that which he thought most likely. "Enough swords to win any war," he answered, thinking of the store in Hrald's treasure room. His eyes went to his own sword, that golden-hilted one of Godwulf's which lay upon a wooden chest by the door.

Cadmar's eyes had followed his. Now the warrior-monk spoke. "Swords do not win wars, my boy. Men do. It is not the sword, but he who wields it, that matters."

A hint of a smile could be seen through the monk's dark beard, and in his twinkling eyes. All they had spoken of last night was still fresh in Ceric's mind.

Cadmar was right, of course. The Dane he had slain nearly slayed him first, and with a weapon no thegn of Kilton would carry.

"Yet," conceded the monk, "in a fight steel is more precious than gold. Let us hope your bride brings much good metal with her, that which will take and keep an edge."

Later that night Ceric recounted in his mind all that he wished to give directly to Ashild. He was standing out in the little pavilion in the pleasure garden, hearing the steady booming roar of the waves as they hit the cliffs far below. The hall was readying for sleep, and soon he must go in, if only as a pretence.

Thinking on those things he would give her brought him pleasure, one deepened by picturing her response as he presented them, one after the next. He had a second silk gown, left behind by his mother, of a watery green that he thought would become her almost as much as the gown of golden silk had, perhaps even more.

His father had a casket of gemstones, now his. Within were loose stones of lapis and garnet, rich in hue and well-cut; lustrous pearls the size of peas, waiting to be drilled and strung into a necklace; and the golden circlet which his mother had worn at table when she was at Kilton; he wore that which had been his father's. He would ask Modwynn to lay that circlet on Ashild's brow the first night she sat at table with them. And the second silver goblet Modwynn had given him would be set before Ashild as she took her place next him. His own already bore his name, incised on the lip, and he would have the silver-worker cut her name into hers. He had wished to have it ready for her, but Modwynn insisted he wait until she herself drank from it; after that he might take the cup to the silver-worker. His lids dropped over his eyes and he smiled, seeing her lift that cup for the first time to her mouth.

In his mother's jewel casket lay all the silver she had arrived at Kilton with, and all the silver and gold she had been given by her husband and his family thereafter. Only one prize was lacking from that casket, the great pearl which she had been given by her new in-laws when they heard she was with child. That pearl was now in the keeping of the Lady of Four Stones. He thought of the second piece of jewellery Hrald's mother now wore, the circle pin of gold he had selected for her when he brought the silk gown to her daughter. He recalled the skillful working of the intertwined beasts upon that brooch, and the delight it had given Ælfwyn, knowing it had been worn by his mother.

His mother. She could not know he had in fact grown to love Ashild. She was not here to welcome her, to make easy her way at Kilton as Ashild moved into her new role. He stopped himself there. Ashild was not one to be spoiled and petted; nor did he think his mother would do so if she were here.

He thought again of the word that applied best to the maid he loved: exacting. She expected, even demanded, much of herself, and of others. She was active and ready and as fit and strong as any of the fillies and colts she loved, and head-strong too, like the most spirited of them. He would be second here at Kilton, but Ashild would help him to always be his best. Maids were moulded to fit their husband's lives; with her it would be different. She would help him find his balance.

A new thought passed through his mind, creasing his brow. The silver hammer of Thor. Did she wear it still? Would she remove it once she came to live with him here? She must know that Modwynn and Edgyth could never see it, and women were much about each other when they bathed and dressed; she could not keep it hid. And Dunnere…

He roused himself. The final torches were being snuffed out at the cooking rings; the men within the hall would be upon their pallets. He must go in to his alcove, act as if he slept. After a while he would rise and dress, saddle his horse and walk him quietly away. He had spent part of the day counting out that treasure he would offer to win Ashild's hand, and this last Moon-lit hour musing on what he would present to Ashild herself. But now he wanted to see Begu. He had something special to ask her.

He had not visited her small house since the night before he had ridden off with Worr to join Eadward; three whole months. She had known of course he was going, had even confided to him during that long and cold last night that she would pray for his safe return. The way she had half-turned her face from him as she admitted this told him that she worried her prayers might be unworthy. Instead he had been moved by it, and had found himself taking her small hands in his and kissing them.

He had been back at Kilton for two nights; by now word would have come to her that he had returned. As he neared the end of the lane that led to her door he felt how much had changed. He had taken part in an ambush, under the command of the Prince of Wessex, and had killed a man, his first. Just as Begu would always be his first woman, the nameless Dane would remain his first kill. He shook his head in the dark, wanting to drive this from his mind. He reined in his horse; he was there.

She was asleep, but came swiftly to his tap and muffled call. He heard the fastening board be drawn back, and then she stood in the open door, her white shift glowing in the little light of the waning Moonlight. She gave a cry, like unto gladness, as he caught her lithe form up in his arms. When he released her she shut out the chill air, and dropped to her knees to kindle straws at her fire-pit to light the cressets.

He said almost nothing, but kissed her long and forcefully, pausing only as he pulled off his clothes. He drew her linen shift up and over her head, revealing the delicate paleness of her body. Her bed, piled high as it ever was with cushions, was still warm, and once in its soft depths he enfolded her in his arms, allowing himself to think of nothing, only to feel and act upon his need.

When they lay still he let out a long and slow breath. The cressets were bright upon the low roof-rafters, giving good light. He watched the flickering shapes the burning oil wicks cast over their heads, content in the silence, the warmth, the release of his desire.

Begu rarely spoke much, and asked no questions. Yet as they lay there, shoulder to shoulder, he thought she must wish to hear of his time away. He did not want to talk of it, and was glad she would not ask.

She turned on her belly next him. He felt her finger trace the scar upon his right arm, at the shoulder. The first time she had touched that scar, she had wondered aloud who had sewn it for him, "A man, I think, to judge the stitching…" It was not a question, but a quiet and tender musing, uttered with no expectation of being answered.

"No," he had found himself saying. "It was sewn by a woman. But she is young, and the light not good where she was forced to work." There was a huskiness in his voice as he told her this, one that surprised him, and soon after he found himself rising and dressing to leave.

Now Begu again traced the length of the scar. His body flooded with the memory of how it had felt to have Ashild hold the arm, how despite the searing pain of the sword cut he had told himself she was touching him as a wife would touch him.

He closed his eyes a moment. Begu withdrew her fingers, and after a while he turned on his side to face her.

"Begu," he breathed. "With a maid…?"

He wore a small half-smile of entreaty, and looked at this moment younger than he ever had.

Her eyelashes fell over her lids. The maid who had sewn his wound was there in the room with him, still present. She remembered how he had said, "But she is young…" not, "But she was young…"

She smiled back at him from the depth of her generous being.

"For a maid, whether she be shy or bold, you must take the time to make her eager, with your kisses and caresses to excite her." She paused, dropping her eyes a moment, before looking at him again. "These things you know well how to do," she assured him.

"She may be fearful; most maids are, but if through stroking her and kissing her you make her eager, the pain she will feel will be as nought.

"Go slowly, watch her face. Do not fear if she winces or cries out; it is the maidenhead breaking. If her arms are about your neck, if she is holding you, she wants you too.

"Then, later, she may be sore the second time. Kiss and stroke her, make her want you."

She ended now, and once more her pale lashes dropped over her eyes.

"You are speaking of your bride," she guessed softly.

"Yes," he confessed.

He thought of the watery green silk gown, which he would bring out at dawn as Ashild's morgen-gyfu, her morning-gift. He smiled to himself, picturing Ashild's face, when Begu spoke again.

"I am happy for you."

She always spoke softly; he did not notice the catch in her voice.

"Thank you. I – I will ride to meet her soon; she is a maid of Lindisse. After that – "

"I know. After that we can never meet."

Since Godwin's death, no one had slept in the treasure room. His widow Edgyth and young Edwin had moved to a newly-built bower house, fast by the stone chapel, and she lived there still. When Edwin received his sword he began to sleep in the hall with the rest of the men. When he wed, the treasure room would be his sleeping place once again.

The bower house where both Godwin and Gyric had taken their brides had sat empty since Ceridwen and Ceric had left for their visit to Four Stones. It was now to be given over to him, as the place he would bring Ashild, and being readied to accept him and his new wife.

Ceric had not often been within the bower house since he had left it with his mother. At length her valuables had been taken up and brought to the treasure room, awaiting the day of her return, a day which never arrived. There had been scant reason for him to enter the little round house. Now it was being cleansed from rafters to floor boards, the walls swept and washed, the wooden furniture scrubbed and waxed. Fresh linens were heaped upon a newly sewn featherbed, and pillows piled upon the frame of the big dragon bed.

He still had memory of his screams as a small boy, emerging from his alcove and seeing the blood upon his mother's gown as she stood in the open doorway during the Danes' first attack on Kilton. Pausing now at the threshold, he could see the slight depression in the wooden floor boards, where the planks had been sanded over and over to remove the traces of blood from the dead serving-man.

He put this out of his mind, and instead looked at the room like the soon-to-wed man he was. It was a fine space, and he could almost imagine Ashild's laughter ringing out, filling the little house with some jest they shared. There were two alcoves for coming children, the one he used to sleep in, and another, which his little sister Ninnoc had not lived long enough to use. The cradle they had both slept in had been made for him, and was still as unmarred as if it had been a year old. The cradle lay beneath one of the two casement windows, not far from the bed. He approached that bed now, the dragon bed that both his uncle and father had taken their brides to. Now he would do the same.

He neared the four posts which rose at the corners of the bed, each bearing at its summit the gaping mouth of a dragon. Each head was slightly different, but each had a painted, carved wooden tongue which flared forth from the opened mouth, like flames shooting above those who lay beneath.

On the wall by the bed were several pegs, pounded in to be handy to hang things at the ready. He looked at the pegs, then found himself unbuckling his seax belt, and hanging it and the shining weapon upon one. His father must have done that at day's end with this very seax. He spent a moment looking at it as lay against the plank wall.

"Some bed," Edwin said behind him. The door was open, and he had not heard his brother enter. Ceric turned to him with a grin. Over the years Edwin had even less reason to enter the bower house, and had in fact almost never been within. Now that it was being readied for his older brother he stopped in. He joined Ceric at the bed rail, and too lifted his eyes at the dragon heads towering above the feather mattresses. The old carved bed in the treasure room was a fine piece, massive and broad, and when Edwin wed it would be his. But this dragon bed Godwin had ordered made had a strength and power his own lacked. As he stood looking at it, his right hand rested on the hilt of Godwin's seax, strapped to his waist as it ever was.

"What – what is this," Edwin asked, reaching forward to one of the bedposts.

Ceric saw for the first time that one of the tall posts bore a knife-cut. It lay on the throat of the dragon at the head of the bed, that side nearest the door. He watched Edwin's fingers go to the cut, saw him run his finger down it. It was deep enough to be deliberate, a single hard thrust, into the throat of the dragon. It was not new, but slightly darkened with age. And it had not been touched; no one had tried to sand or smooth it.

"It was driven, hard," said Edwin. "A seax, I think." He looked to Ceric. "Who would do such a thing?"

"I do not know," Ceric admitted. He lifted his hand and touched the wounded wood himself. He did not know what it meant, but felt it somehow had a tale to tell, which it did by its very presence on the bed.

They heard their grandmother coming up behind them, and Ceric dropped his hand from the cut. He did not think Modwynn knew of this mark, and felt certain if she did she might order it sanded smooth, so all might be as flawless as could be for his wedding night.

"It must remain," he told Edwin, not knowing why. "Do not tell Modwynn of it."

But Modwynn had her arms full of linens, as she often had, and placed them on the table. She went next not to her grandsons, but to the cradle, bending to lay her long hand upon it, and giving it a gentle rock. Ceric turned and went to her, but Edwin remained gazing on the slash in the dragon's throat.

"It is empty," she said, looking down at the bare wooden interior, "and we will leave it so, until Ashild's first babe is born. In the meantime I will sew the plushest feather bed that ever child was laid upon."

As they stood there a serving woman poked her head in the door.

"My Lady, a rider has come, with a letter for Master Ceric."

At once Ceric felt concern. Letters were rare and often times of grave nature. The three left the bower house, following the serving woman past the pleasure garden and into the stable yard. A man strange to Kilton stood there, holding a shoulder pack. He was grimy from the road, and Ceric could see the man's horse was already within the stable, being attended to.

The rider was not a thegn, and he was not a churchman. He was of middle age, wiry, and looking between Ceric and Edwin.

"I am Ceric of Kilton," the older of the two said.

The rider bobbed his chin. "I am Wullaf, Sir, of the household of Tatwine the priest, he who Ælfred bid carry your letter to Lindisse. I have answer, from Hrald of Four Stones."

Answer, thought Ceric. He expected no answer; he was readying to leave for Bryeg to meet his bride and bring her here.

Wullaf was digging in his pack, pulling forth something pressed between two thin boards of wood, which had been bound with cord. He extended it to Ceric, who took it. "I thank you," he managed.

He went to his purse, pulled forth silver for the man. He heard Modwynn speak.

"The kitchen yard will give you food and drink, and refill your packs," she invited, gesturing to the serving woman to attend to the rider.

The man was led away, but Ceric stood with the letter-protector in his hand. Whatever lay within was of import to all of them; he could not take it alone. He led his grandmother and brother away from the noise of the yard, back to the pleasure garden. He laid the letter on the table of the pavilion, hearing the roar of the pounding ocean echoing his own beating heart.

They stood there as he unfastened the cords, took up the single small piece of parchment.

His eyes dropped down on Hrald's words, his friend's large, looping hand recalling the openness of Hrald's face. Then he read the few lines from Ashild.

> I cannot leave Four Stones…The danger is too great to all I love. I cannot now leave.

She is not coming, was all he knew.

He could not read it aloud. He found himself turning the sheet over. There was nothing on the back, nothing but the front face bearing Hrald's brief message, and that even briefer, from Ashild. He stared at the blank side as if dumbstruck.

He looked back to the waiting Modwynn and Edwin.

"She says she cannot leave now. The danger to Four Stones is too great. She invokes Ælfred, and the unsettled nature of Anglia. She does not say when she will come."

"Hrald?" asked his grandmother.

"He writes as well, sorry for the news. Offering hope for better to come," he finished.

He could not say more, and could not stay there, with them looking at him; Edwin was gaping. He took the parchment and folded it in half, hard, something never done with the precious material. He slipped the folded letter into his tunic.

He nodded to them, and left. His waist was bare of his seax and he went back for it, entering the bower house. There it hung, next to the dragon bed. He snatched it from the wall, buckled it on. When he left he shut the door with a slam behind him.

He took his horse from the paddock, saddled him, rode out through the palisade gate. He rode almost slack-reined down the pounded clay road, not seeing nor caring where his horse took him. Only when he realised the beast was making the turning to the hamlet where lived Begu did he stop him. He awoke from his stupor then, turned his horse away. He did not want to see Begu now.

He stood his horse in the middle of the road, then turned him back towards the hall and the main road leading from it. He passed the palisade, went on to the orchard of fruit trees, now coming into green leaf, and showing flower buds where fruit would be. He stopped at the final grove, that of the pear trees, and got off his horse. He stood beneath the open-work branches of a pear, and pulled out the parchment from his tunic. The warmth from his chest vanished in a moment as he held it.

CERIC OF KILTON

All at Four Stones are grateful for your esteem, and the beneficence of Ælfred, great King of Wessex.

I cannot leave Four Stones. Your King himself knows the unsettled nature of our Kingdoms.

The danger is too great to all I love. I cannot now leave.

Please forgive

ASHILD OF FOUR STONES

He read it again and again. There had been nothing hopeful about it, on first reading. But she had said, I cannot now. And he kept returning to her closing. She asked, Please forgive Ashild. Not, Please forget Ashild. He stared at her name, written with a broad and free hand, one that pressed hard upon the quill point.

One of the pear blossoms, dropping before a bee could visit it, did so now, falling on his opened letter, a flower which would never yield fruit.

That night Ceric drank many cups of ale at table. He had eaten little, and the noise of the hall angered him. He knew by the way his Aunt Edgyth and Cadmar looked at him that Modwynn had told them of the letter. There was warm concern in both their eyes, but he kept himself from doing more than nodding at them.

He lay down in his alcove desiring sleep, which would not come. He rose at last and saddled his horse, riding on a Moonless night to Begu.

He rapped hard on her door, not caring which of the neighbours heard him. She came almost at once to let him in, the surprise in her voice clear. He nearly pushed past her, coming into her small house. She fastened the door and bent, as she ever did, to pick fire and light her cressets.

"No," he said.

She rose, the unlit straws still in her hand.

"I can scarcely see you," she said, trying to be playful. He answered not.

"Why do you always wear dark colours?" she asked now. She could just make him out.

He was standing there unmoving, but gave a shake of his head. "I do not know…because my uncle did."

"I did not know your uncle," she said.

It startled him, the thought of the deeper meaning of her words. He let it pass.

"Is there mead?' he asked. There should be, with all the silver he had given her.

"Yes, of course," she assured him. She always kept a supply. He had once teasingly told her that each night with her was a feast, and they should only drink mead.

She felt her way to the cupboard chest, pulled out the crock, found the two well-wrought cups of bronze he had given her. "Here," she said, pressing one into his hand. He sat on the edge of her bed and drank it, almost in one draught.

He had another. The action of her pouring out for him made him think of Ashild, that only when she had sewn his wound had he taken a cup of ale or mead from her hands. Begu sat next him, sipping at the mead, feeling his trouble must stem from his coming bride, but being unable to ask about her.

He was still fully dressed, and she had put on her shift before she opened her door. She had draped a shawl over her shoulders for warmth; he had made no move to take her in his arms. At last he pulled off his boots and swung his legs up on her feather bed.

"Will you not undress, so I might hold you," she finally whispered. She felt him give a shake of his head for answer.

She lay next him, pulling the soft wool blankets up around them both as best as she could.

She heard his breathing soften, thought he slept.

"Are you lonely?" he asked of a sudden. It was a question almost to the dark.

She took a moment before she made answer.

"Yes. I am lonely."

He said no more, but after a time she was prompted to speak again.

"Why do you ask me this? Do you care for me? Or is it just that you care for what is your own?"

There was no harshness in her questions, only pain. She waited a long time for him to speak.

"The maid I will wed…she cannot come now." His voice sounded far away, and when he heard it, he must add to his words, change the meaning. "I must wait longer for her to come," he ended.

He felt her hand upon his shoulder. "I am sorry," she said.

She breathed out a sigh. He would not answer her questions, she knew; he was not even thinking of them. She went on, as gently as she could. "I will be your woman until she comes."

He turned his face further away, into the softness of the feather pillow. Tears pricked his eyes, which he held tightly closed. His head was spinning, and he felt he was drowning.

Begu wrapped her slender arm about him, and sang a murmuring song to lull him to sleep.

Chapter the Nineteenth: What I Already Know

Island of Gotland

CERIDWEN had not known true peace since Rannveig had walked up her hill to tell them she had Danes at the brew-house.

Each day thereafter might have seemed to an onlooker like any day at Tyrsborg. The small stone and timber hall was as rich with fine stuffs as it had been; those working about it as well- treated and content. The laughter of its twinned children still rang out. Bright Fall had gone down to dark Winter, and that Winter darkness had flared green and red with Northern Lights. Snow shrouded all, the crests of it glinting like flakes of sparkling gems in the short and brilliant days. The firewood piled to the roof eaves under the boughs of the spruces shrank tier by tier, keeping warm all within the snug hall. Spring rains softened the snow, allowing the green shoots of new growth to emerge by the roots of water-darkened rocks. The days lengthened.

All was as any new year for the Mistress of Tyrsborg, save this: the steady, and growing, knowledge that Sidroc would leave.

She knew it from the moment he had returned from the brew-house, and she had come upon him, standing in the middle of the treasure room, staring at the wall, and not, she knew, seeing it. Guthrum is dead, Danes had landed in Angle-land, a vast new army of them, he had told her. Most chilling was his certainty that those Danes long-settled there would be forced to fight either with or against the invaders. War could soon sweep over the broad face of that distant island, war that would be fought by their sons. War that could destroy those they had left behind.

Sidroc had not spoken again of what he had learned from the visiting Danes, and she did not ask him to repeat it. The way he had looked when he recounted to her the few facts stuck in her mind, that and his final words on the matter: War allows few choices.

He did not speak more on it, but the thought was with him, always. She saw it in his distraction. Many times when he gazed up into the star-filled sky, or stared into the flames of the fire-pit, she saw it. He was not only considering the goods he was gathering for the new trading season, those things their captain Runulv would carry off to the trading posts along the southern Baltic coast.

More than once she had come into the treasure room and seen him standing before the Wheel of the Year she had drawn there, that calendar to help her mark the days. He had one finger on Jul, those days of feasting surrounding the Winter Solstice, and another counting off the tick marks to the start of welcome Spring. The first time she had asked what he counted, and he had said the days until Runulv might sail. She had not believed him then, but said no more of it.

As the days warmed and lengthened Sidroc's distraction grew. It did not make him restless, rather more sober and alert, more grave. He had never given up his spear-practice, and each year hammered up new target boards that he flung at. This year snow was still upon the ground when he did so. He had pride in his spear-work, in the power and accuracy with which he could throw, but she thought he wore a different expression on his face this year, pushed himself the harder.

He showed his preoccupation when around the children as well. They had now almost nine years, both as healthy and as busy as ever mother could hope. Around Eirian Sidroc took on a new watchfulness, a fresh interest in what she said and did. She was slender-limbed, and would be tall. When she complained to her father that her pony was too small for her he took her next day to Ragnfast's farm and selected a new. Ceridwen might have claimed that he indulged her, but the girl was sweetly grateful, and surprised her father had taken her wish so seriously.

She saw it too with their son. Sidroc was teaching Yrling to throw a light spear himself, and one day as she watched them she saw him drop down behind the boy, arms about him, helping him to sight along the spear shaft for a truer strike. Yrling's head now bent over his shoulder, and he grinned at his father as he asked if he held the shaft properly. She watched Sidroc nod in approval, then saw his face change. He closed his arms about his son, and lowered his head. Ceridwen felt that he had seen the boy Hrald too between his arms, hoisting the spear he had made specially for him.

And alone and in bed with her he was different. The pleasure he had found in her body had never abated, but now his desire for her took on a new urgency. One or the other of them was often wakeful in the dark, and these were times when, in hushed murmurs, their deepest thoughts had been shared, whether of hope or fear. Now when they awakened they spoke less; she could not bear to, and he did not seem to want to. But more often than not he drew her to him, and gave himself to her in a frenzy of passion. It was the same need with which he had touched and handled her in their earliest months as man and wife here at Tyrsborg, but it was not with the same joy. There was something almost desperate in the way he sunk himself into her, clung to her, stroked and kissed her.

One morning, after she awakened and reached for her shift, he pulled her back into the warmth of their bed. The hall still slept; the dawn not yet advanced enough to much lighten the window high on the treasure room wall. He caught up her hand as she tried to slip from the bed, and he tossed the linen shift on her plush weaving that covered the floorboards she had stepped on. In a moment her naked body was pressed against his chest. Then his hands were upon her, wrapping her shoulders, cradling the soft fullness of her breasts, stroking down the length of her waist and belly to rest between the lushness of her thighs. His mouth swept over her throat and face to fasten on hers, as if he might devour her. He lifted her, spreading her knees apart with his own, and hung over her a moment. Then he almost buried himself in her body, as if he yearned to lose himself there within her.

When he drew back she did not lay her cheek upon his breast the way she ever had, her arm cast about his neck. She turned face down to her pillow.

She began to cry. She was soundless, but he saw, from the tail of his eye, her raised shoulder begin to shake. He touched her, turned her to him, his question in his face.

She shook her head, and choked out her words in little gasping sobs. "Because you will not tell me what I already know."

She stilled herself enough to hear his slow release of breath. His hand moved down from her shoulder to lie upon her hip, and rested there, cupping the flesh.

"What is it you know, shield-maiden," he asked, his voice just above a whisper.

She turned her face to him. Enough light was in the room so that she could see him clearly now.

"I know that you will leave. You will sail to Lindisse." She was not crying now, just repeating to him what she had heard within her own heart many times in these past few months. "You will leave."

He nodded his head. "Já," he allowed, in a breath.

His gaze shifted to the flat wooden chest lying atop another against the wall, the chest which held his closely-linked ring-tunic and helmet which Hrald had sent him. He had more than once this Winter opened that chest, fingered the tunic, placed the helmet on his head. He brought his gaze back to her, and again spoke.

"But you must also know another truth. I do not want to leave." His eyes rose to the roof rafters, and he gave a second long and slow sigh. "But I must."

She was propped on her elbows, and now let her head fall down between her shoulders. "I know you must go," she repeated. "Hrald. Ashild and Ealhswith. And Ælfwyn. All of them; all at Four Stones, all your men and folk. I know you must."

She turned to him, her tears still wet upon her cheeks. "I could not love you as I do, if you could stay."

He made a sound now, almost a groan, but softer, a sound of pain and recognition. He pulled her to him, pressing her against his chest, stroking her hair as she began to cry again.

He spoke, his hand upon her bright hair.

"Years ago I made vow to you, that I would not take ship again. Now I must. I waited ten years for you, and Freyja and Tyr together have given me these ten with you. I must break my vow to you, and to them.

"There will be war in Angle-land, perhaps great war. I have had these long and dark months to think on it. I can do no good here, but might do some at Four Stones. If I am granted life I will return as soon as I can. But I must leave with us both knowing I may not come back."

He let her cry; he knew there were months of pent-up tears behind those which stained her face now.

She wept with an openness that gave relief. They had both spoken the truth. It felt a stone which had been lodging in her heart since that day at the brew-house was now dissolved by the salt of her tears. She was able to cling to him, kiss his neck, press her fingers into the firm flesh of his arms, to do these things again with the unguarded abandon she had always cherished in their love-making. Now they could grieve together his leaving, celebrate together what they had known.

She brought her mouth to his ear. "You will come back. You will come back to me. To this. To our children. To all we have built here at Tyrsborg."

"If the Gods grant it, I will come back," he murmured. "If they do not – "

He paused long enough that she burrowed her face in his neck, his hair pressed like a webbing across her eyes.

"If they do not grant my return to Tyrsborg, I will be there, in Freyja's hall, awaiting you, shield-maiden."

His voice wavered at this, finally cracking at the name he had ever called her. "I will await you," he said, in a firmer voice. "I will await you there."

Later that day Ceridwen walked down to the brew-house. She found Rannveig in her brewing shed, rows and rows of thick brown pottery crocks before her, her worn wooden paddle in her hand.

Rannveig nodded and smiled, her still-bright blue eyes crinkling in her face. Her many bead necklaces, strung with glass balls and cylinders of every colour, lay in happy profusion about her plump neck. She moved towards Ceridwen, the mass of bronze and iron keys at her waist jingling with each step. She was about to pour out a taste of the new ale for her friend when Ceridwen spoke.

"Sidroc will sail with Runulv this time. They sail for Lindisse, to the lands where he was Jarl. He is certain there will be war there."

She said this simply, without the rise of tears. Yet the hollowness of her tone betrayed her dread to Rannveig. Ceridwen went on speaking.

"I have had this fear growing in my breast this whole Winter. We were finally able to speak of it, last night. He will go."

Rannveig gave a shake of her head.

"So that has been the trouble," said the brewster, wiping her hands on her apron. "He has not been the same. Nor have you, for that matter. I am sorry I ever told him of those Danes."

"Do not say that. He told me they were as messengers from Tyr, bringing warning."

"Warning – yes. And such sadness, now, to you."

"Já, " she nodded, tears now welling. "But the truth is the truth. It is always better to know it, than to live in ignorance, is it not?"

"When there be those you love at the end of it, já."

Rannveig had taken a step nearer, and now had her arms around Ceridwen. "And your boys," she thought aloud. "They will be of fighting age, themselves."

"Já. And they are of different Kingdoms, Rannveig. Kingdoms no longer at peace."

Rannveig pulled back from her, her hands still on Ceridwen's arms. "You mean they might fight the other?"

Ceridwen could not speak her answer, and only gave a single bob of her head.

Rannveig enclosed her again in her arms. She was shaking her head when she spoke. "Sidroc is forced to leave you, and your sons are in danger. And many others, too…What madness drives men to seek treasure, at the cost of life itself," she muttered, a question with no answer.

Two days later Sidroc saddled his horse and rode to the farm of Runulv and his wife Gyda. Going meant riding down the road of the trading town to the end of the workshops and stalls. All the folk working there were known to him; all looked up and nodded or called out as he walked his black stallion along the way skirting the blue vastness of the Baltic. As he lifted his hand to those he passed he thought again what he had thought many times, of the goodness of this place, a place now his home. At the end of that road he passed the wooden statue of Freyr. He nodded to the image of the God, as if he saw him. Runulv always made some small sacrifice there before setting out; he too would do so, to assure a good return.

Runulv had sailed to trade on Sidroc's behalf these past nine seasons. Early every Spring he had carried what goods Sidroc could amass to the most active of the trading centres within near or distant reach, most profitably to the Frankish city of Paris, built of stone and sitting on a small island in the middle of a broad river. Over the months Sidroc would gather all of value he could buy, barter, or raise – amber and furs and salt and grindstones and honey and precious trained goshawks – and entrust them to Runulv's care. Runulv had more than amply repaid that trust, both in his seamanship, and in his prowess as a trader.

Paris had been the readiest, and wealthiest market for their goods. But when a fleet of Danes had sailed up the Seine and been refused passage beyond it, they had laid siege to the city, and after months of bloody fighting had overcome it. For three years Sidroc had sent no goods there. Last season, deeming the place both safe and prosperous enough to return, he had Runulv again sail to Frankland, then trim his sails South down the great river Seine until he reached it. The trading there had again been good. But after what Sidroc had learnt from the Danes drinking at Rannveig's brew-house, he knew they could not return to the coast of Frankland this year. Marauding Danes would be using it as a staging ground to join that great army already beached in Angle-land. He had told Runulv of this last year, of the Dane Haesten's landing with a huge force in Wessex or Anglia. They had planned instead to send the ship across the water to the several trading posts on the southern Baltic shore. Runulv was readying his ship to leave within a week or two. Sidroc rode now to tell him of a change of route.

Sidroc had had months to consider what Haesten would do, and how Ælfred would respond. Haesten would have but one chance to assume Guthrum's mantle. He would need time to try and win as many of the settled Danes to his side, buying their aid with promises of treasure and lands to come. Sidroc reckoned he would not have much with him, carried off from the now well-defended Frankish coast. But he had his men and ships, and a fame great enough to persuade many others to fight under his command. Even so, he would not, Sidroc thought, move against the Danes of Anglia or engage Ælfred of Wessex until Spring.

He had turned his horse inland after nodding at the great image of Freyr, and made his steady way over greening soil to Runulv's farm. Gyda was out in the warming Sun, her new babe on her hip, her other three scampering about collecting downy goslings which had come running out of a breach in the fence of the big goose pen. She was laughing, and looked up at Sidroc with a smile, gesturing with her head that Runulv was inside the house.

He was, standing before a second trestle table which had been set up, and looking over his sets of scales and weights. He did not expect to see Sidroc, but laughed his welcome, waving his arm at his preparations for the coming sail.

Runulv did not plan to always trade, and felt he would sail only as long as he did so for Sidroc. He thought it would not be long before the Dane was himself content with the treasure he had so gained. This was why Runulv and Gyda were steadily adding to their lands, buying what they could and clearing it, breeding cattle and sheep, building up their herds and flocks so that the silver Runulv now won by trading could come from their own farm.

A serving woman brought them ale from the kitchen yard, and after had each taken a draught Sidroc spoke.

"You will not sail to the lands of the Pomeranie this year. I must go to Angle-land. To Four Stones, in Lindisse. Will you take me?"

Runulv's surprise could hardly have been greater, but he found his answer a moment later.

"Of course."

"We will take goods, be ready to trade in Aros in Danemark on our return trip." He paused a moment before going on with his instruction. "You will stop there and trade even if I am not with you; take what you earn back to Tyrsborg."

Runulv's eyebrows had lifted. "If you are not with me…?"

Sidroc's answer was short, but said in the same even tone of voice.

"I go to fight; to defend Four Stones. I may not return. But all you need do is take me to Saltfleet. I will know more then."

"I will not leave you there," Runulv answered.

Sidroc gave a shake to his head. "We do not know what we will find. Even landing at Salt Fleet might be hard."

In the corner of the house stood two spears, upright in an iron holder; all men of Gotland had thus. Runulv stood and walked over to them, plucked them both from the holder, and returned to the table. He lay them down upon its broad surface next to his scales.

"I will go with you to Four Stones," he said.

Sidroc looked down at the spears, one of which was still rolling, its point dully gleaming in the low light.

"Runulv," he answered, looking back at him. "You are my partner in trade. A good man of business. One of the best captains taking to the Baltic. And you are my friend." He glanced back at the spears a moment. "But you are no warrior. The men I am going to face – they are my brothers. They are in Angle-land for one reason only, to kill enough men to win. After we have landed, I will not let you come with me."

Runulv had straightened up during Sidroc's speech, and now looked quiet defiance at him.

"You gave me your sons to take to Lindisse. Entrusted them to me, in seas full of the same men. I was ready to fight and kill to get them there. Now you tell me I am not worthy of doing the same for you."

Sidroc opened his mouth, began to speak, but Runulv cut him off.

"I have a new ship because of you. We have doubled our lands, have twenty cattle and four score sheep. Gyda wears a golden chain about her neck. All because of you, Sidroc the Dane. I will land you at Saltfleet, and I will go on with you from there. Or I will not take you at all."

Sidroc had never known Runulv to be stubborn. He was fearless at sea in the face of heavy weather, cautious in speech, steadfast in action. Now he stood his ground against him. The younger man had nothing to prove, but demanded this chance to show both his mettle and his gratitude.

"Then we will go together to Four Stones," Sidroc agreed, placing his forearm against Runulv's, and closing his hand over it in embrace.

Sidroc rode next overland, to Tyrsborg's upland farm. It had been part of Rannveig's holdings from her parents, and when she had sold the hall to him, the farm went with it. It had always been known for its apples, and after Rannveig's father had died she and her mother had planted many more sapling trees. Ceridwen and Sidroc had given half-interest in the farm to Ring, Runulv's younger brother. Ring was a steady man and had ever been so, lacking the reasoned risk-taking of his older brother. The maid he had first brought to the farm as his wife, Ása, had died in childbed, along with their unborn babe. Ring had floundered until he wed her sister Astrid, and found happiness again. He and Astrid now had three young ones.

The farm they worked kept Tyrsborg in grain and vegetables, and apples in abundance. But Ring also had care of those trading goods most valued in distant lands. These were the goshawks. They were the offspring of those chicks that Sidroc and Tindr had once robbed from nests perched high in trees and atop stone pinnacles. It was Ring who raised the hawks, cared for them, and with Sidroc, trained them to return to the wrist after downing birds in flight, or seizing upon bounding hares in fields.

Ring was finishing the training of the two goshawks Runulv's ship would carry, building their sturdy wicker-work cages, and also that for the starlings he must net so that the birds would have fresh meat upon the journey. The two selected hawks were a male and female. Sidroc wished to take them as gift to Hrald, so that Four Stones might be able to raise up their own from this pair.

"They are destined for Angle-land," Sidroc remarked as he and Ring left the mews-house wherein the birds lived. "If any can take them there safely, it will be Runulv."

"He does not sail to Paris?" his younger brother asked in surprise.

Sidroc shook his head. "He will take me to Lindisse, as he did with the boys."

Ring was struck by this. "Is there then war?"

Sidroc was scanning the sky overhead, which had darkened. The air about them had grown cooler as well. Sudden squalls blew up quickly this early in Spring.

"I am not sure what I will find," Sidroc returned. "But I thank you for all you have done, with this farm, and the goshawks too."

Ring did not know what to say; it seemed a fare-well. He told Sidroc he would bring the birds by waggon, as soon as he sent word for them. Sidroc was moving to his horse and pulling himself up. A gust of wind sent a clump of dead leaves, twigs attached, skittering at his horse's hooves, making it dance out of the way and toss its head.

The ride back to Tyrsborg was through some of the fields Ring had cleared, and then along the forest path. The colour of the sky had bled steadily from a rich blue to the deep woad shade that plant gives up after long steeping. The wind blew his horse's black mane nearly straight back from his neck. They had almost gained the forest when the sky above him was split by an arcing bolt of lightning. It was close enough to dazzle the eyes, and for Sidroc to feel the charged air moving over his exposed flesh like a phantom hand. His stallion lifted his front legs in startle, one that turned into a plunge at the following crack of thunder, almost deafening to the ear.

He called out to his horse, keeping a firm hand on the reins as he guided him swiftly into the shelter of the many trees of the forest. Sidroc blinked his eyes; they were still slightly dazed from the brilliant white light.

He recalled when he sent his first ship under Runulv's care, a ship sent in high spirits, and hopes for gain. Before it sailed Sidroc had been aboard it, making sure all was ready. Then he walked up the hill to Tyrsborg. His shield-maiden had been waiting at the door, and they had stood together at the well, she in his arms, looking down on the ship as a bolt of lightning had cracked over the Baltic before them.

Odin must envy me, he had jested with her, and might send a lightning bolt to one day end my life.

Runulv told Gyda he would sail with Sidroc to Lindisse, but nothing more. He stressed that on the return they would stop at the large trading port of Aros in the Dane's homeland, but that other than that she should expect him back within the full waning and waxing arc of a Moon.

To the men who often sailed with Runulv, he told more. Several had been those who had been on the prior sail to Lindisse, and knew the additional danger the longer journey and greater exposure posed. They knew as well the greater gain; Sidroc had given Runulv added silver to supplement what he himself paid them as their share. There would, as always, be trading chances for the men who went, and they looked forward to the opportunity to carry on board from their own farms the good Gotland fleece, chunks of amber, or quern stones, and sell them on their own account. To the ten he approached for this trip he told the threat of attack, not only at sea, which they always sailed under; but told them also that once landed the threat might be the greater. No man should join who was unwilling to fight, both for his life, and to protect the ship.

If the weather remained clear they would leave in a few days. At the warehouse by the pier sat a pair of perfectly matched grindstones, ready to be loaded. At Tyrsborg Tindr was readying crocks small and large of his good honey, sealed with wooden stoppers smeared with wax. A pile of small furs, that of fox, martin, and beaver, bought from Osku the Sámi, lay bagged. And under the floorboards of the treasure room were strands of worked yellow amber-bead necklaces, of a smoothness and hue to gladden the heart of the women around whose necks they were to be laid.

The preparation went on as it did each year, but this time with the knowledge that Sidroc himself would go. All that

Ceridwen did to aid the lading or ready the goods she did with a catch in her throat. She stood at one of the kitchen yard work tables, helping Tindr and Šeará with the honey. Their boy Juoksa was running about, and Eirian was chasing after him, tickling him under the chin when she caught him with a long rooster feather. Ceridwen watched the boy, dressed in the softly napped deerskin leggings and tunic his mother had made him. He was a beautiful child, with his mother's pale hair, and large blue eyes peering out from skin of ivory whiteness. In a few months he would have a sister or brother, and the thickening of Šeará's narrow waist told it would be before the snow came.

Ceridwen had told Šeará that Sidroc was journeying far, and hoped that the Sámi girl could tell Tindr more fully of it; Sidroc had gestured to him that he was sailing, but Ceridwen did not think he understood where, or why.

"Your man," Šeará said to her as they stood wiping the outside of the jars. "He is sailing far? Back to his homeland, where the Sun sets?"

"Far beyond his homeland. Both lay in the West, but he is sailing to my homeland, the great island where I was born."

"Then you are from the place where the Sun sets," Šeará said, more than a little interest showing in her soft voice.

Ceridwen must needs smile at this. "Nai, it sets even further West than my great island. I do not think any ship has sailed so far to know where."

Šeará nodded. Her chin turned, as if she herself looked for that distant point. "But he must go, West to your home land."

"Já," Ceridwen said. She did not know what more to tell her, and simply said, "He lived there for some years, has people there…"

"He will visit them, check his herds, and then return to you," Šeará proclaimed. She said this with a confidence Ceridwen yearned to feel.

The Sámi went on, with a look that searched Ceridwen's face. "Your own home – do you not sicken for it?"

Ceridwen paused. She had spent time in marsh-land by the River Dee, on the broad landscape of Lindisse, on strong cliffs above the crashing seas of Kilton, and travelled the breadth of the vast island through its forests. "I lived several places on the great island of Angle-land," she told Šeará. "It is a green and rich place. But there are certain folk I miss, and not the land."

Šeará took this in, and nodded to herself. She had not seen her own northern lands for four Winters. Her father Osku still made the trip each Fall, with the Gotlandic trader Gautvid, and traded furs for grain and cloth and silver ornaments.

Ceridwen saw Šeará's eyes follow her little son as he darted, laughing, about the tables with Eirian giving chase. With her eyes still upon him she told Ceridwen, "Juoksa has had no ren-milk, eaten no ren-meat. He has not looked into their eyes, nor touched his nose to theirs."

Her head lifted now, a head with an almost deer-shaped face, a face of high cheek-bones and slanted eyes, long yellow-white braids descending, crowned with a leathern cap worked over in thread-work of blue and red. It was a face Ceridwen had always found beautiful. "He has not seen nor walked my forests."

The Sámi's voice was tinged with sadness, for all its sweetness of tone. She had paused in her work to place a hand upon her hide tunic, over her coming babe. Ceridwen felt with a keenness that hurt her already-swollen heart how homesick she was.

But Šeará was talking again, smiling at her boy Juoksa, her eyes flitting too to where Tindr stood, absorbed in his work, fitting wooden stoppers on a line of pottery crocks. "All must return home, one time at least. Wolf Eyes too wishes to see my ren again."

At this Tindr raised his eyes from his work, his eye caught by the movement of his boy. His son was laughing, a merry peal that wreathed his little face in smiles, and Tindr smiled too at the joy he felt but could not hear.

Tindr awoke next morning, not feeling called to hunt, but to go into his forest. He had set no snares for small game, and it was early Spring. The stags and boar he hunted were all deeper into the trees, and would stay there until their blood called out for the Fall rut. Deer lay asleep next him, under a coverlet she had stitched of the hides of the animals whose name she shared. Her cap with the bright red and blue thread work was near her side, and her long yellow-white braids fell freely upon the paleness of her throat and arms.

Their son, Bow, lay sleeping in his box bed in his alcove. Tindr slipped from the bed and stood a moment looking down on him, parting the wadmal curtains Bright Hair had woven. The boy lay on his back, arms and legs flung wide under his own small hide coverlet. Bow's hair was as white as Deer's, and his skin as milky. Tindr did not think he had seen any creature so wonderful as Deer, until he saw their son. Bow was a fitting match for his mother, and his eyes were light too, not as light as his own, but near. His mouth was partly opened, and his father watched the small chest rise and fall with each breath.

On the wooden wall above Bow's head hung a small bone whistle. The boy had early learnt to come when he heard the two note, long-and-short call Tindr had devised for him. When he was old enough he begged his father for a whistle of his own. Tindr had carved one, from the fore-leg bone of a stag, just as he carved his own, and after drilling it out and smoothing it, sounded it for Deer. She smiled and nodded her head at its sound. He gave it to Bow, who trilled happily away on it. Tindr went about his other tasks, only to find an angry Bow butting against his legs, face red from puffing away on the slender piece of bone. Deer lifted her head from her sewing, and called to the child. Tindr watched both her lips and hands move as she tried to tell their son that while his father used a whistle to call to him, he could not hear that which Bow used. Now Bow had almost six Summers, and understood these things.

He pulled on his clothing and opened the door to the gathering day, leaving his bow and quiver on the wall. Despite the never-dulling joy of Deer and Bow, and the new child to come, he felt troubled. When he felt thus he knew to allow himself to walk.

He headed out of the circle of birches that hedged their house, and up one of the fern-lined woodland paths. As the Sun climbed he found himself on top of a hill, a place which Deer liked, and which they often climbed together. She would stand and look North, and narrow her blue eyes and tell him with her hands that she saw her ren-deer, far away. He thought of this now, of how this place was his home, and that Deer at times yearned for that place which had been hers. The only time he thought her sad was then.

And he thought of Scar, and Scar's going. Scar had gestured to him that he must go, sail away, and all Tindr could do was nod. Deer had told him more, told him Scar had both kith and kine he must check on, but would be back after he did so.

Tindr did not believe this. Scar would not leave Bright Hair for the sake of his flocks of sheep or herds of cattle, or even ren-deer, if those beasts roamed the forests he was heading to. Tindr had watched Scar kill a man to keep Bright Hair safe, but now he left her. Something was wrong, wrong enough that Scar must leave her.

Standing on the hilltop, he wondered if it had to do with the boys, Scar and Bright Hair's sons, who had spent a Winter with them. They had left by ship, just as Scar told him he must.

He thought of his own son. He would do much, anything, to aid Bow if he was in danger. It must be this that drove Scar away from all he had here.

Ceridwen was sweeping out the hall with Helga, the serving-woman, each aiming for the doors opened to a fine and dry morning. Ash from the fire-pit always blew over the floor boards, even with the larger rocks Sidroc and Tindr had rolled in to hold the fire. And bits of straw, clods of soil, stems and stalks were carried in on all their clothing. The action of sweeping was one that comforted Ceridwen, and gave her birch twig broom a purpose beyond that of mere cleansing.

She stopped at the alcove in which Yrling slept, leant her broom against the wall, and plumped up the feather bed with a shake, then tidied the blankets. When they were tiny he and Eirian had slept in a single alcove, but for the past few years they had had each their own. His was also that in which

Ceric had slept, for those months he had lived at Tyrsborg. That which Hrald had used was next his, and the boys had slept head-to head, sometimes tapping out signals to each other through the wooden wall that divided them.

She sank down on the box bed, and placed her hand on that wall. Of a sudden she was overcome with sadness, thinking on the homely pleasures of those days, and of the dangers facing Hrald and Ceric now.

She rose and found Sidroc, out in the paddock with the horses. Her dun mare was nosing along the withers and back of her dark son, whose front hoof Sidroc let drop. He straightened and moved free of the horses.

"Ceric," she said, as simply as that. She thought how to ask the next, but he answered before she had need to speak.

"He will fight with Ælfred," he said, in way of assurance, "or with the King's son."

"The way his father did," she murmured.

He went on, telling her things she already knew, as a way to give her comfort. "He will be surrounded by the most skilled warriors in Wessex. He will have a fine war-kit, weapons of the best.

"And – I think he will have that thegn, Worr, at his side. Worr is a good man. I would want him at my own."

This held meaning to her, and she looked gratefully at him for it.

"And of Edwin?" she went on.

He ran his hand through his hair. He had never seen the boy, Ceric's half-brother, but he knew he would never get the face of Edwin's father out of his mind.

"He will have a sword now," she went on.

"Then he is old enough to fight." He looked at the paleness of her face, the colour drained from it through worry.

He thought now of Cadmar, the warrior-monk who years ago had bested him at arm-wrestling at Kilton's high table. Ceric had received his earliest training in arms from that monk, and while the boy was here at Tyrsborg let it be known Cadmar was also trusted advisor to the Lady of Kilton. The man was more than capable, and having, as it were, one foot in both worlds seemed imbued with special power.

Sidroc knew Christians had their own magic, a potent one. Danes who had lived amongst them knew this; they used bells and chants and smoking scents to raise spirits and offer prayers. A man like Cadmar knew the ways of the warrior as well as the secret ways of the holy men and women who wore the cross. Both youths would have the benefit of that knowledge.

"I have been twice to Kilton," he reminded her. "I have seen its men. Haesten will have to fight through them to get to Ælfred, or your sons."

He could say nothing beyond this, give no further reassurance. Young and old, good warriors and poor, all will fall on the field of battle if the shield-maidens point their way. This she knew.

She stood looking up in his face.

All of you, she was saying within her heart. I fear for all of you. You who I love beyond counting, beyond measure, you who believed I would love again. Our sons, far from us, and mayhap soon forced to fight, to save their lands and home. Your daughters. And Ælfwyn – she who is the sister I never knew, whose life is bound to mine in every way…

She did not trust herself to speak. She swallowed down the knot in her throat, and forced a smile. She gestured he should go on with his work, turned to go back to hers.

Once in the hall she did not return to her broom. Helga had finished the sweeping and taken it away. The doors to the hall were closed to keep the green pollen from wafting in on the breeze.

She went to the treasure room door, unlocked it, and let herself inside. There against the wall was the chest that Hrald had sent his father, bearing within his abandoned war-kit, his ring-shirt and helmet. She went to the chest, and found herself reaching her arms over it, lowering her head to it, wanting what lay within to protect Sidroc, protect all of them.

She heard a sound, the door closing behind her. Sidroc bent over her, pulled her from the wooden chest. He turned her in his arms.

"Come and be mine," he told her. "It is the only way I can forget I leave."

He lifted her from her feet and laid her upon their bed.

Later that day Ceridwen took a precious sheet of lambskin parchment from a box in the treasure room. She scratched her guidelines in with the sharp point of a steel needle, so that her words would not drift up or down upon the sheet. Then she mixed her ink. By the time she had cut a fresh point on her goose quill words were welling in her heart.

MY DEAREST SISTER ÆLFWYN

> When you hold this letter, may it be as if I am slipping my own hand into yours. For that is the nearness I feel with you, through these words. My fears

for you and your loved ones is great, but will be as nothing compared to those you have suffered yourself. The greatest of these has been our boys finding themselves not the brothers they feel themselves to be, but the enemies that others tell them they must be.

Danes landed here last Summer at the end of the sailing season, bearing news of war to come in Angle-land. Sidroc had not a moment of ease after that, nor had I. That he has sailed now to help defend Four Stones may surprise some, but not, I think, you.

Our lives are in the hands of our Gods. This both you and I believe. Until I have your letter back, know that each day I invoke and bless your name.

YOUR LOVING CERIDWEN

The letter was short, and the sheet of parchment small. She quelled the lump rising in her throat by turning to its protection until it should find its way into the hands of the Lady of Four Stones. Two thin panels of wood were found in the stable, and she slipped the letter within them. She melted beeswax and waxed a piece of densely woven linen, proof against wet. This she sewed tightly over the boards. When she had done she thought of Ælfwyn with her fine sewing shears, nipping away at the lacing she had sewn, and found a smile rising to her lips.

A day later Ceridwen stood alone in the treasure room, combing out her hair. It was as thick as it had ever been, and had continued to grow, reaching now past her waist and to her hips. She thought it her chief beauty, and in the caring for it had always taken pleasure.

Tindr knew her by her hair, had named her for it, a touch of his hand to his own hair, then fingers flung wide, which Sidroc had told her stood for what he had oftentimes termed her tresses: bright hair.

She stood with her comb in her hand, that same comb of veined ox-horn that Sidroc had bought for her their first full day on the trading road. The teeth were widely spaced, the horn smooth and expertly sawn, the work of the mother and daughter comb-makers of the place. Now as she held her hair in one hand and combed through the tips of it she had a thought. Her hair was of her body, yet somehow apart from it as well. A strand cut from her head looked the same as that which still grew; it did not fade nor corrupt. There was power in hair.

She went to her work basket, drew forth the sharp bird-shaped shears of the Idrisid women, had them at the ready. She reached under her hair, deep within by the scalp, and fingered a section, pulling it free. Then she began to braid that strand.

The day before he was to sail Ceridwen and Sidroc told the children he was going. They were untroubled; their father sometimes had need to leave for several days to ride the rough way to the southern-most tip of the island to order or check on mill stones or querns, or to head across the broad body of Gotland to see silver or amber workers on its western shores. Only when they saw the glistening of their mother's eyes did they pause. A quick swipe of her knuckle swept the forming tear from growing, and she smiled at them. Their father said he would sail with Runulv. Well, Runulv always returned, and with bags of silver and sometimes pieces of gold that made their father grin. Now he would come back with the gold himself, they thought.

Runulv's ship lay tied at the wooden pier by the brew-house. The heavy mill stones had been loaded, as had the barrels of water and chests of food stores. All the rest would be carried aboard just as Runulv's men themselves were boarding, laden with packs and the goods they hoped would bring a profit in Aros.

The day was busy. Gunnvor had been up at dawn, stuffing food bags for Sidroc. Helga had helped Ceridwen gather the kit he would need, that for the ship, and that which would be needed to camp on land. And Ceridwen smoothed and rolled his clothing. He was taking little with him, and almost no jewellery; a broad silver cuff he favoured on his wrist, nothing more. But he had counted out much silver in coin the night before, done it before his shield-maiden, and had two purses tucked into his belt.

"All the gold is here," he told her, kneeling on the floor of the treasure room. The short floor board that covered the opening in the earthen floor beneath was lying to one side, and she knelt on a corner of her folded-back plush weaving. He gestured to the many small crocks sunk into the hole.

"That gold which is yours, your morning-gift from me. And all the gold pieces I have earned from trading." He pointed to another pot. "The gold cuff, of the Rus. The larger pots are full of silver, both coins and hack."

She knew all this, but his telling her again gave them both comfort.

"Will you not take some gold," she asked, as he counted out the silver he had chosen for the trip.

"Nai. This will be enough. If it is not, having gold will make no difference."

They would sail next day at noon, on the receding tide. In the grey light of morning Ceridwen was in the kitchen yard, helping Gunnvor with the final packing of food. She lifted her head and watched Sidroc slip into the forest. She thought she knew where he was heading.

He walked alone along the trail through unfurling ferns and mosses looking black in the little light. There had been rain in the night, and the bark of the smooth beeches and birches showed where the drops still ran down. He passed hollows in which a few crusts of snow lay melting, further darkening the clots of brown leaves caught there. He went on a short way, then turned to the place of Offering he had made.

It was where he and his shield-maiden and Tindr and Rannveig had gathered at his first sacrifice at Blót, that blood-month of coming Winter. He had offered seven sows that year, a gift that reflected his thankfulness for coming whole and well and with the woman he wanted to this good island.

Now he stood alone, looking at the low platforms he and Tindr had built, bearing the tattered remains of animals sacrificed there. They had been sent mainly to Freyja and her brother Freyr as thank-offerings, but he had come here and spoken to Tyr as well, that God of justice he had long ago given himself to. Tyr was his God, and had ever guided his arm.

He had need to speak to Tyr now.

Sidroc had made a vow, one made none the less sacred for it being sworn in his own stable yard.

"You are the last," he had vowed, before he delivered the death-blow to Godwin of Kilton.

"Tyr," he spoke aloud, lifting his hands, and looking up into the bare branches of the trees hedging the place. He had ever felt that Tyr saw him, watched him even.

"I made a vow: not to kill again. Now I must break that vow. If I die, I will not blame you. You are the Law-giver, and my death will be the just answer for all the men I have killed. I know that.

"But if I am truly your son, understand what I do. I go to help my own son. His sisters. Their mother. Know that is why I sail. That is why I will kill again."

He had arrived in the grove empty-handed. The God also would have noticed that.

"I bring you no Offering. None but myself. If you deem it, I will be your sacrifice."

He dropped his head a moment, thinking on the moment of his death. He shook that head, lifted it again to the naked branches of the trees. There was a second vow he must break, that he made to his shield-maiden. He had told her would not take ship again, would live the rest of his life here on Gotland. In her kisses she had forgiven him, but Freyja had been called to witness that vow.

"Freyja, white-armed one. You know all that is done between my shield-maiden and me. You marked her to be mine, and at last gave her to me. Keep her safe when I am away. And if I cannot come back, lighten her heart with the knowledge I await her in your jewelled hall."

That hall felt closer to him than it had in many years. His eyes lifted higher, far up in the interlace of stark and reaching branches.

Broken vows brought disaster. Guthrum had once sworn a sacred vow on a great silver arm ring, a vow made before the Gods and Ælfred. Sidroc had sworn it too, smeared with his own blood that mass of silver, as did all of Guthrum's chief men. Then Guthrum, pushed by those men of his who wanted still more, was forced to break his vow, was forced to once again attack Wessex at Æthelinga for a final try at all. There the raven banner of the Danes fell, and they were routed. It was the very same war-flag which had been woven by the great Ragnar Lodbrok's daughters, and it had never failed to do nought but advance upon the enemy. A broken vow heralded Doom.

He shook his head again, driving this away, and stood looking at the dripping trees a while longer. A bird sang out, the clear and hopeful song of one seeking a mate. He turned and made his way back to his home.

At noon the swollen tide began to turn. Runulv had long been within his ship, had the steering oar untethered. He checked and rechecked the lashings of the heavy grinding stones near the keel. His men were clambering back and forth from pier to ship, carrying on goods. Some had wives, and all had parents or siblings, who now crowded the wooden planks, or stood watching from the trading road.

The goshawks, wicker cages covered by tanned hides to keep the birds warm and dry, were aboard, and secured. Tindr's honey, a bundle of furs, the bags of amber, these were in place.

Sidroc had carried his packs on. Then came his black-and-white painted shield, and the two spears he chose, one long, such as the Danes and men of Gotland used, and that light and fast throwing spear taken from the ship of the Idrisids. He saved for last the chest which held his ring-tunic and helmet. He had buckled on his sword belt; it had been long since he had done so.

Once again Rannveig had come out of her brew-house, and summoned a few of those sailing to roll a cask of her good ale on board, as her parting gift.

She had a second gift this time. A smaller cask, of mead.

"Drink it in health, Sidroc the Dane," was all she could say. She stepped back, put her arms about the shoulders of Eirian and Yrling.

Sidroc swallowed, but said with a strong voice. "We will tap it when we turn for home."

Tindr stood there, with his wife Šeará. Their little boy was at their legs, touching both of them as he looked with big eyes at the ship bobbing pier-side.

Tindr stepped forward. Scar looked to him, then lifted his hands. He reached one out before him, then pulled it back, closing the fingers as he did so. With the same hand he tapped his heart. With both he steepled the fingers together, the sign for the steep-roofed hall where Scar and Bright Hair lived. Then Scar inclined his head to where Bright Hair stood.

Take care of them, he told Tindr. Tindr nodded back. Then he extended his own hand, drew it back, closing the fingers as he did so, and tapped his chest. He pointed to Sidroc. Take care of yourself, he said in return.

All was in readiness. There was no further fare-well, save that for his wife. He took a step further down the wooden planks of the pier. She followed.

He stood looking down at her. He had asked her to wear the red gown he had bought her long ago on the Baltic coast, one she wore only for high and happy feasts.

"Shield-maiden," he told her. "If I do not return, I will be with you, always."

She was biting her lip to hold the tears.

"Do not weep, my beautiful one. Freyja, in whose image you were made, prepares a place for you. I will await you in her hall.

"If I come back, we will laugh at this parting, laugh that we could not see Freyja smiling down on us. Think on that day, shield-maiden, when we will again laugh."

His arm closed around her, pressing her one last time to his chest. Then he stepped back, turned to the waiting ship.

They cast off. A cry arose from the throng on the pier, much like that sounded every time a ship sailed from there with men of Gotland heading for a far place. Sidroc stood in the stern, looking back at the cluster of folk from Tyrsborg, fixing his eye on the red of his wife's gown.

Runulv, at his side, kept his eye ahead, as firmly as his hand was on the steering oar. He had never let Gyda come to the pier and see him off; it was too hard. He was glad she did not know the danger he faced.

The coast slipped by, one of bright white rock, and budding trees of tender green set in clusters of dark ever-clothed pines and spruces. Towering rauks, great limestone shafts, stood with their feet in the clear waters.

Late in the afternoon when they had cleared the tip of Gotland, Sidroc opened the pack that held his clothing. There on top lay a slender coil of chestnut-gold hair, tightly braided. A lock of her bright hair, which she had cut as a talisman. He lifted it.

It was bound at either end with silk thread, that same red thread she had sewn the wound on his thigh with. Then she had sewn the ends together. He touched the plait to his lips a moment, then dropped it over his neck, underneath his tunic.

Chapter the Twentieth: Call to Battle

Kilton

"THERE are more than four score Danish war-ships in the Thames basin alone. That is where we will set our blockade, North of Middeltun."

The speaker was Eadward, Prince of Wessex, sitting at the great table on the stone dais at Kilton, in a hall emptied save those he would directly address.

Flanking him as he sat were Edwin on his right, and Ceric on his left. Cadmar, Worr, and four of Eadward's chief men were also there. A lone woman, Modwynn, sat in her accustomed chair of carved oak. Eadward had not had the close personal contact with the Lady of Kilton as had his father, but he granted her the same respect as would the King. She was well-regarded by both men for her wisdom. She also possessed riches in her own right, and Eadward knew this new conflict would demand much silver.

"The blockade will be enacted on land and water. We will sail up the Thames with enough ships to stop the enemy from seeking safety at sea. Half of us will close on the Danes by land, from behind. Any who break through, trying to run overland, will meet the King and his army, ranged about to hold them from fleeing into the countryside."

Eadward paused, looking from face to face of those he addressed. Ale had been poured, but after a single draught sat untouched as the Prince detailed his war plans. He had arrived with a small group of picked men only a short time ago, and would spend but a single night at Kilton. In the morning he would be off to the next burh with his news.

"Ceric brings me twenty men," Eadward went on, turning to his left as Ceric bowed his head to him.

The youth's face wore the same alert but impassive expression that all the men bore. Only the subtle tightening of his jaw, and the tautness of his temple under his coppery gold hair betrayed otherwise.

It was come, Ceric knew. He would soon be thrust into full scale battle, taking his place in a shield-wall on land, or crowding the decks of a war-ship at sea. His hand tightened around the stem of his silver cup, as if it were his sword-hilt. He lifted his eyes again, to see that of Edwin fast upon him, large and round.

The Prince looked now to Edwin. "I would ask you for thirty more."

A slight pause. Edwin commanded the larger part of Kilton's thegns, almost fifty men. Ælfred had for years devised his defences so that no burh need send all its men into the field at once. Edwin had yet to ride out to any skirmish, but a quantity of his men had ever faithfully answered the King's call in the past. Now the Prince asked that more than half of Edwin's men join with those warriors pledged directly to Ceric, and leave now. The request was proof indeed of the dire nature of the Danish threat.

Edwin had been schooled in temperate speech, but a movement of his body towards that of the Prince and Ceric spoke before he opened his mouth. Cadmar was sitting almost opposite him, and he thought he read the warrior-monk's approval in his twinkling eyes.

"They are yours. And I will go myself," Edwin proclaimed. "Thirty-one to join you, and my brother and his men."

Eadward stopped him with a shake of his head. "That you cannot not do," he said with decision. "You are Lord of Kilton, and must remain here. But thirty of your thegns I have great need of. Like those of your brother, I will place them under my direct command."

All at the table knew this would leave Kilton with less than twenty thegns with which to defend itself. Heads shifted, as eyes moved about from face to face, taking this in.

Modwynn's cheek had paled at her younger grandson's offer to ride himself, and was only grateful for the speed with which Eadward had refuted it. After the death of her son Godwin she had shepherded Kilton for a long time, waiting for these two boys to grow. Kilton must never be left Lord-less again.

Eadward's thoughts remained on the challenge ahead. "You must stay at Kilton," he repeated to Edwin. He then added that which none wished to contemplate.

"You will be called for, if there is need."

The soberness of this promise and the thought behind it hung in the air a long moment. Edwin would be asked to abandon his hall only in the most desperate straits, something that Eadward had already been forced to consider.

The Prince took time now to lift his cup to his lips, breaking the tension for all. He lowered his cup and addressed Ceric.

"We will meet at Witanceaster in seven days," he went on. "Be ready to ride in two."

That night before the hall met at table, Ceric begged a word with the Prince. Eadward would spend the night in the treasure room, and was there now, with the four of his thegns who had sat with him earlier. The five were in discourse of their own, but the thegns rose and stood by the far wall as Ceric addressed his Prince.

"My Lord," Ceric began. Eadward too had risen, and now stood before him, just past the threshold. Filled as it was with the Prince and his men the treasure room seemed almost strange to Ceric, no longer part of Kilton.

Ceric had thought of what he wished to say, but felt ill-equipped to make answer if Eadward should challenge him in any way. Though he had only two years more than he, the Prince was old beyond his years. And he was altogether a more forbidding man than his father, who despite his will of iron, had a gentleness about his person which Eadward lacked. Ceric found himself taking a deep breath before he went on.

"I wish to thank you for the trust you place in me and my men. It is the greatest of honours to ride at your side, and to face the enemy in your father's name."

It was also Ceric's pledged duty to offer his life for his King; both knew that, but he must open his request with the formality of gratitude, even should he soon lose that life in the service of Wessex.

Eadward nodded, accepting this, waiting for more.

"It is of Lindisse I wish to speak, my Lord; South Lindisse, and the keep of Four Stones."

Eadward's eyes flitted upwards a moment, in recollection. "That won by Yrling, then held by Sidroc," he summed.

"Yes, my Lord. The jarl there now is Sidroc's son, Hrald, who has eighteen years."

Ceric paused a moment. "I – I know him well; our mothers were close friends. I wish you and the King to know that Hrald will honour the Peace made by your Father the King, and Guthrum. Sidroc signed it too. Hrald will honour it. This I know."

Eadward did not expect this, and shifted his weight slightly in response. He knew the history of every hall of any size which had fallen to the enemy in any of the lost six Kingdoms in the past twenty years; it was his business to do so. But he spoke first from his gut feeling.

"They are Danes, never to be trusted." His tone was as flat as his words were blunt. "A Danish pledge is worthless. They have proved that over and over again."

Ceric's jaw worked, he felt his throat tighten. He could not contradict Eadward, he knew. But he must speak. He dare not tell the Prince that Hrald was a committed Christian; he would dismiss that as well.

"Hrald – he is half-Dane," Ceric said. "As are his sisters," he added, almost blurting it out.

Eadward knew this lineage of the family of Four Stones. He spent a moment considering this, that if any Danish keep would uphold the Peace, it might be Four Stones. He knew Hrald's mother had been Ælfwyn of Cirenceaster. He recalled now that his father had given leave to Ceric to send for the maid of Four Stones, to be Ceric's wife. This changed a great deal.

"You are to wed the daughter thereof," the Prince said.

"I am," Ceric assented. He made his voice firm, though his chest felt hollow at his claim.

"Would that you had already done so," Eadward mused. He gave a single shake of his head now.

"The Danes – Haesten and others – will place great pressure on Hrald of Four Stones," Eadward went on. "I do not think so young a Jarl will be able to withstand it. His own men may rebel against him, wanting to join with Haesten against us."

Here was voiced all the fears that Ceric had secretly harboured. He must reject them, and he did.

"Hrald will honour the Peace his father made," Ceric returned. His voice was low, yet strong with his belief.

All Eadward could do was nod, that and a slight lift of his chin.

"Why tell me this," he questioned. "You cannot know how fares it in Lindisse. We can send neither word nor aid to Four Stones. Hrald is on his own. I pray God he is the man you say he is."

There was unintended sharpness in Eadward's words. In softer tone he went on.

"Fate favours you after all, that you have not yet wed the maid. If so she would be hanging round your neck, crying and begging, in fear that you are soon to face her brother, riding to join those Danes at Middeltun."

Ceric could say nothing to this; he could no more picture Ashild hanging in tears about his neck as he could

Hrald forsaking his vow to honour the Peace. He only bowed his head and murmured, "I thank you, my Lord."

All of Kilton was much occupied with the outfitting of the men who would leave. If Modwynn did not run the hall and yards as capably as she did, such a thing would have been unmanageable on such short notice. But all played their part in equipping the men and beasts who would travel across Wessex to Witanceaster, and from there to the furthest eastern shores of the vast island. His Aunt Edgyth took charge of preparing Ceric's own clothing, just as Worr's wife Wilgyfu did for him. Most of the men riding with them were wed, so that parting must be born.

Ceric's alcove was small, and his war-kit, clothing, and other needful things were being packed in the treasure room. Edgyth had largely finished with clothes and bedding for him, and had left the room. Edwin was there, watching his brother polish the blade of both sword and seax.

"Will you go out tonight," Edwin asked him. His question was quiet, but pointed.

Ceric raised his eyes from his work, and the polishing cloth slowed in his hand.

"Go to see your woman," Edwin went on.

Ceric's lips had slightly parted. Edwin did not mean to make it hard for his older brother.

"I know, of course," he went on. "You have a woman in the village you go to."

Ceric's eyes dropped down to his seax blade, that once worn by his father. "I do not know," he confessed. "All is so busy here."

Edwin thought a moment. Neither his voice nor his eyes were challenging Ceric. "You should go," he prompted.

Ceric let out with a small laugh, one of surprise.

"You should go," Edwin said again.

Ceric sat looking across at Edwin's open face.

"Her name is Begu," Ceric found himself saying. "If I do not come back, give her fifty silver pieces in my name."

Edwin stood up. "You will come back," he returned, his alarm showing in the haste of his response.

Ceric stared at him. "Yes. I will come back. And I will go tonight to see her."

Begu still lay clasped in his arms when he told her he rode to war. She had met him at her door with the same warm greeting she had ever given, and they had drunk mead and undressed the other without haste. He was more quiet than was his custom, but she had seen him in many moods. Yet he seemed more tender to her when he touched her, more thoughtful and considered in his actions. His murmurs were breathed into her ear, and he held and stroked her floss-like hair as he had during their first nights together. When he pulled away from her, he kept holding her still.

"I ride with Eadward, the King's son, on the morrow."

She gave a small cry of surprise; it was not yet time for him and his men to do so. Her hand about his shoulder tightened, but she kept her voice low.

"Then there is war, here in Wessex?"

"There will be a great action." He turned his face up into the darkness of roof rafters. "At last I will be part of it."

His tone was neither boasting nor wistful, a soft statement of fact.

She lowered her head into his shoulder. It was not meet nor fitting that she weep over him, yet it was all she could do to hold back her tears. His arm, still about her, tightened for a moment, pressing her more fully against his ribcage.

Her hand on his shoulder dropped down, felt the raised scar there in the hard muscle.

At once his thoughts went to Hrald, the giver of that wound, and how he had stabbed himself in answer to the hurt he had given him. Hrald had drawn the first blood he had ever shed. Eadward's words rose in his mind, Eadward musing about the Jarl of Four Stones riding to join the other Danes at Middeltun.

Ceric's eyes were wide open, staring up into the dark. The thought of facing Hrald as enemy was impossible to compass. Yet the Prince was right, there was no way to know how it fared in Lindisse, what Hrald might be forced to do.

Begu had moved her hand, off that which had been sewn by another woman, a woman she knew Ceric loved. But the withdrawal of her hand made him think of Ashild.

He kissed Begu's brow, then swung his legs onto the floorboards. He never left so early as this, and as he pulled on his clothes he spoke to her.

"I must go back to the hall and sleep; tomorrow will be full."

She gave the same gentle sounds of assent she ever gave. It was dark enough that he could not see her face clearly, for which she was grateful. But when he stood she could not help but reach her hand out to him, touching his leg. He looked down at her, and lowered himself to sit on the edge of her bed.

He put his arms about her, pulled her close.

"I will see you on my return," he told her. "Keep well until then."

For one fleeting moment he considered telling her what he had told Edwin, that if he were killed she would be well and richly taken care of. But his own throat closed, even thinking this. A man must never say such things, it tempted Fate.

He gave his head a small shake, then rose again. Before he left he set a small pile of whole coinage on the corner of her low table.

After she had barred her door she sat down on the stool by the table, head in hands. Thanks to Ceric she had a growing store of silver in a pot beneath her floorboards. But she would have traded almost her soul for him to have placed some keepsake into her hand.

A troop of one and fifty thegns left Kilton a day hence. The number of men was such that the departure blessing was given not inside the hall, but out in the stable yard before it. The fare-well cups of ale were passed, and emptied. Dunnere the priest went from man to man, beginning with Ceric and ending with the drovers, and blessed each one with his thumb, stamping his brow with the Sign of the Cross. All in the work yards came to watch, even the cooks, endlessly busy, stood silent, their hands in their soiled aprons, biting their lips and looking on. The women of the hall stood together, Modwynn and Edgyth, arrayed in sombre richness almost as if for a feast, but with drawn and loving faces. Ranged about them were the wives of all those who rode. Cadmar stood somewhat apart, watching with eyes both proud and grave. At his side was Edwin, dressed too in fine clothing, out of respect for those before him. A pennon with a golden dragon was affixed to one of the horses, a battle-flag woven and embroidered years ago by Modwynn.

Ceric felt to his core the solemnity of Dunnere's muttered blessing. It was to him more than a request that God receive his soul if he were to fall. In Ceric's ears it was an ardent appeal of his own, seeking to be worthy of his vows, his name, his training, and of his sword. He had his hand upon the golden hilt of that sword as the priest drew his thumb down and across his forehead.

The men mounted their restless horses. For a final time a woman's hand might be pressed into their own, as wives reached up to their husbands.

Ceric had none such. From his horse he nodded to his aunt and grandmother, they who had embraced him lovingly within the hall. But before his younger brother he now bowed his head.

This was the first time he rode to truly defend Kilton, he felt. Despite their ages, Edwin was his Lord. He had bowed to him once, the night Edwin had received the sword and seax of Godwin from the hands of the King. Now he did so again, acknowledging that he rode not only for Ælfred and Wessex, but for Edwin and Kilton.

This troop of fifty men were under his command. He must say that which would be their battle cry as they ran at the enemy, say it so that those left here would know by what cry they would rally. His voice rang out above the horses' snorting and tossing heads.

"For Christ, Ælfred, and Kilton," he called.

An answering cheer from his men, hoops and cries from those assembled. Modwynn's eyes, Edgyth's eyes, both glittering. He turned.

The broad palisade gates were swung open. They passed all the folk of the hall and work-yards who had ringed them. The village too was massed to see them off; never in recent memory has such a number ridden to battle. Every thegn was horsed, and those few men who owned more than one led their second, laden with his war-kit and trappings. Ceric rode in front alongside Worr, the golden dragon banner of Ælfred springing from the cantle of Worr's saddle. There were as well ten additional horses in reserve, trotting alongside the four horse-drawn supply waggons, and six men whose task it would be to guard and keep all the horses on the field of battle when they were taken to the back, away from the shield-wall.

The greening fields and flocks of woolly sheep waiting to be shorn were passed, as were the furthest groves of fruit trees. The village children who had run after them dropped off one by one. The towers of the ward-corns were reached, and one lifted his horn to his lips and blew a long and low salute to those riding by. Further out they were met by mounted horsemen, watchers who had lately been set at all the roads leading to the burh of Kilton. The pounded road snaked into the forest, and they followed it, heading East.

Though it be Spring they were blessed with fine weather on the way, with few rains. It took five days to reach King's hall at Witanceaster. Ceric had been there once before, when he had ridden with Ælfred and Raedwulf to Haesten's stolen camp at Middeltun. It was the largest burh Ceric had ever seen, for not only did the King and his men live here, but the Witan, that group of King's advisors, met at Witanceaster as well.

It was now become a staging ground for the planned action, hundreds of men from all over Wessex filing in by horse and foot. The confusion and noise was like unto a great feast or market-day, but instead of traders opening stalls and farmers selling grain from the back of ox-carts there was troop after troop of warriors. They parcelled out camp sites outside its gates, pulling up tents they would spend the night in, digging latrine trenches, setting up cooking fires. The land around the palisade swarmed with men at work, horses being led to pasture, and folk from Witanceaster proper ducking and dodging their way amongst them.

One of the King's men had met them at arrival, and directed them to a patch of meadow. Looking about Ceric spotted a number of men, who like him, led thegns from their own burhs to join with Ælfred or Eadward. They all looked older, seasoned, and he feared he might be the youngest there who fronted a troop of men. He shook this off, recalling Ælfred himself had been named King here when only two years older than he was now. Age did not equal ability.

He and Worr were pulling up the tent they would share. "Other than the field of battle at Ethandun, I have never seen so many thegns," Worr said, taking a break from pounding in one of the stakes to look out over all those doing the same.

This had been the decisive conflict at which Guthrum and all his assembled Danes had been beaten by Ælfred. Worr would have been about Ceric's age then, and had taken part in the action with Kilton's thegns, led by Godwin.

The tent they worked on was not far from a newly-made road, upon which small groups of men both rode and walked through this hive of activity. Two horsemen neared, and Worr's eye was caught by one of them. He raised his hand to his father-in-law, Raedwulf, Bailiff of Defenas.

Raedwulf reined in, bidding the man with him continue to the palisade gates. Then he was down from his horse, embracing his son-in-law Worr.

"How is Wilgyfu," he asked of his daughter, after the three had made their first greetings.

"She is well," Worr assured him. A slight pause, followed by a quietly proud declaration. "There will be a new child after harvest-time."

Ceric did not know this either, and both men gave Worr good wishes. The horse-thegn of Kilton's life was rich and full, and ever-expanding. For an instant Ceric felt the narrowness of his own existence; and Raedwulf too, while finding satisfaction in the news, was made aware of the constriction of his own affairs.

In the moments that followed the three looked out over the throngs of warriors surrounding them. There was this brief rest of a few hours for both man and horse. On the morrow they would leave, marching towards Middeltun and beyond.

"What…what will really happen," Ceric asked Raedwulf. One who had the King's ear stood before him, and he would not let the chance pass to learn more of what they all headed into.

Raedwulf tilted his head slightly, but with a smile. "I will be with the King," he told them. "We will form an outer barrier, but it is a huge area to defend. The Danes do not like to mass, they will scatter into smaller groups to break through.

"You will go with Eadward, and form the blockade, some on land, some at sea. I do not know how he will assign you," he ended, looking at both of them. "The Danes have brought horses from Frankland in their warships, and have received more horses from those here in Northumbria and

Anglia. And they are the best seaman on any water. Either way it will not be easy to contain them."

How know you this about the horses, Ceric thought, but did not voice. "Ælfred has riders, and runners, throughout the kingdom," is what he said.

The bailiff nodded. "Yes, they are never-failing, his couriers. And there are a few Danes themselves who have come forward with information."

"Those who would keep Guthrum's Peace," Ceric said, aware of the note of hope in his own voice. Raedwulf had helped him win Ælfred's consent for sending for Ashild, and this emboldened him to ask more. "Do you know anything of Four Stones? You have been there, have seen the family thereof. I know they are otherwise unknown to you, but you can judge them."

Raedwulf shook his head, no. As he took his warm leave of the two he answered in his breast, But I too have asked about Four Stones; not for your sake alone have I asked about it.

Despite their weariness Ceric and Worr did not easily find sleep that night. Their tent was snug enough. They had ground cloths of tanned leather hides to keep them from rising damp, and a sheepskin each to lie upon that, and a wool blanket to lie under. There was comfort therein, though not that of the thick feather bed in Ceric's alcove, or the deep bed Worr shared with Wilgyfu.

Men were noisy about them, but even when the grounds quieted Ceric found himself looking upwards at the blotched darkness of the steep leathern roof of their tent. Horses, paddocked at a distance, whinnied and called, and watch-men rode along the trackway outside. Inside their tent Ceric and Worr had laid their weapons between them, within easy reach of their own grasp but not of any other.

In the dark, and even without touching it, Ceric was aware of the presence of Godwulf's sword. He lay there thinking that twice that famed sword had been wrenched out of his grip by a stronger man, a man with better sword skills than he. Ceric had the fine and well-shaped hands of his father, and his grandmother; he did not yet have the strength in his grip he wanted. He had never bested Cadmar, not even once, in arm-wrestling. "You are not come into your full strength yet," the warrior-monk had consoled. But losing his sword twice, once in friendly sparring, the second in deadly combat, haunted his thoughts. He must not let it happen a third time.

"I do not want to fight on a ship," Ceric found himself saying into the dark. His brain had turned from losing his weapon to losing his life. "To be killed there…if your body is lost overboard…"

Worr gave a grunt of agreement.

"I would rather fight on land," Ceric went on. "Have you fought thus – at sea?"

"Your uncle did," Worr recalled aloud, thinking back to the time when Godwin of Kilton had paid for a war-ship to meet the Danish threat.

"He told me of it, told your father and me," Worr went on. "The narrow breadth of it, the deck moving beneath your feet…it is not an easy place to fight. Still," he considered, "it favours quickness, which you have. And you are not so large a target as some of those tall Danes. Could work to your advantage."

Ceric felt his friend was grinning now, the way men do when they are soon to face death.

"What about you," he asked back. "You are tall, like those Danes."

"We will hope Eadward uses us on land," Worr answered. "Now get some sleep."

The family of Witanceaster stood together to watch Eadward's men ride in the morning. Besides the many mounted thegns Eadward had collected from the burhs of Wessex, he had amassed as well a great number of men on foot, who lined up in files of five abreast to march behind the supply waggons. These were not thegns, but free ceorls, able to arm themselves and fight with what weapons best suited them. None had been called from a place so distant as Kilton; they were all from Witanceaster or to the East of it, and nearly all were from the villages of burhs which had suffered raiding attacks from the newly arrived Danish forces. Ceric saw men who carried light throwing spears, archers with packed quivers of fletched arrows at hip or shoulder, and those, youths and boys mostly, with nothing more than leathern slings and a supply of carefully chosen rounded stones with which to assail the enemy. These ceorls must carry their weapons and what little kit they owned on their backs, and walk to the place where they might meet death, unprotected by ring-shirt, sword, or helmet. The greatest personal defence any of these boasted was their round shields, and a hardened cap of leather, strapped over with four prongs of metal. Yet their faces were as resolute, and step as firm, as if some scop awaited at home to sing of the deeds of heedless daring they would perform.

Worr, at his side, had the golden dragon banner of Wessex rising from his saddle. Every troop of thegns carried at least one such pennon, golden creatures dipping and fluttering above the pacing horses. Every pennon was slightly different, each from each, for each had issued from the hands of different women, and the dragons they sported seemed the more fearsome and quick for it. The morning breeze was fresh enough to make the battle flags snap and straighten in the wind as they passed under the King's gaze.

The King himself would not leave until next day, and stood his chestnut stallion before the palisade walls to watch his son march off. Ælfred was dressed as for war, his ring-tunic of bright steel catching the rays of morning Sun, his polished helmet almost dazzling. He nodded his head at the groups of thegns as they paraded before him, seeming to look at each man; at least Ceric felt the King's eyes upon him, saw the grave head nod at him. He thought of Ælfred looking thus upon his own father, and upon Godwin; and then of Ælfred's brothers who had been King before him. He thought too of Ælfred's father, who had given his grandfather Godwulf the sword he now carried in the baldric on his chest. The bond went back for years, and many lives.

He saw Raedwulf and the other King's counsellors and picked men flanking Ælfred, and also a cluster of women. Ælfred's wife was pointed out to him, a woman with clasped hands, looking upon her eldest as he led a host of other warriors to battle. Ceric knew that as a young mother she had once need to flee for her life with the rest of her household, a child in her arms, when their hall was beset by Danes at Twelfth Night. King's wife or no, there were ways in which her life had been one of great hardship.

Chapter the Twenty-first: Golden Cross

THEY were two days on the road. As they approached Middeltun Ceric remembered Raedwulf's words when Ælfred rode to meet Haesten: that they would come here again. Now Ceric and Worr and fifty good men of Kilton had indeed come, joined by three hundred more, all under Eadward's command. It would be here that Eadward would divide his troops, some to take to ships awaiting them further down the coast, others to the brow of that same hill from which Ceric had watched Raedwulf and Ælfred ride unafraid to face the newly landed Danes.

They made camp, took their meal over numberless small cook fires. Then, when there was still light in the sky, Eadward addressed them. He was on his horse, a dusky grey stallion, to be better seen and heard. Just after dawn this new-formed army would part ways.

"On land," he said, "the men of Meretun, and Wedmore, and Winburn, and Kilton…"

The name of his home filled Ceric's ears. He would not fight at sea, on the deck of a pitching ship; he would fight on land. He let out the breath he had been holding, even turned with the ghost of a grin to Worr.

He heard Eadward naming the burhs whose men would leave to take ship. The ships that awaited them were an hour's ride off. There they would set off to form the blockade to try to halt the Danes who attempted flight by sea. Cuthred, a trusted captain of the King, would take command of those afloat, and Eadward detailed that they had enough ships to take the shape of the splayed tines of a comb, one whose teeth the Danes would find deadly to near.

The attack led by Eadward would come by land, calling out the enemy to fight before their stolen fortress. It was early Spring and food stores scarce; the fort at Middeltun could not withstand a siege. The forces of Wessex would seem to have the advantage. It was not known if Haesten was even at Middeltun now; if he were not, so much the better, as the men there were not likely to fight as hard under any second in command as they would for their famed war-lord.

They had camped an hour's fast march from the hill overlooking Haesten's fort at Middeltun, far enough to elude discovery and lend some ease to their final night. Watchmen were set, patrolling the edges of their encampment, and trusted men sent ahead to secretly observe the fort on which they would march in the morning.

It was still dark and Ceric asleep when he jolted upright at the winding of a horn. He heard the running of men, and one cry, "Up and onward! The Danes are roused and taking to ship!"

He and Worr scrambled to their feet, seeing the flickers of torches carried by those crying out to wake them. They had slept half-clad, and plucked at their clothing. They emerged from their low tent. Men all about them were doing the same, some calling out to others. Ceric gaped at the sky as he sat on the damp ground, fastening his boots. The Moon was just setting, and night growing darker for it. Startled awake as he was he felt completely alert. Despite the darkness he felt rested enough that dawn must be nigh.

"We were discovered," Worr was saying, as he leant through the tent flap and pulled out his weapons. "We were not alone in setting watch."

All the orderly plan had been disrupted. As the two stood, arming themselves, pulling on ring-shirts, buckling on seaxes and swords, grasping helmets, Eadward appeared on horseback, flanked by two other riders, each bearing torches.

"Those to sea, to the left," he called. He was fully armed himself, and even in the torchlight his eyes flashed from the eye openings of his steel helmet. There was no alarm in his voice, though his hand had been forced by Haesten. He rode on through the camp, making himself seen, crying out orders, marshalling his men.

A man of Kilton ran up to Ceric, one of the drovers, carrying with him a flask of hot broth and some cheese-stuffed loaves, which he thrust upon Ceric and Worr before retreating to his waggon. Ceric could not take more than a single bite of the bread, but the meat broth warmed him, and soothed his constricted throat. The faint greyish glow of dawn was spreading in the East, slowly lightening what looked to be another fair morning.

A good day to fight, he thought, as he slung his blue and yellow shield upon his back. No rain nor mud to combat, only the enemy. He wished he could say the same aloud to Worr, say it with a lightness he did not feel. Worr's own brow was slightly furrowed as he adjusted his leg wrappings, tightened his seax belt. Worr straightened up, caught Ceric looking at him. The familiar grin flashed on Worr's square-jawed face. "I am on your right, Ceric," he told him, a simple reminder of his steadfast service.

They did not yet know which rank of the shield-wall they would stand in, that first line of warriors pressing almost shoulder to shoulder together as they advanced, or in the second, placed before the line of Eadward's own body-guard. Whichever it was, Ceric would have Worr at his right hand, Worr's strong left hand holding his shield as they moved forward.

Ceric grinned too, and answered, "And I am on your left." They would fight shield-to-shield, and if the shield wall broke, back-to-back.

They must go now, find their horses, and form up before Eadward. They picked their way through the thegns doing the same, skirting a number of ceorls who stood blinking in the growing light. Their round and painted shields lay about at their feet. Few of them had tents, and had slept under the shelter of hides which formed the greater part of their kit. Ceric regarded them as he passed, nodding as he went, returning the looks of those whose eyes fell on the brilliance of his own war-kit. The archers amongst them were checking bowstrings, and not a few of the youths who would wield slings were palming a round stone, soon to be launched from the whipping leather they would swing above their heads. Those armed with throwing spears were the largest and strongest amongst them, men with good arms and two or three light spears each to bring to bear against the Danes.

Bread, cheese, and ale had been passed amongst the men, and hastily consumed, but Ceric was not alone in being unable to swallow more than a bite. Men were warned to refill their water flasks; there might be little chance, once upon the field of battle, to seek out a barrel from the supply waggons.

Ceric's two horses had been saddled, and as Worr attended to his own Ceric mounted and rode amongst Kilton's fifty thegns as they readied their mounts. The men looked up at him, calling out his name as they lifted their hands in salute. Some voiced the name "Kilton" as if it were a vow. Looking down at them as they paused in fastening saddle bags or tightening girths filled him with a deep and spreading pride. He would be led by Eadward, Prince; but he led these men of Kilton, his own pledged thegns, and the thirty of his brother Edwin who had been sent to fight in his name.

When all from Kilton were horsed, they moved forward. They took the same positions they had the previous night when Eadward had divided them for land and sea. Facing them was Eadward and ten of his body-guard, those that would surround him as he stood behind the shield-wall, shouting orders and encouragement, and who, when the wall was breached, would fight to the death that Eadward might live.

Eadward's grey horse pranced beneath him, tossing its arched neck, the light mane shaking, nostrils on the fine muzzle flaring. The Sun had not yet crested the hill behind them, but a few beams of golden light pierced through the tree boughs. The air was fresh, the sky pale blue. As Ceric stood his horse next to Worr, he heard a bird call out from one of those trees, a bird to whom this morning was no more nor less than another day.

"Those to sea," Eadward was saying. "Riders have been sent ahead to our ships to warn them of your early coming. Cuthred commands you. You fight for Wessex, and for Wessex you shall win." Here he looked to Cuthred, who touched his horse's barrel and went to front the waiting men.

"Those on land," Eadward went on, walking his restless horse before the ranks of men. His voice rang out, bell-clear and strong. Like his father, he had a gaze that caught each man in turn as his eye swept over them. "We march in haste to Middeltun's walls. There will be no offer of peace made, no demand of tribute accepted. We march to fight." He raised his voice, moved his eyes to include both groups. "For Ælfred – Wessex – for home and hearth!"

Eadward did not ride with a priest or monk; there was no blessing given, save that made by those men who lifted their fingertips to their brows and crossed themselves. Some breathed prayers, or touched, as Ceric did, his chest, where his golden cross lay resting against his skin. His mind went back to the departure blessing at Kilton, that solemnity with which Dunnere had stamped his brow with holy oil, marking him and the other men who would ride. He thought he felt the oil anew, smeared by the priest's thumb upon his forehead.

"Onward," called Eadward, and was met with an answering cheer from every throat.

The army would march together a short distance until those under Cuthred's command broke off. Eadward touched his heels to his stallion's flank, and his bodyguard closed up behind him. They moved forward as one.

Ceric looked about him. The spear points of the men, held upright, caught the glancing rays of the rising Sun. The sheer number of mounted thegns, the fineness of their horses, the golden dragon banners lifting above them, the line of foremost men splendid in their glittering war-kit, it all held a kind of majesty, fresh, new, and stirring. If he had felt alert before, he felt the heightening of his senses now, aware of the coolness of the breeze upon his face, the animal muscle of the stallion his legs closed upon, the sombre weight of his ring-shirt and helmet, the racing lightness of his breath. He found himself centred in a kind of heart-pounding and unexpected beauty, the glory of men marching to battle.

He thought of the scop, Garrulf, at Kilton. He pictured his dark eyes gleaning all before him, and making of it a stirring and worthy song which told the truth of what Ceric was now feeling. Men, horses, weapons, moving forward as one.

Ceric responded to the beauty of the battle march, though he understood it was an awe-ful beauty: the lines of men with their round and brightly painted shields, the burnished metal, polished again just last night, the great wrought allure of the tools of killing – the blue-bladed swords, over which a weapon-smith had labored for weeks or even months, so that scops saw the scales of dragons dancing as the blade was swung. The glittering seaxes and honed war-axes and spear points incised with delicate tracery, meant to be sunk deeply into another man's body.

All this caught and filled his eyes. The men who bore those weapons became vessels of a rare and manly beauty, thegns in their linked ring-tunics and glinting helmets, and those more humble fighters on foot from whose hands spears bristled and punctured the sky. It all possessed a kind of primitive splendour. There were tales of ancient armies, of conflict brave and bloody, in the Holy Book; warriors led by stern patriarchs battling for more than life. There was grandeur there, and something beyond earthly glory, and Ceric thought there must be a distinct and special beauty to such glory. It had to do with manliness, and perhaps no woman could truly understand it. Men pledged to each other to reach here, thegn to Lord, Lord to King; but the greatest vow was Man to God.

Ashild's face and her stormy eyes flashed in his mind. Perhaps she, amongst all women, would be one to understand.

He felt of a sudden fear-less. Any dread of death, of being hacked down, of his young blood soaking into the warming Spring soil, left him. He rode on in the line of warriors, supported by more than his horse. High-careless, valiant-hearted, strong in faith and surety; that was all he knew. He was part of this vast number of like-minded men, moving forward with dedication to the goal, for Christ, for King, for one's own dear folk and lands.

Those riders headed to sea broke off; Eadward and the larger force went on. Ceric watched the ninety or so men ride away, without feeling their loss, or any diminishment to his own numbers. They would prevail, as would Eadward's contingent, of which he was so fully a part.

The Sun breached the line of trees, trees now giving way to marsh. They reached the swelling rise of land from which they could see their destination, and climbed it. They crowded the rise, an even greater and more impressive troop than that which Ælfred had earlier defined against this sky.

The horses stood, nodding their heads at what lay below, their riders narrowing their eyes above their horse's manes. The foot-men caught up, stood staring down through the morning light at the fortress of Middeltun. The rise gave a vantage, from which could be seen a steady stream of men issuing out from the back of the encircling palisade. Those Danes were headed North, to where lay their ships, beached on the soft banks of the Thames estuary.

Some would flee that way, but half at least would be forced to stay to defend the fortress they had built. Just as Eadward had divided his troops, so must Haesten, and in both places would the Danes be met.

With a few words Eadward again divided his men, one portion to skirt the encampment and stem the flow of Danes from the rear, the other to remain with him and make the frontal assault.

Eadward turned, his back to the enemy, facing his men as he signaled which would ride to stop more Danes escaping to their ships. Ceric's green eyes were fixed upon him, willing the Prince to order Kilton's thegns to remain.

"Ceric of Kilton, you are with me," he heard Eadward call.

Those chosen to ride to the back of the fort had just started off when all heard a blast from a horn, a distant but prolonged sounding. One of the Danish watchmen within the palisade, likely distracted with other tasks, had spotted the army on the hill rise above, and given warning.

"Forward," called Eadward.

They walked down from the rise, the body of them, at a fast walk. The Prince would go so far, determine where to stop, and there, of his troops, form his war-hedge. The horsemen who had been just behind Eadward at the rise of the hill had fanned out, and Ceric and Worr and his fifty men of Kilton found himself in the front rank, just to the left of Eadward. They walked over grassland of tender green growth, flushing not a few ground birds as they went. One fluttered, complaining, before Ceric's horse, and Ceric found himself smiling at it. He was aware of Worr at his right, and his thegn Wistan on his left, a man with as many years and as much experience as Worr, a man who had also fought with Godwin. Most of his other pledged men were closer in age to he himself. Now they would have a chance to prove themselves, as he would.

There were Danes on the ramparts on the palisade before them, and the horn that had sounded had scarcely stopped in its winding. All within knew of the approaching threat, and could see as well the second part of Eadward's forces as they cantered, rounding the arc of the fortress to close up the path to escape. The numbers of men on the ramparts grew, as more and more Danes craned their heads at them. Ceric scanned the line of small figures, wondering if Haesten himself be amongst them.

Eadward grew closer. There was still a small rise on which they stood, and he would claim that advantage, forcing Haesten to rush upwards on the slight grade to reach them. Closer to the fortress, the land sloped gently downwards to the closed palisade gates. Eadward turned to his men to ready them for when those gates should open.

He gestured them off their horses, but kept his to be better seen and heard. "First rank," he called, naming those who would form the initial shield-wall, that which would take the brunt of first contact. "My own men in centre. Wedmore, to the right of them. Meretun, to the left."

"Second rank, and third ranks. Kilton, behind my own men. Winburn, to the right of Kilton. Englafeld, to the left." He looked at Ceric, and at the two lords of Winburn and Englafeld. "Split your men in two ranks. Behind the second of them will be me, and my bodyguard.

"Wait for my battle cry," he went on. The power in his voice matched the look in his eyes as he scanned the faces of the men before him. "Do not forsake the shield-wall. Do not break rank unless you hear the horn sound thrice. Do not run after any Dane. Do not stop to strip for booty, or to aid any injured of our own, until I signal.

"Archers, sling-men, and spear-men," he now called, addressing that throng. "You will stand behind the foremost rank. When the enemy is within range, let fly at my command, three volleys of missiles, as quickly as you can discharge them. Then clear that rank, at a run, heading to the rear. Make ready there to come forward and fire more at my command."

These were the orders, clear, direct, given once. Every pair of eyes was set upon Eadward's face as he looked down upon his troops. A moment's pause, as his own swept over men and boys. Then came a single nod of his head in affirmation.

"Horses to the rear," he called last.

He swung off his own. Ceric and all the rest led their horses to where the supply waggons rolled in. Here the drovers, and those men brought to keep and guard horses and supplies took charge of them. No one spoke; it was all done almost soundlessly, save for the snorting of the horses. Ceric gave his stallion a pat on the glossy neck, as if he had just come in from a morning's ride. He watched other men do the same to their mounts. He checked his war-kit one more time. He heard

Sidroc's voice in his head, telling him and Hrald to secure their clothing, check their leg wrappings, and he did so, as he had when he was but a lad with Hrald.

He took his shield from his back and threaded his left arm through the support, his left hand closing around the grip in the iron boss at the round's centre. The shield was of alder wood, light and strong, with a leathern covering which had been wetted and shrunk to fit the wooden disc. The face of it had been painted in two bright halves, yellow and blue, the yellow to echo the golden dragon banner of Wessex, the blue to recall the foaming waters beneath Kilton's hall. The inside was lined too in leather, and padded to lend protection to bracing left arm, shoulder, and knee. Unlike some men, Ceric had not painted nor drawn any figure or symbol within his shield, something to look upon when it was raised in his left arm. Worr had painted an open eye in his, telling Ceric it reminded him the Almighty Watcher saw him, and to do his best. Other men carved or painted marks in theirs: crosses, or runes. He thought again of Sidroc the Dane, and his red and black shield, and the bind rune painted therein.

A brass horn sounded, one blown by Eadward's herald, and all like thoughts fell away. The men formed up. Eadward stood in direct line from the palisade gates, for from there would the opposing force issue. He would be the Dane's prized target, the man they most sought to kill, just as Haesten would be theirs. His picked bodyguard surrounded him, twenty of his best warriors. Ceric and his men stood just before these. As he took his place Ceric heard the Prince's words in his mind again, distinguishing him thus. Eadward had picked him and Kilton to stand with Eadward's own best.

Another man was at Eadward's side, one but a youth in Eadward's train. He wore a tunic of leather, but other than a long seax carried no weapon. In his hands was held a staff bearing the large battle flag of Wessex, nearly twice the size of those carried by the horses, now sent to safety in the rear. His role was one of honour and of danger, to stand as near to Eadward as could be, holding the fluttering banner aloft, marking the place where their Prince stood and fought. Eadward would call out orders, urging his men, directing their efforts, but in the noise and clamour of battle those outside ear-shot could but glance up and see the dragon pennon aloft and know their Prince still lived. The pennon, and the man it marked, was the rallying point for all to come.

The foot-men were in place, just behind the foremost rank of the shield-wall. Ceric and Worr and Wistan and the others were in two ranks behind them. One of the foot-men turned and looked at Ceric, a wide-eyed lad of no more than fourteen years, he thought, holding his sling in one hand, his leathern pouch of river stones on his hip. He thought of a sudden of the youth he had given the sword and knife to, after he had killed the Dane in the forest ambush.

He felt with keenness how much better was this than those cramped confines amongst the trees, where he had taken that first life. The Danes who had died in the ambush suffered squalid deaths, pulled from their horses unawares and run through. At least his man had a chance to fight back, to defend himself. But this, today, on a field, was ever to be preferred. The expansiveness of pitched battle made the men themselves taking part larger. A bigger sky loomed over their heads.

Ceric had let his men choose which rank in which to stand; that nearest to Eadward and his defending body-guard, or that closest to the first shield-wall. Ceric looked back and saw Eadward, almost directly behind him, his picked warriors already glaring out from under the eye holes of their helmets. Turning back to the palisade walls of Middeltun he saw that few of the Danes who had been watching from the ramparts could be seen.

The Sun was now high enough in the sky to cast shadows that rapidly shrank as it climbed.

All that was left was to call out the foe. The brass horn of the herald sounded, long and low.

Eadward bellowed out his challenge. "Take your stand, Haesten, and meet death at my hand!"

Silence. Eadward's men stood about and around him, holding their shields and weapons, waiting. One long moment passed into another.

Then one of Eadward's body-guard, standing at his very right, struck the iron rim of his upheld shield with the flat of his sword. The sound of metal on metal rang out. Another man did the same, and another, one sword after the next rapping against the iron-bound rim of a waiting shield.

Ceric had heard this before in sparring, done it as well, but it was a taunt acted almost in jest. The rattling sound of scores of warriors doing so sounded no jest. He joined the jarring, rhythmic rattle, beating the flat of his sword, Godwulf's sword, against his shield-rim. He felt the strength in his wrist, in his grip, as he did so. No man would fling this sword from his grasp today.

The palisade gates swung open.

"Stand!" called Eadward, behind him. They must not advance until the order was given.

Out at a trot came a doubled file of Danes on foot. At first sight of them the rattle of Saxon swords against shield-rims grew louder, and was joined by voiced calls and hoots of derision. Ceric found himself swaying slightly as he held his place in the shield wall, and saw other men doing so as well, shifting lightly from foot to foot in anticipation as their swords clanged and taunts flew.

He watched as the Danes quickly spread into a single rank ranged before them. They were as well armed as were Eadward's troops; perhaps the men who had been sent to the ships were those lesser warriors without the protective gear and weapons of their brethren who had remained to defend the fortress.

Now he saw the line of the Danes change again, even as they kept on trotting towards them. The single line compressed, became a wedge fronted by a single warrior, with two behind him, then three, four, five; an ever growing and ever denser wedge of men aimed for the centre of their shield wall.

It was the formation the Danes called boar-snout, meant to punch through the staunchest wall of thegns. Their greatest champion took the single position in front, with men of nearly equal repute behind him.

Haesten's answer was clear. He would not match his warriors one-to-one in a shield-wall of his own, but would at first assault attempt to penetrate Eadward's ranks, forcing a melée.

"Men of Kilton, close up, double-ranked!" came the order from behind. Eadward would try to absorb the shock by piling his own men together.

Ceric felt Worr move closer to him, and he too closed up the slight distance lying between his shield and Wistan's shoulder. He knew his men at the furthest edges of his rank had pulled in, doubling their numbers, to act as a damper to the coming assault.

His eyes were riveted ahead, but he saw Worr's helmet from the tail of his right eye. The Danes were trotting forward with steely precision, aiming right at him. His ears were filled with the racket he and all other of the thegns were making. Yet an odd quiet filled him, that, and a flush of gratitude for Worr's devotion. Why, when they were arming, had he not turned to Worr, and embraced him as a brother? Now he could not. He could not break the spell, that spell of standing under orders which was part of the bond between those waiting in this wall.

He stopped his slight shifting of his weight, and braced himself against his shield. He stilled his hand, aware that the rattle all around him had also died down, as they awaited Eadward's next order.

The long line of archers in front of the men of Kilton had nocked their arrows. The youths with slings had them ready loaded and were whirring them over their heads. Those with throwing spears had taken their stances, prepared to launch.

The order came. "Foot-men!" cried Eadward.

A volley of arrows arced over the heads of the shield-wall, sleeting down upon the advancing Danes. Round stones the size of plums were flung at speed, able to kill a man if they hit face or head, or break the largest bone. Throwing spears were lofted with grunting oaths by the spear-men. All these took their toll, and as the missile-throwers ran back and out of the way, they heard the cries of those Danes who had met what they had thrown.

Still they kept on, the boar-snout fortified by new men. The apex of that snout was no more than fifteen paces away now. Eadward's battle cry would come at any moment, and his men would answer back and stride forward as a man to meet the onrushing Danes.

The Prince's battle-cry was of the simplest, and that which had already sounded in Ceric's ears, the single word which was his father-King's name.

"Ælfred!"

They all responded, repeating the name of their King. An answering cry rose from the Danes bearing down on them. Ceric opened his mouth again, with his battle-cry for Kilton's warriors.

"For Christ, Ælfred, and Kilton," he yelled.

The words were hot in his mouth, his cry drowning out all else in his ears. Then he was moving forward, as if in a leap, following the strides made by the shield-wall in front of him. He could see the face of the champion of the Danes now, that man who formed the point of the boar-snout, coming almost at a run. They must absorb the brunt of the wedge, diffuse its force, forbid a rent in the war-hedge surrounding and protecting their Prince. To compress themselves too much meant leaving their flanks open to be run at, and around; the men of Wedmore and Meretun would find that their task. But Kilton's men and the others at the centre must withstand the boar-snout, and the sword-tusks charging at them.

Ceric as he moved saw the bared teeth of the Danes who rushed at him, saw men with yellow or brown hair falling down from beneath their helmets, and the eyes that gleamed from iron eye-holes in those helmets. He glimpsed Danes already felled by spear or arrow from the foot-men's volleys, some trying to rise to their feet, others lying still upon the grass behind the onrushers. A blur of leather before him, steel blades, the pressing rounds of shields in every colour yet drained of hue. Then the thegn in front of him fell; Ceric did not know how, but he nearly stumbled over him. He leapt to the side, knocking he thought into Worr's shield; he could not turn his head to look. There were screams now, screams and oaths; and the hacking of weapons into wood, clanging against other swords, and finding human flesh.

His eyes were always forward. He knew to pick his man, and one at the edge of a rank of five in the boar-snout presented himself. The Dane was coming faster than his brethren in his line, and Ceric had but to lunge to his right to place himself before him. He surprised the Dane, who answered with a grin and a quick nod of his helmeted head. The Dane was both older and taller than Ceric, but no more powerfully built. Besides his helmet he was protected with a ring-shirt, and in his hand was the longer sword oftentimes favoured by the Danes. Ceric's left hand, holding his shield, moved crosswise across his body as he extended his sword arm. The Dane's eye fell upon the bright hilt gripped by Ceric, fell upon the gold there, freezing him a moment as his eyes filled with that treasure.

It was enough. Ceric thrust his shield forward and to his left, and with his right slashed upward on the common iron of the Dane's half-extended sword. It did not fall from his fist, but was driven up enough that Ceric's next drive was to the wrist itself, hacking against the naked flesh of it. A gasping cry uttered from the twisting mouth of the Dane, and a spurt of blood, warm and thick, spattered across Ceric's face and chest. The man dropped, screaming, holding the maimed arm in the air as he did.

Down your man, then kill him, Ceric heard in his head, direction given him by every man who had trained him. With force he pressed his booted foot on the Dane's hip, then rammed his sword through the neck opening of the man's ring-shirt. The upheld arm fell.

He straightened up, drew breath. It had happened so fast, been done with such ease. Two strokes and he had killed one trying to kill him.

He turned his head to left and right. The shield-wall had been breached, thegns no longer arrayed shield-to-shield, but caught in their own contests. There was Worr, still to his right, fighting it seemed two Danes. He sprang to Worr's shield side, taking the man there. He startled all three by doing so, but saw too Worr's grateful look as he glanced at him. The horse-thegn of Kilton was a powerful swordsman, but here he faced two men of unequal height, hampering his ability to coordinate action of shield and sword. The Dane Ceric opposed was the shorter of the two, and one who moved with the agile quickness of a youth. He could be no older than Ceric, perhaps a year or two younger. A sideways look at the other man told Ceric that he and Worr faced son and father, or nephew and uncle; there was a likeness between the two men. The young Dane took him in, in the moment Ceric readied his sword. The eyes of the youth widened, looking on him. Ceric's face and chest was splashed with blood, Danish blood. Ceric could smell it, and when he had shook his head after the killing he felt it run from his cheek down his chin. He knew the tribes of the Old People had smeared themselves with pigments before going into war: here before this invading Dane was a man of Wessex in war-paint issued from his own blade.

Worr had stepped aside, away from Ceric, drawing the older man with him, giving Ceric room. It worked to Worr's advantage, as the elder, distracted by his concern for the youth, tried to edge his way back to him. But Ceric had the youth fully involved. The young Dane was a good swordsman, and used his speed to advantage, raising his black shield with the same quickness to block Ceric's blows as he used to deliver his own rapid thrusts. The Dane's sword beat against the upraised blue and yellow shield, leaving gashes both shallow and deep, and striking more than once the iron boss, making Ceric's clenched hand behind it tingle.

Cadmar had taught Ceric about such swordsmen, taught him to take a number of blows, offering none, until the man tired. And he had taught him more, about using the shield and its pointed boss as a weapon in itself. When, after Ceric had deflected a number of rapid sword blows, the Dane's blade tip lodged itself for a moment between wood and iron rim, Ceric had his chance. He lunged forward behind his shield, placing all his weight against it, and knocked the Dane first back, and then down, the point of the boss raised now at the man's collarbone. The Dane staggered, his back knee touching the ground, and fought to bring his now-freed sword to bear, but Ceric swung his own, edge-first, against the side of the man's helmet.

A sucking gasp; nothing more. Ceric had struck at the jaw-line, hitting metal, yes; but severing into the neck under the chin as well. There was no need for Ceric to deliver the mercy killing-thrust; the Dane's eyes rolled into his head as he crumpled before him.

A yelp from the older man turned Ceric back to Worr. Seeing his kin go down made the Dane redouble his efforts. But Worr had already made a hit; Ceric saw blood running down the man's left leg, some wound to shield arm or torso. The Dane was yelling, fighting wrathfully and in pain, and Worr was hacking away, silent save for his grunts. He advanced only, never gave ground, fought steadily, without show and without stopping, sword thrusting, shield blocking. As the Dane he fought tired Worr's own strength seemed to grow.

This Dane will ask for quarter, Ceric thought, he will drop his sword and ask for life. But he did not. He kept on, parrying Worr's sword and trying to bring to bear his own. A few steps brought them closer to where the body of the young Dane lay; the older could not help but see the grievous wound to the head which had ended his life. A look downward. Worr's sudden and much faster lunge, sword held low, driving into the older Dane's waist at the hipbone. A final feeble swing of the Dane's blade. He fell, still holding it, the fist spreading only when he toppled upon the youth's body.

Worr pulled back, turned to Ceric. He was breathing heavily but mastered his voice. "What happened," he asked, gesturing with the wrist of his sword-hand to the blood Ceric bore, a broad stripe of glistening red that showed even on the darkened steel of his ring-tunic.

"Not mine," Ceric told him.

Worr himself looked unmarked. There was little fighting about them; they had been at the fore-edge of it, and the contest was now all behind them. There was the dragon banner of Wessex, held aloft, waving furiously from the centre of a thick knot of warring men. Fragments of the shield wall could be discerned before and about that knot, three or four men shoulder-to-shoulder, blocking the way of equal numbers of Danes trying to pass them and reach the banner and who it flew above.

They broke and ran to them. They could not move fast; Ceric was now aware of the heaviness of his ring-tunic, the weight of his sword and shield, the fact that his arms had not the spring nor his legs the speed with which he had begun. They could not move fast for the bodies they must skirt, lying in heaps, locked after fatal combat; or sprawled, legs flung, like bloodied sleeping men. Ceric saw the opened brain-pans of thegns, the hacked torsos of the enemy, unknown faces smashed to pulp by the hammering skeggox; what had been living men was so much torn and ghastly meat. It was no more than what he had seen as a child at Kilton, save that he himself had driven some of these wounds.

Those still alive moaned, or screamed in anguished pain, or tried to drag themselves, heedless to further danger, from the gore they lay in.

He and Worr had nearly reached a line of four thegns, one of them of Kilton, who faced off against five Danes. As they neared Worr bellowed out a wordless cry, forcing the

Danes to pause and look over their shoulders to see who ran at them. This gave the beleaguered thegns the chance to close up and stride forward, and Ceric, at Worr's shoulder, saw one of them at once find flesh in the Dane he had been fighting, and saw the Dane drop.

Ceric was raising his sword to attack the Dane closest to him who had whirled to Worr's challenge. As he did he was hit by a crushing blow from behind.

Something smashed down upon the back of his right shoulder, doubling him over from the impact. He dropped to his left knee, his lowered sword tip piercing the grass he knelt on. He struggled to lift himself, expecting every moment for sword blade or skeggox to hit him in the back of the neck. Somehow he found his feet, using the edge of his shield to push himself up. The pain in his shoulder and upper back was such that he must stare at his sword blade to make it rise; he could not at first feel his arm. He heard Worr's voice call out, three words: Ceric of Kilton, yelled as a rallying cry. Worr, battling a man trying to kill him, yet had voice to shout resolutely to Ceric.

He staggered upright. He was surrounded by men fighting, both the thegns he and Worr had come to aid, and fresh Danes, who had either broken out of the larger conflict or come anew from the palisade. He saw Worr, trying to work his way towards him.

He hugged his shield tighter in to his body and turned. Two Danes were there, fighting two thegns, both of Kilton. He thought he had been hit unknowingly by the swung shield of one of the Danes, or even one of his own men. If a Dane had hit him, he had not had time enough to finish the job.

He raised his sword, his shoulder feeling as though a burning brand consumed it from within. His men saw him, and one cried out, "Kilton" even as he fought off the Dane he traded blows with. Ceric was so plainly dressed, so blood-smeared and filthy, that he did not look an heir of a great burh of Wessex. Only the sword of Godwulf, gift of Kings, betrayed that. Any set of eyes which fell on the dancing waves of patterned steel, or glimpsed the hilt and guard, saw it as such. His presence encouraged his men and emboldened his foe. He heard an answering grunt from the Dane nearest him; here was a prize indeed.

The Dane was quick to leave the thegn and come after Ceric and his sword. The man's eyes were even fixed upon it as he neared, his brow furrowed on a helmet-less head. A hissing breath fell from Ceric's lips, as he expelled that held in his tightened chest. His left side was unharmed, and he angled himself to the Dane to favour his right. Shield held firmly and high, he invited the blows of Danish steel upon its painted face. He braced his left shoulder against the padded leather of the shield's curve, and left knee too, making of himself a shield-wall of one.

The Dane hacked and swung, slicing up the leathern facing, driving gashes into the alder body of it. He hit the iron boss, making his sword recoil, and Ceric's hand within ring like the bright and deadly noise sounding from the blow. The whole time Ceric withstood this, he was gauging the strength in his sword arm. It was folded close to his body, extended just slightly for balance. Worr was fully busy where he stood; of his other men, one had fallen and the other battling a Dane swinging a skeggox. Unless other men of Wessex could run to him, he would have no aid.

Another blow, and Ceric heard the rent of wood. A cry of victory from the Dane as Ceric's shield split, the right side of it hacked away. It hung a moment from the severed rim of iron banding at its edge, then dropped to his feet. He was left with little more than half a shield, his left hand and arm firmly in the boss, but his right side wholly open to attack. He must raise his sword if he were to live.

Riding here he had thought of pomp, of ancient armies, of the splendour of the march. Now the men whose beauty he had celebrated were dying one by one. He had killed two men, two men perhaps as united in bonds with their fellows as was he. His shield was mostly gone, his sword arm uncertain, and this Dane was near to killing him. Here was the sudden reality of death, the smell of it, its breath hot on his face. Now he felt it. No beauty or nobility remained of his earlier dedication, even the sacrifice for kin, King, and God seemed impossibly distorted and distant. All that was left was his animal desire to live.

The Dane kicked the fallen part of Ceric's shield out of his way. Ceric dropped his eyes to his blade, stared at it. By its edge would he live or die. He lifted the weapon, the cross piece of the guard coming to his gaze like the frame on which Christ was nailed.

I am wrong, he thought. If he could not now think of Kilton or King, one thing yet remained. That was God. His vow to God mattered, still made sense. If he died, he would go to God. Either way in the contest, he would win.

He knew his golden cross lay against his skin, under his linen tunic, under that of leather, and that of linked rings. He pressed the forearm holding his shield tighter to his chest, pressing that cross to his flesh. He felt the muscles in his forearm, the force of his grip, and the pain too, in his right shoulder and back. It was all his. Give over to it, he told himself; give yourself up to it, the strength, the fury, the silence, and the tumult.

He might have one or two good blows in his sword arm; he must not waste them. Nothing would be wasted, he heard within him, as if in answer. Even should he fall he went to something larger than he.

He swung his sword up, purposefully high and to the right, making the Dane track it with his shield. His teeth were clenched in pain as he lifted his arm thus, but such was his intent that it was a pain almost outside of his body. The Dane's eyes followed his sword's transit, latched onto the golden hilt in Ceric's fist. It gave Ceric the chance to leap forward with his shattered shield, wielding the pointed boss as a weapon. He was able to hit the Dane's unguarded left shoulder with it. The man stifled his cry of pain; Ceric had punched through the ring-shirt as if he held a bodkin. The red shield dropped uselessly from the Dane's arm.

As Ceric moved in again with his sword tip, the Dane dodged to his left, then swung a booted foot up and kicked the sword out of Ceric's hand with a blow to his forearm. The sword fell upright between the two, its point buried for a moment in the soil, before falling. There was no chance to bend and retrieve it; all Ceric could do was draw his seax from the sheath at his belly. His right arm was almost numb with pain, but the lighter seax freed what strength he had left in it.

Deprived of his shield, the Dane moved to draw his own knife in his left hand, an action which slowed him enough for Ceric to lunge forward, nearly straight-armed, with both shield boss and seax. Neither met flesh; but what was left of his shield pushed the man's sword up into the air, while his right arm closed down upon the Dane's left, forcing it next to his body. They fell backwards together, grappling to the death, Ceric trying to turn his seax in his wrist enough to enter the man's body, while holding the Dane's own sword aloft. His helmet rolled off. Their faces were but inches apart, the smell of the other's sweat full and pungent in their nostrils, a closeness both awe-ful and terror-making. He felt the man's desperate strength beneath him, but felt his own even more.

His arms, his whole body, shook with effort. Give yourself up to it, Ceric heard again from within.

"Not me, but you," Ceric told him, looking into the widened eyes of a man who did not understand his words. "Not Woden. Christ."

It was said in gritted triumph. He had freed his wrist enough from the Dane's weight to turn it, and by rocking hard against the man's body had wedged it into the small of his back. The man shrieked, then shuddered. Ceric withdrew his seax, gripped by a hand which no longer trembled. He pulled away so that he knelt at the dying man's side. The Dane was gurgling wordlessly, head back, chin thrust in the air, suffering, Ceric knew. He would end it, and did, with a quick thrust of the blade to the man's windpipe.

"Not Woden, Christ," Ceric repeated; a form of prayer. He looked at the blood upon his blade, that seax of which the scop at home sang songs. He wiped it on the grass, slid it back slowly into its sheath. His sword was almost at his feet. He reached for it, held it upright, saw the Holy Cross in the guard piece.

His lips moved again. "For Christ, Ælfred, and Kilton," he breathed. Then he touched his lips to that cross.

Chapter the Twenty-second: The Toll

CERIC spent a moment kneeling there, his sword hilt before his face. He lived; he was alive. The joy of finding himself thus flooded into his breast. He had not been called after all. His eyes, when he lowered his sword hilt, were filled with the tenderness of the soft and vivid grass before him, a patch springing undefiled from trample and blood.

His thoughts spiraled down, tumbling with dizzying speed from the exulting heights of communion with Christ, to these tiny growing shoots beneath him, offering their Earthly loveliness. And the image of Ashild filled his mind. Ashild whom he would soon find his way to, and soon wed. He took a deep breath, filling his lungs, smiling despite the pain he felt in doing so.

No fighting was near him, but now, as if his ears had been unstopped, the sounds of conflict washed over him. He gave his head a shake. He heard the war-cries of attacking men, oaths lobbed in answer, the clang of iron coming to bear against iron, and beneath it all, the wail of the wounded.

Worr was coming to him now, holding his sword in a bloodied hand, his face begrimed, one of his leggings ripped open at the knee. "You are hit?" he asked, his voice a panting breath. Worr's eyes travelled from Ceric's face to the body of the Dane he knelt next to.

Ceric shook his head. "Or – not badly. My back and shoulder aches."

"Can you fight," Worr asked now, lifting his eyes beyond Ceric, to where a mass of men still struggled. "Do not say Yes, if you cannot lift your sword." The urgency in Worr's voice told Ceric that every arm must count.

He pushed himself up. "I can fight," he said. He retrieved his helmet where it had rolled, placed its heaviness back on his head.

Worr took him in more fully, saw the remains of the shield. He picked up the dead Dane's red round. "You need a shield; leave that which you have."

Ceric obeyed, but set it upright by the Dane. "I dropped him with it," he told Worr. "I will come back for it. I must take it to Cadmar, proof that I listened well." This seemed of sudden importance, that he bear such witness, as if the warrior-monk had foretold of Ceric's survival by the use of his shield boss.

He took the shield Worr offered. "Your hand," Ceric said, awake to the wound there. He saw that the blood from the gash above the wrist flowed freely enough to wet his friend's palm. "Let me wrap it."

In his belt he had a roll of linen his Aunt Edgyth had pressed upon him. He felt for it, but it was gone. He saw the pouch that carried it upon the grass, dislodged during his struggle with the Dane. He cut a length and bound the gash on Worr's arm.

There was time for nothing more. They lifted their weapons. The golden dragon banner of Wessex was still aloft, but quiet against the brilliant blue of a clear and nearly cloudless sky. They made for it, and the two score of men fighting underneath. But they had not gone more than a few steps when a horn sounded.

It was not that of Eadward's herald. It was higher pitched, and blew once, a horn which came from deep within the struggling men. The men beneath the battle flag seemed to separate and dissolve. Danes began running, coming not only from the numbers fighting near the flag of Wessex, but from all around the field. They were leaving, running towards the opening gates of the palisade. The Danes were fleeing.

They ran with purpose, not stopping to engage any thegns who gave chase, or tried to bar their way. Few Danes were seen even to pluck at anything upon the ground. Ceric and Worr stood watching with opened mouths. Then, mindful they would be needed, they made their way as quickly as they could to where the banner beckoned. The carnage only deepened as they neared the spot where such a short time ago they had stood in ranks fronting Eadward and his picked men.

A feeling like ice in his veins gripped Ceric. What if the bodyguard had failed, and Eadward was dead? Yet if that were true, why did the Danes retreat? And there was the golden dragon, hanging in the cool morning air, not captured, not torn down.

Now they were close enough to see men of Kilton, thegns of other burhs too, standing and looking in to where Ceric hoped Eadward stood. Only when they entered the inner ring of men did they see him, sword in his hand.

He had himself fought; it was clear from the dampness of his brow and the hacks to his shield he had traded blows. The fighting was hot indeed around him for this to happen, for his bodyguard to fail in this way. Yet the Prince looked unhurt, though his anger was clear. Ceric watched the Prince hand his shield to one of his men, and then slide the naked blade of his bright sword back into its baldric.

Ten or more dead men lay about him, most of them Danes, attesting to the heat of the battle about the Prince. One of his bodyguard was moving amongst those fallen Danes, ramming a spear point into the breast of any who still lived.

Ceric saw one raise his hand in supplication, a plea which was denied. These Danes had tried to kill the Prince of Wessex.

Ceric shifted his gaze to the dragon banner. Its staff had been thrust into the ground. The youth he had seen this morning holding it lay dead upon the grass. His eyes went back to the Prince, his flag-bearer slain, his bodyguard breached. The Danes had fled, but this was hardly a great victory.

"Just as we are winning out, they run," Eadward said. His face showed his dismay, one bordering on disgust.

"Those who can still ride, follow me," he told them. "Those unfit, stay and help gather the injured and the dead. I leave half my remaining men here to keep the Danes within. The rest of you fit enough to fight will join me as we track down those who escaped as we arrived."

As they stood listening a rider approached, on a horse well lathered. "My Lord," he called, as he flung himself down from his saddle. "Those Danes who left the field leave now, from their rear gate."

"Are all our men dead?"

"No my Lord, but they rode after those who early escaped."

"Leaving none to hold the gate," Eadward finished. If he had been angered before, he was near rage now.

"Enough," he said aloud, but as if to himself. He looked to the man who rode as messenger. "The tracks of many horses will be easy to follow in this soft soil.

"Bring the horses forward, waggons too," he ordered now. "We will gather the wounded."

He scanned the faces of the warriors who stood about him. "Strip the Danes, taking what you will. Collect the dead," he went on. His chin turned to where the youth who had held his battle flag had fallen. His voice dropped. "Put Ecgulf in my own waggon."

Eadward's herald pulled his brass horn from his shoulder, turned to face the gently rising ground upon which the horses and supply men waited. He blew the summoning calls, a sound as mournful as if it had been for retreat.

The men began to look about them, seeing who lived and stood, and to find their lords or leaders. Other thegns, able to walk but with injuries, were still coming haltingly towards them from the field, heading for the dragon banner. Ceric and those gathered before him must walk now to meet them, and all return to the places they had fought, find the men they had killed, take what battle-gain could be had.

As the thegns of Kilton presented themselves before Ceric and Worr, he tried to number them. Fifty-one fighting men had ridden from Kilton, and all had taken part in the action. He saw nine and twenty now before him.

Others must live, he thought, looking out at those men who still walked slowly towards the banner. He looked to Worr, who he knew had been counting as well. Adding themselves it made thirty-one men standing. There must be more.

"Wistan. Where is Wistan," Ceric asked. "He was on my left."

"I saw him, after the shield-wall broke," Worr said, lending some hope.

They all began heading for those places where they had downed men. Wounded thegns were still rising from the ground, or trying to. The men were so scattered that the warriors of one burh now lay near that of another, who had been many paces away when the boar-snout had rushed at them. The thegns of Kilton dropped off one by one, going to aid their injured brethren, searching for the Danes they had felled.

Worr and Ceric walked past Ceric's shattered shield, resting upright against the body of the last Dane he had killed. They continued on; they had always been near to each other. They scanned the bodies as they passed them, some of which they need roll over so their faces could be seen. They found eight dead thegns of Kilton this way, and several more of other burhs.

"Wistan," said Worr, turning over a ninth. The ground was soaked with his blood, the broad rent on his right arm showing where the head of a war-axe had sliced through the ring-tunic as if it had been little more than loops of women's thread-work.

Ceric looked down on the lifeless form. Wistan had a merry, rusty-haired wife who was plump, and three nearly grown daughters, and a young son. It would be Ceric who must tell her how her husband fell.

"His sword," Worr was saying, eyes travelling all around the dead thegn. "Where is his sword." The voice, always so steady, held now a plaintive edge.

Wistan was the most seasoned of thegns, had won treasure in the service of both Godwulf and Godwin. He was liked by all, but was Worr's friend. When Worr had fought to defend Kilton as a young man, it was Wistan who stood by him, urging him on as he put to use all the hours of sparring they had done together. Worr knew Wistan's fine sword almost as well as his own; it was one Godwulf had presented to Wistan as reward when he was no older than Ceric was now.

They kicked over the bodies of dead Danes and pulled over those of the thegns of Wessex, searching. Wistan's sword was not there. It had been carried off by the retreating Danes. They looked at each other, not needing to speak. Wistan's body had not been defiled through having been stripped by the enemy, but this was the sole consolation. There was no sword to pass into his widow's keeping. They would take his seax and any slight valuables, and bring them to her; it was all they could do.

Waggons were coming now, some for the dead, others for the wounded. They walked back to where the Danes had first hit them. Ceric looked up above a distant line of trees, blinking at the brilliance of the Sun, still climbing in the sky. The whole battle had been brief. He knew in the past pitched battles had gone on for hours, short truces called while men retrieved weapons, found whole shields, took refreshment, had their wounds bound up. But this had been over in the space of an hour; the Sun was not yet overhead. It was hard to take in.

He found the first man, he who had been in the fifth rank of the boar snout. His blow had not severed the wrist entirely, and the opened hand hanging by a flap of skin was the more grisly for it. The hand and its arm lay folded up near the Dane's shoulder, and Ceric moved to the man's other side. He could see without reaching that the Dane wore no neck chain. No bracelet encircled the man's left wrist, which was still inside his shield. He unbuckled the weapons belts and lay them in his upturned shield, then dragged it by its shoulder strap to where Worr knelt, working over those he had downed. They worked back to back, Ceric stripping the body of the younger man, Worr of the older. He heard Worr's sharp intake of breath, and turned to see him pull a thick cuff of silver from the man's left wrist, concealed behind his shield. It was a worthy prize.

The younger man had little, weapons serviceable but of no great worth, and next to no silver in his worn purse. Ceric had no need for any of this, and the act of stripping a dead body gave him no satisfaction, as it did to other men, sealing their victory over them. Nor was he likely to find something that he would wish as keepsake, or had such value that he would wear or use himself. But everything he took would be given out as reward to his remaining men, or given to benefit the poor of Kilton. It was proof of prowess on the field, yes; but it was a vital part of the circle of war. His men would offer the best of what they took to him, just as he would do so to Edwin. This Winter Ceric would at some upcoming Yule feast dole out treasure to his pledged thegns, just as Edwin would grant him some rich gift for his own service to Kilton.

He moved to the last man. Worr had gone on; Ceric knew from the number of stops he made that he had killed at least four. He would give Worr his pick of the best horses at Kilton when they returned; a stallion and mare both. Four men killed in a single short battle was a champion's tally. Most men were glad to place a blow, maiming or killing one, and coming alive themselves from the action. Worr was indeed a fine warrior; all said it, and now Ceric had seen it. He did not himself think at this moment that he, in his first open battle, had killed three.

He turned his attention to the Dane before him. He placed the remnants of his shield into that of the dead man's; there was a grim justice that Ceric now used it to collect his battle-gain. He forced his eyes up to the man's throat, which he had pierced with his seax. The tunic had shifted as the man writhed in his death-agony, and a silver chain could be seen there.

He moved behind the man, lifted the head with one hand, with the other plucked at the chain and pulled it over. Something caught on the man's chin and nose as it came. Ceric found himself holding a silver chain from which swung a hammer of Thor.

He turned his face from it. An image of Ashild filled his eyes, pulling her father's own hammer from her gown and showing it to him and her mother in the stable yard of Four Stones.

He let his eyes drop to his hand. This hammer was smaller and less finely wrought than that of Yrling's, and its proof against the enemy just as faulty. He knew his uncle had ripped the hammer from Yrling's neck, but thought only of she who now wore it.

He wiped the clotted blood from the links and slipped the hammer into the pouch at his belt. Not Woden, Christ, he had told the man. He would have the hammer melted down and the silver given for the poor.

When he had finished with the Dane he walked to where a waggon loaded the wounded. He tried to lift the upper body of a groaning thegn, but the pain in his own shoulder and back made him lower him again. "I am only bruised," he assured a thegn who questioned him. Worr was come now, dragging a quantity of battle-gain, stuffed into a leathern pack he had found.

They went to the waggons of the dead, made sure that what treasure could be taken back to Kilton was lifted from the bodies. Some of the thegns had downed the enemy before themselves being downed, and their brethren stripped those bodies for them, booty to go to widows and sons. The men themselves would end their Earthly sojourn in Witanceaster; Kilton was five days beyond that and too far to take them. There in the burial ground by Ælfred's fine church would they greet the day of Resurrection.

They all walked further up the rise. Eadward's horse had been brought to him, and he came last, stopping by the waggons into which the dead of Wessex were hoisted, moving his horse slowly as he looked upon the plundered and abandoned bodies of the Danish dead. The foot-men waited there at the top of the swelling hill, those who had fired the opening volleys of missiles, and whom, given the disorder of the conflict, Eadward had never used again. They had seen all from their vantage, and knew this day would not be one of which songs were made.

One of the drovers from Kilton came to Ceric, bearing a basin of cold water. The man gave a jerk of his head to the basin, and a muttered, Sir, as invitation. The water dropped down bright red as Ceric splashed it over his face; the blood drying on his face running again to liquid, nearly as bright as when it had pumped from living veins.

Bread, meat, and cheese was passed, and casks of ale tapped. Ceric dropped upon the ground with all the others and found himself shaking with hunger. He sat there on the grass, almost cramming food into his mouth, mindful of those dead who would never taste again.

Then they must move on. The extra horses, and some of those of the dead thegns, were transformed into pack animals, the supplies that would be needed on the road quickly loaded on to their backs. The waggons were all in use, to cart back the injured, and the dead. Ceric would move on with the living, under Eadward's command.

Chapter the Twenty-third: A Landing

Four Stones

"ONE here," Gunnulf was saying, pointing at a clump of trees and brush. "Plenty of cover, and it gives a clear view up and down the stream bed."

Hrald, Jari, and Gunnulf were riding the full perimeter of Four Stone's lands, looking for points at which new watch-posts could be set to advantage. The roads leading to the keep had always had watch-men. But there were places where a whole body of men could move quickly and unobserved, bringing them near enough for surprise attack. This stream and its grassy banks were one such vulnerable path.

It was the morning of their second day out, and this stream served as one of the borders with the keep to their North, Turcesig, that held now by Thorfast. The hall of Turcesig was still many hours' ride away, and these lands uninhabited by any small trevs or hamlets from either keep. Along the way they had noted several places where new patrols could be stationed.

Hrald was glad to have Gunnulf with him. He was swift to spot and size up a possibility, his reasoning sound, and with his older, more seasoned brother Jari could argue for one or another new watch-post, pointing out advantages and disadvantages to each. And Gunnulf was good company. Jari was sometimes prone to moroseness, and Gunnulf with his quick wit kept him on a lighter footing. He was a favourite amongst the men, tossing his long yellow hair as he jested with them. Gunnulf had ever had a striking boldness about him, and cut a fine figure on the half-trained horses he favoured. Riding out with him in company with other men, Hrald began to feel the easy closeness he had once had with Gunnulf to be repaired, even if it could not be fully restored.

Besides Jari and Gunnulf, ten other warriors rode with Hrald as they circled their borders. No word of war had come to Four Stones; in fact the lack of riders bearing news had made the hall almost as anxious as if panting men on lathered horses had reined up, sounding an alarm.

Asberg thought he knew why one of Haesten's chief men, or Haesten himself, had not ventured to Four Stones to speak to them, and had shared his concerns with Hrald and Jari. He thought it likely that word had been sent to Haesten from Thorfast, or some other neighbouring war-chief, that Hrald would not take up arms against Ælfred, would in fact honour the Peace. Haesten or his captains did not wish to force the issue, Asberg ventured. Avoiding a confrontation before the conflict began left the door open. Whether it was left open for later direct attack, or for reconciliation, they could not know.

Either way, with the coming of good weather all at Four Stones were now on alert, and new watch-posts surrounding it deemed necessary. Asberg had remained at the hall, where men drilled daily in the arts of spear and sword, shield-blocking and skeggox-wielding. But Asberg had sent his two young sons to join their cousin Hrald on this border patrol. Indeed, the lads had begged to come. For them it was a worthy adventure in itself, a chance to ride with Hrald and his best men, to camp overnight in the fair Spring nights, to view parts of their lands they had never seen. Ulf, the older of them, had just received his sword, while Abi, two years younger, was armed with a knife. Both lads also carried spears, sized for their height and strength.

"Hrald," Ulf was petitioning now, lifting his arm to the fairness of the place. "When you send back men to take up their posts, send Abi and me here." Abi took this up at once, chiming in on the appeal to their cousin.

"There is water, places to shelter in the trees, good grass for our horses, dried wood in plenty for our cook-fires," the younger was numbering.

Hrald laughed, as did Gunnulf. "I did not choose it as a joy-camp for you two snare-setters," Gunnulf told them. Hrald had shown the lads how to fashion snares, and several times had taken them out, until they themselves were skillful enough to return from their runs with small game.

Hrald shook his head, but the boys were so hopeful that he could bring himself to say no more than, "We shall see."

They moved on in their route, Ulf and Abi riding behind Gunnulf, and calling out to him, pleading their case that he should put in a good word for them when Hrald assigned the new patrols.

In truth, there was no chance that Asberg's sons would be exposed to this danger. Their father knew this, as did Hrald. Watch-men were easily overwhelmed by invaders, and if caught, the first to be killed. If Hrald should die, his closest male kin was his uncle, Asberg; and after Asberg, his own two sons. Ulf and Abi did not yet grasp their importance to the future of Four Stones.

Hrald's small troop rode on. They were cresting the northern-most border of their lands when two strange riders came into view, travelling at an unrushed canter. The men whistled out to them, a three-part whistle that Thorfast used. Hrald whistled back, gesturing with his arm that they approach.

Thorfast was near, they told him, and on his way to Four Stones to see him. They followed his advance riders North, into the edges of Turcesig's southern borders. They soon found Thorfast, riding with six of his own men.

"You are wise to fortify yourself in this way," Thorfast said to Hrald, after he had told him of his current mission. Jari had made way for Thorfast, dropping back to ride with Gunnulf, so that he and Hrald now rode side by side. "Fore-warned is fore-armed. Even an hour's warning can make the difference in an attack."

Hrald nodded. He had not seen Thorfast since Yule, when he had come to spend a feast-night with him at Four Stones. "Haward and I do the same, extend our watch-posts," Thorfast went on, speaking of his younger brother who lived at the old family hall to the East of Turcesig.

They had left the stream banks and were now at the edge of a mere. The only border markings were dolmens of stone, the height of a man and so widely spaced as to be out of sight of each other. Thorfast had come specially to see him, Hrald knew; they must head back to the hall, and finish their circuit another day.

As they rode Hrald wondered as to the nature of his neighbour's visit. At Yule they had refrained from war-talk, as much as was possible given the uncertain times. Thorfast had not asked to speak privately with Ashild, but had greeted her with good humour, dipped his head respectfully when she filled his cup, and made handsome compliment to the gown she wore. As the newly large party approached the palisade Hrald knew she would be surprised by his early arrival, and by who he brought with him.

Ashild was up in the weaving room with her little sister, standing at a loom. She was beating up the woof of a growing length of wool, when Ælfwyn walked in.

"Thorfast is here," is what she said to them.

It was Ealhswith who spoke first. "Did he bring you another horse," she asked her sister, blue eyes brighter than usual.

Ashild gave her a half-smile, pressing her finger to her own lips to bid the girl's silence.

"I was in the kitchen yard when he rode in, with Hrald," her mother went on. She was still standing in the doorway, making no move to spindle or loom; she must of course attend to her guest.

"Hrald is back early," Ashild considered, watching her mother's face. "Is there then trouble?"

"Not from how they greeted me." She spent a moment taking in her two girls, the elder still holding her weaving-sword. Left unspoken was the word But, upon which all might hinge.

Ashild slid the tool between the warp strings and stepped nearer her mother. Other than the single letter from Ceric, and that she and Hrald had sent in answer, they had had no communication with Kilton, or indeed, all of Wessex. They knew as much as Asberg and Hrald did, that a vast army of Danes had landed, driven out of Frankland from lack of gain, and was now massed to attack here in Angle-land. Whether their plan was to march West to Wessex or North through Anglia remained to be known. What was known is that certain Danes from as far North as Northumbria were aiding the newly arrived; had in fact thrown in with Haesten. It placed halls like Four Stones between two hostile forces.

Ælfwyn was watching her daughter's face. The stresses of the past year had touched her; the girl had grown more serious, even grave. What she said next surprised her mother.

"I want to live my life here, at Four Stones. And die here, too," she proclaimed, as a small child might. Ashild had lifted her hands slightly before her, spreading the fingers as if she warded off her future. But there was little insolence in her pensive manner.

Ælfwyn was not sure how to take it. "Ashild," she chided, in her gentlest tone. "Do not ask for that which can never be." Her eyebrows lifted in question, and she gave a light laugh. "Whom would you wed?"

She cast about in her mind, looking for an example to make her daughter also laugh. "Gunnulf? He likes horses as well as you…"

Ashild was shaking her head, but her mother had forced a smile to her lips. "Gunnulf is a friend, like kin…" She lifted her head, straightening her shoulders as she did so. "And I know I cannot wed any from the keep. I must bring treasure, an alliance…"

It pained her mother to hear Ashild outline her greatest role, her most pressing duty, as true as it was. "The alliance formed, the treasure exchanged, is between halls. It is not on your head alone, my sweet."

Ashild seemed to waver. Even her body rocked slightly forward and back, and her brow was scrunched in thought. She knew her mother must go back down, play the hostess, order the meal. She could stay up here, safe with Ealhswith, beating up the soft wool with her weaving-sword…

"I will come down with you," she decided.

They found Hrald and Thorfast by the wall on which hung the long dragon banner, standing with Asberg. Jari and the rest of the returning men were seeing to the horses and kit. Hrald's own packs lay by the edge of the fire-pit, where he had dropped them. Ale had been brought, but only Asberg now held a cup in his hand. As the two women approached they saw the men were eyeing each other, and not speaking.

"Ashild," said Thorfast. It was clear he did not expect to see her so quickly after his arrival. Yet he lifted his hand to her, and the smile which spread upon his lips seemed genuine.

No one spoke. Whatever was next said might cast all which came after on a path which could not be retraced.

The Lady of Four Stones took a quiet breath. Her lovely hands, which she held clasped before her at her waist, barely moved from the gentleness of the air she drew.

"Thorfast of Turcesig," she began. All eyes were upon her, but the formality of her address made those before her fix her in their gaze.

Ashild stepped forward, shifting the eyes of the others from her mother to herself. She gestured to the treasure room door, slightly ajar. Whatever would be said now would require the privacy of that inner stronghold. They went to it.

Burginde was within, with Ælfwyn's sister Eanflad at her side, refilling the oil cressets from pottery jugs, making the careful pours of the costly oil that both women were known for. Burginde had heard the voice of Thorfast in the hall, and had suspected he and his hosts might be heading for the treasure room, away from the passing serving folk of the main hall, and the women who stood spinning by the opened doors. She moved to the stool by the broad bed, ready to plump down on the cushion there as soon as Ælfwyn gave the sign, and summoned Eanflad to stand at her side. But perhaps because of her sister's presence, Ælfwyn gestured they should both leave. Burginde cast a lingering look at Ashild as she did so, and from the tension on the maid's face it was all she could do to refrain from clucking her teeth in sympathy as she passed her.

Now that all were inside at her invitation, Ashild did not know what to say. The five of them stood just within the closed door. Ashild's eye flitted to the battle flag she had made for Hrald, threaded upon a staff, and resting in a corner. Thorfast had been watching Ashild's face as well, and smoothed the way for her.

"I am glad you join us, Ashild, for what I am here to say concerns all of us, and you perhaps most of all." He turned his head now, so that his eyes met in turn those of Hrald, Asberg, and lastly, Ashild's mother.

"There will be war," he announced, "within weeks, or perhaps days."

The heads of those before him lifted the higher at his words. "My cousin, Agmund, Guthrum's son, has told me this. He is joining with Haesten."

He let this hang in the air before going on. All were staring at him.

"I am here because I myself am undecided. But I would face whatever is to come with a greater force, and not a lesser." He looked to Hrald. "A single arrow is snapped like a reed in the hands of a man, but a bundle of them, held together, cannot be broken by the strongest fists.

"Will you Hrald, join with me, so that we are both the stronger? Let me wed Ashild, now, to bind our halls together."

Asberg was the first to speak. "We are ready for war," he claimed. His hand had moved to his sword-hilt, a sword he wore now even within the hall.

But Thorfast shook his head. "You do not know the strength of the forces Haesten has gathered. Over three hundred ships full; and now he has been joined by many of us who settled here after the Peace was made. Agmund has heard that Ofram in Northumbria rides to join Haesten. It will not be one battle, one siege, but wave after wave. We here in Lindisse will be at the heart of it.

"And Haesten will not deal kindly with those Danes who he feels have betrayed their own kind."

This spurred Hrald. Thorfast's voice had grown steadily louder, its tone more strident. They had ever been on friendly terms, but he must make reply to this last, which fell on Hrald's ear as a threat not only from the invading Haesten, but from Thorfast too.

"I am half-Dane," he told Thorfast. "I also am half-Saxon. And I will not war against Wessex. Not break the Peace which my father signed."

He took a step closer to him he faced, ready with his own demand. "Would you join with me, Thorfast, knowing that? You say you do not yet know which way you will fight. But I do. To uphold the Peace your uncle made." Hrald stressed these last few words.

Thorfast's lips parted slightly, and his gaze dropped a moment before returning to Hrald's face.

Ashild caught her mother's eye. The love in that returning glance gave her courage to speak.

"I would have a word with my brother," she began to Thorfast, ending by a look to Hrald which had him already turning to the door.

It must be this way, Ashild said to herself, as she turned from her mother and uncle. It must be Hrald and I who make decision; none other but we two.

"Hrald," she pleaded, once they were in the hall. "I must wed. Ceric is far away, Thorfast near at hand. He is rich, and ready to join with you. To join with us," she forced herself to say.

She knew her brother would speak now, and went on, to stay his words. "You had two spears made for me, and taught me how to use them. Hearing Thorfast speak of the war to come I thought one thing: that if I am willing to kill for Four Stones, I should be able to wed for it, as well. I will go in and tell him that if he vows to uphold the Peace, I will wed him."

Hrald reached his hand to her, placed it on her wrist. "Ashild, wait. He told me once that you would be thrown away at Kilton."

Her face betrayed that she had heard the same from Thorfast's lips. Hrald's dark blue eyes were locked on hers as he went on. "But if he does not resist Haesten with his men, if he does not observe the Peace, then you will be thrown away at Turcesig. That must be his decision, not one made because of promise of marriage with you. He must decide, first. I do not ask for Ceric's sake – I do not. I ask for your own."

She made a sound, a stifled groan, one of real and wrenching pain.

"Delay him," Hrald urged. "Delay him again. We must know which way he will turn. Ask for a fortnight in which to make your decision, and promise it then. Please."

Hrald had been deprived the presence of his father for some years, yet his instincts proved him to be Sidroc's son. Hrald would not push Thorfast; he felt without being told that to push an undecided man was dangerous. He wanted Thorfast as an ally. He was asking him to be patient, and he would do the same; he would not press Thorfast for his own decision.

She had closed her eyes, as if against his words. When she had asked her brother to leave the room with her she had resolved they would act together. She had declared to him she would become Lady of Turcesig. Hrald now made request of his own, and she must honour it. If she must beg Thorfast to wait again, even so brief a span as fourteen days was much to ask. But she nodded, and placed her own hand over that which clasped her wrist. They went back inside.

"I am disposed towards you, Thorfast," she began, "and say it freely before my beloved kin. But I beg a fortnight in which to make my full decision. Grant me only this, you who have been patient with Ashild."

This was said with such earnestness that Thorfast could do nothing but incline his head in assent.

Ashild stopped her mother on the landing outside the weaving room. Soon she would travel these steps no more, save for when she came to visit. She had been watching Thorfast's face, not her mother's, when she had spoken. She knew her uncle was pleased, and her mother sorrowed, by what she had promised. She turned to her now.

"Forgive me mother. I know you wanted me for Ceric."

Ælfwyn's arms reached about her. "Hush, my darling. It is a sacrifice for you, either way; this I know. If you do choose Thorfast, you will be close to me, a great balm."

"And if there is war against Haesten?"

It took all her mother's courage to fight back her fears and answer with assurance. Perhaps Ashild could sway her new husband where her brother could not. "If there is war, it will be as Thorfast has told us: Four Stones and Turcesig united are an army of its own."

Three days out, Runulv's ship hit a patch of weather so foul that even he began to fear for her seaworthiness. The storm struck as they entered the straights of Dane-mark, and at one point thickened into a gale so fierce that they beat into a cove for a full two days. They hauled her ashore in blinding rain, and took what shelter they could in her lee. They huddled, soaked through and cold, able only with difficulty to finally strike and light a fire to warm their food, and thaw their numbed limbs. The goshawks and the starlings had the best of it, for the one must be kept alive to feed the other, and if any amongst that ship's number knew comfort, it was they.

The weather had settled but slightly when they set out once more, sail furled, every man at the oars, and Runulv and Sidroc both hanging on to the steering-oar, guiding her prow so she was not swamped as they made their way through foaming seas. These two alone welcomed the weather, and as they struggled under glowering skies gave thanks to the Gods for it, for it kept the dragon-ships of the Danes on shore during this point of greatest danger. When they broke into the clear they were all much worn by their efforts, but the wind and waves had propelled them so that the two lost days in the bleak Danish cove had been more than made up.

They would not coast after rounding the northern tip of Sidroc's native land, finding each night some deserted stretch of beach to land, and rest overnight. They would instead set course by the stars straight out in open waters across the North Sea, as Runulv had years earlier when he had returned Hrald and Ceric to Four Stones. This sea was kinder than the Baltic had been, and although staying at sea meant both chilly nights and cold food through lack of fire, Runulv's ruddy-sailed ship skipped over the waters with the grace and speed of a great red swan. When, six days later, the coast of Angle-land appeared on the western horizon they all let loose a cry of gladness. They gaped at its dark outline. It was vast, seeming without end, filling the eyes from corner to corner, which told those men who had not made this journey before how great an island they aimed for.

Both wind and tides brought them down from the North, slipping past a green and empty coastline, the shores of which teamed with great forests to the water's edge. It was strange for Sidroc, standing at the gunwale, to lay eyes upon it after so long an absence. There was no landmark yet to pick out, but the very shades of green, and shapes of trees, had a familiar cast about them. Then he saw a river outlet he knew, and then, with a sense of recognition that made his eyes widen, he spied the bluff upon which he and his shield-maiden had been walking when they awaited the ship which would return her to Kilton. They never saw that ship, for they had been spotted by the crew of one quite different.

"Saltfleet," he heard Runulv call out. He himself could say nothing, only watched as they glided past the bluff, rounding into the bay that held the wooden pier he had built as Jarl of South Lindisse.

Runulv was focused on his steering-oar and the depth of water skirting an outcropping of rock, then at last gave the order to drop sail. All the men, even those busying themselves with sail or line, had one eye fixed on the small cluster of buildings at the shore end of the reaching pier. Two men were standing there, holding both spears and shields, and as they watched they were joined by four others, coming hastily from one of the timber buildings.

When they were near enough Sidroc put his fingers to his mouth. The whistle he sent their way pierced the air with its shrillness. Three of the men had begun to make their way down the pier, then stopped when they heard it. Sidroc whistled a second time. A pause, then spears were lifted straight up overhead, lifted in greeting. He stood there, grinning across the shrinking expanse of water at those who now hurried down the pier to greet him.

"Freyr, who carried me over the seas through sea-god Njord's dangers, I thank you. To you Freyr, and your sister Freyja, I will make rich Offering." It was said aloud, but Sidroc meant it for the Gods he thanked. He was not alone in murmuring so; every man of Gotland gave thanks to be delivered safely after such a passage.

The line was thrown; the straked hull of the ship pulled alongside the pier.

"Sidroc!" called one of spears-men. He and his fellows were setting down their weapons in readiness.

The man so named had vanished a moment behind the gunwale, to appear with shield and spears in hand, which he swung over the ship's side and into the reaching hands of those waiting.

He leapt out. "Thidrick. Holmgaut." He passed from embracing arm to arm of his men, calling their names, and looked at the two youngest standing before him, watching in puzzlement. They had been boys when he had been taken.

"You have come from Gotland," Thidrick asked.

"Já. And to Gotland I will return, as the Gods allow."

His men took this in, looking at Sidroc, more than ten years gone, and then at each other.

"Where is Haesten," Sidroc asked now, surprising them with his knowledge.

"Massing somewhere down the coast. But he has got help from Ofram in Northumbria, and other jarls."

"Ælfred?"

"He and his son have an army each, we hear; but we do not know where they are."

"And of Four Stones?"

"Your men still number above two hundred," Thidrick told him.

"Not mine," Sidroc corrected. "My son's." His tone sealed his words.

"And Hrald has not broken the Peace?" he asked now.

Both Thidrick and Holmgaut shook their heads. "He has said many times he will not break what you and Ælfred made."

Then Ælfred would still be friendly to Four Stones, Sidroc thought.

Runulv's men were now climbing over the gunwale to touch the solid planks of the pier, all save the captain himself, who was ever the first man on, and the last off.

Sidroc looked to where he stood, securing the steering-oar.

"I recall your captain," Thidrick said. "He brought Hrald home."

Sidroc nodded. "And now Runulv and I ride to Four Stones. Give me two of your best horses, but you yourselves must stay here and help guard the ship. It holds things of worth that must be kept ready for my leaving. And there are goshawks aboard, a gift for Hrald which we will send for later. The men know how to care for them."

Sidroc's packs and those of Runulv were put ashore, and the captain himself leapt down upon the wooden planks. He gave a final word to his men, and he and Sidroc turned their backs on the stout ship which had borne them so many leagues.

Thorfast left Four Stones after a single night's stay, and Hrald and Asberg had been quick to act. By the blowing of a horn from the ramparts crowning the palisade wall which circled Four Stones, they summoned all the villagers. They walked out and met them, with Wilgot the priest, at the tall stone preaching cross outside the walls, and there gave their instructions. Men and women left their plough-bats and weeding hoes, spindles and wash tubs, and gathered with their blinking children about them to listen. All beasts from far pastures must be brought close in; all food-stores packed so as to be readily transported. Rumour of war had risen and then ebbed for several seasons. Now it was made real by their young Jarl standing before them, warning that soon they might have need to herd all they owned inside the keep's timber walls.

This accomplished, Hrald, Jari and Gunnulf rode off to resume their circuit of Four Stone's borders, this time taking a troop of men large enough to leave well-supplied watch-men in their wake. Hrald rode over the objections of Ashild, who did not think he should be a moment away from the hall. But he forced a smile to her face when he inclined his head to the spears bristling in their iron hoops flanking the long dragon banner, and told her she and their uncle could hold the hall just as well.

Asberg again stayed behind, and this time forbade Ulf and Abi from riding with their older cousin. But the Lady of Four Stones made glad the boys' hearts by asking her nephews to come with her and her daughters as they walked out themselves to speak to the villagers. "They are affright," she told Ashild and Ealhswith as they readied themselves, "and if our showing our own calmness can serve them, we will do so."

In truth, Ælfwyn's words were far steadier than her thoughts. As a maid she had come to a devastated village and a ruined hall, and had shared in that suffering, even as she worked to rebuild what had been thrust upon her. Four Stones and its folk had known such peace since then that the threat of nearing war might now have choked her with fear. But she arrayed herself, and went out with her two daughters and Burginde. Four women, two of them but maids, thus showed themselves to the anxious villagers. For escort Ælfwyn chose her two nephews, one only old enough to bear a sword, and proud to be asked to accompany their aunt. She walked amongst her people as they made preparation, beginning at the hut of Meryth, the stable-man Mul's mother, a woman who had been one of Ælfwyn's first allies in her early days at the keep. Her folk had ever loved her, but the act of walking amongst them as a woman, vulnerable and brave, lent more courage to those she greeted than if all of the warriors of Four Stones poured forth from its gates to defend them.

That night as Ælfwyn knelt to say her prayers, she drew, as she often had, her Psalter from its hardened box, and held it. She had no need to turn the pages, knowing every psalm as she did by heart. She merely held it as she whispered her prayers, deriving comfort from the saying of them, the rhythmic rise and fall of well-loved verses. Then she prayed for the health and safety of those she cherished. Eyes lowered on the silver cover of the precious book, she prayed as well for the King who had given her this rich gift; and prayed also for him who had delivered it.

Ashild was riding back from the stand of elm trees where hung her target-shield. She had her two spears in her right hand, guiding her mare with her left. Her practice had been solitary; Hrald was not yet returned from his circuit about their lands, but was soon expected. As she neared the old place of Offering, a movement glimpsed through the trees stopped her eye. Some man vanished through the shrubs, alerted perhaps to her nearness. Gaining the place fully she saw why.

Before the rotted carving of Odin an old hay-fork had been thrust up, tines to the sky. Caught in those tines was the sacrificed body of a fowl.

She stopped her horse. Her breath came in a long and quiet sough from her opened lips. All of the men at Four Stones had received the Cross, all of them. The back-sliders who had made Offering when the great long-tailed star had appeared in the sky had been roundly scolded then by Wilgot. Once the beaming light had faded from view, this trench and its mute figure had been once again ignored.

The late afternoon breeze ruffled the fowl's speckled brown feathers as if it still lived, but the bird's broken neck hung limply between the iron tines. Ashild's eye travelled down to the pit from which rose the hay-fork. Another bird lay there, and one not long ago sacrificed.

"Odin," she said aloud. Her naming the God almost startled her. She was in fact not alone here at Four Stones; there were others who again gave thought to their old Gods. All-Father he was named, just as the Christian God was. Odin who knew all, who traded an eye for a sip of well-water to grant him that sight...

Her father's hammer of Thor rested between her breasts, its silver weight ever-present. Thor was fearless in his courage, and had magic of his own. But he lacked fore-sight of what was to come. No mind, she told herself, nudging her mare forward. It is courage that is most needed, now.

Chapter the Twenty-fourth: Another Offering

Gotland

CERIDWEN sat with Rannveig in the brew-house. It was not yet open for the day, but the weather was mild enough that Rannveig had rolled up the heavy canvas awnings from the low wooden walls, and she and her guest sat looking out upon a placid Baltic. Eirian sat between them, as slender as a willow sapling, her thin fingers flying at her work, her dark head bent slightly down. All three were braiding waxed linen thread, to serve as wicks for Rannveig's beeswax tapers. It was a pleasant task, done in the strong and good light of mid-day, and in welcome and loving company.

A ship came into view, one of Gotland's broad-beamed fishing fleet, and they all looked at it a moment as it headed with its catch towards the wooden pier. Eirian did not return to her work, and after studying the ship she wondered aloud.

"Why does father's ship not come back?"

The Mistress of Tyrsborg paused a moment before making answer. Eirian's rich blue eyes went from the sea to her mother's face. "Runulv is taking him further than he generally sails, all the way West to the great island of Angle-land."

Eirian nodded, a quick bob of her chin, and went back to her finger-work. She had asked this question before, as had her brother Yrling, and had before been satisfied with the reminder of the distance to be travelled.

The brewster was still thinking on it, though. "It has been –" Rannveig thought aloud.

"Seventeen days," Ceridwen answered. Every hour of them had been marked on her heart. She did not let herself sigh, but in holding it in, stifled herself just the same.

A few days after Sidroc had sailed a storm of unusual ferocity blew from the West, one that wrenched trees in full leaf from the soil they stood rooted in, and ripped the sedge thatching from peaked roofs. It knocked over boats which had been hauled ashore on the rocky beaches, canting them as if they heeled with sails unfurled in driving winds. When the storm calmed Ceridwen came down to the trading road. The newly-blue sky seemed to mock the violence that had been, and she shivered in the fresh breeze. She looked upon those boats, nearly overturned yet on dry land, and wrapped herself in her own arms, thinking on what Runulv's ship may have faced. As she stood there she heard the door of the brew house, behind her. Rannveig came up at her side, and placed an arm around her.

She must for the sake of her children and household greet each day with hopeful cheer, busying herself with the normal demands of early Spring. She walked the forest paths with the children and little Juoksa, willow baskets in hand, to pluck tender birch leaves to boil the tonic she favoured, and which she forced on all for whom she cared. She and Helga turned out every featherbed of the hall, beat them well, darning up any faults in the ticking, and re-stuffing those whose down had crushed beyond re-fluffing. Ring had shorn the sheep at the farm and carted to her the raw fleece to be cleant, combed, and spun, a task which would busy her through Summer. Through careful husbandry Tindr and Šeará had made great increase in the fowl and geese of Tyrsborg, and Ceridwen and Helga and the cook Gunnvor numbered the chicks and goslings, and picked out those larger to be sent to the trading road for sale and barter.

Tindr was busy two days running carrying off all the Winter ash from the hall fire-pit. He shovelled it out into a drag sling, much like that he strapped to his waist to haul back the stags he took. Now the ash would be used for scrubbing, and spading into the vegetables. In his wake, the birch twig brooms held by Ceridwen and Helga and young Eirian were active sweeping up the fine powder of the burnt wood that had warmed them during the cold. Of all she did during the lengthening days of Sidroc's absence, this was perhaps the hardest task, that of sweeping away the Winter's ash of the fires she had sat with her husband by. These had been the warming flames they had stared into together, and held their chilled hands to until their palms tingled. They had spoken together before these fires, of children, farm, and hall, and done hand-work or carving by the grateful glow. The heat from those logs which Sidroc and Tindr had hewn and stacked was long spent, and now to sweep away and dispose of the last relics of these warming fires felt an unlooked for and additional loss.

When Rannveig determined that she had enough linen wicking for the tapers she would make, Ceridwen walked back up the hill with Eirian. The girl skipped ahead to their neighbour Alrik's house, spotting his own daughter and running to join her, and Ceridwen continued on alone. The view of Tyrsborg's steeply gabled roof had always filled her with quiet happiness. Now its sharpness felt a stabbing blow to her breast. Sidroc was not there. Sadness flooded her, so that her next breath was no more than a gasp. This is what being a widow will be like, her heart told her; returning to my hall, without my man. This is what Rannveig had to bear when her Dagr took ship and did not return alive…

One morning, awakening before dawn, she found her arm stretch out, into the half of her bed where Sidroc should be lying. Her fingers met no solid warmth, only more smooth and cool linen. She gave a stifled cry. She could not fully recall her dream, but knew he had been with her. She reached her hand over her head, touching the headboard into which he had carved the knot she had drawn. Then she drew her hand back, over the silver disc bracelet on her left wrist. She squeezed her eyes to shut out the pain of awakening alone.

She must rise, turn from her fears. She swung her legs onto the softness of her plush weaving and began to stand. As she did so the floor rose up to meet her. She fell back, in a wash of dizzy sickness. She reached her hand again to the headboard, her fingertips feeling the depth of the carved spiral arm of the pattern. It steadied her, and she again rose. The dizziness once more, and her mouth feeling as if she might retch.

She sat, then curled herself back into the warmth of the bedclothes, her hands coiled by her heart. It was pounding in her breast. She knew she was shaking, but she was not cold. Hope overtook her, more fully than despair had before. After the birth of her twinned children she had not been able to conceive again. It had been an unvoiced grief to her, for she welcomed the thought of more children with Sidroc. Yet she must not be greedy in her happiness, she had told herself over the years. Eirian and Yrling were hale and hearty, as good as any active young could be, and had brought both her and Sidroc joy.

But now – now with Sidroc gone, she knew she was with child again. He was gone, but had left her this.

Moving slowly but with calm assurance, she pulled on her gown and shoes. The hall was still quiet, but once out into the stable yard she found the pail of cow's milk, faintly warm, that Tindr must have lately left. Milk, that mother's gift of sustaining love. She took a small copper pail from Gunnvor's stock and dipped it into the creamy stuff. Then, with the sky lightening overhead, she slipped past the spruces.

She had never visited the place of Offering without Sidroc. He made Offering for the household, and came here too alone at times, to speak to his Gods. She knew he had come here to do so before taking ship. No one would have been back since his visit, and to enter the small tree-ringed clearing after him heightened her sense of his babe growing under her heart. She walked as if called, and stood in the centre of the sacred space and lifted her head to the ever-growing light.

"Freyja," she said aloud, "I give you thanks for this gift." Her throat caught at her next words, those she must say, though they be uttered through her tears. "Sidroc may be even now in your hall. But he, and you, have left me his coming child."

She bent and poured out the milk, describing a circle about her with its foaming white stream, a circle of protection at her feet.

Chapter the Twenty-fifth: Yrling's Daughter

HRALD had returned, and six days passed since Thorfast had left them. Ashild had but another week in which to give her decision, and, as her brother kept insisting, Thorfast the same in which to make his own.

It was mid-morning, the day cool and damp, with a Sun struggling to pierce a scrim of thinly layered pearl-hued clouds. A mist hung about the air, one which neither resolved into rain nor vanished under the ever-lifting Sun. Hrald was in the treasure room with his uncle, sorting through the weaponry kept there. They had earlier spent some time with Jari, numbering all the spears standing at attention against the inner walls of the hall. Ashild was with her mother and sister up in the weaving room. Its windows gave out over a portion of the palisade, and it was because of this that Ashild heard the whistles, followed by the winding of a horn, even before her brother did.

She looked at her mother, but neither spoke. They put down their weaving tools, and Ælfwyn followed her daughter down the creaking stairs to the hall. Hrald was by now outside on the step, Asberg and Jari at his side, awaiting whatever rider was being ushered though the gates. They swung shut behind a single man, a watch-man who Hrald had posted not a week ago at Four Stones' north-west border.

"A rider of Thorfast found us," the man panted out. He had dropped from his horse, who was near to foundering from the hard ride. "Armies from the North are coming, coming our way, mounted and on foot, to join Haesten."

"From Northumbria?" Asberg asked. "Is it Ofram and his men?"

The rider was shaking his head. "They do not know. But they are Danes, heading to Haesten in the South."

"And sweeping all they can before them," Hrald said.

"And Haesten will, I wager, send some of his own up to meet them," Asberg offered.

If so it could be what they had feared, movement from both South and North. Hrald's mother and sister were now at his side, and he took them in in a long glance. Burginde was in his mother's bower house with Ealhswith and Eanflad. Both his little sister and aunt were fearful, had suffered the night-mare already. He was glad they were not standing there, seeing the alarm on the faces of those of hall and stable yard who surrounded him.

The next words were uttered by the Lady of Four Stones. Her eyes were widening at the recognition of what may lie before them, and though she kept her panic from her voice, the note of full urgency was there.

"Oundle," she said, looking to her son. "Mother – Sigewif. We must protect Oundle."

Oundle lay South and West, in the direct path of those coming as these armies might be.

Oundle was led by the esteemed Abbess Sigewif, peopled by nuns and monks, two priests, and devout serving folk. Hrald's own grandmother, who had known war-time horrors, was there. And Oundle held rich treasure.

"We must split our men," Hrald decided, looking to Asberg, "half to Oundle, half to remain here."

They both turned, gave orders to ready the men. Shouts and whistles sounded throughout the yard. Then they headed for the treasure room. Just behind them were Ashild, and then

Ælfwyn. The hall itself was already alive with serving folk, alert to new demands.

Hrald went to the flat box which held his ring-shirt. His eyes were swimming in his head as he began to gather his war-kit. Asberg too was moving about the room, opening chests.

"I will ride to Oundle," Hrald said.

"Never," answered his sister. He looked to her. She had followed him so quickly that her skirts were still gathered in her hands. "You must stay here, here at Four Stones."

"Já, she is right," their uncle agreed. "You are Jarl, you must stay here and defend your hall."

"Asberg and I will ride to Oundle," Ashild went on. "You and Jari here, and Uncle and I there."

A cry came from her mother, and a sputtering denial from her uncle.

"Já, I will ride to Oundle, but you will stay here, with your mother and aunts and sister."

Ashild's quiet defiance sounded in each word of her answer. "You are not my father," she told him. She turned to her mother, still white-faced from her daughter's declaration that she would ride to defend the abbey.

"We do not even know if either enemy will stop there," Ashild told her. "We do not know what we face. But we must send a force to Oundle. Let me ride with Uncle. I am of the family of Four Stones; your daughter, you who made Oundle what it is with your treasure."

Ælfwyn began to protest, only to be cut short by her daughter.

"Grandmother. Sigewif. All the women consecrated there," Ashild pressed. "Think what it will mean to see your daughter ride to them."

Her mother spoke through her tears. "You do not know what you are saying…"

But Ashild would not relent. "Four Stones has protection enough. But the folk at Oundle –all its women. Let me ride to them. I will not allow the women there to suffer a Fate I am not prepared to suffer."

Ælfwyn looked to her brother-in-law, and then to her son, with growing helplessness. Both men stood silent. Ælfwyn was shaking her head, and ready to speak again when her daughter took a step closer to her.

"Do not forbid me, mother," she asked, and now her voice began to waver. "I would go with your blessing, and not your curse."

Hrald spoke now. "Do not forbid her," he seconded. "She will only find a way to ride after Asberg."

His sister beamed at him for taking her part, even as her heart was racing in her chest.

Ælfwyn was staring at her, her hands now framing her temples. "I beg you not to do this," she pleaded.

"All the women there," Ashild repeated. "I will defend them, as a woman."

"You are but a maid," her mother countered.

"And many of them are but maids, though they be of all ages," she returned. She spoke with growing strength. "I will not let them be taken and raped. And if they are, it will be my Fate as well. I share it with them."

Her words were so dreadful to hear that she herself turned from them.

She looked now to her uncle. "Asberg, you won this hall with my father Yrling. Many of our best warriors here did the same, and are ready to fight again. I am Yrling's daughter. They all of them know this. Much of Yrling's treasure is held at Oundle. Let us ride together with our good men, to protect it."

Asberg's hands lifted before him, as if he tried to somehow contain, or even measure, the force of will issuing from the young woman standing there. Her call to protect what Yrling had won was a potent charge. The maid had drawn a straight line from her father's prowess to the holy folk at Oundle, with her in the middle of it. She connected the glories of that dead war-lord with the need to protect what his treasure had built. Yrling had made Asberg rich; now his daughter demanded her right to protect the place where the bulk of Yrling's wealth resided.

Asberg took this in, and did not have time to gather his thoughts to counter her words. Her mother was giving answer, reaching her own hands towards the maid who stood resolute, and with eyes shining, before them all.

"Go," nodded Ælfwyn, her tears falling from her eyes. She tried to call down what she herself could not provide. "Blessed Mary, the Mother of God, will protect you."

Ashild let herself be enfolded in those arms. She was still in her mother's embrace when she spoke again.

"The horses," she remembered, and broke from her mother to face her brother and uncle.

Hrald knew what she meant. Their wealth of horse-flesh was Four Stones' great asset, and one that could be driven off by a determined foe. "We must protect them," he agreed. It seemed their forces would now be split in three ways, and not just two.

"Twenty mounted men to the valley, to guard the horses," Asberg decided, looking to his nephew.

Hrald made quick reckoning, and then nodded. There were already thirty men there, those who lived at the hall in the valley. "One hundred warriors to hold the hall," Hrald said. "Fifty to protect the horses. And fifty to ride to Oundle." He could only hope that fifty would suffice.

"Fifty to Oundle," Ashild repeated. "We must bring as many spears as we can carry," she now urged. "The men – and women there, who wish to take one up, must not be denied." She did not foresee a nun or monk doing so, but the number of lay people who lived there should have the means to defend themselves, and those they served.

"I will ready myself," she said, "see Mul, and pack my kit." Her mind now buzzed with all that lay before her, but she gave each of her kin a kiss before she left to make her preparation. Her first stop was just outside the treasure room, retrieving the two lightest spears from their iron holder.

The hall was filled with folk. Æthelthryth, so unswerving in seeing to the needs of Four Stones, left the kitchen yard and found her husband. Word had come to her ears that he would ride to defend the abbey at Oundle; an honour, if a fearsome one. Their sons Ulf and Abi crowded round them, the boys begging that they be at their father's side wherever he stood. Both lads were smaller versions of Asberg himself, yellow-haired, blue-eyed, their broad brows now darkening with dashed hope.

"You will defend Four Stones," their father told them, placing the best face on it. He thought then to add that which would make them grow in understanding.

"If Hrald is killed, if I am killed, you are next in line, Ulf."

His wife made gasp at this truth, one she had known, but never heard sounded. The boys looked open-mouthed at him, then at each other. They must hear it too, and so consider their value to Four Stones.

He left them then, hurrying to tell those chosen men that they would ride to Oundle's defence. He made one additional stop, that to find Wilgot, who was at that moment at the bower house of the Lady of Four Stones, comforting her sister and younger daughter.

Ashild did not credit her uncle with great powers of reckoning, but now Asberg bethought him that the priest would be certain to object if he knew that the elder daughter of the hall was riding to front a troop of armed warriors, even if it were to defend an abbey. Wilgot could be forceful in his own right, and might so rail against this violation of female propriety as to spook the men with threats. Asberg had been sprinkled and blessed long ago, and at Wilgot's hands, so that he might wed Æthelthryth; it was the only way she would have him. And Asberg had nothing against the new God nor his priest. He even wore a small cross his bride had given him. But he felt the justness of Ashild's desire, even if he did not strictly approve of its expression, and would keep her from priestly hindrance.

All within the palisade was in enough turmoil that folk knew battle was being prepared for, and Asberg determined that Wilgot need not be there to bless those men who would soon ride off to Oundle. It was a simple matter to call the priest aside, and mutter to him that dark and forbidden sacrifice had been made at the old place of Offering, and encourage Wilgot to go see for himself.

The priest's brow clouded. A heathen horde was likely headed their way, he knew, and now his own flock was again turning to those false idols he thought he had taught them to forsake. His hand pulled at the rope tied at his waist, and he pulled up the cross of carved wood that hung there at his hem. With it in hand he squared his shoulders and made at a fast walk to the kitchen yard door, the nearest to the place of Offering.

As Asberg watched him disappear through the door he recalled something he had forgotten to admit, and so said it under his breath, not wishing to be proved a liar in any God's eyes. "And one of the dead roosters is mine."

Ashild stood before Mul, at the wide mouth of the opened stable doors. His young sons and many others worked within, carrying out saddles and bridles to the paddocked horses, or bringing forth those beasts stabled within which now were wanted. She would ride to Oundle, ride quickly, and need decide which of her several mounts was best suited for the task, the faster and more steady of her mares, or the white stallion Thorfast gave her.

The stallion caught and held the eye; men would kill to capture such a prize. But the stallion was akin to a landmark, easy for the men of Four Stones to see. And on him she was so tall; she felt safe. With his power he could cut a swath through the enemy, she was sure. Thus it was the white stallion she asked Mul to ready for her. He looked at her, gripping the two spears in her hand, and gravely nodded his head at her order.

Then she was up to the weaving room. All she needed could be found there; she had no need to go to her aunt's house, where she spent her nights. She always had a change of clothes at the ready, and something else she had made herself. Once inside she took an old gown of hers, laid it on the table, and with the sharp weaving shears cut it off at the waist. The skirt dropped off the table, leaving her with something very much like a man's tunic. She untied her head-wrap. Then she tugged off her shoes, and then her own gown, and her linen shift. The hammer of Thor about her neck came up about her chin as she did so, before falling back against her naked skin. She pulled on the remnants of the gown she had cut down. Then, from one of the storage chests, she drew on a pair of dark leggings she had sewn. She put her shoes back on, then tucked her tunic into the laced waistband. She ran her fingers through her mussed hair, then plaited it in one thick braid down her back. She drew a breath, and picked up a silver disc mirror of her mother's. She held it before her, looking at herself, thus dressed as a man would be. She had made the leggings months ago, and sometimes wore them, her skirts tied up around her waist, at the elm trees when practicing alone with her spear-work. No one, not even Hrald, had seen her thus attired.

She took her mantle of blue wool from the peg on the wall. She could think of nothing else to bring. She would be at Oundle, surrounded by women, they would have a comb and other necessaries she could use. And the kitchen yard would pack food and drink for her saddle bags. Her eyes swept the room, stopping at the wooden crucifix mounted on the wall by her mother's loom. When Ashild did not wear her small golden cross, she often times left it at the base of this carving, for safe-keeping, resting by a strange small silver coin always there. Now she went to the carving and took up the cross her mother had given her in girlhood, and slipped it over her head, dropping it inside her tunic next to the silver hammer.

Sound arose from outside the window: horses whinnying and men calling, barrels being rolled, folk scurrying about. She had heard no general alarm, no call to the villagers to come and seek shelter, and felt that Hrald was wise to delay until the troop for Oundle had ridden forth. The congestion in the work yards was great enough.

She went back down into the hall. Jari was there, pulling spears from the holders, passing them into the hands of a cluster of Four Stones' men. The men were rushed, yet oddly quiet, and she wondered if they were amongst those readying to ride to Oundle. The door to the treasure room was open, and she stepped through it.

Her mother and Hrald were still within. Hrald was laying out his full war-kit, and had his helmet in his hand. He pulled the sheepskin wrapping from it, and placed the shining metal dome on the table, atop the new ring-shirt which had been the gift of Ceric. Ashild knew that other than to try it on, Hrald had never yet worn the heavy shirt.

Her mother was speaking as she walked in but fell silent as Ashild stood before them, now ready to depart. Ælfwyn's pale face paled further, and she let herself drop down into a chair.

Her uncle came in behind her, wearing his ring-shirt, his helmet upon his head. Seeing her thus, attired as a man ready for war, spears in hand, forced Asberg to speak. She was little bigger than his younger son. Despite his earlier leanings he felt the foolishness of her act, and, he feared, the foolish wastefulness of it.

He looked from Ashild to her mother, and then to her brother. "Forbid her to go," he said.

Ashild did not wait. "I am safer dressed like this; I do not look a woman."

Hrald took her in, and nodded his head.

"I will not stop her," he told his uncle. He turned to his mother. "And you must not stop her. She will find a way to be there, one way or the other." He spoke again to Asberg. "She is safer riding in the thick, with you, than creeping through the woods to try to join you at Oundle."

He faced his sister. "Only make me a promise. If you find real danger on the road, or before the gates of Oundle, swear to ride back to us, so we may join you if we can." He could not keep a smile from cracking his lips. "I know you are a better rider than any of us. I want you to come yourself with the news. Will you swear this, Ashild?"

"I swear it, Hrald," she murmured.

"You have your spears," he went on, in way of agreement.

"Your spears?" her mother asked in a faint voice.

Ashild raised her fist slightly. "They are mine, Mother. And Hrald and Asberg both taught me how to use them."

As Ælfwyn was taking this in, Hrald was looking about the treasure room. "You need a real knife," he told her, going to one of chests. Ashild had tied at her waist the small women's knife she wore every day; he would have her carry more than that. He sorted through half-a-score of good Danish knives. One different caught his eye, and he brought it forth.

"A Saxon seax," he said, holding the leathern scabbard and belt before her. She saw red copper wire beaten into the grip of it. He pulled the gleaming blade out to show her. "Worn across your belly. It will be easier to grasp, on horseback."

She knew the advantages of the Saxon weapon such as Ceric wore. Indeed, he almost seemed to be in the room with them, between the ring-shirt he had given, and the seax of his people her brother wished her to wear.

She set down her spears and buckled the seax on. Hrald had spotted something else, his boyhood shield, hanging on the wall, that which his father had made for him on Gotland.

"Here," he said, handing it to her. "Its size is perfect for you. Sling it on your back for now. If you are threatened when you are mounted, pull it across to protect your chest. With your reins in your left hand, and your spear in your right, you can clear a path before you."

"I will be at her side, each moment," her uncle assured him. He said it with some little force, making clear he had reconciled himself to the risk to her, and the responsibility for him.

Asberg now bent over a large woven basket, and turned back to the young people. In his hand was a cap of hardened leather, strapped over with thin iron bars. "A helmet is heavy," he told her. "But wear this. It gives protection, and you will look less a maid."

She placed it on her head, stiff, but well-fitting enough that she felt it would not slide off.

The three of them were looking at her, mother, uncle and brother. Save for the roundness of her hips she almost did look a man of small stature, and once she was upon her horse no one need know otherwise.

Hrald thought of what else he could tell her. He had urged his mother and uncle of her right to go, and now the truth of her riding into danger was made real, and awe-ful. "If you are engaged on the way, stay on your horse at all cost. And stay at the edges of any fight," he ordered. "With your horse and spear you can harry the men, scatter them, knock some of them down."

She nodded, tried to smile. Behind him in the corner was the raven battle-flag she had made him. "The banner," she asked now. "May I take it, so that all may see the coming of the raven."

He turned and seized it. "I will have Mul fix it to your saddle," he said, pulling the square of fabric from the long staff.

Then they were out, walking through the crowded hall, and into the stable yard where the warriors who would ride were gathering.

Most of them were still at their horses' sides, looping saddle bags through tie rings, checking girths, bidding fare-well to wives and children. Asberg had himself picked the chosen for Oundle, and they fully expected to see him and Hrald appear now; their young Jarl to send them off, Asberg to rally them with fitting boasts of glory to be won. But a seeming youth stood between them, one they did not know, a shield on his back, spears in his hand. Asberg's sons waited to one side, and themselves stared at the newcomer. It was only when he pulled off the leathern cap and spoke that they knew.

There were sounds from those before her; her name being spoken aloud and in wonder, and a few snickers of surprise, uttered under the breath of the crowd.

"I am Yrling's daughter," Ashild told the waiting men. She paused a moment as they considered this, letting her eyes travel amongst them, beginning with Jari on her right, across the body of the troop, and ending with Gunnulf on her left.

"Most of you recall him, and served as his brothers in the battles he fought to make Four Stones your home. I am his blood. His own.

"Oundle is a place he never knew, yet much of his treasure lies there. We go to protect it, to protect our lands. Just as those who stay with my brother protect our hall."

She raised the hand that held her spears to her uncle. "No warrior is more stalwart than Asberg. He fought at my father's side, and at the side of Hrald's father. Today he fights at my side, to defend Oundle. But what I ask of you is not for me, but for my father. Those of you who ride now, recall Yrling who won this place for you."

She put the cap back on her head, moving once more from maid to warrior.

The men were staring at her, some of them open-mouthed. But she was not done. Her left hand rose to the neck of her tunic. She pulled the silver hammer of Thor out, and lifted it by its chain so all could see it swinging before them. Then she let it drop upon her tunic, uncovered, where it would lie. "It is Yrling's hammer of Thor," was what she said.

"For Yrling. For Oundle."

There was a restless shuffling from men and horses, though Ashild's cry still rung in the air. From the edge of the crowd Mul was coming, leading her white stallion by the bridle. A few whistles arose from the men, whistles of admiration for the showy mount she would ride into danger. Hrald had the banner in his hands and stepped to Mul, bidding him bring it back with a staff to fix to her saddle cantle.

Burginde had appeared. She had taken both Eanflad and Ealhswith to the weaving room, but Ealhswith would not stay there, and had scampered down the stairs after her. Now nurse and daughter stood on either side of Ælfwyn, and each took one of her hands in their own, looking on Ashild with astonished eyes.

Gunnulf had been watching with the others. Now he stepped forward, a broad smile on his face, and gave Ashild the boost up she needed to gain the saddle. It was a slight action, but one in which he showed to all his approval of her riding with the troop. Then he spoke to her, privately.

"If Hrald had not asked me to stay here with him, I would flank your other side," he told her. There was no mockery in his voice, rather esteem, tinged with only the slightest note of surprise.

Gunnulf turned and spoke in a loud voice to all the men. "Is she not like white-limbed Freyja, in her guise as the angry sow?" he prompted. "Let men who do not value their lives throw themselves in the way of a female boar."

He looked up at her, seated on the great beast, a maid of just over twenty years who had transformed herself into a warrior. If the boar-spirit could enter any earthly woman, it would be Ashild, and it would be now. He was almost grinning at her, seeing her for who and what she could be. She found herself mouthing his name, so grateful was she for how he commended her.

The men, hearing Gunnulf speak thus, began nodding their heads. Then Mul returned with the pennon, which Hrald affixed to her saddle. The first-born of the hall of Four Stones was now armed, rode a noble horse, and bore a battle standard.

Hrald must seal it. He stepped back from Ashild's horse, and spoke to all.

"The battle-flag you ride under is one Ashild herself wove. You know the flag which the great Ragnar Lodbrok carried was made by his daughters. There was power and force in its threads. A battle flag woven by a maid carries magic within it. Follow the raven. Be of the raven. Protect Oundle and its riches, and the holy folk therein."

Now a cheer arose from those mounted, and from those watching, even from throats tightened by worry.

Hrald gestured the gates be opened. Asberg rode a dun stallion, almost yellow with a dark mane and tail, and brought his horse alongside Ashild's. She looked down at her brother, his arm still lifted, having given her a sendoff any tried warrior would covet. It was only the firmness of Hrald's mouth that told her of his inner fears. She wrenched her eyes from him, to her mother, who now was clutched in the arms of Burginde, though her gaze was set upon her eldest daughter. She had never seen her mother look as stricken as she looked now, not even the day that Hrald's father had vanished. Over the pang in her own heart she forced herself to smile down at her. Then she turned her head, and put her heels to her stallion's flank.

The villagers, aware that the earlier rider had brought tidings, now stood staring from their crofts and fields as the answering warriors cantered by. She and Asberg fronted the two files, and she turned her head to see the raven banner fluttering out behind her. A mad joy filled her breast. She was part of it, though she be neither trained nor tried. She was of this troop of warriors, had won the right through the blood in her veins and her own demand, to ride with them. The gleaming weapons, the power of the great stallion beneath her, those whom she loved she rode to protect; it was all made hers in a way she could never have owned without being of it, as fully as she now was.

At Four Stones Ælfwyn returned to the weaving room, Burginde and Ealhswith at her side. Eanflad stood at her loom, working with swift fingers, and Ælfwyn knew it gave her quiet sister comfort to be so absorbed. Burginde walked to the floor near the table, and picked up what remained of Ashild's cut-down gown. The nurse began to cluck her teeth in censure, but instead, still shaking her head, she clutched the fabric to her breast. She plumped down on one of the beds and began to sob, lifting the scrunched cloth to her face. Ealhswith went to her, worming her way into Burginde's arms, which made the nurse stop in her tears. They held each other, and looked to Ælfwyn.

"Let us say a prayer," Ælfwyn offered. She could not show her fear to her young daughter, nor to her sister, who had suffered so cruelly at the hands of those who had destroyed their own hall. All she could do now was to offer her love, and her fear, to God.

She turned to the crucifix mounted on the wall. She was crossing herself before it when she noticed the empty base. This morning Ashild's small cross had glimmered there. She went to the wall. Only the tiny silver coin of the Idrisids lay there. The cross was gone. Ashild had slipped it on, at least taken it with her.

"She wears her cross," she said aloud, finding the first comfort of the troubled day. If her daughter should fall, she would do so wearing the cross of Christ, and not only the heathen amulet of Thor.

Chapter the Twenty-sixth: The Fight for Oundle

THE troop headed to Oundle cantered and walked, walked and cantered. They stopped twice at stream and lake-side to water and rest their horses, but otherwise drove them as hard as they safely could, hastening the hour when they should reach the abbey. The bright flare of joy Ashild had felt when leaving her own gates damped into a flicker. Resting her horse, she felt a target, one of a group which could be easily hit. The fear of meeting an oncoming enemy force, one which might boast it had already despoiled Oundle, haunted her mind each moment they were not driving forward.

But they met no one. They rode into noon, past noon, and saw nary a shepherd nor goatherd. Then came a final stand of ash and elm trees which crowded the road on both sides, a place of sudden dimness and seeming menace until they were out into the open once more. When the abbey's brown palisade walls rose up from the fresh fields of oats and rye fronting it, the land lay quiet. Oundle had no village of its own, all was enclosed within its stout walls, with only a few huts, now seemingly empty of folk, which served as shelter for those who watched over the grain. Off to one side, between margin of forest and field, lay the abbey burial grounds, a small plot enclosed with densely-branched yew trees, symbol of immortality. The gates in the palisade hemming the abbey were shut, as they never were during day. Soon they heard a clanging alarm issue from within those walls; a watchman on the ramparts must have spotted their approach.

Asberg had a horn hanging from his saddle and held it now to his lips, blowing out the four notes that signaled a rider from Four Stones. As they neared they made out figures on the ramparts, men clambering up to look upon the visitors. At a distance behind the timber walls the squat stone tower of the church could be seen, crowned with its cross of iron. Ashild found her eyes caught by the skeletal framework of that wrought metal. It recalled her to the hammer of Thor around her neck. Her hand rose to that amulet, and she dropped it beneath her tunic collar.

Those up on the ramparts, knowing both the sounded notes and the look of their horses, began calling out to them. The doubled gates were swung back, and one-and-fifty riders from Four Stones cantered in.

Sigewif stood there before the door of the woman's hall, with Mildgyth, the prioress of the place, at her side. Oundle's two priests made haste to join those gathering to meet the arrivals. Ashild watched Sigewif raise her hands in welcome to the horsemen, and saw too the relieved concern on the abbess' face.

They crowded in, filling the space between halls and barn with the swirling vigour of stamping horses. Ashild looked about her, and guided her horse to the mounting block at the wall of the barn. There she could dismount unseen; the numbers of riders about her in the forecourt would shield her from view. She knew her garb was a gross breach of womanly modesty, showing as it did the contours of her female form, unswathed by yards of flowing fabric. It had been one thing at Four Stones, a hall created by and for warriors, to appear thus. It was quite another at Oundle, a realm of women, raised out of nothing by the noblewoman who stood before the hall's door. Here Ashild had entered a realm of consecrated, devout, and self-effacing females who numbered far more than their male counterparts on the monk's side. And now she herself was dressed as a man.

She lowered herself from the stallion, and hung her shield on the saddle. She saw that a boyish Hrald had marked the shield on its inside with the rune Sigel ᛋ, victory, but that next to that was scrawled a Christian cross.

Then she drew her mantle about her, covering her lower limbs and cloaking her boldness. She went to join her uncle where he stood before the abbess and prioress. Sigewif was telling Asberg that Oundle had heard no word of war, but been wary since a watchmen Hrald had lately posted had ridden to tell them he would be at their western-most point. Oundle was well aware of its vulnerability, and more than grateful for the troop of warriors now ridden to secure it.

The eyes of the abbess went to her as she took her place at her uncle's side. It was clear from Sigewif's face that it took her a moment to recognise this young stranger for who she was. The war-cap on her head and the leggings peeking out from beneath the mantle did not disguise her long. Ashild lifted her hand to her cap, to remove it in respect, when she realised this would leave her with an uncovered head. Her hand froze. Sigewif's eyes widened as she took Ashild in. The stern set of the abbess' jaw tightened, then with a nod of her large head, relaxed.

"Ashild," she acknowledged. Her eyes shifted to the girl's uncle, who let his own eyes roll slightly up in his defence. His niece was not to be stopped; not easily, and the abbess knew it.

Ashild pulled off her cap and bowed her head. She let her mantle fall open, showing more fully her leggings-clad body.

For answer Sigewif lifted her hand and laid it upon that tousled mass of loosened hair, hair the colour of old and damp oak leaves.

"Your dear mother knows you ride here?" Sigewif asked, when Ashild had straightened up and stood before her, battle-cap in her hand.

There was no severity in her question, and the abbess touching her head as she had had lent her own blessing to the endeavour. Ashild nodded.

From amongst the folk of hall and work-yards Ashild now saw Bova, garbed in the dove-gray gown of a novice, and fidgeting like the sparrow she had once been named for. Bova was staring, looking in wonder at her. Then, over Bova's shoulder, she saw her own grandmother, in her dark nun's habit and white head-wrap. Sigewif gestured her forward, and in an instant Ashild was her arms. Given the threat of attack the daytime rule of silence had been suspended by the abbess, save for when she bid it, and Ashild was enfolded in the murmuring caresses of her oldest kinswoman.

Then the horses must be seen to, and Ashild herself went to lead her stallion to the paddock fence, and unsaddled him before passing him into the keeping of one of the barn's stablemen. When they had finished, a hand-drawn wain had been pulled by a serving man into the forecourt of the woman's hall. Bova and an old nun stood at it, dipping pottery cups into the first of two great ale crocks, and handing them to the riders. Ashild went up last to claim hers. Bova's dark eyes again fastened on her, but she bowed and said, "Lady," as she handed her a brimming cup.

"I thank you for coming, Lady," she managed further, when Ashild had lowered her cup. Bova's eyes flitted about the work-yard, moving from one heavily armed man to the next, never resting on any one. She was biting her lower lip, and her small brown hand, which had touched Ashild's when she handed over the cup, was clammy, as if with fear.

"Warriors might come," Bova told her, with quavering voice. "Warriors...they hurt me."

"I know this, Bova," Ashild told her. "They hurt my aunts, and grandmother, too. That is why we are here, to save Oundle's treasure, and to help spare us all."

Bova swallowed, and nodded her head. Ashild reached and took Bova's cold hand in her own and gave it a squeeze. Then she went back to Sigewif and her uncle.

The men could sleep in the monk's hall, and they had each ridden with provision for two days, so that the food stores of Oundle might remain for the moment relatively untouched. Many of the men had carried extra spears, and these were now being collected and placed in two empty barrels, one near the door of the monks' hall, the second by that of the nuns'.

"What now," Ashild heard Sigewif ask her uncle.

"Now we must wait," Asberg answered.

The Sun had reached high above the trees when Sidroc and Runulv took horse. The road leading out of Saltfleet was a broad one, made so by the ox carts and waggons filled with stuffs being drawn to and from the landing ships. It was also one on which an army would travel North.

"There are side-tracks we will take," Sidroc told his captain, leading him up a more coastal route. At times that afternoon they came in sight of the road, and made haste to reach the next thicket of sheltering brush or stand of trees. They were about to emerge once more into a meadow-land, when Runulv, riding behind Sidroc, gave a hiss. They both reined up, pulling their horses back behind the darkness of a clump of spiked hawthorns.

Up on the road, heading North from behind them, rode a triple rank of horsemen. They each numbered the files, three, six, nine, twelve, fourteen files of three riders each; two-and-forty men, armed with swords and shields, their spears laced onto their saddles. They carried no banner, nor trailed supply waggons, just cantered steadily ahead on their dust-caked horses.

"Danes," muttered Sidroc.

He had never before wished to meet a troop of Saxon warriors, but he did now. If these had been men of Wessex on his lands they would have for once been his allies.

He and Runulv stood their horses, looking after them. The road would fork not far ahead, offering a choice: the broader way to Four Stones and points beyond; the narrower to the abbey of Oundle. Sidroc had not meant to stop at Oundle, but to ride as quickly as he could to Four Stones, camping overnight when it became too dark to ride.

"We will trail them," he told Runulv.

They did so, moving not upon the road but from the scant safety of the tree-cover. At the fork they watched the Danes shun the larger road and head for Oundle.

The Sun was setting as they neared the final bend in the road. There was a small woods, into which the road cleaved and then emerged. Once out of the trees Oundle would stand plainly upon the land, fronted by its growing fields.

Sidroc and Runulv watched the Danes stop. They seemed to know where they were heading, and now made their preparation to spend the coming night amongst the trees.

Sidroc weighed his choices. They could either attempt to skirt the men unnoticed, ride to Oundle, and gain entry without alerting these Danes, or stay here, and on their tails.

He shook his head, dismissing the first. Oundle's watch-men used a loud-voiced brass gong to signal approach of any stranger. He dare not risk alerting all the Danes behind him by having his own arrival announced. They would stay with the Danes.

Within the walls of Oundle, Asberg had told Sigewif there was little to do but wait. Asberg dined with the abbess and Ashild in the women's hall, then left to return to that of the monks. Oundle's own watch was joined that night by men of Four Stones, and Asberg made command that though careful watch be made, no alarm be sounded if any untoward activity be detected; instead, he should be sent for in all haste, but silence otherwise be observed.

They need not wait long. Under cover of dawn the enemy began creeping in. Nuns and brothers both had risen in the dark for Lauds, and while in the stone church offering their first prayers of the new day, watch-men on the ramparts had detected movement across the fields.

Ashild, asleep in an alcove in the women's hall, was roused first by the glare of an oil torch which pierced the parting of the woollen curtains screening her bed. She felt blear-eyed, uncertain of where she was. It was Mildgyth the prioress, who slept in her own small cell, but had been called from Lauds to fetch her.

"Lady," she urged, "Asberg is up, the men are arming. The enemy gathers outside our walls."

Ashild tumbled out of the alcove. She had slept in her tunic and leggings, and now pulled on her shoes. She took a moment to run the comb she had been lent through her hair, then plaited it with fingers flying. Mildgyth was going from alcove to alcove, where still slept the lay-women of the place, and from each emerged a frightened, and even tearful, woman, who Mildgyth begged keep quiet.

Mildgyth had returned to Ashild, who was now pinning on her mantle. The torch in the prioress' hand cast ghostly shadows upon the walls and curtains, and on the face of Mildgyth too. "I go now back to Abbess Sigewif," she told Ashild, who followed her out.

Enough light was now in the East to see the yard filling with folk. The warriors of Four Stones were already mostly armed, and Ashild could see her uncle with his yellow hair struggling a moment as he pulled his ring-shirt on over his leathern tunic. Even with another man to help they were awkward to handle, and Asberg was shrugging his way into his alone. The door of the stone church was open, and women, both nuns and serving-women, were hurrying within. The score or more of monks stood outside the door, gesturing they move in haste. From around the back of the garden, where the single cells lay, Ashild saw two monks bear an aged nun on a litter, carrying her within the confines of the sanctuary.

Horses were being drawn from barn and paddock, and saddled and bridled. Ashild's stallion was easy to pick out, and when she reached him found one of her own men, Byrgher, cinching up her saddle. She muttered her thanks and led the animal by his reins to where all those were gathering.

She found her uncle. He nodded ruefully at her, but otherwise treated her as any of the other warriors readying themselves for what was to come. She followed him to one of the ramparts-ladders. The abbess was at its base, one of her own watch-men speaking into her ear. Asberg would see for himself what he had been told, and Ashild was quick to follow him up the ladder, with Byrgher, and a few other men.

The Sun was lifting enough so that they dare not show their heads above the palisade and risk discovery. But there were many small lookout holes at that height, and they crouched down and peered through them.

Walking down the road towards their walls was a score of men, each burdened with something in their arms. At a distance were a number of horses, and more men. As the men neared they saw that some balanced small wooden casks on their shoulders, like unto those used for mead. Others had arms-full or backs bent under piles of wooden faggots and thick tufts of dried, strawy grasses.

It was all too clear what their intention was. Asberg looked again at the cask perched on one of the men's shoulders, then breathed a single word, "Oil."

They crept down the ladder, and stood before Sigewif.

"Is it true," she asked, her voice as calm as it was firm.

Asberg nodded. "They think to burn us out, Lady." He took his eyes from her, let them glide over the expanse of wooden wall which was their only barrier.

Bread was now being hastily passed amongst them, and Ashild found her uncle thrusting a loaf into her hands. "No one fights long on an empty belly," Asberg urged, tearing into his own loaf.

After what she had seen from the ramparts and heard her uncle say it was hard to take something so dry as the crusted loaf into her mouth and swallow. She saw the hand-wain that had been pulled the day before, again with crocks of ale within, and joined those who went to drink. The older nun was there, but Bova's place was taken by a serving man.

"Where is Bova," Ashild asked the woman, barely able to form the words aright.

The old nun pushed a stray strand of hair back under her head-wrap. "Inside the church, poor child, and half-mad with fear." Ashild's eyes widened, and the woman went on. "She is like a beast, going to slaughter, dumb but full of terror."

Ashild made a move to the church door, still open. If she could comfort the novice she would do so. But something within her stopped her from going. She was not sure she could face her own fear, and Bova's too. Instead she looked back to the nun.

"Will you be with her? Stay with her?" she said, her words more demand than question.

"I will go to her," the nun said.

Ashild nodded her thanks, took a gulp of the ale, and returned to her uncle. Mildgyth was now at Sigewif's side, and the men of Four Stones stood in half-circle around Asberg and the two holy women.

"There are no more than two score of them," Asberg was saying in a hoarse whisper. "They are near to our own numbers. Less than our numbers," he added, though Ashild did not see how he had counted them so closely as this. "They do not want any losses. We look a ready target."

Sigewif was an imposing woman in bodily form, and now straightened herself even taller, as if to object to the low estimation afforded her by those outside her gates.

Asberg went on, voice more urgent. "These are not many, who threaten us today. But are more on the way?" He scanned the faces looking at his before he gave answer. "We must rush them now, kill those we can, scatter the rest, show them we are no easy mark."

Stifled grunts and nodding heads greeted his assertion, that and the sure sign of hands gripping the hilts of their swords.

But this place was Sigewif's, and she must make decision. She did so by speaking not to Asberg, but to Mildgyth, her prioress, who now stood at her shoulder with the two priests of Oundle. "Holy Fathers, dear Prioress," she murmured. "I give into your keeping all the women of Oundle. Lock yourselves into the church, along with any of the brothers who would join you, and wait on God's will."

The priests crossed themselves and turned to fulfill her order, but Mildgyth did not turn with them. "Allow me the privilege of standing by your side, Mother Abbess," she asked.

But Sigewif shook her head, albeit gently. "You serve me best by leading those in the church, strengthening, and guiding them. We all of us have our single tasks to do, as we await God's mercy."

Tears were in the eyes of the prioress, but she took the hand that Sigewif offered, kissed it, and left.

"On your horses," Asberg now said. Ashild had yet to place her battle-cap on her head, and as she lifted it found herself swept into Sigewif's arm, and a kiss planted on her brow. The abbess held her by the shoulders and looked her full in the face.

"Will you not stay here, to help guard the women?" she tried.

"I cannot, "Ashild answered. "I come from Four Stones with my kin, to defend Oundle and its treasure. I must do what I came for; fight with our men."

Sigewif released her, but her eyes latched more firmly, and more warmly onto Ashild's.

"There were warrior-women amongst the noble race of Israelites," she told her, "women who would in their courage sever the head of the greatest war-chief for the deliverance of their folk. Go, under the shield of God."

She did not say more, and Ashild saw that the abbess' own eyes were now glistening.

Sidroc and Runulv stood with their horses in the shadow of the burial ground's yews. They had been there since before first light, working their way through the margin of forest, and then to the back of the burial place. From there they watched every movement of the invading Danes. What vexed Sidroc was the utter quiet of Oundle and its precincts. The few ward-men's huts were empty; the fields, though untrampled, untended; and the ever-vigilant and raucous ramparts watch-men seemingly silenced. The place had seen no violence, and he could not believe that the entire community had sought shelter at Four Stones. Something was afoot, something he must wait to learn.

They had each had little sleep, and had made a meagre meal of the mess of cold browis and bits of roast pig his men at Saltfleet could offer them. They had filled their water-skins with good ale, though, and were able to water their horses at a trough within the burying place. Now, watching the Danes approach and begin to lay the makings of a fire at the base of Oundle's walls, they once more checked their battle-kit. Sidroc had ring-shirt, seax, sword, helmet, white-and-black painted shield, and his two spears. Runulv had a leathern tunic, his long knife, two spears, and a steel war-axe, hung on his saddle. Three of the men at Saltfleet owned helmets, but knowing they were in danger themselves kept Sidroc from asking one for his captain. And he hoped they were there to watch, nothing more.

As if he read his thoughts Runulv now spoke, his eyes moving from the men shouldering piles of brush-wood to Sidroc.

"What...what will we do," he muttered.

"What we can," returned Sidroc. "We are two. They are two and forty."

He pulled himself up on his horse, and Runulv did the same. They made final adjustment to their kit. Sidroc thought for one moment of dying here, fighting to defend a Christian settlement. His eyes rose to the pale sky, as if seeking answer there. And his hand lifted to his neck, touched for an instant the slender braid of bright hair tucked into his tunic. He looked again at the warriors across the field from him.

"But one man," Sidroc went on, "can send a broad-beamed boat of four oars over. We will see if we can be that one, reckless man."

"Byrgher, you will flank Ashild on her right," Asberg said, helping her spring up into her saddle. She pulled the shield from the tie ring, and held it before her as she shortened the strap so that it would hold tight to her chest.

She looked about her. The door to the church was closing. Two score men, monks and serving folk alike, stood outside it as safe-guards. Ashild knew that amongst these monks were men who had once been warriors of Lindisse. A few of them, facing this new threat, proved their lineage. Some had taken up spears; others, forbidding themselves a true weapon, held wooden clubs, or hoes, as if they were staffs.

Sigewif's eyes too swept over this, and then at the troop of warriors ready mounted before her. From over their heads one of the watch-men hissed down to them. "The enemy is just without; lays wood at the base of the wall," he said.

As if in response a dull thud was heard, a thud that most within the walls knew as the sound of a spear hurled forcefully into wood. One of the doubled doors of the gate shuddered slightly from the impact.

"Open!" bellowed a voice from without.

The four strongest of the serving men of Oundle stood just inside those doors, ready to pull them wide at Asberg's order. The man closest to the struck door had given a jump, but the spear-point had not driven through.

Sigewif looked at those serving men, and at the armed troop ready to defend them. Bloodshed and death at Oundle's own gates, thought the sister of slain King Edmund. She crossed herself, and by doing so confirmed in her courageous breast, So be it.

The abbess' gaze settled on Ashild, and then Asberg, fixing them each with eyes the hue of steel. She closed her hand about the cross of walrus ivory ever resting over her heart. The enemy was just without, her watch-man said. She gave her answer, her voice low and firm.

"Let me speak to them, draw them near."

Asberg could not help his grin. He knew this woman came from warrior-stock; now she proved it. She did not say more than that, nor did she need to.

She turned from them, and faced the wall. As she did Ashild reached within her tunic and once again brought forth the hammer of Thor that lay against her skin. Her fingers touched as well the small golden cross, gift of her mother, that also lay there. She let it remain where it was. One for within, one for without, she thought.

The troop of mounted men from Four Stones watched as the abbess clasped hand over hand on the ladder leading to the ramparts. She rose in her dark gown, stately as a raven, until she gained the narrow walkway above.

"Open," the voice outside again demanded, "or we burn your walls. We have oil. Open now, or we will make of them a warming fire."

Those within her walls saw Sigewif straighten herself to her full height, her head and shoulders exposed to view from the road without. She was looking down at two men who stood shoulder-to-shoulder, their helmets gleaming dully in the morning light. Shields were upon their left arms, covering their torsos, lest an arrow try to find them, but they brandished as yet no swords. One of them held something small in his outstretched hand; a flint and striking iron, she guessed, from his threat. A number of other intruders ranged behind them. Her eye dropped to the outside of her gate, and the long spear stuck there, its shaft still quivering.

Her answering call was as stern as any war-lord's who faced a taunting enemy.

"I am Sigewif, Abbess of this place. I command you to leave my walls. You do not frighten me with talk of fire. Any fire you strike will be as nothing to that kindled of your souls in Hell, for if you harm us you shall burn eternally."

"A woman!" cried one of the two warriors. He turned his face to spit upon the ground, then raised the hand with the fire-starter at her. "A woman, in a hall of women!"

He nudged the man he stood with, then spoke to him, what, she could not hear. He looked back at her. "Know your place, woman, and get off that wall. If you do not, you will be the first to die."

"My place," she echoed in anger. "I am sister to Edmund, King and Saint. My place is here, protecting the servants of God."

As she spoke, Sigewif saw the other men coming closer, trying to make her out. Most were armed with swords, and many carried spears as well. Several men had left their shields and spears on the road, and were still at work, bundling piles of brush at intervals against the wooden palings of her wall. At running distance down the road she saw the men's horses, being held in safe-keeping by five or six men. She gauged the warriors who threatened her. Only a few donned helmets, and ring-shirts were even rarer. The two in front were certainly their leaders, wearing both helmets and ring-shirts. The man who spoke did so in the tongue of Angle-land, but with the accents of a Dane.

"We serve the one and true God, live lives of study and quiet. There is nothing for you here."

This was met by a hoot of laughter. "There is silver, somewhere. And you have women within!"

Her voice became even more firm. "If seek treasure, you must go to the halls which house it," she argued.

"There is a hall just North, one great with treasure, but others are headed for it," he returned. "Just now, we are here, before a hall of silver-bearing women."

Sigewif gave a single shake of her large head. "Tell me your names," she challenged in a ringing voice, "so I may offer a prayer for your souls when you are cast to damnation."

The man she addressed snorted with laughter. "I tell you nothing, woman, but that you have seen your last day. Take your prayers and crosses to your Devil. I have been here since Guthrum came, and fear them not. These men are come from Dane-mark to join Haesten, and I throw in with them."

All the time he spoke the warrior standing next him was watching, telling Sigewif the second spoke not the speech of Angle-land. Even less could she expect him to respect the property and persons of consecrated women.

Inside the stone church, Bova pressed herself against the rough wall of the bell-tower. She had fled within this tiny space with the old sister who had been the abbey's former brewster, and closed the wooden door behind them. There was no way to bar it, and in an effort to calm Bova the old nun herself leant against it, as if her slight weight might keep an intruder from trespass. The tower was lit from above, opening to the sky as it did at its top, but it was dim enough within. The thick hempen rope to the single bronze bell was looped up on an iron hook on the wall, the bell itself a dark void high above their heads.

Outside the narrow confines of their rock-bound cell, in the body of the church itself, the nave and chancel were crowded with nuns and serving women, standing huddled together holding each other, or kneeling in prayer. Oundle's priests knelt before the altar, upon the very slabs of stone that hid the silver and gemstone treasure of the place. Prioress Mildgyth moved amongst her charges, white-faced herself, but lending ghostly comfort where she could.

Bova was panting in her fear, her eyes locked Heavenward, focused on the scrap of pale sky she saw beyond the darkness of the bell. She was breathless and light-headed, giddy with a terror that made it impossible to feel her feet. She wished to be that moment up and into the air, like the small birds she envied, free and uncatchable. I will not be trapped and caught, she told herself. I will call those feathered Beings down on us, call the Angels to our sides.

She reached her hand to the hempen rope of the bell, freed it. She had watched the monks ring it, summoning all to Holy Mass, and knew the bell had its own strength. She lunged at the rope, at a point high above her head, grabbing it in both hands as she pulled at the weight of bronze above. Her feet came off the stone pavers of the floor, touched down again. She was pulled up, heard the mighty clang of the metal tongue against the inside of the bronze dome, a sound that with the door closed filled every particle of her body with its bright ringing. Another pull, carrying her, gasping, up so that her toes left the floor; then the brief and more rapid descent, seeing the astonished face of the old brewster, clapping her hands over her ears. Another, greater peal from the deep-hearted bell, and another. She kept pulling, being pulled herself Heaven-ward, and the bell was loud in answering. The Angels would hear them; they would come.

Sigewif was about to speak again when the bell in her church began ringing. After the muffled and enforced silence of the past hours it had remarkable effect. The bell pealed without ceasing, wild and insistent, a tremendous clamour rising from within, and far over, Oundle's walls. Sigewif looked down on the Danes who threatened her, seeing their twisted and distracted faces. Asberg, below and behind her, was spurred by the uproar, and gave signal.

The gates were flung open.

Asberg had just time enough to turn to Ashild on his right. "Stay with me, my girl," he told her. "Do not let yourself get surrounded. Stay at my side."

Then he turned his face ahead, and from his opened mouth came a piercing scream of anger.

Her left hand gripped her reins, her right her spear. She tightened her knees around the great beast. Then she was plunging ahead with Asberg and Byrgher, ahead and out through the gates.

Behind the dark cover of the yews Sidroc heard a shrill, two-part battle-cry erupt from the opening gates, a cry he knew: Asberg. No one else made battle-yell like he.

He gave answering yell of his own, and dug his heels into his horse's flanks. Runulv was just at his side, finding his own voice, sudden and full-throated, adding to the din of the clanging bell. There was a score of Danish warriors before them, scrambling to pick up their shields or spears, drawing swords, looking about with darting eyes, some already running away, to where their horses were being held.

Ashild, between Asberg and Byrgher, hurtled towards the two lead Danes on the road outside the gates. Both men had time to draw their swords, but both found themselves caught under the churning hooves and proffered spear-points of the three horsemen who ran over them. The men ranged behind them took defensive stance with their spears, but, on foot as they were, found themselves unable to hold. And other horses were now bearing down from the trees on their right; men yelling who had come from nowhere. They were being hit from both sides; from within the gates, and without.

Ashild's stallion had struck one of the men with a forefoot, and though the warrior slashed his sword in the air as he fell, had missed her horse; he stumbled not, but kept carrying her onward. She looked back, had a glimpse of her own raven banner streaming out over her stallion's broad white rump, his tail a second streamer; and saw too the ranks of her men behind her, driving spear points into the downed men.

Her horse slowed as she looked back, and turning her head she saw her uncle pulling ahead of her. Some of the enemy stood, taking aim with throwing spears; others fled, running towards their waiting horses, now being rushed towards them by those who held them at a distance.

Stay with him, she thought in panic, seeing that she had let her uncle outride her. Her heels dug at her stallion's side again. Then a shock hit her, an impact great enough that she almost lost her seat, and the spear held in her lowered right hand nearly dropped from it.

A light spear had been thrown at her, hitting Hrald's shield. It had been thrown close enough to lodge itself firmly in the painted face of the shield, and though the point barely penetrated the surface, it knocked the wind from her. The realness of it, the fact that the inch or so of linden wood had saved her life, snapped her head back to where the spear had come. There was the man, standing, looking after her. She wheeled, making the stallion dance on his hind legs an instant before plummeting down again. She lifted her own spear, and threw.

Her target was young, with brown hair in plaits that hung down his shoulders. Over that hair was a battle-cap much like her own. He wore a leathern tunic, but no ring-shirt, and had lowered his shield as he looked. He was gawking at her horse, she knew; trying to knock her off so he might claim such a prize as was the stallion.

Her spear hit him in the right breast, just under the collar-bone. His jaw dropped open. His knees buckled beneath him as his head fell back. She saw his battle-cap drop and hit the soil a moment before the head did. He lay there, her spear stuck in his breast, pointing to the sky.

She knew a noise was coming from her own mouth, some sound she did not recognise. Men were yelling oaths and battle-cries, and some, screaming out in pain. Horses, in their fear and hard usage, were whinnying their shrill cries of distress. Above it all the church bell kept clanging, masking the din of turmoil eddying about her.

Sidroc and Runulv had charged across the field fronting the burial ground, on to the road, and now across it. They both held spears lowered before them, spears which had cleaved only the air.

I have killed no one, Sidroc thought. It struck him almost with wonder. He had charged, spear foremost, but the action of doing so had thrown the Danes into such confusion that he had never reached them. His spear had met no flesh; his horse had trampled no man.

A big white horse was before him, ridden by one who had been in the first rank of attackers.

Ashild turned her horse to see a man she did not know, mounted on a strange horse, coming to her, followed by a second. She had seen the movement of horses from the direction of the burying place, but could not know who they were. Her second spear was hanging under her knee; it would take a few precious moments to free it, moments she might not have. Instead she gripped the spear embedded in her shield just behind the iron point, and wrenched it out with a twist of her wrist, ready to use it against him.

"Who are you?" she demanded. She could see her uncle turn his horse back to her, and Byrgher, who had gone after and felled another spears-man, wheel also.

The stranger jerked his horse to a halt.

"I am Sidroc."

His shield was painted black and white, in swirls from the iron boss. She recalled Hrald telling her of this shield, on his return from Gotland. It was very like the one of black and red hanging on the wall behind the place Hrald sat each night, the shield of his father.

She pulled the cap from her head.

He saw the rider was a woman. "What daughter of Freyja are you," he found himself asking.

He eyed her as if she were come from a Saga.

"I am Ashild."

"Ashild!"

She had been a child when last he saw her, but it was surely her. She was daughter of his own warrior uncle, Yrling; that was bloodline enough. He had raised her as his own, the first nine years of her life, but she was woman now.

Little could have shocked Ashild as much as seeing him. A wave of near-forgotten longing swept over her, almost impelling her to fling herself at him. It was followed just as swiftly by a flare of anger at his abandonment.

Asberg reined his heaving horse up before them. Beyond him she could see the Danes who had escaped riding away at full speed.

"Sidroc!" Asberg called, bringing his horse in head-to-tail with that his old war-chief rode.

"Brother," answered Sidroc. He was only slightly less startled to see a grown Ashild and Asberg pour forth from the abbey's gates as they were to see him.

"It was you, who came at them from the side," Asberg exulted. "You are back!"

But Sidroc shook his head. "Only for this," he corrected. "Where is Hrald?" he asked, looking at the men gathering about them.

It was Ashild gave answer. "At Four Stones, defending it," she told him.

Sidroc scanned the remnants of the invading troop. Perhaps twenty men lay dead or dying around them. A few of the invaders' horses had gotten loose and were now being led back to where Asberg and Ashild stood with the two newcomers.

Sidroc looked again at Ashild, sitting upon a horse fit for a King. "You are as bold as your father," he told her. "He would take pride in your courage and skill, as I do." He looked to Asberg. "She killed a man," he said.

"I saw," answered her uncle. "It was Hrald and I who taught her to throw."

Sidroc was still looking at her, in admiring disbelief. He saw the hammer of Thor around her neck, and knew it for whose it had been.

Ashild was staring back at Sidroc. "Why did you come," she demanded, her tone no question, rather a challenge.

"To protect you," he answered. He raised his hand, as if to the heavens. "Not that you needed it."

I needed you every day, she thought, almost as much as Hrald has needed you.

The bell, which had rung so loudly and without ceasing, now stopped. It gave a single, slower clang, and fell silent.

Sidroc looked over at Oundle's walls. "Is your mother within?"

"Within? She is at Four Stones." It was only after she answered she realised he thought her mother had gone for a nun.

Asberg's men had swept the area, and now circled them. Their gain was twelve horses, an unexpected windfall, and whatever booty could be taken from the bodies of the fallen enemy. Only two of their men had been hurt, one thrown from his horse and stunned; the second a slash, not deep, to the forearm. It was rich return for their efforts.

Sidroc was waving Runulv up by his side. "This is my ship captain, Runulv. He carried me in heavy weather from Gotland, to ride with me here."

Asberg was quick to reply. "So it is. And he will have his share of the battle-gain," he promised. He took in the seaman, a ready-looking enough man, face flushed with action. Along with Sidroc he had charged, yelling, at the enemy, and helped rout them.

They let the bodies lie and turned back to the gates. Sigewif was still upon the ramparts, and had seen all. She vanished from view, and then came to meet them, striding on foot to stand before the yawning opening. Some of the horsemen had dismounted, to help the two injured within, or to ascertain, spear in hand, that all the Danes were dead. Ashild and Asberg headed those still astride.

The abbess looked as solid as a mountain to Ashild, unshakable and fearless. She kept her eyes upon Sigewif's face as she approached, knowing that riding just behind her was the man she had called Father; that behind her also was the body of a Dane she had killed; and knowing too that she had almost been knocked from her saddle. If she had fallen she very likely would be dead now.

She slipped from her horse, not waiting to gain a mounting block. Her knees folded a moment under her own weight and the firmness of the pounded ground. She did not know if she was red-faced or pallid, but she worked hard to control the trembling she felt overtake her body. When Sigewif opened her arms to her she feared she might sob. Instead, once enclosed in that strong embrace, she found a refuge of warmth and stillness. She was held but a moment, then the abbess pulled her back, strong hands on Ashild's shoulders, and peered into her face. The searching grey eyes dropped an instant to the heavy silver hammer around Ashild's neck. The expression did not change, but returned to Ashild's own eyes.

"Judith was no more courageous," she muttered, as gently as mother would to babe. Her lips pressed themselves once more to Ashild's forehead. The voice now, as firm as that kiss, went on. "Wilgot will hear your confession. And hear too, of your valour."

Sidroc was now off his horse, and hung his helmet on his saddle-bow. Sigewif had watched the two horsemen dart from behind the dense cover of the yews. Now one turned to her.

"Jarl Sidroc," she said. Her steel-coloured eyes had widened.

He inclined his head to her, as he always had. The years fell away in that simple gesture. She pressed her hands together, made her slight bow. "I thank you for your timely help."

He shook his head. "It was Asberg; Asberg and Ashild."

The folk of Oundle were drawing near, crowding around them. Sidroc saw cassocked monks gripping spears, and watched them slide those weapons back inside the barrel they had drawn them from. White-faced woman held each other and looked on.

"That bell," Sidroc began, his eyes travelling up the squat church tower to the top. "Who thought to ring it deserves a warrior's share."

Ashild scanned those fronting the church. The crowd parted, and one of Oundle's priests came through it, holding Bova in his arms, whether dead or in a faint could not be known. But the old brewster was there too, at Bova's head, chafing her brow and speaking to her.

"Was Bova, dear Abbess," the woman now said, "Bova who took the bell, as if it were life itself, and made it ring."

Sigewif took her novice's limp hand in her own. Bova's eyelids began to flutter.

"We have all played our part, and offer great thanks to God for our deliverance," said the abbess. She placed Bova's hand into that of the old nun. "Take her to her cell and keep her warm; I will be with you soon."

Asberg spoke now. "We must leave for Four Stones," he told Sigewif. He made reckoning of who he could spare. "We leave our injured with you, and ten men to help guard you."

He looked to Sidroc. They could not know what might await them at Four Stones, or on the way there. Leaving twelve of their number behind was a risk, but Asberg hardly saw how he could leave Oundle with less.

Sidroc gave a slight gesture, one which conveyed that Asberg still commanded.

"The dead," Sigewif said now. The bodies of the two enemy leaders lay at the margin of road and field. Her eyes went from them to those others dotting the broken furrows. "After you have taken what you want, we will give them decent burial."

But Sidroc countered this. "We claim the bodies, Abbess," he told her. "You must leave them to us. They will be justly dealt with."

Sigewif's lips parted, then closed. "As you wish," she conceded.

Asberg lifted his hand, gesturing his men to follow. Ashild remained at the side of the abbess. They watched the men from Four Stones and Sidroc and his captain go from body to body. Asberg and Byrgher stopped first at the richest prize, that of the two leaders, and with quick and knowing hands stripped swords, ring-shirts, helmets, knives, purses, and silver arm-rings. Ashild saw Sidroc and his man walk a distance to where a spear stood upright from a dark form. She watched Sidroc pull the spear, and plunge the tip into the soil. Then he knelt down at the side of the body. She brought her eyes back to the ground in front of her, and kept them there.

Her uncle was before her now, pulling an overturned shield full of glinting metal. "You have share in this," he told her. His eyes were flashing in joy of his own gain, and in pride of her actions.

Sidroc was come as well, with weapons-belts and more. "This is yours outright," he said. "The sword is middling, but the knife is well-wrought." He had her spear in his hand, and now passed it to her. "And your spear, that made a clean kill. It has tasted blood and will be hungry for more." There was also a small pouch of worn leather. "His purse."

She accepted this mutely, with a nod of her head. The booty was stuffed into the saddle bags of their horses, and the dead Danes slung two each over the backs of those beasts they had captured.

"We will send word back to you from Four Stones," Asberg told the abbess. They stood with her looking back at the walls. Her serving folk were already at work, gathering up the fire-stuff the Danes had deposited there as their threat.

One of the two small casks of oil had fallen and been smashed, darkening the soil with its costly contents, but the second sat upright and untouched. Sigewif eyed the quantity of brushwood and faggots heaped up by the enemy. Her voice was dry, and not without a hint of triumph. "Good of them to have left us so much kindling."

Riding back to Four Stones their first stop was just outside the small wood of trees. They passed through it, but then Sidroc, in front with Asberg, reined to a halt. Ashild stayed on her stallion as Sidroc and Asberg hurled the bodies of the dead Danes off the captured horses. Working in threes and fours she watched the warriors of Four Stones clamber up into the ash trees there, pulling up the bodies of the dead, hanging them from the stoutest boughs on either side of the road. Any approaching Oundle would be met by this gruesome party of earlier callers.

Runulv did not take part in the hanging, but stayed upon his horse and near Ashild, an act for which she was silently grateful. She recalled Runulv from when he had brought Hrald home, and knew Hrald liked him. As Sidroc jumped down from the tree he was in, Runulv asked her a question.

"He is your father, já?"

She watched Sidroc straighten up from where he had landed, and his face lift to the man he had left hanging in the ash. The ugliness of the sight made her look away.

"No," she told him in Norse. "And yes."

When they were done and the men remounted, they spent a moment looking back at their handiwork. Both she and Runulv joined in a final glance. Ash trees were sacred to Odin, and the source of the best spears. These had received the offered burden without complaint.

"Fair warning to avoid the haunts of Christians," Sidroc said, for all of them.

Chapter the Twenty-seventh: Hrald of Four Stones

FOR the first part of the ride Sidroc remained side-by-side with Asberg. Ashild, riding just behind with Byrgher, heard snatches of their talk. They rode back as they had come, pushing their horses, and after they had stopped to water them Ashild found Sidroc dropping back to ride next her.

She had her battle-cap once more on her head, and the spear he had pulled from the man she killed in her hand. Of the two Hrald had made for her it was the one she liked better. Now it felt oddly heavier in her hand, and as she rode her eyes often times dropped to the steel point of it, held low and by her stallion's right shoulder. It cannot be made heavier by that man's blood, she told herself; I am only weak from having not eaten.

"That is the shield Hrald used at Tyrsborg," Sidroc offered, of the disc of wood upon her back. They had ridden some time in silence, and were now passing through open meadowlands.

She gave a quick nod of her head, but said nothing.

"You wear a seax," he said next.

"It is one of yours. Or rather Hrald's. He gave it me, from the knife chest in the treasure room."

Feeling as dull in body as she did, it took effort to keep her anger at the high pitch she had known when she first recognised him. A seax, she thought, such as you wear. Or Ceric. And you live at your hall Tyrsborg, with his mother. You, who have been away from us so long.

She turned her head now to look at him.

"Why did you forsake us?" The sudden tears pricking her eyes could not soften the rage filling her breast, white-hot and painful within her.

"Forsake you?" His voice held the note of true surprise. "I was captured, at the point of a sword. Six of them."

"You could have returned! Mother and Hrald – all of us…"

But he was shaking his head. "No. I could not." This was a simple fact, spoken without anger of his own.

"Why are you back now?"

He took a breath. "I had to come. Danes landed on Gotland. I learned Guthrum was dead, and that Haesten had marshalled a huge force. I feared Hrald would be – "

"Hrald! You feared for Hrald. Hrald, who is now Jarl. Hrald, who as a boy was allowed to come to you, as I longed to."

He was quick to protest this last. "You could not make that voyage; the danger was too great."

"Not too great for Hrald and Ceric. Only for me."

"Ashild. You were a girl. And the man they travelled with – Kilton – he was mad."

Yet he saw now, and for the first time, what spending those months with him might have meant to her.

She was looking straight ahead now, over the creamy mane of her horse's head, looking at the red ribband of road they followed back to the home she loved, a home she was, as a woman, destined to leave.

She thought of he who rode next her, living in peace and plenty with Ceric's mother, and thought too of the new children he had fathered with her, the twinned boy and girl Hrald recalled with such fondness. And she thought of her sister Ealhswith, who had been a toddling child when her father had vanished.

"Ealhswith has never known you," she pronounced.

"I cannot hope for her to recall me," he allowed, in a mild voice. "But you do.

"Ashild. I could not live two lives. The Gods drove me far away, and I chose to stay, believing that it was my Doom to cross their will for me. But I did grieve for you. Know that if I had come back, I would have had to face Kilton here." He paused a moment. "It might have meant war."

She searched for more to challenge him with. "Why is your Doom any different now?"

"It is not," he answered, his voice low. "I cross the will of the Gods to be here."

He thought of what he could add to this, and looking at her, spotted the hammer of Thor around her neck. She would not be wearing it now unless it held meaning, beyond it having been that of Yrling. His next words carried his conviction with them.

"The Gods move in you, too, Ashild," he told her.

Hrald and all else at Four Stones were expecting news, from Oundle, points South, or West. What he did not expect was one of his own riders, posted to the North, coming to him to say that Thorfast and his brother Haward were on the march with their combined halls, heading for Four Stones with near two hundred men.

They were not far behind, and Hrald and Jari must make quick decision as to the meaning of the visit. To summon the villagers into the hall yards seemed untoward and could lead to panic; to begin to assemble his men to ride out and meet him might trigger aggression where none was intended.

In the end they let the village be, but alerted all within the walls. They had fifty men in the vale of horses, guarding that treasure, and with Asberg's fifty gone to Oundle they had a hundred men remaining.

"'Tis a hot-head; I always knew it," Burginde grumbled. "Them that act so cool are hot beneath."

Ælfwyn turned to her as they crossed the floor of the hall. "We do not know that of Thorfast, nurse," she returned, trying to assure herself as much as Burginde.

They had just left Hrald and Jari, who remained in the treasure room. Her son had summoned her down from her weaving with the news, but had been able to give her scant comfort as to the meaning of it. She did not know if she should be preparing welcome in the kitchen yard, or gather her daughter and sisters and warn them of danger. At any rate, she must go up and speak to them, trying to mask her own concern.

The palisade wall was well-stocked with watch-men its entire length, and it was not long before alerting whistles were sounded from over the section behind the kitchen yard. The Lady of Four Stones came down, Burginde at her side, to meet her guests.

Hrald was wearing his sword and knife, and Jari the same. Gunnulf was about the yard, and he stood with his brother. Ten or more of the warriors who sat at table with

Hrald stood behind them. The rest stood in clusters of ten or twelve, eyeing the small party ready to step outside the gates. All within the yard, whether warriors, workmen, or serving folk, stopped in what they were doing, and waited.

They could hear the horses come, riding the perimeter of the walls, and the jangling of bridle metal and weaponry when the lead men stopped. Hrald signaled the gates be opened. He stepped out. Jari was at one side, and his mother and Burginde at the other. A score of his best men filled the space behind him.

Thorfast was there, sitting on a black stallion, his younger brother Haward next him on a bay of equal worth. They were fully armed as if for imminent battle.

"Thorfast," said Hrald. He was making no move to dismount.

Thorfast's eyes moved behind the openings of his helmet, looking at the men and women who stood off to one side.

What he said bore the note of near unbearable boldness.

"Ride with me now to join Haesten, or be crushed."

It was challenge so sudden and unyielding that every ear it fell upon rang with it. Ælfwyn could not stop the gasp that issued from her throat. Her hand went to the pale skin there, and Burginde's to her own mouth. Yet both women felt a surge of anger at the wildness of this threat.

"Haesten!" answered Hrald. "What does he offer that is not already yours?"

"The chance to keep what is mine."

Hrald took a step nearer to where Thorfast's horse stood shaking its mane.

"I will not ride with you," he said, his voice as steady as the hand that now rested on his sword hilt. "I will not join Haesten. I will not break the Peace."

"I want you as friend, not foe," Thorfast answered.

"You are the one to decide that," Hrald said. "I am unchanged. I will not break what my father and your uncle made."

"You are a fool, and you are young," Thorfast said, glaring down at him. "Turcesig and Four Stones would have been joined long ago, if not for your delay. You cannot even control your sister. How do you think you will hold onto your hall." He was turning his head now, as if he looked again for she who was missing.

"Join with me now," he ordered. "When we return, I will wed Ashild."

"I will not take arms against Ælfred, or any who uphold the Peace. And you will not wed Ashild unless she wants you."

The fury Thorfast felt thrilled through his voice. "Then fight me now. Here. The men of Turcesig against that of Four Stones. Let it be decided now."

Hrald's chief men had closed up behind him during this, and now an answering hoot was sounded from amongst them.

Thorfast went on. "It will serve as practice for when we face Wessex. Our men will fight line to line, Saxon-style."

Hrald was looking at him in disbelief at the slaughter he threatened. He shook his head in wonder.

It only angered Thorfast more. "You will fight me, or never leave these walls alive," he claimed.

"I would never throw my men away as you would," Hrald returned.

He found himself looking up, as if for answer. "No. Hand to hand, three of us, three of you. You and your two best men. Me, and mine."

Thorfast looked struck by this idea, then seized on it. "Three on three, to decide all."

Now Hrald would sum the challenge. "The men, the hall, whatever lies within is forfeit, to whoever wins."

"Name your men," Thorfast said next.

Asberg and Jari, Hrald thought at once; two of the strongest and ablest warriors at Four Stones; and one of them kin. But Asberg was not here, and there was no knowing when he would return from Oundle. Hrald could not have his uncle at his side.

He was aware that Jari had taken a stride forward.

"Me, of course," he assured Hrald. The one who had served as his body-guard since Hrald's boyhood was again ready to die for him.

Hrald gave the slightest of nods. Jari had been his most constant sparring partner, and now would stand shoulder-to-shoulder with him. Other of his men were crowding forward, some in haste, others with deliberate step. Asberg's oldest boy Ulf was one.

It was Gunnulf who broke through. His face and voice were more earnest than Hrald had ever known. "I must be your third, Hrald. No fighter is as strong as Jari, but you need speed as well. Let me take your other side."

Jari stared at his younger brother, as if sizing him up. "Já, Hrald. Gunnulf as your third. The two brothers to flank you."

Not all behind him agreed, Hrald saw that. Gunnulf was only a little older than he, and though quick with his sword, more known for his bold jests and pranks. Others of his men extended their hands to Hrald, asking to be named. Behind them he saw Onund, looking with despair at Gunnulf. But Gunnulf was looking back at Hrald and Jari.

"The two brothers," Hrald repeated. He nodded at them both, these two who committed to fighting to the death with him.

He did not say more, for coming down the pounded clay road was a small troop of horsemen, riding at speed.

It was well past noon when they approached Four Stones. They had met no one on the road, save for the three patrols posted by Hrald, who had nothing to report from the South. Some of the men so posted were too young to have good remembrance of Sidroc, but those who did greeted him with the same awed surprise that Asberg had shown. They left each patrol more wary than they had found them, telling of the body of Danes who had made attempt on Oundle, and warning of more to follow.

The road to Four Stones curved up a slight incline, one that all the riders knew well, but that hid the full extent of the landscape just around the keep. Thus it was with a shock that the troop approaching saw an army of men before the walls.

They stopped, their horses jigging and prancing in the suddenness of their reins being pulled.

"What –" breathed Sidroc. Ashild was now between him and Asberg, in the first rank. Asberg had grunted, and was trying to control the head of his stallion, who lifted his front legs in protest at the hard stop. Ashild's mouth had opened, and she stared first at the army of men, then at her uncle.

Sidroc was scanning the road ahead. "They never came this way, not with that number of men and horses," he judged. Neither road nor huts were disturbed. They were not far from the croft furthest from the walls, and the cottar's huts sprung up more thickly after that.

"From the North," Asberg surmised.

"Thorfast," answered Ashild, almost to herself. "It is Thorfast."

A lone figure, one of the cottars, now appeared from a milking-pen, holding a staff in his hands as if to defend his milk-ewes. He stood a long moment looking at the new riders behind him. Then he let himself out of the pen and came down the road to them.

"Brave man," Asberg muttered. He watched the cottar's face, saw how it was fastened on Ashild. "He sees your horse, Ashild, and knows it to be you," he said in satisfaction.

The man now came at a trot to them, to say it was indeed Thorfast who had come to call, with his entire hall of warriors at his back. The cottar had been up by the gates when Thorfast had ridden around from behind. He had not liked the look of things, and had made haste for his sheep, ready, if not to defend them, to drive them to safety.

"Well, it is a friend," Asberg said, as they watched the cottar head back to his fold.

Ashild said nothing.

Sidroc spoke. "Thorfast, son of Amundi?"

He had known a few slight boundary conflicts with Amundi in his first years of ruling Four Stones, nothing of grave import, though in one a man had been killed. He knew Thorfast was also nephew to Guthrum, and had been a boy when he left.

"The same," Asberg answered. "Now he wants Ashild to wife, a match that would benefit both halls. Guthrum left him Turcesig in his will."

Sidroc took this in, and turned to Ashild. Her face was canted down, looking into the white mane of her horse. She looked no starry-eyed maiden at the sound of her suitor's name.

"Is he your choice as well," he asked. He had forfeited right to have say in such matters, but not his right to care for her happiness.

"I told Hrald I would wed him," is how she answered. She had not raised her face to his.

"Your mother…?"

Now she looked at him. "Like Hrald, she wishes me to wed Ceric of Kilton."

He could not be surprised. It was what his shield-maiden always desired, and no two women had ever been of one mind more than she and Ælfwyn. And he could not believe her mother and brother would wish this for Ashild if she herself were not disposed towards the young Saxon. He would risk another question.

"But you would wed Thorfast for…your own sake?"

She turned her chin and snapped her answer at him. "For the sake of Four Stones."

She did not want Thorfast, that was clear. Her eyes glinted, not with tears, but with anger. Her mouth was set almost as if she gritted her teeth.

His eyes lifted a moment to the sky. He had not been the father to this girl he had promised to be, but he might aid her now.

"Then let us ride to Four Stones' door and see what he wants," was what he said in return.

He swung his shield around, and the others did the same.

The mass of men they approached were mostly mounted, and a number of supply waggons at their rear were stopped upon the road. They must thin their own ranks to ride two-by-two, and Ashild and Asberg went first. As they neared they saw the army turn towards them, almost a wave of movement as their approach was spotted; and saw the two foremost riders be recognised and a parting made to admit them.

Sidroc saw the vastness of the force assembled, as great as that of Four Stones. He was riding just behind Ashild, the raven banner springing from her saddle cantle fluttering behind her. The Sun was on its downward path, casting strong shadows from their horses and upheld spears.

Standing there before the walls Hrald saw the white stallion canter towards him, then the figure in its cap upon its back. It was Ashild, alive and upon her great horse. He wanted to rush to her and pluck her from her saddle and into his arms. Then he saw his boyhood shield, a deep rent in its face from the blow it had taken. It made him catch his breath, thinking what it had stopped. He knew the wooden disc as no longer his own shield, but his sister's.

Another shield caught his eye, that fronting a warrior who was now coming up to flank Ashild.

Thorfast had turned his horse to face the arriving troop. It took a moment for him to see the figure upon the stallion was none other than she he had given the beast to. He almost laughed, a thrill of pleasure rippling through him at her spirit.

Looking up from where they stood Ælfwyn and Burginde also saw Ashild. Ælfwyn's fingers rose to her brow as she crossed herself in thanksgiving for her daughter's return. They saw the girl try to smile down at them. Ashild always had good colour, but now her cheek was as white as her mother's.

It was Asberg spoke first. "Oundle was attacked, just after dawn, by newly-arrived Danes who follow Haesten. We sprang, and routed them; two only of our men have hurt. They remain there with ten others."

"There is battle everywhere," Thorfast answered. "You are in time to see more. Hrald has challenged me and my chosen two men to combat, three on three. The winner claims the hall and men of the loser."

Asberg's howl was loud and immediate. But the rider on the other side of Ashild now pulled his helmet from his head.

"Hrald," called his father. "Is this true?"

Hrald's mouth dropped open, and he took a step nearer Sidroc's horse. He could scarce speak, but looking on his father's face, made answer.

"He wanted open battle. I would spare our men."

"Sidroc," Thorfast said, squinting at the newly arrived warrior. The name was repeated again, flowing through the ranks of those within the gates. Sidroc was returned.

"Hrald has set the terms," Thorfast went on, still staring at Sidroc. "Swear that you will abide by them."

"Then I fight for you," Sidroc said instead, eyes fixed on his son.

"That you cannot," Thorfast answered. "We have picked our men."

Sidroc gave a flick of his head, as if he could shake off this claim. His eyes returned to Hrald. "Who fights for you," Sidroc asked.

"Jari and Gunnulf will join me."

Asberg again gave voice, and from the ranks of men behind him came confused utterings and oaths, as word spread of the sudden bargain that had been struck.

Sidroc looked to his son. The boy was tall and rangy, and had less than twenty years. Thorfast was a man, who if not battle-hardened himself, was come into his full strength. Such a combat was a champion's role, not a youth's. He had not known what he would find in Lindisse, but never thought to find Hrald ready to throw himself into the teeth of almost certain disaster. He felt a clenching coldness in the core of him, the numbing chill of loss and destruction.

His voice was low and urgent, his eyes trained on those of his son. "Hrald. Let me take your place."

Hrald's eyes shone back at him. He had prayed to see his father again, and now here he was. But he had made the bargain and would adhere to it.

Thorfast, watching them, spoke his anger to Sidroc. "You have no part of this," he said.

Sidroc's eyes shifted in his head; much was forfeit, and out of his control. As he had wanted it. But his young – he would not forfeit them to a Fate marking them for death or enslavement.

Hrald turned to Thorfast. They must finish setting terms.

"If you win, my hall and men are yours," he vowed. He worked to keep his voice steady as he said this. "My mother and sisters, all my kin, must be free to go."

"They may go. All but Ashild. Ashild will be my wife." Thorfast had turned his head to glance at her. The very horse she was riding showed him she wanted him.

"I will not wed a man who has killed my brother," she spat back.

"That we shall see," Thorfast answered, still smiling at her.

"I demand same for Haward," said Thorfast next, looking to his younger brother. Haward dwelt in the hall of their fathers.

"Haward will not be denied his birthright," decided Hrald. "His hall remains his. But if I win, Turcesig, that which Guthrum gave you, and the men thereof, becomes part of Four Stones."

Thorfast nodded.

"Then it is settled," Hrald ended.

"Where?" Thorfast now asked. His horse was restless under him, and he pulled hard on his reins as it danced.

Sidroc's mind was whirling, but he spoke. They stood in the shadow of the stone preaching cross that the priest was so proud of. This combat must be held in a place equally suited for its purpose.

"At the duelling place," Sidroc said. "Around, past the beech, and the old place of Offering." He gestured with his hand from whence Thorfast had come. "We will meet you there."

Thorfast nodded. Sidroc looked at the army behind him. "Ten men to witness, for each side. No more."

"Ten," agreed Thorfast.

Ten would be witness enough to swear the fight had been an honest one.

"Leave the rest of your men here," Sidroc ended. Thorfast again nodded.

Those who had come from Oundle began to pass inside their own gates. When all were inside, the doors were swung shut. The horsemen climbed down from their mounts. Those who would fight or witness must soon leave for the appointed place, but now the yard was filled with questioning murmurs. Stablemen appeared, holding the heads of the horses. Hrald had walked at the head of Ashild's horse, and now helped brace her as she dropped from the saddle.

Sidroc was next her, but stayed on his horse a moment, watching the two. Asberg, already on foot, had come up to his niece and nephew, and now raised his voice so all nearby could hear.

"She killed a man, with a thrown spear, right in the chest. We watched him fall, Sidroc and I."

"Thrown truly, and well," Sidroc added, with grave respect.

All near them were looking at her. She kept her eyes on her brother.

"Your shield told me something had happened," Hrald said. He looked at it, now hanging from her saddle, and the deep puncture in its face near the iron boss. It added to the unreality of the day, hearing of her act. Except for slashing Ceric in their sword play, he had never done more than bruise his opponent. Ashild had killed a man.

"It was a spear you had made for me, Hrald," she told him, holding it slightly towards him.

Wilgot the priest was one of those near them, and his eyes had fastened on Ashild.

Asberg could but raise his voice again. "To protect the women and treasure of Oundle," he asserted, looking at the priest. Wilgot, flustered, lifted his hands as if in benediction.

Ashild turned to one of her saddle bags, from which a sheathed sword protruded. "This is yours, Hrald."

"Your battle-gain?"

"You are my Jarl; it is rightly yours."

A smile forced itself to his lips. "You shall have rich reward at the mead bench, Ashild."

Now her mother and Burginde had come to her, and she was taken up in their arms. Ælfwyn had love of scented oils, and Ashild had always found being in her mother's embrace akin to holding a bouquet. Her smell was one of the things she loved about her, and the familiar sweetness of her was never more welcome than it was at this moment. Ashild was unwashed, her hair tangled, her clothes slept in. But more than that, her mother's scent told of home.

Ælfwyn was now holding Ashild's hands to her face and kissing them. These rein-roughened hands had thrown a spear that had found home in a marauding Dane's breast; her girl had killed a man. Ælfwyn felt startle, but not the shock she might expect. Ashild had fought for the defence of those defenceless; that and to protect the treasure dedicated to God's works. Ælfwyn knew she herself, if cornered, would take up weapon and try to kill to protect her own; but Ashild, with so little training, had stood with the warriors and done so.

"My dear, dear girl," her mother told her. "How grateful Sigewif must have been at your coming!"

Tired as she was Ashild managed a smile. "She likened me to Judith," she told her, and both her mother and Burginde could hear the note of pride in her voice.

Hrald had neared Sidroc's horse. His father swung down, and they stood staring at each other.

Hrald felt he could not move. More than seven years had passed since he had seen him. Sidroc took the final stride to his son, bridging the last distance of the leagues he had travelled to be at his side. He opened his arms to a young man now his own height. Those strong arms closed around Hrald.

Hrald felt the strength in those arms, and the power and prowess in the body of his father. He felt a stripling next an oak; one that could never have the stature and skill of this man that held him.

His eyes were squeezed shut, thinking of what he had done, and that now his father was here to witness what might be his first and final battle.

He forced his eyes open. There was Ashild. He summoned her with his eyes, bidding her to come to where he stood in his father's embrace.

She could not, for Hrald's sake, stand apart; such pain was in his face. In a single movement she cast herself at them, to find herself in their joint embrace. Their arms moved to take her in. She felt the strength of both of them surround her. Yet what little she had left she wished to give to Hrald, to help him in his coming conflict.

They dropped their arms to see trays of ale being passed. Men drank deep around them, thirsty from long riding, and the strain of what must soon be faced. Then Ashild's mother was there before them, with a small silver tray holding silver and gilt cups.

She offered the cups without speaking, and Hrald and Ashild each took one up and moved away. She was left facing Sidroc, the salver between them.

"You have come." Her tone was as soft as it was grateful.

"I heard there was danger. The children. You. I could not but come."

"Ceridwen?"

"She is well. I carry her letter to you."

They fell silent. "You have scarce changed, Lady," he told her.

Warmth rose, not to her cheek, but the warmth of memory, remembering when Sidroc had leant over the table and addressed her during her first nights at Four Stones. "You are beautiful, Lady," he had told her then, after she became Yrling's wife.

She sat that night with Ceridwen, in a hall filled with strange men, who one by one became less fearsome to them. This had been the best of those men, he who had kept her from destroying her own life, had redeemed her enslaved mother and sisters, and had given her two of the three children she cherished.

"Nor have you," she returned, in simple honesty. The strand of grey at his left temple was the brighter, the eyes showing a few more lines about them, but in form he was as lean and forceful as he had ever been; there was no creeping softness about him. And when he smiled, as he did now, the long and pale scar on the left side of his face folded in, as it had always done.

Chapter the Twenty-eighth: The Duel

SIDROC would not go within the treasure room; it was Asberg who went with Hrald, Jari, and Gunnulf to help arm them. What lay within that stronghold belonged to Hrald, and he would have his son be armed amidst the treasure he owned, without the distraction of his lately returned father.

When the three stepped out into the hall those waiting fell silent. Hrald, the tallest yet the leanest of them, wore for the first time the shining ring-shirt Ceric had brought him. He knew the weight of doing so, had sparred several times wearing another, but had saved Ceric's gift for that time when actual battle was demanded. As his uncle helped him into it and the weight settled over his shoulders, he recalled what Ceric had told him on the day he left, when he had tried to thank him for it. Do not get it dented, his friend had said. For one moment he allowed himself to think on Ceric, and what his own ring-tunic had known since their parting.

Upon Hrald's head was his helmet, a striking piece with long-legged creatures like wolves etched into the sides of it; and over the eye-holes and extending down the nose-guard a design like the gaping head of a raptor. His long knife and sword completed his kit, that and his red and black shield.

Jari and Gunnulf were equally protected, with ring-shirts over their leathern tunics, knives, and swords. Gunnulf had no helmet of his own, but now wore one from the store of weapon-treasure owned by Hrald. His long yellow hair fell down from beneath it, and his bright eyes flashed from the slanted eye holes. Jari, with his sword on his right hip, wore a helmet he had won long ago fighting with Sidroc, one of blued steel that looked almost black upon his reddish hair. All three so arrayed looked formidable, and awe-ful in acts yet unexpressed.

Sidroc had been sitting with Runulv on a bench not far from the treasure room door, awaiting them with the rest. His old shield of red and black swirls hung upon the wall, to the left of the long raven banner Ælfwyn and Burginde had worked years ago. When his son stepped out holding a shield coloured like his own, his throat caught.

It was, in a way, like seeing himself as a young man, and all which this sensation drew forth, of hope dashed or realised. When he had embraced his son in the yard he had wondered at the boy's beauty, a face far more good looking than his had ever been, even before the knife cut to his cheek. But then Hrald's mother had beauty, and had been generous in passing a manly measure on to her son.

Those men who would witness were Hrald's father and uncle, and eight of the warriors who sat each night at table with their Jarl. Three women were there as well, insistent on their right to be present: Hrald's mother, older sister, and Burginde, never to be parted from the side of her mistress.

"If Thorfast objects we will stand apart and away, but we will be there," said Ælfwyn. Asberg had looked to Hrald, expecting him to reject this claim, but he nodded.

"I thank you," he near-whispered to the three. The man and woman who had brought him into this world would witness his contest, and if he should be called from life to death he would die surrounded by those who he knew loved him.

He would embrace his mother now; he could not do so once outside, and before so many. He pulled his helmet off. She was wordless as she held him, her slender body like that of an aspen, trembling against the mass of metal which made up his war-kit. He bent his head so she could press her face against his.

He pulled himself away, her long fingers sliding over the links of the sleeve of his ring-shirt. He too could say nothing, and had kept his eyes closed as he had breathed in her scent.

He moved to Ashild, for whom he had words. He put his hand on his sword hilt and spoke. "When I chose this sword you took it from me and touched the tip of the blade to my brow. Do you recall? You told me to be worthy of it. Now I ask that I may be."

It took every scrap of strength to master her voice and make answer.

"You are worthy now, brother," she told him.

He took them in, his mother silent and white-faced in Burginde's arms, his warrior-sister acclaiming his merit. He gave himself a long moment, then turned from them.

The walk through the hall and yard to the gates felt amongst the longest Hrald had ever made. He walked flanked by Gunnulf on his right and Jari on his left, the way they would stand in the contest. Behind him came Asberg and his father and his other witnesses, and then the three women. Every man, woman and child of Four Stones was there to watch them pass. There were murmurs and sighs, and he was sure, whispered prayers. If he fell, these folk would be ruled by Thorfast, and his family cast out of Four Stones. He steadied himself when he remembered Thorfast saying he would wed Ashild. After hearing of her actions outside the gates of Oundle, Hrald had no fear she would submit to a man who had laid her brother in his grave.

He shook his head slightly to clear it, glad for the sobering weight of the helmet which shielded his eyes, glad for the weight of the ring-shirt and the thought of the man who had given it. He turned his chin left and right, taking in the warriors who would stay behind, and the gathered folk of the yard. There amongst the kitchen-women was Milburga, she who had pulled him into the grain hut. The brief moments spent between her thighs had been the only taste of a woman's flesh he had known. Now he thought not of the haste and sordidness of those moments, but his gladness that no woman he loved as wife or sweetheart watched him go. He wished to be wed, to sire children, but now he was glad he had yet to do so. Milburga's hand was to her mouth and she was weeping, just as all the kitchen-women were. Looking at her wet cheeks and running nose he felt pity for her, and her fears.

The strangeness of it, of seeing this woman, and walking now with Gunnulf at his side, was met with the surety that just now his body was his own, on which no one could lay claim, save death. He could lose his life fighting the man who awaited him at the duelling ground, one older and more skilled than he, a man he had been prepared to welcome as kin. All could shift in a moment. These thoughts came before him and he passed them, like those he passed who stood here, watching him on his way.

Just outside the gates Wilgot was standing, a shallow bowl in one hand, his other already extended towards them.

Of course, Hrald thought; he must be blessed. He might die soon, and would have the priest's benediction on him as he did. Hrald believed in Christ and in life eternal. His own death was one thing, a small matter of one soul, gone home to Heaven, as Wilgot liked to say. It was what his death would mean to so many others that called Four Stones home that made large his death.

The three of them passed their shields to others so they could lift the helmets from their heads. Wilgot said prayers over each, dividing the air before their faces with his hand as he signed the cross. Then he anointed their brows with a smear of holy oil rubbed from his thumb.

He blessed Hrald last, and muttered, "May God protect you, my son," when he was done.

When he took back his shield he saw the symbol he had inked upon the leathern lining when this shield was given him, one meant to hearten him as his eyes dropped on it before he raised them to the enemy. It was a Christian cross he had painted there, just above the hand-grip in the iron boss which his hand would close over.

Then they were off. Those who were not chosen to witness fell back, Runulv amongst them. Hrald had seen and acknowledged him; looking on him Hrald felt Runulv carried everything that was out of reach of the island bourne of Gotland with him: his few months at Tyrsborg with Ceric, their time with Tindr in the forest. It felt a lifetime ago.

Thorfast's men were ranged upon the road, and the path the party from the hall took was purposeful in moving past them. It would have been shorter to reach the duelling grounds from the door by the kitchen yard, but it was meet to show themselves in this way to the men who might soon be either taking over Four Stones, or fall under Hrald's command.

They left all behind, Hrald and his train skirting the palisade, dropping down with the terrain, passing the stream where it flowed out of the opening now high above, finding level ground, marshy to one side, which they took to the designated place. The Sun had lowered enough that the shadows of the trees they passed stretched far away; good light was still in the sky, but not for long.

It came into view, a cluster of horses held to one side, a cluster of men awaiting them.

The duelling ground itself was nothing but a level patch of ground, one which had seen many men fight there, but never to the death. It was a no-man's land outside of the hall, and outside too the place of Offering, where men came to settle disputes. Hrald had sharp memory of being brought here as a child by his father, the Summer Ceric first came to stay, and of holding onto his father's leg in fear as two men hacked at each other until one was bloodied and yielded.

Now his father took the center of that patch of soil, and turned to both groups of warriors. "I will mark the ground," he told them, "and set the corners with hazel wands, as the Gods demand. All men fighting must stay within the bounds so set. He who is driven out, or steps out, is forfeit to the action, as if he were killed."

He looked to his son, who nodded in agreement, and to Thorfast, who did the same.

Sidroc walked to the hazels hedging one side of the place and drew his seax. He cut eight long wands, and with his seax tip dug holes so that two sprang out into the air at one edge of the duelling ground. Holding the others in his arms he paced out thirty broad paces, stopped, and dug two more marking wands in. He repeated this twice, until he had described a square. Now that it had been made, no one could enter save those who would fight within.

The two sides approached him. Thorfast had spotted the women as soon as Hrald's men had fanned out. The females of Four Stones had stopped at least fifteen paces from the duelling field. Sidroc saw him looking. If he were to object, claim that a woman's gaze would blunt his weapon with her magic, Sidroc would shame him as a gullible fool. But Thorfast did not object. Ashild stood in the middle of her mother and the old nurse, and Thorfast let his eyes fall upon her. He was too cunning to give insult to her now, and before her brother; he did not want some awakened rage to surface in the boy, as he fought to protect her. He merely looked at Ashild, looked and smiled.

Sidroc stopped him by his words.

"Give your names so all will hear," he ordered.

"Thorfast of Turcesig," he answered, his voice sounding in the stillness.

"Gnupa of Turcesig," said the second who stood with him.

"Odinkar of Turcesig," said the third.

Sidroc turned to his son, gestured he speak.

"Hrald of Four Stones."

"Jari of Four Stones."

"Gunnulf of Four Stones."

Sidroc drew breath before he went on.

"You fight for the other's hall and men. To yield is to lose claim to both, as if you had fallen. The victor determines if one who yields may live."

He scanned the faces of the six before him, their eyes masked by their helmets, but jaws set.

"If you have question, ask it now."

None spoke.

He looked beyond them. "You who witness pledge not to interfere, and to abide by the outcome." Heads nodded in agreement.

There was nothing more he could say.

"Ready yourselves," he finished.

Thorfast turned back to his men, and moved with them to the far side of the duelling ground. Asberg came forward and with another of his men began at the feet of the three, checking toggles on boots, tucking leg wrappings, tightening weapons belts, making all secure. Asberg was muttering under his breath the whole while, some nameless calling down of protection, or some way to busy his own mind as he readied his nephew and his companions for mortal combat.

Gunnulf was as cool as if a sparring-match awaited; aided Asberg in his helping work, even cast a grin when the older man over-tightened a belt, and redid it himself. Jari was silent, the heavy jaw clenched. He stood still as an ox as Asberg, his companion in many a battle, went over his war-kit once more. Asberg could not look in the face of his friend, but gave a solid thump on the metalled shoulder when he was done.

Jari narrowed his eyes at the two young men he would fight with, and for. They were both completely untried in actual battle. Both had sparred endless hours with him and with others, but the only bloodshed they had witnessed were the rare fights between men. Well, he thought, looking at Asberg, and so were we untried, once.

Hrald was foolishly young for this, but Jari understood why he had offered himself to spare so many more. Hrald, like his lady-mother, followed Christ, and it was the Christian thing to do, to sacrifice oneself. To the Gods war was an act of devotion, almost of prayer, but that was no way to live when one had mostly laid down the sword and taken to raising horses, and had a wife, as Jari did, who listened to Wilgot and believed.

Hrald's face was pale, what could be seen of it, but he stood up well, straight and with chin held high, under that bright helmet. Sidroc was come too late to stop this, but was here none the less to look upon the boy, and Jari knew Hrald had much of his father in him. If Sidroc's skill and boldness flowed in Hrald's blood, all might come right for the young jarl.

And Gunnulf, his own brother! Nothing bad could happen to Gunnulf, nothing ever did, his life was charmed, he who should have broken his neck ten times over on his half-wild horses and wilder dares. No, it was he himself, the old man with the marred hand that would fall. But not before he had taken his man out. It would be the greatest battle lesson given of his life, and he would give it before the twenty best men of two halls.

The three from Four Stones now stood, looking across at the three from Turcesig. Like Hrald, Thorfast stood flanked by his two chosen. They had but these last moments to try and gauge their strength and skill. Hrald had only slight knowledge of Gnupa and Odinkar; they had come from Guthrum when Turcesig was given over, and as Thorfast had picked them to fight at his side, he could wager they were from the late king's bodyguard. Hrald knew that now he must forget their names, forget even they had names. They were no longer the men of one once friendly to him; they were the enemy.

Asberg was the last to step away from his nephew. When he did Sidroc came forward to Hrald. His boy was a few breaths away from entering the sacred space of the duelling ground, a place he could not follow. He placed his hands on his son's shoulders. They were eye to eye. Sidroc's words were slow and clear.

"Hrald, listen to me." Each word sounded in Hrald's brain, and his father's eyes bored into his own. "You do not fear them. They fear you."

That was all; that was enough.

He released his son, stepped back.

"At the fall of my sword," Sidroc called, drawing his blade and holding it outstretched before him.

Hrald turned, stepped past the boundary line, his men at his sides. Thorfast did the same. They faced North-South, so the setting Sun would not blind them. Their shadows were now huge on the ground they stood upon.

Jari saw Gnupa, the man he faced, regard him, and note the shield held in the right hand. He had fought a Tyr-hand before. No matter, Jari thought, I will drop you, before I myself fall.

Gunnulf made a gesture at Hrald's side, turned to him. "I thank you," he told Hrald. The almost ever-present smile was there on his lips. Gunnulf turned back to face the man he would soon draw sword against.

I thank you, thought Hrald. I thank you for putting my life in such jeopardy. For giving me the chance to prove myself before the best warriors of these halls. I thank you for keeping the silence you promised. He could not guess the meaning, but Gunnulf spoke with honest ease.

Jari, silent the whole time, had been thinking now on Thorfast. He turned at last to speak to Hrald, a final prompt to all his training. "Use your height, Hrald. Your long reach. Use it."

They lined up, strode forward. Fists tightened about sword hilts as blades were drawn. Shields were lifted, elbows braced. Sidroc looked on all. His eyes rose to the sky. Then he dropped his sword, in one swift movement.

Six mouths opened and gave battle cry, the final release of coiled nerves before metal bit metal. There was a whooping yell from Gunnulf, a mighty oath-warmed grunt from Jari, and from Hrald a piercing call.

Then they struck.

Thorfast lunged hard at Hrald, his sword laying the first blow on Hrald's shield. As quickly as it had hit, the blade was withdrawn and with shortened swing came again, as Thorfast jumped at him. The shield Hrald used was painted in two wedges of opposed black, on a red face, and the blows Thorfast had placed almost followed the line of black leading up to Hrald's left shoulder. He drove at him with such energy and speed that Hrald found himself giving and giving ground. Thorfast's eyes glared from through the eyeholes of his helmet, intent on finishing his task as quickly as possible. Hrald was pushed relentlessly back. He saw Jari and Gunnulf many paces ahead of him, standing much where they had drawn their swords, hacking away at their men. He had already vanished from their view as Thorfast drove him near the hazel boundary.

He could hear men shouting, confused cries and oaths, coming from those who watched. Each time he gave ground, Thorfast redoubled the speed with which he leapt and swung. Hrald must break this onslaught. He had scarce brought his own weapon into play, and his shield had taken several solid hits, one which gave the crack of alder being rent. It had a fault, somewhere. As Thorfast levelled his sword again, Hrald leapt to one side. Thorfast tried to twist to meet his mark, but missed, his blade catching nothing but air. It gave Hrald time to turn. Now it was Thorfast's back against the hazel boundary.

It changed a great deal. Thorfast was winded from the force with which he had pursued Hrald, and now angered that he had lost the chance to push him out of bounds and win the forfeit.

Hrald attacked. He did not yet have the strength that Thorfast possessed in his arm and shoulder, but he had his reach, and he too was quick with his wrist. Fighting starts with the feet, his father had taught him as a boy, and he stayed light upon his heels, ready to pivot and spring. One, two, three solid blows he landed on the face of Thorfast's blue and black shield. His blows were aimed high, high, and low, so that Thorfast was kept moving the wooden disc, unable to guess where the next strike would fall. As they swung and blocked they moved together, coming a little away from the boundary line, with first Hrald and then Thorfast looking back to the centre of the duelling ground.

A loud cry. Hrald was facing in and saw Jari had lunged forward on one powerful knee, saw the man Gnupa he was facing standing unnaturally still before him. Jari's sword had found home in the man's bowels. Jari reared back, withdrawing the blade, and Gnupa pitched forward, sword dropping from hand.

Jari had no sooner straightened himself than a second roaring cry rose from those outside the pitch. Gunnulf had found ample challenge in attempting to best Odinkar, and it was only Gunnulf's speed that kept the more powerful man's blows from hitting more than wood. Odinkar had shattered Gunnulf's shield in the last strike, and he was left holding little more than the boss and the quarter-piece of wood that still hung to it. Gunnulf had never stopped grinning at his opponent, and had several times laughed in taunt when Odinkar had missed or shown effort. The loss of his shield made him laugh again, a hearty laugh at himself. Then he flung the crippled thing at Odinkar's head.

It was so bold a move that those watching gave a yell of astonishment. Odinkar staggered back, and Gunnulf had his chance. He drove for the man's torso, now unprotected by his lowered shield.

But Odinkar had not been one of Guthrum's own bodyguard for nought. As he fell back he kicked his right leg out and forward. It caught Gunnulf on his own right leg, and tripped him. Gunnulf fell before him, and it was the act of an instant for Odinkar to drive his sword into Gunnulf's back.

Jari, heavily winded from his own contest, had watched all, standing with lowered sword and shield as the enemy sword tip plunged into his younger brother. He gave a howl so deep that all other cries were silenced under it. He lifted his blade and shield and ran the few paces to where Odinkar stood over Gunnulf's body.

A rage overtook Jari, his disbelief that he lived and Gunnulf had been felled. His anger was fuelled by the manner of Gunnulf's death. All was fair in battle: tripping, grappling, hidden weapons, but to be tripped and run through in the back seemed a Fate bitterly unworthy one who was known in life for his deft grace.

He came at Odinkar like two men, he himself, and his brother's vengeful shade. There was no display of especial skill in the way in which he wielded his sword, just the immense and raw power of his anger. He swung, hacking at Odinkar's raised shield, and howling like a blood-hungry hound. It was a strength that could not long be withstood, and Odinkar found his knees buckling under the rain of blows. Another hack and his shield had splintered into yellow and green fragments, from which he shook his left hand free. It left him, two handed on his sword hilt, blocking Jari's blows with his blade.

If he would yield he would ask for it now. But Odinkar would not ask, and Jari would not have granted this boon to

Gunnulf's killer. They went on for two blows more. On the third Jari got in at the hilt, carrying off the sword and several of the man's fingers with it. As Odinkar stumbled Jari drove a final time, into the torso beneath the heart. With his power behind it, the ring-tunic crushed and broke, rivets sundered apart, useless against a driven sword-point. Odinkar dropped, and Jari placed his booted foot on his back and drove his sword a second time, in between the shoulder blades.

Hrald, trading blows with Thorfast, had seen all this; it had taken place with the lightning speed of a few rushed heartbeats. Gunnulf was dead, but Jari had killed both Gnupa and Odinkar. Thorfast saw it too. All that truly mattered was if Hrald fell.

For an instant Hrald's eyes lifted to the edges of the duelling ground. On one side stood Haward, almost at the edge of the hazel boundary, leaning anxiously forward and towards his brother. Thorfast's men were several paces behind him, rigidly upright, hands on weapons-belts as they watched.

Hrald's gaze returned. He blinked at the three bodies tumbled on the ground. Gunnulf was dead, his helmet rolled off, his long yellow hair fallen around him.

My friend is dead, Hrald inwardly repeated. Salute, and move on. This is what I have been taught. I have my own task: this man before me wants to kill me; I must kill him first. It was what Asberg and Jari and his own father had always told him, to stay alive you must kill him first.

For the first time Hrald felt fear. He had been fighting Thorfast, fending off his blows, bringing his training to bear, the fruits of all the sparring he had done. When he had been forced near the hazel wands he had known a thrill of recognition: he would be forfeit if he stepped outside. But now faced with the baldness of the fact that he must kill Thorfast to himself live, he felt fear.

He raised his chin a moment across the field, to where his father stood. He knew all eyes were upon him in this final contest, but those he sought were Sidroc's. He was there, taller than any other man, his eyes hooded in their keenness as they stared back at his son.

He recalled Sidroc telling him of when he was young, in one of his first battles, of how he took fright and dropped his sword in surrender. His hamingja, his luck-spirit, had felt his fear and begun to flee. He went on to kill the Saxon who had picked up his sword. Ceric thought it was all dishonour, but now Hrald knew what his father had known.

He felt fear unto terror at what he must do, and do before all. And he felt a caged beast, forced to fight before those who watched, though it had been he himself who had decreed this contest.

He did not want to kill. Naming it like this, as if it were a choice he could make, made it the worse; he had no choice. His fear flared up inside him, yet he felt cold. His hamingja must be even now leaving him.

"Christ help me," he muttered. "Christ, help me."

The few moments they had passed in watching Jari fight Odinkar had ended. Thorfast, hearing Hrald mutter something, squared up against him.

They started again, thrusting, blocking, feinting, lunging. The iron bosses of their shields rang from their blows, as did the fists holding them. All the time Hrald was speaking, first to himself, then to One outside him, or to one within. "Christ, help me," he kept repeating.

His teeth were clenched, and tears ran from his eyes. He swung his blade and blocked with his shield, gave and received blows, all knowing nothing but the prayer he recited. It breathed in him as he drew breath.

Jari came into view, moving slowly and with effort, but coming to Hrald's side. "Nej," came from Hrald's lips. He prayed for help, but not to lead another faithful to him to his death. He must end this contest with Thorfast as he had begun it.

Ashild, watching with her mother and Burginde, could not close her eyes before it. She saw how her brother struggled, returning the blows that came from Thorfast's sword. At times the two men almost fell in each other's arms, or their heads were brought close, side to side. She had thrown her spear from afar and killed her man; Hrald was hard upon his, hand to hand, face to face, an intimate and horrible closeness which she had not suffered.

As they moved together in their lethal parrying both men began to slow. Hrald was tiring, his shield forearm and shoulder tingling with fatigue, his sword arm heavy as it rose or swung. But so too, he saw, was Thorfast. The lightning advances he had used against him at the beginning of their contest were replaced by a steady holding of his ground. His war-cries were now grunts of effort as he blocked Hrald's sword thrusts and tried his own. Hrald knew one of them would die soon, and could rest. Perhaps Christ would help him to that rest.

His eyes flicked to the cluster of men from Four Stones, none distinct. But there at the edge stood his father, unmoving from when he had last spotted him.

His father's words came to him, those which he had said to him before he stepped onto this sacred ground.

Hrald's lips moved again. "I do not fear you," he found himself saying. He was speaking to Thorfast, but seeing Death.

Something rushed back at him, at speed unimaginable, Christ's hand over his head, or his sense of his hamingja, that fleeing luck-spirit, being called back. He felt something enter him, flowing back like a river of living water. This river swept out his fear and doubt, and even his exhaustion, so that something else could come in. Whether it was his luck-spirit, or the Christ-spirit; that of his ancestors or that of the Source, he could not know.

He no longer felt the blows his shield took, nor the ache in his arm from those he gave.

"I do not fear you," he cried in words slow and deliberate. His voice was loud enough that all watching heard, though they could not make out what he said. Only Thorfast did.

His opponent had once more lashed out with his sword, and was in the act of returning his shield to cover his torso. Hrald's cry arrested his motion, and Hrald stepped forward in the heart-beat Thorfast's guard was down. A plunge of Hrald's sword drove the point deep into Thorfast's body.

The sword fell from Thorfast's hand. He stood there with widened eyes, staring at Hrald an arm's length before him, and his sword hand began to move toward the blade connecting him to his killer. Then Thorfast's legs crumpled, and Hrald found himself stepping back to avoid being hit by his falling body.

A great and roaring cry arose from those behind and around Hrald. He stumbled, went down on one knee, then pushed himself up and away from the vanquished.

He was still within the sacred ground. He must speak. He dropped his shield, pulled off his helmet with his left hand, let that too fall. His sword alone he held.

His panting breath slowed, and his words sounded steadily across the field of death.

"Thorfast is defeated," he called out to all those watching him. "His brother Haward and all other witnesses will attest to our fight.

"Those of you who would join with Haesten, go now. You are free to leave. If you do, know that we may meet again." He glanced now down to the body of Thorfast, at his feet.

"Those of you who pledge to stand with Four Stones, I bid you now to return to Turcesig and await me there. Haward, if you will stand with me and uphold the Peace as your father did, tell me now."

The younger brother's face was ashen. "I will uphold the Peace, Hrald," he answered.

"Then take your dead, and tell all the men of Turcesig what I have told you."

That was all. He lifted his sword, ran it back into its scabbard.

Men came to him across the field, his father foremost. Hrald found himself once more in his father's embrace, a meeting as wordless as had been that before the hall, but imbued with power. Then he felt the arms of his uncle too about him. He knew he swayed as they held him.

They turned to where Jari knelt at the side of Gunnulf. Jari had turned his brother over, and was blowing great breaths as he held him by his lifeless shoulders. Gunnulf's long hair streamed down from his head. The wound in his back had bled but little, and his handsome face was totally unmarked. No fear nor horror shown there; the blue eyes fixed but still moist, the mouth held in a look of almost amused surprise.

All the witnesses from Four Stones were crowded about, but now one who had not been of their number pushed his way through. Onund must have crept through the trees and been watching from a distance. He threw himself down at Gunnulf's boots, and clasped onto his ankles, bent double in grief.

Jari's arms slid under his brother, and with a heave he lifted him in his arms and rose to his feet. He stood there alone, Gunnulf's trailing hair and arms falling down from the body Jari cradled. Onund, having been deprived of his friend, turned to Hrald.

"He died for you," Onund choked out. His brow was deeply creased, and his dark hair limp upon it.

"Já," said Hrald. "And for Four Stones."

After claiming his brother's body in this way, it took Asberg to get Jari to relinquish it.

Haward was at the side of Thorfast's body, and the field now crowded with folk bringing broad planks of wood on which the dead might be carried. The bodies were loaded, and the path retraced along the palisade wall, a solemn procession of the quick and the dead. Hrald walked first, with Jari at his side. Then came the board bearing Gunnulf. It took only the sight of Hrald to tell Thorfast's waiting men of the outcome.

It was dusk when the group from Four Stones passed through the gates and into the hall yard. Hrald's mother and sister had held him in loving embrace when they had returned through the gates, waiting until they were within the hall to do so. Burginde had grabbed him with devoted might, and looked almost ready to scold through her tears. Then, sniffing, she took Ashild away to the bower house, threatening her with a good scrubbing.

There was much still to do, the most vital of which was attending to the dead. Jari's wife Inga was joined by the Lady of Four Stones in washing and wrapping Gunnulf's body. Ælfwyn herself would serve in this hallowed task, for Gunnulf had died in service of her son. Beyond this was the affection she held for both Jari and Inga, and her desire to do honour to them all by the work of her hands. Moving in tender silence, the women completed their sorrowful charge. Gunnulf's body was washed, the yellow hair of which he was so proud combed and plaited. He was bound in new linen, and covered with a shroud of the same. Then he was carried by Jari and Asberg and Sidroc and Hrald to the house of Wilgot, and laid out there for the night, awaiting burial. Another came with them; Onund, who asked the priest that he might keep vigil through the night.

"His closest friend," Jari said, as they left the priest's door. His voice was hoarse with lament.

"Já," Hrald answered.

Hrald was now alone with his father in the treasure room. They had ale-cups in their hand. Hrald was still unwashed and in the clothes he had fought in. His father had helped him take off his ring-shirt, which had withstood the contest well. Hrald's lip twisted in a smile, thinking on he who had given it. "Now I can tell Ceric I did not dent it," he told his father.

Sidroc smiled back, and regarded his son.

"Hrald," he began. "What you did there, I will ever be proud of. And what we all saw, none will forget."

He watched his son's chin drop, the dark lashes fall over the eyes as he looked down, warding off his praise.

"I thought I would die," Hrald confessed. "I felt terror of death. I begged Christ to help. Then I almost wanted it, so I could stop. So I would not have to kill him.

He swallowed, his eyes still downcast. "Then I remembered what you had said. That was what I called out to him: I do not fear you.

"I wanted to live, but it almost did not matter. The fear left me. Something else came."

Sidroc had been looking at his son's downcast face all this time, and now Hrald raised his eyes to his father. A shield-maiden had not touched ground before Hrald, pointing her spear at him, summoning him to the halls of Odin or Freyja. If she had, Sidroc did not know if he would have seen her; mayhap it would seem a winged angel, calling him to Heaven. Neither place had called to him, and Sidroc could not think of what it would have been to have travelled so many leagues to witness his son's death upon his arrival, nor what that death would have meant to all of their lives after that moment of profound loss.

He thought his boy had felt the flight of his hamingja, that luck-spirit running out on him, as men who were losing at dice complained. If he had, she had returned, he had called her back, and that was all that mattered. He leant towards his son, and answered him.

"What came was courage, which flanks fear, runs alongside fear, always. Without fear there is no courage."

The words filled Hrald's head; he let them settle. And he let himself smile.

He must ask his father the next. "You will leave us soon?"

He nodded. "I came to see what manner of man you had grown to. Now I know."

The colour had risen to Hrald's cheek under this praise. His father had fought hard to win his way to the life he lived, and worked hard to keep it. Hrald had seen that life, and understood his father's desire to return to it. And he had left Four Stones to him, demanding nothing.

Even the thickness of the oak wall and door could not hide the sounds of the hall being set up for their delayed meal. It would be a feast, one as great as could be mustered given the shortness of notice. They must both ready themselves for it.

"Tonight you will sleep here in the treasure room, Father," Hrald thought to say.

But Sidroc shook his head. "This room and all in it is yours. I will sleep in the hall with the rest of the men."

He turned his head at the treasure-bearing chests and barrels, baskets, and shelves. Doing so made him remember the precious things he had brought for his son.

"I have a pair of Tyrsborg goshawks for you, at Saltfleet," he said. "The offspring of those you flew with Ceric."

They grinned at each other, recollecting those days on the island. "They will be the pride of the falcon-house," Hrald said.

Sidroc now looked as well at the broad bed, covered with the wolf pelts.

"One day you will bring your wife here," he said, a hint of teasing in his voice. "Is there some maid who has caught your eye?"

Hrald's cheek again flushed. "None," he admitted, and Sidroc recalled there were a dearth of nearby halls which counted likely maids amongst their offspring. If Guthrum still lived, a match with one of his daughters, or even with a noble maid of Wessex, might be explored by Hrald's mother and uncle. All this would have to wait until peace was once again established.

"Whoever you choose, I hope she is as good a woman as your mother," Sidroc ended.

Just before Hrald would take his place at table, he called his mother into the treasure room. He had donned a fine tunic, one on which she had devoted hours in embellishing neck opening and cuffs. His hair was still damp from the dousing he had given it, and lay long and dark upon the shoulders of the deep brown tunic.

His mother was arrayed as for a great feast, in a gown of pale blue wool upon which tiny pearls had been sewn at the neckline, like a sprinkling of snow. So eager was she to embrace her son again that she rushed to his side when she entered. She had washed the body of one young man; here was her own, alive and whole before her. She remained holding onto his forearms as he spoke to her.

"Mother, I would have something for Ashild, something choice to give her."

He had been considering the gifts he would soon present to his men for their service of arms this day. But he had nothing fitting for his sister.

Ælfwyn closed her eyes a moment in thought. It was true she had given to Oundle every jewel that Yrling had ever bestowed upon her. But Sidroc too had carried back to Four Stones plunder in way of gems and silver and gold-work; and had been given bracelets and neck-rings and other prized pieces of metal from his men as tribute to their war-chief, just as he shared out booty in swords and knives and horses to them. There were amongst these things ornaments she had given to Ashild and kept by for Ealhswith, and more remained with which Hrald might adorn a future wife. But nothing, she knew, of especial nature, or unknown to Ashild's eyes.

But now she remembered something else.

She turned to a locked chest which held within it another, resting at the bottom under a bolt of cloth of purple. This was one of the chests she had first found in the treasure room, when she had come as a bride. What she drew forth was a piece of gold treasure, one she had kept back from giving to the abbey, for she felt it was of the original treasure of Four Stones, that of the dead Merewala. She had admired its beauty, but it had not been anything she wished to herself wear. Now she brought it forth and pressed it into her son's hands, to present to Ashild.

It was a thick fillet of pure gold, a band meant to be worn about the brow of a great lady; a queen, even. If it had truly belonged to an earlier Lady of Four Stones, it was fitting that it be bestowed now on one who had fought to preserve the keep, and its religious house.

He almost laughed at the sight of it. "She will never take it off," he predicted.

Once back in the hall, Ealhswith ran to her to mother. The day had been long and filled with fears, and the hall was crowded and growing noisy. Ælfwyn hugged her youngest, who clung to her. Sidroc was standing with Asberg and Jari by the long raven banner. The battle flag Ashild had made was hanging there too, stuck into a rush-light holder. The three men were speaking together, a number of others leaning in and listening to the returned Sidroc.

"You must greet your father, Ealhswith," Ælfwyn told her. She took her by her hand and led her to the group. Sidroc wore one of the dark blue tunics he favoured, upon which his jewel-hilted seax gleamed. His face was shaven; Ealhswith, if she had memory of her father, had never seen him without the dark beard he used to wear.

He fell silent as they approached. The maid was of twelve or thirteen years, and in her slender and fair beauty was an almost perfect copy of her mother. She had been little more than a toddling child when he had been captured.

Ealhswith's face was uncertain before the tall stranger, but her curtsy was unrushed and sincere. Sidroc raised his arms to his daughter, and she came to him.

Hrald came out the treasure room door to see his little sister being held by his father. He saw his father's dark head bow over that of the flaxen-haired girl. And it brought to his mind Siggerith, half the age of Ealhswith, who was Thorfast's daughter. She was wholly orphaned now, and would likely be taken with her serving woman to live with her young uncle Haward. She would barely understand it all, but in years to come when she saw him, she would know Hrald as her father's killer; that would be on Hrald all the rest of his life.

He thought of the hall of Turcesig, and what lay ahead of him there. The holdings of Four Stones had in one day been doubled in size. Someone must be sent to live at Turcesig, command the men, and run the hall; his uncle, Asberg and his aunt, Æthelthryth...He shook his head, thinking on all that must be decided.

For now he must take his place at table, and address his hall. Serving folk were ready with platters of food, and stood waiting with ewers of mead in their hands, ready to be swirled in eager cups. His mother held her ewer of silver and stood behind her chair, waiting for when she would pour out for him and the rest of their table. His father would sit there, on the other side of Asberg, and Runulv too was given a place at the high table.

Within the treasure room Hrald had asked his father to be the first to address the hall. But Sidroc had shaken this off. Hrald was Jarl, the victory his, the duty and honour his.

As he was moving Ashild walked in, with shortened step, hastening to her place at the women's table. Late as it was, the hall was lit only by fire-light; that of the oil-soaked rush torches jutting from the walls, the oil cressets on the tables, and on the table at which his family sat, long tapers of beeswax. In this light Ashild glimmered and shone, for she wore the gown of golden silk which Ceric had brought her. Her hair, the hue of Winter-dark honey, fell smoothly under a fine head-wrap of thin linen, flowing like a veil down her back. She had her skirts in her hands, fistfuls of the precious stuff gathered up to speed her to her seat. Her eyes were shining as she looked across to the table at which Hrald stood. A moment later she found her mother's eyes also upon her, smiling as she grasped the silver vessel of mead.

The hall began to quiet. The Lady of Four Stones carried her ewer about her table. It was ever the lady's role to determine in which order mead should be poured out, to whom should go the greatest honour. She began tonight with her son, who was ever first, save when Guthrum had dined with them. She paused then at the outstretched cup held in the hand of three-fingered Jari. Next she crossed to Sidroc. An appreciative murmur went round at this, and he smiled up at her as she dipped the silver over the cup before him. Next she served Asberg, then Byrgher, Wilgot the priest, and those remaining at her table. She poured out last for herself, and as she did so all the cups in the hall were filled by the serving folk.

All eyes were now on Hrald, finely arrayed, standing straight before the treasure room wall, the two raven banners of the hall to his left, his father's red and black shield behind him. He took a calming breath and began.

"We have known today two victories," Hrald said. "The price was the life of one who will be greatly missed in the hall, and in the field. I raise my cup to Gunnulf, who took my part, and the part of Four Stones; a hero's part. Hail, and fare-well."

He brought the cup to his lips and drank, the strong and potent sweetness of the mead filling his mouth, warming him, as it warmed all who so partook. All there echoed his fare-well. Hrald looked over to Jari, grief-stricken and proud, who had stood at his words, and Hrald tipped his cup to him.

Now Hrald must award treasure to his men. He first turned to Jari, still standing and looking to him, who had fought valiantly, and over the body of his fallen brother.

"To his brother Jari, who felled Gunnulf's killer and his own man too, and who has been ever at my side, I award any sword, any helmet, and any knife from my store."

Whistles and the stamping of feet arose through the hall at this, the men signalling their approval. Hrald leant to his body-guard.

"I give this as well, Jari," he added, passing him an open circle of gold-chased silver, a broad pin for fastening his mantle. Jari clasped Hrald's hand with his own marred one, and took the rich piece.

The young Jarl of Four Stones went on, handing out reward. To his uncle, he gave the forest lands to the East of the vale of horses, and all rights pertaining to it; it doubled what Asberg owned in his own name. He called Byrgher forward, he who had ridden next Asberg and Ashild, and offered him his choice of Hrald's fine horses. Then in loud voice he promised a measure of silver to all who had ridden to Oundle and repelled the invaders.

He must look beyond his own table now, to that where the unmarried women sat. "Ashild of Four Stones," he summoned.

She rose, her gown of golden silk rustling as she moved. She passed her own table, and saw the loving eyes of Ealhswith and Burginde upon her.

She stopped before her brother. He had ever been tall, overtaking her own height when they were but children. Tonight, despite his youth, he looked almost fully a man.

And in this gown, she thought, I feel a woman, and one who is loved by my folk.

He looked at her, standing before him in Ceric's gift. It was her finest gown, of course, but he hoped her choosing it for tonight carried greater meaning, as well. She smiled up at him. She wore no gems nor pins, but he saw about her neck the chains of two amulets, one silver, one gold, hidden beneath the bodice of her gown, those she had worn as she had ridden away a day ago.

Now Hrald looked to those who watched them both.

"To Ashild, who rode in the foremost rank at Oundle, and who made a clean kill there from true aim, I give this circlet of gold."

It lay on the table before him. He lifted the filet in both hands and placed it over her head. It rested over the fine linen draping her head, and settled just above her eyebrows, a band of pure red gold.

All the champions had drawn acclaim from the hall. Again it erupted in cheers and whistles. Ashild lowered her eyes a moment to her brother, then raised them. She felt her cheek was aflame, but knew that such honour as this might never again come her way. She might one day be revered, as her mother was, for being the Lady of a hall, but acclaim such as this was a warrior's portion, and she had won it. Her brother's words, the cheers of her folk, wholly filled her. She let herself look out at all those before her. Her mother's eyes beamed, and she held her hands clasped as if in grateful thanksgiving. Sidroc was grinning at her in open approval. Asberg was holding his silver cup to her in salute.

She returned to her table. Hrald looked as if he might gesture the serving folk forward. But the men of Four Stones wanted more.

"Sidroc! Sidroc!" they called. He rose, raising his arms to them, and they howled their welcome, stamping and cheering.

"I tell you what I told my son. I came to see that Four Stones was in certain and steady hands. All of us have proof that this is so." He let his eye move about the place. "The men – and women – of Four Stones are like none other. I return to Gotland, secure in that knowledge."

His eye landed on the shield behind Hrald. "I know my shield was hung upon that wall by Hrald. Now he must replace it, with his own, that he held today."

An uproar of cheers greeted this. It was broken only by a demand from the middle of the hall.

"But you will tell your tale," a man shouted. Others of them took it up.

"Já, já, we will hear of your adventures, of the Idrisids and all that came after!"

"You shall hear all," Sidroc grinned. "We will eat and drink, and you shall hear all."

They had eaten beef boiled with dried plums and cherries, and thickened with chunks of toasted oaten bread. There were ripened ewe's cheeses, and great baked custards of beaten eggs and new milk, sprinkled with ground walnuts, a rich and tender delicacy of Spring's bounty. Much mead had been drunk. Sidroc had told his tale, one which was met with calls and hoots when he described the dragon-ship of the Danes bearing down on that of his captors, and enslaving them in turn. All leant towards him as he recounted this, his words holding them in a kind of spell. Likewise his listeners were riveted by the tale of the second sea battle, in which Sidroc had but an instant to decide which group of Danish raiders to fight for. Cups were raised to him, and more than once, during the telling.

After this dice and counters were brought forth, and the men and women of the hall ranged from table to table, gaming and watching those who did. The cressets were renewed, and as it was a day of such high note, the wax tapers on the high table replaced with others, that all might bask in generous light.

The night thinned. Ælfwyn's day had seemed without end, and she was weary. She must stay a while longer, but looked forward to kneeling by her bed in her bower-house, holding her Psalter in her hand as she said her grateful prayers.

One by one folk began to take themselves off. Wilgot the priest was amongst the first to leave, to keep vigil with Onund beside the body of the fallen Gunnulf, who must be buried in the morning.

Ashild too felt that soon she must know sleep. Sidroc was at this time standing at a table not far from her, ready to take up the dice in his fist. He saw her rise, then laid down his dice, and followed her to the door which led to the stable yard. He wanted a moment alone with her. They paused there, inside the hall, but out of the height of its noise.

The flickering candles and cressets and the sheen of her silken gown cast all in dimly gleaming light. The newly placed band of gold about her brow also caught this warm, uncertain glow. He considered her now; the two, so long apart, facing the other. She had made clear her anger at him on the ride back from Oundle. And in her later embrace, when he held both her and Hrald in his arms, he felt that anger be replaced with as much affection as his absence could allow. Nothing could return the lost years, but he would have her know that he esteemed her courage, and wanted her happiness.

He regarded her a long while, while she held her face, looking back on him. She did not have her mother's beauty, but had instead allure of her own, a kind of fetching attraction about her. She took after her father, had his colouring and stature. And, he knew now, she had Yrling's firmness of purpose. But studying her in the little light, he began speaking of what she wore.

"Your gown..." he began. This gown of golden silk was known to him.

"Ceric brought it to me," she said, looking down at the gorgeousness of the stuff it had been sewn from.

"She who is his mother – and my wife – wore it, years ago, at the hall of Kilton. I saw it when I went there with Guthrum. She wore it a second time, when she visited here; you and Hrald were children."

She almost laughed; the history of this gown encircled three women.

"And before that, it was mother's," she told him.

He had recalled Ælfwyn's gown of red silk, which she had worn for her hand-fast day with Yrling, but not her wearing this one of yellow.

"And now it is yours."

He wondered if she too would one day wear it at Kilton. He spent another moment looking at her.

"I do not know that you will find any man to be your match, Ashild." It sounded praise, but he meant it as fact. "Has Ceric grown into such a one?"

She let a long breath escape her lips, not quite a sigh, but a sound of deep thoughtfulness. "He was my first choice, though it was hard to admit it. I do not want to leave Four Stones. But if I must, I will go to Ceric."

"That will gladden your mother."

"And Hrald as well. Ceric is dear to him as any brother could be."

He would not, in respect for her, spare her his next thought; and he felt that she was thinking it as well.

"Then his greatest fear will be to face him in battle."

She nodded in grave agreement. "I would do much to prevent that," she murmured.

Sidroc awoke just before dawn. He lay there on a straw pallet on the floor of Four Stones, amongst a score or more of its unmarried men, just as he had when his uncle, Yrling, had ruled here. A few cressets left burning on the stones of the fire-pit lit his way as he rose.

There was someplace he must go, and he headed there now. He made his way through a kitchen yard waking to a new day. A few kitchen staff, the bakers and the boys that stoked the bread ovens, were already bending over the hot baking pans, or trundling more wood. Soon the torches they had lit to aid their work could be rubbed out; dawn was nigh.

He let himself out through the palisade door there, and walked, slowly given the low light, along the path. His goal was the place of Offering. He passed the dank growth of the marshy area, and went on. To the left the path would take him to the duelling ground, where yesterday the Fate of Four Stones had been held in the hands of his son. This morning he went straight on. The Sun was risen enough so that the tall wooden carving of Odin was clear before him. It stood where it had always been by the trench in which men had made sacrifice of both animals and weapons. The night he had killed his sword was fresh in his mind, walking here burning with fever to bend back and snap with a steel hammer the blade which had failed him.

He stopped a moment before the visage of Odin. The carving was rotting away, any Summer storm to come might topple it. But before it he saw that a hay-fork had been driven into the ground, and that its tines held a fowl. At the base of the carving there were other animal remains, fresh ones. He would be back, to make Offering of his own, but did not expect the evidence that others were as well.

Where he headed was the great beech tree, off to one side of the place. The smooth trunk was such that two men could not clasp hands about it, and the canopy of new purple-green leaves spread dense and broad above it. He stepped under that leafy roof, and lifted his face to it, looking. Far over his head he saw something slender dangling from a bough, the silver chain he had hung for his shield-maiden so long ago. It was beyond his reach; the branch he hung it on had grown and uplifted, holding it closer to the Gods.

Years had tarnished the silver black, but beneath lay pure metal. He extended his arm towards it, driven by his yearning.

"Shield-maiden," he said aloud. Water was in his eyes.

"I live."

Here ends Book Six of The Circle of Ceridwen Saga

The Wheel of the Year

Candlemas - 2 February

St Gregory's Day - 12 March

St Cuthbert's Day – The Spring Equinox, about 21 March

St Elgiva's Day - 18 May

High Summer or Mid-Summer Day- 24 June

Sts Peter and Paul - 29 June

Hlafmesse (Lammas)- 1 August

St Mary's Day -15 August

St Matthews' Day – The Fall Equinox, about 21 September

All Saints -1 November

The month of Blót – November; the time of Offering

Martinmas (St Martin's) -11 November

Yuletide - 25 December to Twelfthnight - 6 January

Winter's Nights – the Norse end of the year rituals, ruled by women, marked by feasting and ceremony

Anglo-Saxon Place Names, with Modern Equivalents

Æscesdun = Ashdown

Æthelinga = Athelney

Apulder = Appledore

Basingas = Basing

Bryeg= Bridgenorth

Caeginesham = Keynsham

Cippenham = Chippenham

Cirenceaster = Cirencester

Defenas = Devon

Englafeld = Englefield

Ethandun = Edington

Exanceaster = Exeter

Fearnhamme = Farnham

Glastunburh = Glastonbury

Hamtunscir = Hampshire

Hreopedun = Repton

Jorvik (Danish name for Eoforwic) = York

Legaceaster = Chester

Limenemutha = Lymington in Hampshire

Lindisse = Lindsey

Lundenwic = London

Meredune = Marton

Middeltun = Milton

Readingas = Reading

Sceaftesburh = Shaftesbury

Snotingaham = Nottingham

Sumorsaet = Somerset

Swanawic = Swanage

Turcesig = Torksey

Wedmor = Wedmore

Witanceaster (where the Witan, the King's advisors, met) = Winchester

Frankland = France

Haithabu = Hedeby

Land of the Svear = Sweden

Aros = Aarhus, Denmark

Glossary of Terms

Bova: a seventh century saint of Frankland, known today as Ste Beuve.

brewster: the female form of brewer (and, interestingly enough, the female form of baker is baxter…so many common names are rooted in professions and trades…).

browis: a cereal-based stew, often made with fowl or pork.

chaff: the husks of grain after being separated from the usable kernel.

cooper: a maker of casks and barrels.

cresset: stone, bronze, or iron lamp fitted with a wick that burnt oil.

dísir: female household spirits, celebrated at Winter's Nights feasts.

ealdorman: a nobleman with jurisdiction over given lands; the rank was generally appointed by the King and not necessarily inherited from generation to generation. The modern derivative *alderman* in no way conveys the esteem and power of the Anglo-Saxon term.

fulltrúi: the Norse deity patron that one felt called to dedicate oneself to.

fylgja: a Norse guardian spirit, always female, unique to each family.

hackle: the splitting and combing of fibres of flax or hemp with opposing brush-like tools.

hamingja: the Norse "luck-spirit" which each person is born with.

joik: (also, yoik) A chant-like Sámi song, evoking the essence and spirituality of a person, animal, or landscape element, and unique to each recipient.

Judith: in the Old Testament *Book of Judith*, the beautiful Hebrew slayer of the enemy Assyrian general Holofernes, who had put her town to siege.

kith and kine: kin – family members – and cattle.

Máttaráhkká: The Sámi mother Goddess, creator of human bodies, who lives under the floor boards of Sámi dwellings. She is the mother of Sáráhkká, patron of female fetuses, menstruating women, and those in child-birth, whose domain was under the hearth fire; Juksáhká, guardian of male fetuses; and Uksáhkká, patron of children. These last two Goddesses lived by a door.

morgen-gyfu: literally, "morning-gift"; in Angle-land, a gift given by a husband to his new wife the first morning they awake together.

nålbinding: a form of early knitting or crochet, using one's thumb and threaded needle to form interlocking loops.

rauk: the striking sea- and wind-formed limestone towers on the coast of Gotland; the one on the cover of Book Four, *The Hall of Tyr* is at Fårö, Gotland.

seax: the angle-bladed dagger which gave its name to the Saxons; all freemen carried one.

scop: ("shope") a poet, saga-teller, or bard, responsible not only for entertainment but seen as a collective cultural historian. A talented scop would be greatly valued by his lord and receive land, gold and silver jewellery, costly clothing and other riches as his reward.

skep: a bee hive formed of coils of plaited straw, built up into a conical shape.

skeggox: steel battle-axe favoured by the Danes.

skirrets: a sweet root vegetable similar to carrots, but cream-coloured, and having several fingers on each plant.

skogkatt: "forest cat"; the ancestor of the modern Norwegian Forest Cat, known for its large size, climbing ability, and thick and water-shedding coat.

skogsrå: "Lady of the Forest"; a womanly wood spirit who protected woodland animals, and yet guided hunters she favoured.

strakes: overlapping wooden planks, running horizontally, making up a ship's hull.

symbel: a ceremonial high occasion for the Angle-Saxons, marked by the giving of gifts, making of oaths, swearing of fidelity, and (of course) drinking ale.

tæfl or **Cyningtæfl** ("King's table"): a board game of strategy.

thegn: ("thane") a freeborn warrior-retainer of a lord; thegns were housed, fed and armed in exchange for complete fidelity to their sworn lord. Booty won in battle by a thegn was generally offered to their lord, and in return the lord was expected to bestow handsome gifts of arms, horses, arm-rings, and so on to his best champions.

thrummy: from the noun "thrum", meaning the rough, uneven ends of the warp strings left behind on the loom when the fabric is cut free. "Thrummy hair" would then be tousled, uncombed, or uneven.

trev: a settlement of a few huts, smaller than a village.

wadmal: the Norse name for the coarse and durable woven woollen fabric that was a chief export in the Viking age.

verjuice: "green juice"; an acidic juice from unripe grapes or crabapples, much used as we would vinegar.

woad: a free-growing herbaceous perennial plant, its leaves used for its astringent, antiseptic, and blood-staunching properties, and to produce the colour blue for fabric dying.

wither: the highest point at the top of the shoulder of a horse or deer, marked by a projecting knob.

withy: a willow or willow wand; withy-man: a figure woven from such wands.

wool-wax: (also wool-oil, wool-fat) All earlier names for lanolin. Lanolin was extracted from sheep's wool by boiling washed wool in water. When the pan was left to cool, a milky white grease would be floating on top - the sheep's waterproofing. The globules were further refined by squeezing them through linen cloths. Lanolin was invaluable as a simple remedy for chapped and roughened skin. Blended with powdered or crushed herbs, it served as a medicinal salve.

Acknowledgments

This novel was begun in the lilac-ringed garden of Ängen, part of the Ingmar Bergman Estate on the Baltic island of Fårö. The month I spent there as an Artistic Fellow in 2016 will stand as a highpoint in my creative life. I express my sincere gratitude to the Board of Directors of the Bergman Estate, and to Kerstin Kalström of Fårö, for a magical and productive stay.

Three readers have distinguished themselves during the creation of this book, and are owed special thanks: Ellen Rudd, whose discerning eye and feel for the psychological moment occasioned many discussions between us; Suzanne Gunter-Sheppard, Texas Star, for bringing me to an image of the Staffordshire Cross (c 675-725 CE) which became the model for the gold cross which Ceric wears; and Kimberly Gerber Spina, for all past favours and the gift of the old word "thrummy".

Silver Hammer, Golden Cross benefitted from an exceptionally dedicated, articulate, and passionate group of First Readers. Your feedback and encouragement made this a richer book, and I am indeed grateful for your continuing loyalty to my work. Carla Aeiker, Anne Malphrus Bailey, Jeanne Dorsey, Angela Elder, Dawn Fernald-Spruill, Lisa Graham, Sylvia Melancon, Cyndi Messina, Barbara Odgers, Mary Ann Quirk, Ellen Rudd, Suzanne Gunter-Sheppard, Tina Simmons, Cheryl Anne Snider, Nina Snyder, Kimberly Gerber Spina, Jennifer Stetson, Ali Teague, Frances C. Yancey, and Beth Garison Wylie – my deep and sincere thanks.

You've read the books - now enjoy the food! Your free Circle of Ceridwen Cookery Book(let) is waiting for you at octavia.net.

Ten easy, delicious, and authentic recipes from the Saga, including Barley Browis, Roast Fowl, Baked Apples, Oat Griddle Cakes, Lavender- scented Pudding, and of course - Honey Cakes. Charmingly illustrated with medieval woodcuts and packed with fascinating facts about Anglo-Saxon and Viking cookery. Free when you join the Circle, my mailing list. Be the first to know of new novels, have the opportunity to become a First Reader, and more. Get your Cookery Book(let) now and get cooking!

About the Author

Octavia Randolph has long been fascinated with the development, dominance, and decline of the Anglo-Saxon peoples. The path of her research has included disciplines as varied as the study of Anglo-Saxon and Norse runes, and learning to spin with a drop spindle. Her interests have led to extensive on-site research in England, Denmark, Sweden, and Gotland. In addition to the Circle Saga, she is the author of the novella *The Tale of Melkorka*, taken from the Icelandic Sagas; the novella *Ride*, a retelling of the story of Lady Godiva, first published in Narrative Magazine; and *Light, Descending*, a biographical novel about the great John Ruskin. She has been awarded Artistic Fellowships at the Ingmar Bergman Estate on Fårö, Sweden; MacDowell Colony; Ledig House International; and Byrdcliffe.

She answers all fan mail and loves to stay in touch with her readers. Join her mailing list and read more on Anglo-Saxon and Viking life at www.octavia.net.

CPSIA information can be obtained
at www.ICGtesting.com
Printed in the USA
BVHW031806231119
564646BV00001B/114/P